DEAD
FIND

Also by T. F. Muir

DEAD FIND

T. F. MUIR

CONSTABLE

CONSTABLE

First published in Great Britain in 2022 by Constable

Copyright © T. F. Muir, 2022

1 3 5 7 9 10 8 6 4 2

The moral right of the author has been asserted.

A CIP catalogue record for this book is available from the British Library.

ISBN: 978-1-40871-653-3

Typeset in Dante MT byHewer Text UK Ltd, Edinburgh
Printed and bound in Great Britain by by Clays Ltd, Elcograf S.p.A.

Papers used by Constable are from well-managed forests and
other responsible sources.

MIX
Paper from
responsible sources
FSC
www.fsc.org
FSC® C104740

Constable
An imprint of
Little, Brown Book Group
Carmelite House
50 Victoria Embankment
London EC4Y 0DZ

An Hachette UK Company
www.hachette.co.uk

www.littlebrown.co.uk

For Anna

AUTHOR'S NOTE

First and foremost, this book is a work of fiction. Those readers familiar with St Andrews and the East Neuk may notice that I have taken creative licence with respect to some local geography and history, and with the names of some police forces, which have now changed. Sadly, too, the North Street Police Station has been demolished and a block of flats constructed on the site, but its past proximity to the town centre with its many pubs and restaurants would have been too sorely missed by Gilchrist for me to abandon it. Any resemblance to real persons, living or dead, is unintentional and purely coincidental.

Any and all mistakes are mine.

www.frankmuir.com

CHAPTER 1

10.20 a.m., Thursday 7 August
The Old Course, St Andrews, Fife, Scotland

Detective Chief Inspector Andy Gilchrist lifted his face to the
sun, and revelled in a stirring breeze as the electric cart bumbled
its way across the fairway, its driver seemingly oblivious to golfers on the adjacent tee, taking practice swings with careful deliberation. The start of that week had been unusually warm, even
hot, with temperatures in the mid-twenties – or eighties in old
money, as Gilchrist preferred to say – and with another cloudless
sky and not a breath of wind, the forecast for that day was to be
a scorcher.

Of course, in Scotland, it could be blowing a gale by the
weekend.

'Run it through me again,' Gilchrist said to the driver. 'How
you found the body.'

'Oh, it wasnae me that found it. It was Jimmy. I was just telt to
pick youse up.'

'So who's Jimmy?'

1

'Jimmy Carter. No the ex-president, mind.' He laughed at his joke, and added, 'He's head of maintenance. Good guy, Jimmy. You'll like him.'

Gilchrist had to tighten his grip on the seat as the cart took a sharp turn onto a tarred pathway, and raced northwards in the direction of the Eden Estuary. 'So in the course of doing maintenance works,' he said, 'Jimmy came across the body?'

'Aye, that's right.'

'What kind of maintenance works?'

'I couldnae tell you exactly. We do maintenance all over the place. The Old Course one day, Jubilee the next, the New the next and so on. But we was laying a new waterpipe to an upgraded sprinkler system out along the side of the twelfth.'

'By hand?'

'What?'

'Do you dig the trenches for the pipe by hand?'

'Naw, we've got all sorts of machines for that now.'

'So Jimmy was driving the machine when he came across the body?'

'Naw, Jimmy's the gaffer. Someone else was driving it.'

'Which means that Jimmy never found the body at all, then. Someone else must have.'

The driver scowled at the pathway ahead, as if stumped by the question, then said, 'Aye, he must have, I suppose.'

They drove on in silence after that, Detective Sergeant Jessie Janes in the rear of the cart, her back to the front, facing the way they'd come. Gilchrist glanced over his shoulder and saw she was on her mobile, fingers tapping a message. The cart rocked to the side as the driver pulled off the pathway, and bumped across another fairway. Jessie never missed a tap.

2

Ahead, the Eden Estuary came into view, a wide channel that widened farther as its waters spilled into the shallow expanse of St Andrews Bay, then beyond to the North Sea. With the tide out, the estuary sands lay dark and uninviting, but where it touched the bay, beach sand spread like sheets of gold either side. Across the waters to the north, the sands of Tentsmuir shimmered like a mirage in the morning heat.

'This is as far as I can take youse,' the driver said, pulling the cart to a halt. 'Youse'll need to walk it from here.'

'Right, where is it?' Jessie said, sliding from the cart, slipping her mobile into her back pocket.

The driver nodded to a group of four individuals, huddled beyond a crop of gorse bushes in a tight group, like co-conspirators hatching some ominous plan. They wore the dark green outfits of the St Andrews Links Trust maintenance crews. Cigarette smoke swirled around them like steam.

Out of the cart, the air seemed to still and the temperature to soar. Gilchrist removed his jacket, slung it over his shoulder, and set off into the rough, Jessie by his side. One of the crew gave a quick nod to the others, and cigarettes were nipped between thumbs and fingers and slipped into pockets, out of sight.

When he reached the group, Gilchrist held up his warrant card. 'DCI Gilchrist of St Andrews CID, and my associate DS Janes.' To keep things simple, he said, 'We were told Jimmy Carter found the body?'

'That's me, aye,' a voice shouted from behind them.

Gilchrist turned to face a man he would put somewhere in his fifties, shorn head and face sun-burned a deep tan – or maybe weather-beaten – shirt sleeves rolled up to his elbows to expose tattooed forearms as colourful as paintings. He walked towards them from behind a gorse bush, as if he'd taken refuge to relieve himself. A firm handshake with a rough grip, a quick nod to Jessie, then, 'It's this way.'

Gilchrist and Jessie followed, while Jimmy explained that morning's events.

'We're upgrading parts of our irrigation system. It's an ongoing project. Nae problem. All going well. Making good progress. When we comes across some material.' He lifted his hand to his crown and scratched it. 'Looked like an old jacket, or something. Thought it was maybe someone's old clothes that had been dumped or buried.' He stopped alongside a roll of black plastic pipe on the ground, which tailed to a narrow trench, no more than twelve inches wide, with vertical sides two or so feet in depth. He tapped the roll. 'This is what we're putting in; sixteen-mil high-density polyethylene – HDPE. Miles of the stuff. It's often laid using a pipe router. But out here, it's quicker and cheaper just to excavate and lay it in a trench by machine.'

Gilchrist followed Jimmy's line of sight to a mechanical device that stood abandoned at the far end of the trench, wheels either side. Not that he'd ever used one, but he thought it looked like a narrow rotavator of sorts, the kind you might use on a domestic vegetable patch.

'I don't see any old clothes,' Jessie said.

'Over here.' Jimmy strode towards the excavator, kneeled on the ground, picked up a length of tattered dirt-covered fabric, and laid it on the grass alongside the trench. 'There's more of it over there, and some on the blades, too.'

'So where exactly did this come from?' Jessie said, as she kneeled on the grass, and peered into the trench.

'Just about where you're looking.'

Jessie removed her pocket torch and shone it into the trench. 'Not a lot to see,' she said. 'So why do you think it's a body?'

'Well . . .' Another scratch to the crown. 'We found that.'

Gilchrist followed his line of sight again. At the edge of the trench by the side of the machine lay what looked at first glance like a loose collection of scattered tree roots, or pieces of a vase that had been shattered by the blades of the machine. Most were caked with sun-dried dirt and discoloured from age, but one piece had been rubbed clean, perhaps with a cloth or a gloved hand, to expose a gold-filled tooth on the edge of a shattered jawbone. He thought he saw how it happened, how the machine driver at first must have thought he'd turned lucky, that he'd found some hidden treasure, some lost jewellery perhaps, his initial excitement turning to horror as the realisation of what he'd just dug up hit home.

Gilchrist kneeled on the dry grass for a closer look, brushed his fingers over the other pieces of bone with care. The metal blades had done a proper job of shattering the skull. If not for the gold filling, the body could have gone unnoticed in the course of a busy day laying pipe – torn rags and scattered bones almost indiscernible from clumps of discarded waste.

Jimmy said, 'Andy got the shock of his life when he came across it.'

'Which one's Andy?' Gilchrist said.

'The ponytail.'

He glanced at the group of four, who were eyeing them with concerned looks, as if wondering what was going to happen now the police were on the scene. 'We'll need a statement from him.'

'Of course, aye.'

'You, too.'

'Aye.'

'And the others.'

'Nae problem.'

Gilchrist nodded to Jessie, who already had her notebook out and was striding across the dune grass. 'Hey, you with the ponytail . . .'

Gilchrist returned his attention to the shattered skull. He counted four teeth in total, attached to pieces of bone. Other clumps of dirt could be parts of teeth, or bone, but it wasn't up to him to identify what was what. The SOCOs – Scenes of Crime Officers – could collect every piece for a full forensic examination. He peered into the trench to estimate its depth. No more than three feet, as best he could tell, deep enough to protect the irrigation pipework from the worst of Scotland's frosts.

He pushed himself to his feet, rubbed his hands together for a quick clean, and looked around him. Out here, at the edge of the golf course, ten yards from the nearest fairway, no more than three feet deep . . .? You didn't have to be a genius to work out that the maintenance crew had uncovered the body of a murder victim buried in a shallow grave.

He removed his mobile phone from his pocket, and called it in.

CHAPTER 2

By mid-afternoon, the SOCOs had exposed the body in its entirety.

Wearing a full forensic suit, Gilchrist stepped inside the crime scene tent, Jessie by his side.

'Bloody hell,' she complained. 'It's hotter than the Sahara in August.'

Gilchrist resisted the urge to remove his mask. Sweat was already working its way down his neck to trickle the length of his spine. Protected from the elements, and acting like a greenhouse, the temperature had to be in the nineties – Fahrenheit, that is – maybe more. The air hung as dead as that in a coffin. Light through the fabric walls infused the scene in a quiet yellow.

A trench some six feet long and three feet wide, no more than three deep, had been excavated in the centre of the area to reveal the tattered skeletal remains of the victim. The narrower trench made by the pipeline excavator ran across it at an angle, and cut through the victim's skull. Another six inches or so to the left, he thought, and they would have missed it altogether, and no one would have been any the wiser that a murder victim lay buried within inches of the pipeline.

He leaned forward for a closer look.

The SOCOs had done a fine job of exposing the body without disturbing it, the only damage being where the excavator had churned through the right shoulder and the lower part of the skull. The skeletal body of a male, if the clothes were anything to go by; bold checked suit, striped shirt with a tie still knotted around the bones of the neck. The right arm lay across the stomach in a Napoleon pose – no rings on any of the finger bones – while the left was twisted under the body. The legs, too, were crossed at the ankles, as if the poor soul had been dumped into his grave by killers in a hurry.

'Nice brogues once upon a time,' Jessie said, leaning down to inspect them. 'Leather soles? You wouldn't wear leather soles in winter, would you? Not in Scotland.'

'So you think he was killed in the summer?' Gilchrist said.

She stood upright. 'Don't know what to think, to be honest, because if you're stupid enough to wear a plaid tie with a striped shirt, you're stupid enough to wear leather soles in the snow.'

'Which gets us where?'

'Back to the beginning?'

'Body skeletonised. Clothes not fully deteriorated. Which puts death at . . . ten to twenty years ago?'

'Could be. But we might get a handle on that from the suit. I mean, look at it. Big checks. A bit flashy. Don't think you'd find this in Marks & Sparks.'

'If it's made to measure, we might find the name of the tailor.'

'Maybe,' she said, but from the tone of her voice, she didn't sound hopeful. She leaned down by the head, tugged at the collar of her forensic suit. 'Bloody hell, I'll need a right dooking in the sea when I get out of here.'

'It's warm, I'll give you that.'

'Master of the understatement.' She stilled, then kneeled closer. 'Uh-oh, what've we got here?' She had reached down and touched the top of the skull, which lay intact despite its lower half being mangled, and was running gloved fingers over it, as if testing the bone for strength. 'If I'm not mistaken,' she said, 'I'd say this is what killed him.'

'Him?' he said, just to gauge her reaction.

'Unless she liked dressing in men's clothes.'

Gilchrist kneeled beside Jessie as she prodded the side of the skull.

'Difficult to say with the skull caked in dirt,' she continued, 'but it feels like a nice clean entry wound, more than likely made by a bullet.'

'Bullet to the side of the head, then buried in a shallow grave? What does that tell you?' he said.

'Again, just thinking, but I'd say it's murder.' She chuckled at her own joke. 'But Queen Becky'll give her royal opinion on the post-mortem table, no doubt. Where is she anyway? Shouldn't she be here by now?' She exhaled a gasp through her facemask, then said, 'Jeez, I need to get out of here before I melt.'

Gilchrist let her go. He was struggling with the heat himself, but rather than follow her, he found himself touching the skull – bullet hole would indeed fit the wound – feeling through the victim's clothes in the unlikely expectation of finding some form of ID – wallet, business card, addressed envelope – you never could tell. But the suit fabric fell apart from the slightest tug, and he realised it would be best if he left the body intact for a post-mortem examination.

9

If the victim had indeed been shot, the next question was where? Had he been shot somewhere else, in his home, or in town, and his body then transported for burying? Or had he been shot *in situ*, so to speak, and buried at the scene? Something told him it was the latter. A bullet wound to the side of the head sounded more like an execution, and if so, it would be much more convenient to shoot the victim at the site of his final resting spot. For all anyone knew, the victim might have dug his own grave.

But to the side of the head? Not the back?

What did that tell him? Not a lot, came the answer.

And what about the angle of entry? If that could be determined – maybe from the exit wound, if there was one – it might give them a clue as to how the victim had been shot, meaning that he could have been on his knees then shot, which might give them a chance, a slim one, to find the bullet. But the side of the head suggested – at least to his mind – that the victim had been standing upright, in which case they would have little chance of finding the bullet in the wider expanse of dune grass and gorse. Still, at this stage of the investigation, it might be prudent to expand the crime scene.

Of course, all of it could add up to the square root of eff all.

He pushed to his feet, and had to stand still for a few seconds to let a disorienting sense of dizziness pass. He hadn't told Jessie, in fact he hadn't told anyone yet, but Doctor Rebecca Cooper, Fife's foremost police pathologist, had taken leave of absence, maybe even resigned. Not that she'd had the courtesy to give any notice. According to Smiler – Chief Superintendent Diane Smiley, Gilchrist's boss – Cooper had departed Bell Street Mortuary yesterday morning after a phone call with person unknown, during which she was heard cursing and shouting at the top of her voice. *Absolutely furious, she was.* A phone call from Cooper to the Hospital Director later that afternoon had confirmed that she needed to take time off work for personal reasons. She would be in touch.

Gilchrist had the uneasy suspicion that her on-again-off-again marriage with her ex- or not ex-husband, Max, might be the cause of such distress. But he'd kept those thoughts to himself. Despite the inference that she might return after some time off, he thought he knew Cooper well enough to know she would never come back. She was gone for good, moved on to pastures new, maybe overseas, or perhaps simply retired from the profession altogether.

Who knew? Certainly not him.

He stepped from the forensic tent, stumbled some yards over the dune grass towards the sea, before stripping out of his suit. Despite the absence of wind, and the temperature still high enough to burn, the fresh air felt relatively cool. He swept his fingers across his brow, raked them through his hair. His shirt stuck to his skin, and he loosened a couple of buttons and flapped the material.

When had it last been this hot in Scotland? Most summers you were lucky if you got a run of a few days in the sun, but this heat-wave had gone on for well over a week now. He remembered one summer, when Maureen and Jack were still young – six and four, if his memory was correct – and Gail was still in love with him, they'd spent one Sunday, a full day on the West Sands, from nine in the morning until four in the afternoon. It had been Gail's idea, and he hadn't thought he would like it – a whole day at the beach. But Gail told him he needed to spend some time with the kids; *You hardly ever see them. All you ever think about is work.* He found himself eyeing the distance, looking for the spot on the beach where they'd spent that day. But the sands were hidden from view by an expanse of fairways, course rough and dune grass, and he realised that day had likely been the most time he'd spent with his children at a single sitting.

His reverie was broken by raised voices behind him, and he turned to see a slender woman in white skin-tight shorts and a loose top being confronted by two SOCOs trying to prevent her from crossing the tape and entering the crime scene. Her head seemed bald, and she carried a backpack. They all quietened as Jessie approached. It took several seconds of face-to-face discussion before Jessie lifted the tape to let the woman under, then pointed to Gilchrist. Looked like Cooper's stand-in had arrived.

CHAPTER 3

When she reached Gilchrist, she said, 'Hi. I'm Sam Kim. I was
told you're the SIO. DCI Gilchrist. Is that right?'

She wasn't bald after all. Her blonde hair was tied back in the
tightest of ponytails, which from a distance gave the impression
of being shorn. Her eyes were liquid pools of the darkest brown
with a hint of the epicanthic fold of the orient.

'It is, yes.' Her grip was firm and dry, making him aware
of his own sweaty palms. Even though he knew she had to
be Cooper's replacement, she looked far too young to have
completed the seven-year medical degree course. She'd offered
no professional ID, so just to be sure, he said, 'And you are here
because . . .?'

'Oh. Sorry. Yeah. I'm the police pathologist. I understand
you've found a body.'

Her accent was nondescript – educated Scottish with no local
dialect strong enough for him to place – and he said, 'I take it you
were called out at short notice?'

She giggled, which only made her seem impossibly younger. 'I
was in the gym, getting some exercise in before I started. Didn't

pick up the call on my mobile until after I'd showered. Would've been here earlier otherwise.'

He nodded. 'Before you started . . . ?"

'Work.'

'I see. Which is where?'

'Well it was going to be Glasgow, but it looks like it could be here now.'

'Could be?' he said, not sure he'd hidden his surprise.

'I was informed that Doctor Cooper's had to take time off for personal reasons, and that there's an immediate opening for a police pathologist in Fife. So, here I am.' Another chuckle.

'So,' he said. '*Start* . . . as in start work for the first time?'

'Yes. I sat my finals in May.' She looked around her as if taking in the pastoral scene, before her eyes settled with a glint of excitement on the crime scene tent.

'Good results?' he enquired.

Perfect teeth set off a smile that sparkled with youthful energy and something else . . . unbridled confidence? 'Top of my class.'

'Excellent. And have you ever carried out a post mortem before?' he tried.

'Only assisted. As a student.' She slipped her backpack from her shoulders. 'Shall we get started?'

He struggled to still the niggle that worried deep inside him. As SIO, he had control over all aspects of the crime scene and its investigation, but he'd never had the need to insist on a more experienced pathologist. She looked no more than sixteen, for crying out loud. And no practical experience to speak of. Her input at this stage could jeopardise his investigation. On the other hand, the chances of her doing something wrong with a twenty-year-old skeleton were pretty slim, he supposed, and if it came

14

down to it he could always find someone else to do a second PM, just to be sure. Besides, in this heat, they needed to get the body removed and back to the mortuary without any delay.

'Something wrong?' she said. 'You look worried.'

'Well . . .'

'Don't worry. I'm excellent at what I do.'

It was on the tip of his tongue to remind her that in real terms she'd done nothing at all yet. But wisely, he said, 'Why don't you suit up, while I have a chat with the SOCOs.'

Without a word, she unzipped her backpack, and removed a sealed Willis Safety pack – Kappler disposable coveralls, Nitra gloves, Tyvec overboots and Solway disposable mask.

Well, at least she'd come prepared.

When Gilchrist reached Jessie, she said, 'I wasn't sure how long we'd have to wait, so ordered a small generator, fans and an AC unit, in case the body dissolved in the heat before she got here. Now she's here, do you want me to cancel it?'

'No. Let's see how she does. She might welcome it.'

Jessie glanced at Sam Kim, now suited up in full forensic outfit, and about to step inside the crime scene tent. 'So what's going on with Becky?'

'She's taken some time off.'

'That's a pity. For a moment I thought you were going to tell me she'd been fired.'

He ignored her comment and said to Colin, the lead SOCO, 'I need you to expand the crime scene, say by another ten or twenty feet.'

'What're we looking for?'

'A bullet, if we're lucky.'

'Will do.'

Colin walked off to the SOCO van parked at the edge of the fairway, which was as close to the victim as it could be driven.

Jessie said, 'So when did you find out about Cooper?'

'Smiler told me this morning.'

'So it's only just happened?'

'It seems so.'

'And when were you going to tell me?'

Gilchrist stared off to the horizon. He didn't particularly care for being challenged by Jessie, but she and Cooper had never hit it off, and he didn't need Jessie to get off to a bad start with Cooper's replacement, whomever that might be. Surely not Sam Kim. No practical experience to speak of, and for such an important position any candidate would need to go through an intensive and rigorous interview process. No, he concluded, Sam Kim was temporary, good enough to be called in at short notice during the holiday season—

'Earth to Andy, hello-oh.'

He looked at Jessie, almost surprised to see her still there.

'So when?' she said.

'I wasn't going to tell you until you needed some cheering up.'

She chuckled, and said, 'You smarmy bugger,' then her face dropped. 'Uh-oh, this looks like trouble.'

Gilchrist turned to find Kim walking towards them, peeling the mask from her face, shaking her head as if to release her ponytail, and looking somewhat flustered. When she stood before him, she said, 'I'm going to take some photographs, then we need—'

'The police photographer's already been and gone,' Jessie interrupted.

'I always take my own photos, in case they miss something. Once I'm done, which will be in about ten minutes, I'll need the remains taken to Bell Street Mortuary right away, including all the soil that's been removed from the grave. The heat could be destroying any recoverable DNA. So can you organise that for me?'

Gilchrist nodded. 'Sure.'

'I also want all the soil beneath the body, to a depth of no less than six inches, put in separate containers. One for the soil beneath the head, another for the chest, and so on. It's important to keep it in order. Can you get that organised, too?'

'Can do, yes.'

'Good.' She walked away, pulling her mask back over her face.

'Bloody hell,' Jessie said. 'I thought Queen Becky was bossy, but she's—'

'Let's not get off on the wrong foot with her,' Gilchrist interrupted. 'Come on, we've got work to do, starting with you cancelling that equipment delivery.'

Jessie chuckled. 'That'll teach her.'

CHAPTER 4

North Street Police Station, St Andrews

By 8 p.m. that night, Gilchrist had a preliminary post-mortem report emailed over to him from Kim. Cooper had always complained that he was too pushy, that post mortems took time, despite which she'd done what she could to comply with his demands, even if she had made him feel guilty at having done so. Well, if Kim was Cooper's replacement, for how ever long or short a period, she would have to get used to his demanding ways. So, he'd insisted on having a draft PM report emailed to him by eight that night.

And here it was.

As he read through it, he realised that Sam Kim was indeed excellent at what she did. Her PM report stated that the victim had been killed about fifteen years ago – a bone density analysis would be ordered for a more accurate time of death – and not only gave a detailed account of cause of death – not one, but two bullets to the head – but also included information to assist in identification of the victim, and her hypothesis on the manner in

18

which the victim had been killed. She'd also taken DNA samples from the victim's bones, with a note that she'd instructed it to be fast-tracked through the system as high priority.

After a quick skim-through, Gilchrist read it again, taking his time to make sure he understood exactly what Kim had determined. Two entry wounds had been found, still in good enough condition to estimate the size of the bullet – 0.32 parabellum – with a sketch that showed entry and likely exit wounds.

Two entry wounds to the skull, one at the back of the head, the other to the right temple. Preliminary analysis suggests that the back headshot was the first and the fatal wound, with exit most likely through the mouth. The lower mandible was too badly damaged by the excavation machine to confirm this, and a reconstruction of the fragmented jawbone and teeth (which will take some time) . . . slipped in for his benefit, no doubt. He might be demanding, but there was only so much she could achieve in the time available. He read on: . . . *might confirm this. The second bullet to the temple entered the skull post mortem.* No ifs, ands or buts about it. Sam Kim seemed remarkably confident in her assessment. But could he trust her? And how much of it was really conjecture? From experience he knew that angles of lines of fire, and similarly, blood-spatter analyses, could be particularly fickle.

Still . . .

Comparison with the exit wound beneath the aural cavity confirms that this shot was fired at an angle, suggesting that the shooter stood over the victim and aimed the barrel at a downwards angle. Okay, he might buy that, but if the shot to the back of the head did in fact kill the victim, then the angle of the second shot would depend on the manner in which the body had fallen to the ground, surely. In his mind's eye, he visualised the man on his knees, gun to the back of the head, shot being fired, then the body toppling into the ready-dug grave.

That stopped him.

He turned his gaze to the window and stared out at the shifting skies. Clouds edged with a hint of pink seemed to be thickening for the evening. *Red sky at night, shepherd's delight*, which promised another good day tomorrow. If the body had toppled into the grave, and the second shot was fired, then it was possible – no, make that *likely* – that the second bullet must be in the grave. But the body was lying supine, face up, which didn't fit with his imagined execution. Even so, he felt a thrill of excitement at the possibility that the second bullet might still be in close proximity to the body. He pursed his lips, and shook his head. Finding one or both bullets would be helpful, but without the gun that fired them, all they could confirm was where the victim had been murdered. So he shouldn't focus all his efforts on locating them.

He turned back to the report, scanning the pages until he found what he was looking for, and decided that this is what he should put manhours against.

Clothes: Nothing was found in any of the suit jacket or trouser pockets. The material was wool, in a heavy check (burgundy and blue as best I can determine, as the material is too deteriorated to confirm the colour), but definitely not tartan. The suit buttons are unusual, not plastic or metal, but a hard material, probably stone, with a marbled effect, suggesting a flamboyancy in the victim's dress sense. The suit is likely made to measure. A tag stitched to one of the inside pockets bears the name and address of the tailor: Hugh Cannon, Specialist Tailor, 114 West Nile Street, Glasgow. Well, there he had it. The suit was indeed made to measure. It had to be. *Specialist Tailor.* You didn't live in

St Andrews and drive to Glasgow to be fitted for a suit, although it wasn't out of the question. So although not conclusive, the victim most likely lived in Glasgow or the surrounding areas. But if so, why drive all the way to St Andrews to murder the victim and dispose of the body? Because no one would expect him to have been buried in Fife? Was that it? That aside, a chat with Hugh Cannon in the morning would be a good start.

But was the *Specialist Tailor* still in business?

Gilchrist clicked his mouse, moved the cursor, and typed in *Hugh Cannon*, only to be presented with a waterfall list of Cannons, none of whom were tailors, specialist or otherwise. He tried *Specialist Tailor* and up popped another list – *Bespoke Tailors; Specialist Sewing and Alterations; Shirt Makers; Tailor Jobs* – none leading him to the tailor he was looking for. Another fifteen minutes of combinations and variations led him nowhere, and a quick effort on Google Maps brought him to the front of a darkened sandstone building on West Nile Street that looked as if it was abandoned and waiting silently for demolition.

Back to the PM report.

Another stirring of excitement at the discovery of a piece of jewellery.

A single diamond ear stud was located in the soil beneath the victim's skull. Despite my request that the soil be removed with locational care, there is no way to confirm if it was from the left or the right ear. Gilchrist gave that some thought. Not like Colin or his team of SOCOs to be lax. But did it matter which ear was studded? Years ago, when men wearing jewellery was far from the norm it is nowadays, ear studs were recognised as a statement of sexual orientation. But for the life of him, he couldn't remember if it was left or right. And did it matter? In current times, male ear studs were more common and often stated nothing other than the fact that the wearer liked to spend money on jewellery.

Still . . . a visit to a jeweller's might be worth making.

By 9.20 he'd found nothing more in the PM report that could help ID the victim. He'd sent an interoffice email to Jackie – researcher extraordinaire – with instruction to find all she could on Hugh Cannon, Specialist Tailor. He might have moved away from West Nile Street and be working from new premises. Or maybe he'd retired or even died. No matter the whats or the wheres, Jackie would track him down.

He powered down his computer, pushed back from his desk, and stood. He stretched his shoulders, rolled his neck, trying to ease the stiffness that seemed to inhabit his body on a more permanent basis these days. He'd taken up jogging along the West Sands again, but despite his best intentions to do so daily, the relentless presence of work had interfered. Several missed days in a row ended up being a missed week, and in the end the promise of a daily jog had become a thing of the past. He needed to be much more strict with his personal fitness regimen, and made a mental note to enquire about membership in a local gym.

He pushed through the door onto North Street, mobile to his ear, and smiled when Irene answered. The sound of her voice often sent a pleasing shiver through him.

'Sorry I'm a tad late,' he said to her.

'That's all right. I was watching telly.'

'Anything exciting?'

'If you can call watching a recording of Nigella Lawson cooking shrimp exciting, then yes.' She chuckled at that, a soft sound that he always thought should come from someone so much younger.

'I'm heading home and thought I'd have a quick pint,' he said. 'Would you care to join me?'

'I'll pass,' she said. 'I've got an appointment in the morning that I can't miss.'

He entered College Street, and walked towards Market Street, the Central Bar on the corner as good as any magnet. He couldn't remember Irene mentioning an appointment, but he'd noticed that his short-term memory was nowhere near as good as it used to be. Rather than query her, he said, 'Tomorrow's Friday, and I was thinking it might be nice to have a quiet meal somewhere. Just the two of us. Nothing special.'

The line seemed to hiss with digital silence.

'If you're up for it,' he pressed on, 'I'll book a table, and give you a call?' He wasn't used to ending his sentences with a question, but something in Irene's silence – he hoped it wasn't Irene's *reluctance* – gave off the sense that all was not right.

'That would be nice,' she said at length. 'But won't you be busy with that body they found on the golf course? It's been on all the news channels.'

Sometimes the speed with which the local press picked up news surprised him. But he should have expected that the extraordinary police activity on the Old Course in the form of crime scene tape, SOCO van, and a gangload of forensic-suited SOCOs going about their gruesome task would not go unnoticed. Strictly speaking, he wasn't allowed to discuss an ongoing murder investigation with anyone outside his team. Even though he knew Irene could keep a secret, he didn't take the bait, and ignored her question.

'How about the Dunvegan? Haven't been there for a while. Six o'clock for seven work for you?'

The line remained silent for a few seconds, before she said, 'Yes, that would be nice.'

'I'll come round at five-thirty, and we can have a few drinks before we eat.'

'See you then,' she said.

'That's great.' But the line had already died.

He slipped his mobile into his pocket, and stepped into the Central Bar.

CHAPTER 5

Not yet the weekend, and the place was heaving. Thursday seemed to be the new Friday. Or maybe that rarest of rare events – a hot Scottish summer's night – was excuse enough for everyone to throw responsibility to the wind and be willing to suffer a hangover at work the following day.

He squeezed his way to the bar, but if he thought he would find a seat he was sorely disappointed. Three deep, he managed to catch the eye of a barmaid, and shouted, 'A pint of Belhaven,' pleased to see she either had excellent hearing or could lipread.

A minute later, with pint in hand, he found a less crowded spot closer to the door to Market Street. Not the best of places to have a drink, but at least it gave him the option to slip outside if the din and congestion became unbearable. A youthful couple, all white teeth and tanned faces, pushed past him to the bar. He caught the American accent, and found himself puzzling, as he always seemed to do, at St Andrews' magnetic pull for global tourism. But with such popularity came higher prices, although as a local Gilchrist received *local* rates for beer, and was well enough known in the Central to keep a monthly tab.

As he took his pint to the halfway mark, he happened to make eye contact with a young woman – late twenties, early thirties, if he were a betting man – standing in a small group at the far corner of the bar. When she smiled and gave him a quick wave, he smiled in return, struggling to recall where he'd seen her before. As if reading his mind, she waded through the crowd to introduce herself.

'Hi,' she said. 'Fran Patten.' She chinked her glass to his. 'Cheers.'

'Cheers,' he said, then added, 'I'm sorry, but I can't . . .'

'I'm a friend of Jessie's. We met briefly at a seminar in Glasgow about eighteen months ago. But you got called away in the middle of it. Some emergency, or something.'

'Ah, yes,' he said, as his memory peeled back the fog of the past. He and Jessie had been obliged to attend a seminar on the need of funding for the mental health of survivors of abuse, or some such thing, but he'd made an excuse to miss the afternoon session – not an emergency at all, just his dislike of sitting through lectures on a subject he considered was of no benefit to him – or members of his staff, for that matter. Not that the mental health of survivors of abuse or other such crimes was of no import, but he often thought that funding could be better spent at the front end of the equation – the police and other forces deployed to prevent crime in the first instance – rather than at the back end, or the aftermath, where it seemed as if it should all have been avoided.

'Haven't seen her for ages,' Fran said. 'I'm up in St Andrews for a few days with some friends . . .' A quick glance at the corner had him thinking it must be a hen party '. . . and thought it would be good to catch up with her.' A frown, then, 'She's still working in St Andrews, isn't she? With the police?'

'She still is, yes, and are you?'

'Me?'

'Still working for the police?'

'No, I'm not in the police. I work with the local council. Glasgow District.'

'I see.' He raised his glass, in a cheerio sort of gesture. 'Well, it was nice meeting you again, and I'll let Jessie know I bumped into you.'

'Do you have a number for her? A mobile, or something.'

'I can't give out her number,' he said, with the finality he felt it needed.

'I understand. Protocol and all that. Here.' She slipped her hand into the back pocket of her jeans. 'Can you give her this?' She handed over a dog-eared business card. 'And have her call me?'

'I'll certainly ask her.'

'Great. Thanks. Can't wait.'

Gilchrist watched her return to her friends, then whisper something that must have been funny, because two of them laughed and threw a glance his way. Somehow, that simple action killed his pint for him. It no longer tasted welcoming, as if it were the last of a bad batch. He placed it on the bar top, quarter full, nodded to one of the barmen, then turned and walked into the night air.

It felt wonderful to be enveloped in a warm ambience, rather than the chill that often accompanied nightfall in Scotland. All the tables on the pavement were taken with customers having a late bite, or celebrating the weather, or maybe the early start of the weekend. Most tables were stacked with empty glasses – beer, wine, gin – and he wondered at the laziness of it all, why no one carried their empties back to the bar any more. A faint smog of

27

cigarette smoke clouded the air, and he found himself resisting the urge to breathe it in as he side-stepped past. He turned into College Street, back towards the Office, and in North Street walked through the pend to the car park in the rear.

He clicked his key fob, and his car winked at him.

Once out of St Andrews on the road to Crail, he called his daughter through the car phone. 'Hi, Mo,' he said, when she answered. 'Haven't heard from you in a while. What's new?'

'Oh, the usual, you know.'

He almost said that he didn't know what the usual was because they hadn't spoken to each other since . . . when . . . the start of last week? He often felt as if he didn't know either of his children at all. When had he last spoken to Jack? Two weeks ago? Three? And as for Mo, it was often hit or miss. He knew she'd finished her Open University course, which seemed to have taken years, and, as best he could work out, was on the verge of graduating. But what did he know? It sometimes seemed as if she didn't want to share her life with him, as if she wanted to leave St Andrews at the first opportunity. Graduating with a degree in criminology was one way of doing it.

'Any luck with the job front?' he tried.

'I wondered how long it would take you to find out.'

Find out? 'I'm sorry, Mo, you've lost me. Find out what?'

'Haven't you heard?'

'Clearly not.'

'I've been offered a job with Strathclyde Police. I start on Monday.'

A flurry of mixed emotions swept over him. Disappointment that she hadn't shared her success with him. Delight that she'd found a job at all, especially in today's market, and with the police, too, what with all the cuts going on. And surprise at the quick start. Next Monday, only three days to go?

'Well, that's great, Mo, I didn't know you'd even had an interview.'

'I didn't want to tell you, Dad. I wanted to get a job off my own bat.'

'You didn't want me putting in a good word for you, is what you mean.'

'Yes . . . I suppose so . . . I'm sorry.'

'It wouldn't have mattered what I'd said, Mo, or how much I praised you up. If you weren't suitably qualified, you wouldn't have got the job. End of. So well done you. That's great news.' He had a pile of questions to ask her – when was the interview, where was it, who had interviewed her, and where exactly was she going to work? – but that was too much too soon, so instead he said, 'I think that's cause for celebration. What're you doing tomorrow night?' The words were spoken before he remembered he was going out with Irene for a meal that night.

'I can't, Dad, I've got too much to do.'

Too much to do sounded like she was giving him a body swerve, that she'd applied for the job all by herself, taken and passed the interview off her own bat, as she'd said, and now wanted to move to Glasgow all on her own – an independent woman in her own right. But it had him thinking.

'Can I help you with anything?' he tried. 'Drive you to Glasgow, take care of your flat in South Street—'

'I've rented the flat out, Dad, and the new tenant moves in on Monday.'

He found himself easing his foot off the pedal as he took in this news. Where the hell had he been when all this graduating,

29

interviewing, house-moving, wheeling and dealing and flat-letting was going on? All of a sudden he felt so far out of Mo's life that he wondered if he'd fallen out of favour with her, that perhaps he'd done something wrong, the kind of thing that only women know, and men have no idea about. It struck him then that Mo was more like her mother than he could ever have believed possible.

'Well,' he said, almost lost for words, 'if you need me to do anything, help you in any way, just let me know. I'm here for you.'

'Thanks, Dad.'

'Love you, princess,' he said, and listened to the cold click of a dead connection.

He drove on into the darkening night, troubled by his feelings. He should be pleased that his daughter was striking out to her own future, making a new home and a new career for herself. But even so, those thoughts did little to lighten the heaviness in his heart.

CHAPTER 6

Back at Fisherman's Cottage, his home in Crail, he stripped off and threw his clothes into the laundry basket. Even though he'd been suited up in full forensic attire, the smell of death always managed to creep into the tiniest of crevices of a person's being. He turned the thermostat up as high as he could suffer and, despite the warm evening, stepped into a piping hot shower.

He lathered his body from top to toe, poured shampoo into his hands and washed his hair, then rinsed himself clean, revelling in the sharp pinpricks of a hot, hard shower. He gave his body another lathering, rubbing soap all over as if trying to cleanse himself not only of the smell of death, but of all upsetting thoughts.

Maureen troubled him, or perhaps more correctly, her attitude troubled him. At times she could be the most loving daughter, as if she were unable to live life without her father's presence. But when some idea settled into her head, some thought that she had to come to terms with, she could be unreachable. Had he upset her in some way? Should he have called her more often? Had he missed a birthday, a special event, an anniversary? But no matter how much he churned it through his mind, he stepped from the shower none the wiser. He dried himself off, his mind set that he would call her tomorrow, and again offer to help.

He pulled on a pair of cotton shorts and a loose-fitting T-shirt, opened a cold bottle of Budweiser from the fridge, and stepped outside into his back garden. The sun was down, and the night air enveloped him, as still as a warm blanket. A number of solar lights, which had been given to him as a gift out of the blue by Maureen, cast soft beams of white onto the stone boundary wall, up a trellis of honeysuckle, over a sprawling wisteria. He eyed the dog-eared business card, and phoned Jessie.

'Don't tell me it's an emergency,' she said.

'Am I not allowed to call you up for a night-time chat?'

'Aye, that'll be right. What're you after?'

'Fran Patten,' he said. 'D'you know her?'

'Fran who?'

'Patten.'

The line hung in silence for a few seconds before she came back with, 'Short blonde hair as tight as a dyke's?'

'Well, that's one way of describing her. But her hair was more orange than blonde.'

'She dyes it.'

'So you know her?'

'Barely. What about her?'

'She's up in St Andrews for a few days, and would like you to give her a call.'

'Why?'

'You'd need to ask her. I met her in the Central, and she gave me her phone number. You interested?'

A pause, then, 'Yeah, why not?'

He read it out to her, and said, 'Got an early start tomorrow, and a busy day. I'd like you to check out a piece of jewellery.'

'Oh, that's very kind of you, but my birthday's been and gone.'

'A diamond ear stud,' he said. 'Recovered from soil under the deceased's head. It's currently with Sam Kim, so you can pick it up from her in the morning. Find out what you can about it. Maybe it's nothing more than a trinket, but something tells me it could be valuable.'

'And if it is, what does that tell us?'

'It tells us that some jeweller might recognise it, or remember someone buying it.'

'*Some* jeweller,' she said. 'Anyone in mind?'

'The Argyle Arcade in Glasgow. Isn't that place full of jewellers?'

'It is, yes.'

'So that's your first stop.'

'Hang on, Andy, you're losing me. Why Glasgow?'

He told her about the PM report, the specialist tailor's suit tag, the two shots to the head, and his thoughts on the second bullet.

'And this specialist tailor,' Jessie said, 'Hugh Cannon, with a business in Glasgow. You've already got Jackie researching him?'

'Yes.'

'And you'll want to have a chat with him, no doubt.'

'Yes.'

'Well, why don't we go down to Glasgow together?'

'Because I don't know what Jackie will find out, or when she'll find it.'

'Ah, right, so I'll make a head start with the ear stud.'

He took a mouthful of Bud, then said, 'You don't sound happy.'

33

'No, it's okay, it's just that my wee car's developing a cough, and I need to take it to the doctor.'

'Have you checked the oil level?'

'The oil what?'

'For crying out loud, Jessie,' he said, 'you've got to . . .' then stopped when he heard her giggling.

'Of course I've checked the oil level. Well, Robert has. He knows a bit about engines, and thinks it just needs a right good service.'

'When was it last serviced?'

'Aye, well, I'll tell you about that another time.'

He took a sip of his beer, and found himself smiling. Jessie'd had her car for a couple of years, as best he could recall, a Fiat 500. But small-engined or not, you still needed to have it serviced on a regular basis. This next service would likely be its first.

'Look,' he said, 'why don't you collect the ear stud from Sam Kim first thing, bring it back to the Office, by which time Jackie might have something on this Hugh Cannon, and we can drive to Glasgow together? Does that work?'

'Can I take my wee car to the doctor's, too, and you can pick me up there?'

'Sure.'

'Thanks, Andy. You're a sweetheart. I'll call you in the morning.'

She hung up.

Gilchrist looked at his mobile for a few seconds, wondering if he should text Jackie and ask her to prioritise Hugh Cannon. Then he decided against it. Jackie was a civilian, a hardworking individual with severe physical disabilities – a pair of crutches to help her get around, and a stutter so bad she was as good as mute.

34

She worked all hours of the day and night, and for all he knew, she could already be on it.

He finished his beer, and was about to return inside, when he decided to phone Colin, the lead SOCO. But the call went to voicemail, and he left a message asking Colin to meet him on site first thing in the morning – 7 a.m. – and to bring a metal detector, explaining that with two shots to the head, one of the bullets could be in close proximity to the body. Finding the bullet might not help them ID the victim, but it could lead them to the killer.

He ended the call, picked up the empty Bud, and returned inside.

He poured himself a good measure of Aberlour, a Speyside whisky recommended to him by his son, Jack, of all people. Jack Gilchrist, the same guy who used to guzzle vodka shooters as if they were sweeties, and who now had an art gallery in Edinburgh and a wee baby girl four weeks old. For years, he'd always worried that Jack would fail as an adult, that he would never find a job, that he would always be a penniless artist living in abject poverty all for the sake of his passion, his art. But here he was now, the father of a beautiful baby girl, partner to an older woman, a Swedish beauty with a criminal background, and a successful – or so it seemed – businessman, running an art gallery in Edinburgh. And for these same years, he never worried about Maureen. She'd recovered from her horrific attack all these years ago, and was making a new life and a new career for herself. But now . . .?

Now he wasn't so sure.

He sat in front of the TV, put it on mute and clicked on the closed captioning. He took a sip of the Aberlour, loving its smooth heat as it slipped down his throat. Then he picked up the draft PM

35

report and flipped through it once again, searching for anything that might give him a clue. But alcohol at the end of a long day, and the hot summer spell, were too much for him, and fifteen minutes later, as sleep overpowered him, the pages slipped through his fingers and fell to the floor.

CHAPTER 7

Friday morning

Gilchrist woke stiff-necked to a black-screened TV. Without pulling himself from his chair, he looked around to gather his thoughts. Daylight shone through the blinds on his front window. The TV remote sat on the side table next to a half-empty glass of Aberlour. Pages of the draft PM report lay scattered on the floor. He couldn't see his mobile phone, and couldn't remember where he'd left it. He pulled himself to his feet, straightened his back with some painful care, then tidied up the mess.

In the kitchen, the clock on his microwave told him it was 05:17, an awkward time if you thought about it – too late to go back to bed, and too early to go to work. He found his mobile on the breakfast bar – out of charge – and plugged it in. Next, he filled the kettle and switched it on, opened the back door, and stepped outside.

Not a cloud in the sky. His back garden was protected from the wind by walls on three sides, and acted like a sun trap. Not that there was any wind to speak of, and the temperature had to be already in the high sixties – in old money, that is. He sat at his garden table, and turned his face to the already risen sun while he waited for the kettle to boil.

Five minutes later, mug of tea in hand – little milk, no sugar – he flipped through the PM report again, regrouping his thoughts, setting out the day's schedule in his mind. From the kitchen he heard his mobile beep, and returned inside to check it out.

Two text messages, both from Jackie. He checked the times – 02:42 and 02:53 – and felt a flush of guilt course through him. He hadn't intended for Jackie to work overnight, had expected her to work on it at the Office in the morning. But Jackie being Jackie, whose entire world it seemed revolved around her job with the police, had put all personal matters to the side, and jumped on her task right away. You couldn't ask for a better employee, and he made a mental note to thank her personally in some way.

He opened the first text, which gave him Hugh Cannon's full name – Hugh Bonar McInley Cannon – home address – some street with a Glasgow postcode – and date of birth, and to save him the bother of calculating it, his age at seventy-three. No mention of any death certificate, so it seemed that Mr Hugh Cannon, Specialist Tailor – presumably retired – was still alive. The second message was a short text advising him that while preparing a more detailed report she had discovered that Cannon had a criminal record, and she would have to finish her report later that morning once she was able to access his files. Gilchrist knew that access to the PNC – the Police National Computer – could be granted only through computer terminals at the Office, so Jackie had taken her research on Hugh Cannon as far as she could from her computer at home.

But what she'd provided thus far, had him thinking. Hugh Cannon, a specialist tailor with a criminal record? But specialist tailor to whom? Who would let a tailor with a criminal record measure them up for a suit? But would you really know your tailor from Adam, let alone that he or she had a criminal record? Not necessarily. You'd let yourself be measured for your suit, return for a final fitting, then pay for it, ignorant of your tailor's criminal past. But somehow that didn't sit well with Gilchrist. A tailor with a criminal record would most likely make made-to-measure suits for the criminal underworld, or at least some of them. And if the deceased was indeed a criminal, could his DNA already be in the system? Not so sure about that one. He'd been murdered fifteen or so years ago, when DNA analysis was pulling itself out of its infancy, so if he were a betting man, he would have to concede with some reluctance, that it seemed unlikely. Still . . .

He put his mobile back on charge, and returned outside, surprised by the warmth and humidity in the air. It seemed surreal to be walking about the garden in the early hours of a Scottish morning, neck sticky with sweat, the air heavy with the promise of another hot day. He noticed his potted geraniums by the back shed were drooping, and a closer inspection of them and the rest of his garden confirmed he'd been remiss in taking care of it. He unrolled the garden hose, and spent the next fifteen minutes soaking every plant and bush and blade of grass he could find, including random weeds – they could be pulled out later. He was reeling in the hose when his mobile beeped from indoors.

The call was from a number not memorised in his contacts list, so he answered with a simple, 'Hello?'

'DCI Gilchrist?'

'Yes.'

'This is Sam Kim. I'm sorry to call so early, but I need to inform you that I missed something in my draft report. I don't know if it makes any difference or not, but I thought you should know about it first-hand.'

Well, the high-flying super-confident Sam Kim with the excellent exam results was human after all. 'I'm listening,' he said.

A deep intake of breath, then, 'I've carried out a microscopic analysis on what I at first thought was natural deterioration of the left ulna, one of the main bones in the forearm, it's the thinner of the two, and discovered that the deterioration was not natural at all, but evidence of an earlier trauma. So I checked the right ulna, and found that it showed signs of a similar trauma.'

'Trauma like they'd been broken sometime in the past?' he said.

'No, DCI Gilchrist—'

'Call me Andy, please.'

'Okay . . . Andy.' A pause, then, 'No, not broken, but fractured. And not fractured from some accident, but from . . . and here I'm making an educated guess . . . but fractured from repeated beatings.'

'Couldn't he have been involved in a car accident, say, and fractured both his arms?'

'Possible, but I don't think so.'

'Why not?'

'I also checked the fibula and tibia in both legs, the main bones that connect the knee to the foot, and they all show signs of trauma.'

'So you're suggesting that this poor guy's suffered numerous fractures to both his arms and his legs.'

'No, what I'm suggesting is that this poor guy's been beaten senseless, time and time again. I'd even go so far as to say he's been tortured.'

As the impact of what she was telling him worked through his brain, he struggled to understand how knowing this could help his investigation. If the victim had been tortured as Sam Kim was suggesting, what did that tell him? That the victim had possibly spent time in prison where beatings were often handed out as prisoner-to-prisoner punishment? Maybe he was a masochist who beat himself, or maybe he liked rough masochistic sex—

'Are you still there?'

'Sorry. Just thinking,' then said, 'Did you find anything else that might help ID him?'

'I've completed the post mortem now and found nothing more on his clothes, other than to say that the material was high quality; remnants of silk lining in his waistcoat and suit, expensive-looking buttons, and lots of them; four on each sleeve, pockets buttoned inside and out, his fly was buttoned, too, which I thought was odd. All in all nineteen buttons, all of a marble-like material. His shoes, too, were handmade, with one heel thicker than the other—'

'As a result of the beatings?' Gilchrist offered.

'No. From an older injury to his hip, which I'm surmising altered his gait. I think most people would likely live with a limp, and just get on with it. But not this man. I'd say he took care of himself, and was likely vain in his appearance.'

Well, well, well, he thought. All this from a skeletonised body. She'll be telling him what the victim had for breakfast next. 'What about DNA?' he said, just to bring it back to reality. 'I need you to expedite it. I have a sneaking suspicion that he might have been part of the criminal element. His DNA could already be in the national database.'

'I'll chase that up first thing. Anything else?'

He couldn't think of anything to ask her, and said, 'Just get back to me as quickly as you can with the DNA, thanks.'

She grunted what he took to be a Yes, then hung up.

He refilled his cup of tea, zapped it for twenty seconds in the microwave to heat it up, then returned outside. The air smelled warm and fresh from his heavy watering, and reminded him of early morning walks when he holidayed in Spain. When had he last been there? Five years, six, more? He couldn't say. What he could say was that this extraordinary hot spell had him longing for more, that he needed to take time off for a well-earned holiday. Maybe he and Irene could have ten days in Majorca. She'd told him that was one of her favourite places for a holiday. Should he suggest that to her tonight?

But that thought troubled him.

What would the sleeping arrangements be?

He'd been seeing Irene now for what . . .? Five months? And in all that time, they'd never spent the night together. Not that they'd never made love. In the heat of the moment, they could have been desperate teenagers on their parents' sofa. But as for staying the night, something always seemed to hold Irene back, as if she had to overcome some awful memory, force whatever had happened to her to the back of her consciousness before she could let go. He'd broached the subject only once before, about six weeks ago, in an attempt to help her. She'd listened to him with quiet intent, before telling him that he shouldn't worry, it would all be fine in the end, then changing the subject. It was not in his nature to press her for sexual favours, or to enquire into her personal thoughts. He enjoyed her company, and she his, and as long as they continued to spend time together, enjoying their companionship, then that was perfectly fine with him. He would book a table for two at the Doll's House that evening, have a nice meal after a couple of pints in the Dunvegan; something to look forward to.

Even though it was the start of a murder investigation, when his team would normally be racing against the clock – the first forty-eight hours being the most critical – the fact that this victim had been killed years ago made it less urgent. Still, he needed to move it forward, find some way to ID the poor soul, and, if possible, work out why he was killed, and who killed him. He picked up the draft report and his cup of tea, and returned inside for a shave and a shower.

Then he would head off to the Office.

CHAPTER 8

Jessie pulled herself from bed and stumbled into the bathroom, trying to avert her eyes from the mirror. She hated how her body had turned out, even though she'd lost some weight, down from eighty-five kilos to seventy-three, last time she'd checked. But at five six, maybe less – she hadn't measured her height in years – she felt as if she was still more dumpy than slender.

She turned the shower on, and brushed her teeth while the water heated up. Normally, that simple action would liven her up, bring her back to life after a good night's sleep, but not that morning. She hadn't slept well, which was not like her, but had lain awake most of the night, drifting in and out of sleep as her mind replayed last night's conversation with her son, Robert. Well, conversation might not be the correct word as Robert was stone deaf. He had been all of his life, and would be for the remainder of his life, because his auditory nervous system had never developed at birth. She couldn't remember what the proper medical term was, some fancy word that the doctor had for it, but all that mattered to Jessie was that her wee boy would never hear her tell him that she loved him.

And how she loved him, her wee boy who was wee one moment then six foot two the next, and working as a joiner. And how they could talk to each other, using sign language that worked as good as any linguistic tool. And how he was so like his mum's personality, with an innate sense of humour that he used to chase his personal dream of becoming an author. He'd managed to find a publisher who wanted to take him on, but it turned out to be one of those vanity publishing companies that take your money then do eff all for you after that. But he'd taken advice, and walked away. Jessie had been so proud of him when he'd done that. Here was a chance to start his dream for real, but he'd been pragmatic and sensible, and so mature about it, that she sometimes wondered if he really had come from her. And he always seemed upbeat, no matter what life threw at him. Which was what was now worrying her. For last night, he'd come home from work, later than usual, didn't want anything to eat, and after a quick shower slipped into his bedroom without his usual nightly chat with his mum. She'd stood outside his bedroom door for several minutes, and thought she could hear him crying.

And that's what had kept her awake most of the night.

Her wee boy was hurting, and she didn't know what was wrong with him. She ran a thousand scenarios through her mind, until in the end she'd made herself sick with worry. But all that was going to stop, for this morning she was going to talk to Robert, and sort it out.

A subtle shift in the flooring, felt through her bare feet, and a sharp creak from another room as the old house complained about the start of a new day, had her switching off the shower, throwing on her bathrobe, and scurrying downstairs. She wanted to make sure he didn't leave for work without speaking to her.

In the kitchen, she followed Robert's morning routine upstairs by the noise from the ceiling. He'd had his shower, and was now dressing above her, over there, in the corner of his bedroom. The floorboards cracked as he crossed the room. Any second now his bedroom door would open, and he would come downstairs. She had the kettle on, and two slices of bread in the toaster. Like Jessie, Robert wasn't a big breakfast person, preferring something light first thing, until the body became accustomed to a new day. Then she heard his bedroom door open, and the upper hallway flooring grunt and crack, and just in case he decided not to have any breakfast at all and slip out for work without so much as a Good morning, mum, she eased to the door, casual like, as if she was checking up on mail, and caught sight of him as he swung around the half-landing.

She smiled at him, and signed, 'Good morning, Robert, and how are you this fine sunny day?'

'Okay.'

'Fresh toast's about to pop up, and the kettle's boiled.'

'I'm not hungry, Mum. I'm running late for work. We've an early start.'

She barred his way to the door, and stood with her arms folded. He frowned at her, as if to ask what she thought she was doing, and in his eyes she could read his pain, almost feel his hurt at something that was upsetting him.

'I'm late, Mum. I have to go.'

She unfolded her arms. 'We need to talk.'

'Not now. Later.'

'Now,' she signed, and gave him one of her looks that told him he would either have to do as she asked, or physically lift her out of his way. 'I want to know what's wrong. I want to know why you're not talking to me.'

46

His face tightened, he shook his head, and his arms hung loose by his side as if he was unable to lift them and form any sign language.

She stepped forward then, pulled her wee boy's face down to her, and whispered into his ear. 'I love you, Robert, my wee boy. I love you so much. I'm here to help you, and I'll do whatever I can, if you'll only let me in.' Even though he couldn't hear her, she knew that he could feel the vibration of her voice, and know that she was speaking to him, maybe even know what she was saying.

When she pulled back, Robert ran a finger under his eyes, and turned away from her in case she saw he was crying. She followed him into the kitchen, and sat opposite him at the small oak table. She reached across and took hold of his hand, and he squeezed back, still unable to look into her eyes.

She released his hand. *'Are you going to tell me what's up?'*

'It's Niamh. She's finished with me.'

Jessie could've jumped for joy. Her wee boy didn't have terminal cancer after all, or wasn't about to be fired from his job. In fact, nothing had happened at all, only that his girlfriend had given him the boot. But Robert and Niamh had always seemed good together, although there was just that something about Niamh that Jessie had never warmed to, as if she were too perfect to be true. She didn't want to minimise Robert's hurt by telling him that losing a girlfriend was nothing to worry about – it happened all the time – and he'd get over it and find someone else. Instead, she signed, *'That's awful, Robert. What happened?'*

He hung his head, couldn't look her in the eye.

'Did you have an argument?' she tried.

He shook his head.

'What happened? Can you tell me?'

47

He lifted his head and stared at her. Mixed emotions swept behind his eyes like waves in a dark sea – anger, despair, hurt, puzzlement. But anger won as he stabbed and signed, '*She slept with someone else,*' then jumped up from the table, and stormed from the kitchen.

Jessie didn't have time to respond or stop him. Instead she just sat there, listening to her wee boy's rushed departure; the rattling from the hall cupboard as he picked up his bag of tools, a hard thump on the wall as the cupboard door closed – or he'd punched the wall, she couldn't say – the hard click of the outside door opening, and the thunderclap shudder as it closed with such force that the letterbox clattered and a mounted photograph fell to the floor. Which was so unlike Robert. Despite all the difficulties he'd faced because of his deafness, she'd never once seen him angry. He'd been upset before, of course, cried, too, been sad as well. But never angry. Never once had he shown her his temper.

So this was a first for her, and for Robert, which she hoped she would never see again. For at six-two with shoulders out to here, and biceps like tempered steel from working in construction, her wee boy had no idea of his own strength. And now Jessie didn't know how he would cope with that most volatile emotion of all – jealousy. As a detective, she'd been called to numerous scenes of domestic violence, witnessed first-hand the senseless devastation caused by a husband or partner enraged by the other's infidelity. She didn't know who Niamh had slept with, but she was going to make it her business to find out.

For God help the poor bastard if Robert ever laid his hands on him.

CHAPTER 9

Gilchrist drew to a halt outside Jessie's house in Canongate. She'd called him earlier that morning to announce a change of plan – her car wouldn't start, and she'd arranged for someone from the garage to have a look at it later, and could he pick her up? They'd agreed a time, but he'd had to call ahead to let her know he was running ten minutes late. Before his breakfast, he'd decided enough was enough, that he needed to exercise, and on the spur of the moment had gone for a short run down by the harbour. After showering, he felt refreshed, his muscles aching in a pleasant way, which told him he should get back into his early morning jogs along the West Sands, and get into some sort of shape before he became too old.

The passenger door opened, and Jessie bustled in. 'Go,' she said. 'I need a coffee. And forget the latte. I want a double espresso. Make it a triple.'

'Rough night?' Gilchrist said as he drove off.

But Jessie seemed more interested in her mobile than explaining her feelings, and a few minutes later, as he accelerated through the mini-roundabout at the West Port, she said, 'Got you, you wee bitch.'

'Anyone I know?' Gilchrist said.

'Shouldn't think so. It's Robert's girlfriend. She's dumped him, and here she is on Facebook posting photos of herself with her new boyfriend.' She held her mobile out to him, but he was too busy negotiating traffic to take a look. Back to scrolling her mobile. 'Here she is again. I mean, look at her, she's almost topless, for crying out loud. Aw, for God's sake, there's another one. Is she kissing him or eating him?' She slapped her mobile onto her knee. 'I don't get it with the younger generation, this social media crap, Facebooking this, Twittering that. I mean, who gives a toss?' She pulled out her notepad, and scribbled into it. 'Ward Peterson. Never heard of him. Looks a right smarmy wanker, too. What does she see in him? More tattoos than the Edinburgh bloody Festival.' She slapped her notebook shut and stuffed it into her pocket.

'Good morning to you, too,' Gilchrist said, pulling up alongside Costa Coffee. 'You really want an espresso?'

'Nah, just the usual latte. But I'll take a muffin. Cranberry if they've got it.'

'Thought you were on another diet.'

'Don't you start. I'm not in the mood.'

Gilchrist found a space in the car park of the St Andrews Links Clubhouse.

'We'll walk from here,' he said, and took a sip of his latte.

Jessie had almost finished her muffin on the drive to the beach, and stuffed the rest of it into her mouth before getting out of the car. She took another slurp of coffee to wash it down, then said, 'Why are we here? I thought we were picking up some jewellery.'

'I wanted to have another look at the murder scene.'

She looked over the fairway dunes and greens. 'Couldn't you get any closer? We're miles from the estuary.'

'It's a lovely day for a walk.'

And it was. Even at that time of morning, the sun rode high in a cloudless sky. He'd caught the weather on the TV; a cold front was moving in from the west, with thunderstorms and heavy downpours forecast for Sunday morning. He looked across the West Sands beyond St Andrews Bay. The horizon was no longer crystal clear, but harboured the hint of a sea haar running off the sands beyond Tentsmuir. Maybe the weather was about to break earlier. Another sip of coffee, then he turned towards the course. They crossed a fairway, found a tarmac pathway, and walked side by side in silence.

'You're quiet this morning,' Jessie said at length. 'What're you thinking?'

'I was wondering why you wrote Ward Peterson's name in your notebook.'

'So I wouldn't forget.'

'I'm thinking it's so you could check him out.'

'That, too. He looks a right scumbag.'

'I'd say you're biased.'

'Just protecting my wee boy. Making sure no harm comes to him.'

Gilchrist thought it odd that Jessie would say that. He didn't know Robert all that well, but he'd seen him often enough, and where his own son, Jack, was slim to the point of skinny, Robert was the epitome of a strapping young lad. 'I'm sure Robert can look after himself,' he offered.

'It's not Robert I'm worried about. Well, I am really, but not in the way you're thinking.'

'Which is?'

'That if this Peterson punter's thinking of giving Robert a doing,' she said, and shook her head, 'I'm worried that it could be the other way round.'

Gilchrist frowned. He'd never heard Jessie speak of her son in any way other than with pride. But here she was, talking about him as if he were about to start a fight. 'I always thought Robert was a nice young man,' he said. 'He's never been violent in any way, has he?'

'Not at all.' She finished her coffee, was about to toss the card-board cup into the gorse before having second thoughts, then let out a heavy sigh. 'This morning, something clicked in his brain. All to do with this Niamh bitch putting it about behind his back. I'd never seen him like that before. His eyes, Andy. They were wild. And he was angry. Really angry. And hurt. I think that's what worries me the most. The pain in his eyes. I just . . . I don't know . . . he looked so wild, I thought he was mad enough to . . .' She paused, as if to gather her breath, then rattled out, 'I thought he was mad enough to kill someone. There. I've said it.'

'And that someone could be Ward Peterson?'

'They told me you were good.'

'Joking aside,' he said. 'Is Robert on social media?'

'Who isn't at his age?'

Well, he supposed it had been a silly question. But Jessie's concern for Robert was real, not just as a mother, but as a police officer. Like her he'd witnessed enough scenes of domestic distur-bance to know that jealousy and infidelity were the dominant reasons for violence. And a person's upbringing didn't seem to matter. When relationships failed, all sense of rationale evapo-rated. Anything could happen. And often did.

He remembered one of his earliest murder investigations, where a woman had been clubbed to death in her living room. When the police arrived, her husband – a retired bank manager, who'd never had so much as a speeding ticket in his sixty-odd years – had been sitting on the settee watching the TV, his wife's battered body by his feet. He'd turned the TV to mute when Gilchrist entered, then stood, hands held out for cuffing. His motive for murdering his wife of thirty years? She'd wanted him to move into the spare bedroom, because she was losing sleep over his snoring.

'Do you think talking to someone would help Robert?' he said.

'I can't see him doing that,' Jessie huffed. 'Talking about all his personal feelings isn't him. He's like me in that way, in fact he's like me in so many ways it's scary.'

'Are you capable of murder?'

'I've been angry enough to think about it,' she said. 'But I know I could never go through with it.'

'Well, there you are. If Robert's like you, he'll have the same feelings. He'll get upset, angry, feel mad enough to kill, then with time it'll pass, and he'll settle down.'

'You think so?'

He didn't want to say anything that would destroy the sense of hope he'd caught in her voice, and instead said, 'I know so.'

'Good.' She nodded. 'That's good.'

'But you need to talk to him,' he added. 'Just to make sure.'

She cast him a wary glance, as if undecided, then fixed her gaze on the estuary as they strode on.

CHAPTER 10

Colin, the lead SOCO, was already at the site, having set up a wider police perimeter, with his fully suited team setting out lines across the grass, to ensure nothing was missed as they swept the area with the metal detector. 'That work for you?' he asked Gilchrist.

Gilchrist eyed the scene, some fifty yards by sixty or so, he thought. With budgets slashed and bean counters watching costs like eagles over rabbits, he had the sudden sense that his search for the bullets – a super-longshot at best – could be manhour intensive.

'This way.' Even though the body had been removed, the forensic tent was still in place. He entered it. 'Let me run this past you.'

Colin nodded. Jessie looked on in puzzled silence as Gilchrist kneeled on the ground next to the grave site.

'I'm thinking that whoever killed the victim would not have done so remote from this site, but killed him here.' He looked from one to the other. 'Agreed?'

Colin shrugged. Jessie said, 'Why lug a body over the grass when you can get him to dig his own grave for you? Seems as good a way as any. Okay, agreed.'

'So,' Gilchrist said. 'Two shots, and according to Sam Kim, the shot to the back of the head was the fatal shot, right here.' He placed a finger to the nape of his neck.

'How do you know which way he was facing?' Jessie again.

'I think he would be facing this way when he was killed, because this was the way his body was found – head here, feet there. He would've fallen forward, then all they would have to do was roll him into the grave.' He reasoned, 'Why turn the body around, head for feet, when a shove was all that was needed? It's all conjecture, I know. But hear me out.' He lay forward, on his stomach, head to one side. 'Now, the second shot is through the right temple.' He pointed with his finger.

'Why shoot him if he's already dead?' Jessie said.

'Coup de grâce? Two bullets to be doubly sure? I don't know. But what I do know is that two shots were fired into his skull. He placed a finger to his right temple. 'So if the bullet went in there, it would come out here.' He lifted his head, and slapped his hand to the ground, then stood. 'I would concentrate your search around this area first, Colin, extending out in a line from the grave. If you find nothing, then try the same on the other side of the grave. He could've been shot there, and rolled in from that side.'

Colin nodded, then said, 'And if we find nothing in the end, do you want us to continue with our search outside?'

This was where it could all fall apart, with manhours piling cost upon cost, and all for what? The slim possibility of finding a bullet? Which might help identify the gun, but after fifteen years, would they ever locate that weapon? All this, and a thousand other questions flew through his mind with electrifying speed to reach a weak conclusion. 'Give it until midday,' he said.

Back outside, he walked with intent back to his car, Jessie almost trotting beside him.

'What's the rush?' she gasped.

'If the bullet's not by the grave, then it'll be like looking for a needle in a haystack. I don't have any budget set yet, and I can't see Smiler agreeing to us combing the whole of the Old Course on the off-chance of finding a bullet that might not get us anywhere. Get hold of Sam Kim,' he said, 'and let her know we're on our way to collect that ear stud. Then find out if Jackie's come up with anything more on Hugh Cannon.'

'You've got his home address though, right?'

'Yes, but it would be good to know a bit more about him before we talk to him.'

'Got it. But I'll wait until we're in your car. I can't do anything on the run.'

Gilchrist glanced at her, thought she looked out of breath, then slowed down. 'When you contact Jackie,' he said, 'why not ask her to check if Ward Peterson's on the PNC in any shape or form?'

'Thanks, Andy. I was going to do a bit of background checking myself. But rather than tie up Jackie, it might be better to have Mhairi look into him for me.'

'Sure,' he said. 'That's even better.'

Once back in the car, Jessie removed her mobile and tapped the keypad, as Gilchrist accelerated around Bruce Embankment.

They first drove to the police mortuary in Dundee and collected the diamond ear stud from Sam Kim, shower-fresh and already at her desk despite having had only a few hours' sleep. She also gave

Gilchrist a plastic box that contained the nineteen buttons, every one like a polished slice of grey and white marble, and each with an individual pattern.

By the time Mhairi phoned Jessie with what she'd found on Ward Peterson, they were in the outskirts of Glasgow on the M80. Gilchrist set the speed control to the 50 mph speed limit, and listened to the call on speaker.

'Nothing major,' Mhairi said. 'He's had a couple of ASBOs, and runs around with a bad crowd.'

Gilchrist didn't like the sound of that. Anti-Social Behaviour Orders were issued to individuals who harassed or caused harm or distress to others, and were often an indicator of that person's latent criminality. Peterson might not have a criminal record yet, but if he was running around with quote unquote, *a bad crowd*, then it might be only a matter of time.

'One ASBO for breach of the peace,' Mhairi said, 'and being drunk and disorderly. Another for taking a leak on someone's front doorstep. Both of them after football games.'

'Let me guess,' Jessie said. 'Local derbies in Dundee?'

'Don't know. Would you like me to find out?'

Gilchrist said, 'No, it's not important, Mhairi. Anything else on him?'

'Not on him, but one of his friends, the crowd he runs around with, was charged with possession of a weapon, which turned out to be one of those credit cards that you pull apart to reveal a concealed blade. Said he used it only when he went fishing, for cutting lines, that sort of thing. He was given the benefit of the doubt and sixty hours' community service.'

'Okay, thanks, Mhairi. Is Jackie there?'

'She's at her desk. Want me to get her for you?'

'She's looking into something for me. If she has anything more on Hugh Cannon, can you have her send it to me as soon as? And if Peterson's name crops up any time soon, I want you to let me know.'

'Will do.'

Jessie ended the call as Gilchrist pulled off the M80 heading for the city centre. 'I'm going to have to talk to Robert tonight, and make sure he knows to keep away from this Peterson guy. He could be trouble.'

Gilchrist nodded in agreement. 'Good idea.'

They hit traffic on Castle Street, and Jessie removed the ear stud from its wrapping. 'If this is a real diamond, I'd say it's worth close to a thousand. What do you think?'

'It's been a long time since I bought any diamonds, so I haven't a clue.'

'How are you and Irene getting on?'

'That's a bit of the quantum leap. Why would you ask that?'

'Don't know. Just thinking.'

'Right,' he said, and eased through a set of traffic lights. He couldn't remember the last time he'd visited Glasgow, and it seemed to him that the architectural landscape had changed. Modern flats now stood on what had been vacant ground, and whole sections of tenement buildings that looked as if they could last for another century stood derelict, as if waiting for the inevitability of demolition. He worked his way through the confusion of the city's one-way system, taxi- and bus-only lanes, and eventually managed to drop Jessie off close to the St Enoch Centre.

As she opened the door, he said, 'You know where you're going?'

'Any woman who's lived in Glasgow knows the Argyle Arcade.

Aren't diamonds a girl's best friend?' She gave him a smile and a toodle-do wave, then set off.

He was working his way back out of the city centre when his mobile rang – ID Colin.

'You were right,' Colin said. 'We found one of the bullets: 0.32 parabellum on the other side of the grave. About eight inches deep.'

The ground must have been soft, he thought, for the bullet to enter and exit the skull and still have sufficient velocity to power itself into the ground to a depth of eight inches. 'Is it in good condition?'

'Good enough. The lines are clear enough for a match to a gun.' A pause, then, 'Do you have a gun to match it to?'

'Therein lies the problem.'

Colin said, 'And we also found what looks like a metal clasp, like the piece that clips an earring in place in pierced ears.'

'Lying on the surface?'

'More or less.'

He gave Colin's words some thought. If it fitted the diamond stud Jessie had with her, maybe the killers, or one of them, had ripped the stud from the victim's other ear before he was buried. Which would explain why the clasp was found on the surface, but not why only one diamond stud was stolen, and not two. And what did this tell him about the victim? He wasn't sure, but it did tell him he had an opportunity to save on his budget.

'Okay, Colin, wrap it up. We're unlikely to find that first bullet. It could be anywhere. Send what you've got to Bell Street, and I'll have Sam Kim have a look at the ear studs.'

He ended the call, and followed the slow-moving traffic through the busy streets.

CHAPTER 11

Hugh Cannon lived in Eastburn Road in Balornock, an inner suburb of Glasgow, in a semi-detached house in what had once been a council estate before Margaret Thatcher's government introduced the right-to-buy scheme. Once identical houses, every home now had its own identity stamped on it in the form of front porches, tiled roofs, solar panels, painted fences, and hedges trimmed and shaped to perfection. Cars lay parked on slabbed driveways that ran to side doors.

Cannon's home was distinctive in that it seemed to be the only house without a porch, and no car parked in the driveway. A tufted lawn, in dire need of watering, fronted the home in straw-coloured patches. Opened windows on the ground level told him that Cannon was at home, or at least should be. Or maybe it was a safe neighbourhood.

He rang the doorbell, and waited.

A minute or so later, he tried the doorbell again, gave the letterbox a hard rattle for good measure. His peripheral vision caught the flicker of a window blind, then through the front-door-panel window he watched a shadow shift along the hallway, until the door cracked open to reveal an elderly man stripped to the waist, barefooted, wearing what at first looked like shorts more suited to the Caribbean than darkest Glasgow, but were in fact swimming shorts. The oily fragrance of suntan lotion lifted off wrinkled skin that was more burned than tanned. White chest hair as thick as wool matched an uncombed head of hair as wild as an Aboriginal's. And not a tattoo in sight.

Well, that was the older generation for you.

He held out his warrant card, introduced himself, and said, 'Hugh Cannon?'

'Aye.'

'Can we talk?'

'What about?'

'In private, if you don't mind.'

'And if I do mind?'

'I wouldn't want us to get off on the wrong foot, if you get my meaning.'

'Aye, I do. Round the back.' And with that, the door closed with a dull thud.

Gilchrist stepped to the side of the house, and followed a narrow slabbed walkway to a wooden gate, which creaked open on rusted hinges. Cannon had already settled back into a sun lounger and was busy anointing his body with oil.

'Pull a seat over,' Cannon said, nodding to a set of plastic garden furniture parked in the far corner next to a covered barbecue.

Gilchrist did as instructed, and positioned his chair next to Cannon.

'The neighbours'll be pleased,' Cannon said.

'Why's that?'

He snapped the waistband of his shorts. 'I usually sunbathe starkers, but I wouldnae want to embarrass an officer of the law now, would I?'

Gilchrist looked around the garden, at low hedges and open fences and overlooking windows that afforded a row of neighbouring homes a clear view. No privacy at all for any nude sunbathing. 'Don't the neighbours object?' he said.

'They used to.'

'Are you not concerned about them, about young children perhaps—'

'Fuck the neighbours.'

Well, he supposed that put an end to the subject.

Cannon settled lower into his sun lounger, shuffling and shifting until his body was just so, then he closed his eyes, and said, 'So . . . what have I done wrong?'

'Nothing, as far as I'm aware. I'm here to ask for your help.'

'Well that's a fucking change. You bastards harassed me for years, and now youse want me to help?' He gave a throaty chuckle. 'Wonders'll never fucking cease.'

'Why would we harass you for years?' he asked, just to find out if Cannon would open up to him.

'Youse lot thought I was laundering drug money through the shop. I was nae use at keeping books up to speed. That's all. Ended up owing money to the taxman. And once these bastards get their teeth into you, they're worse than drowning rats with fucking lockjaw.'

Not all truthful, according to Jackie, but a reasonable start. 'You're a tailor,' he said.

'Used to be.'

'Used to have a shop in West Nile Street, too.'

'Youse've been doing your homework, I see. Well done.'

'When did you retire?'

'I didnae retire. I had to file for bankruptcy to pay the fucking taxman.'

'Death and taxes,' Gilchrist said. 'The only certainties in life.'

'Aye, and once I'm deid, then I'll've paid my dues. So why don't you tell me what the fuck youse want? Then you can fuck off out of it and gie me peace.'

Gilchrist removed one of the victim's suit buttons from his pocket, and held it out. 'What type of buttons are these?'

Cannon open one eye, squinted at the button in Gilchrist's hand, then piece by piece stirred back to life. First his other eye opened, then his head lifted, and his mouth opened as if to speak, and with slow deliberation he reached for the button as he pulled himself upright.

Gilchrist let Cannon take it from him, long-nailed nicotine-stained fingers turning the button over and over, rubbing the surface, as if expecting a genie to emerge and grant him his wish. Then he glared at Gilchrist, blue eyes as cold and hard as tempered steel.

When he spoke, his voice was as rough as gravel in a mixer. 'Where the fuck did you get this?'

'Let me ask the—'

'I said . . . where the *fuck* . . . did you get this?'

'I'm afraid I can't disclose that yet—'

'But you found it here. *Here?*' he pleaded. 'In *Scotland?*'

'We did, yes. That and another eighteen, all sewn onto an expensive-looking suit and waistcoat, with silk lining, tailored by you.'

'Jesus fuck.' Cannon shook his head, staring at the button again. 'I fucking knew it.' Then he looked at Gilchrist, eyes wild as if his mind was filled with fierce thought. 'Was he murdered?'

Gilchrist hesitated, then said, 'We believe so.'

'I knew it, I knew it, I told them, but they wouldnae listen to me.'

'Who wouldn't listen to you?'

Cannon stared at him as if he were crazy. '*Youse* lot.' Then he turned his gaze back to the button and shook his head. 'He'd gone off to the Far East, was what youse tried to tell me. I said youse were thicker than a week's worth of shite, could youse no read the writing on the fucking wall? Rab wouldnae just get up and leave like that. It wisnae in him. He loved this place. I know he talked about going to Thailand and the Philippines, but that was just for a holiday, some place he wanted to visit, no go and live there? But aw naw, youse were right, and I was wrong, and when youse showed me a faked manifest on a slow boat to China, or some such fucking place, youse then told me to fuck off out of it. Wouldnae even put him down as a missing person. Just told me to piss off and get a life.'

'Rab who?' Gilchrist tried.

Cannon lifted his head. Tears glistened in his eyes. His lips seemed to shiver as he said, 'Rab Shepherd.'

The surname sent a tremor of recognition through Gilchrist. But surely never.

'Big Jock's wee brother,' Cannon said, as if reading his thoughts.

Gilchrist felt ice tickle his neck. Big Jock Shepherd, now deceased. Not so long ago he'd been Glasgow's crime patriarch, although many would say *Scotland's* crime patriarch, with criminal fingers that stretched the length and breadth of the UK. He'd been known to run his businesses with a fist of steel during a formidable reign of over forty years, and had no doubt presided over many a gruesome death. And in all that time, not once had Gilchrist ever heard mention of big Jock having a brother.

He had a vague recollection fifteen or twenty years earlier, not long after he'd joined the Force, of catching some story that had run for a few days, of a series of Glasgow gangland shootings. At the time, the media had described it as a territorial dispute between two criminal families, the Shepherds and an Italian-named group that fell into abrupt anonymity thereafter. Had big Jock's wee brother, Rab, been killed as part of that feud?

The timing seemed about right.

His thoughts were interrupted when Cannon held up the button. 'Rab bought a bunch of these from some guy, an American salesman or something. Three dozen I think he bought. Told him they were rare as fuck, and Rab being Rab had to have them. Paid over the odds for them, but I had to make two suits for Rab that month, just to use up all the buttons.'

'And what are they made of?' Gilchrist asked, just to satisfy his sense of curiosity.

'Some sort of stone, but no a rare marble as Rab was told. They're original enough,' he said, holding the button closer, turning it as if to catch the light. 'Polished to a fine sheen. Every one of them slightly different. Every one unique. Beautiful though, aren't they?'

Silent, Gilchrist watched Cannon admire the stone button, a hint of a smile tickling the corners of his lips, as if he was remembering happier times. He had no reason to believe that Cannon was telling him anything other than the truth. That being so, then the victim now had a name, but it would be useful to have a date. He would have Jackie dig into the archives to confirm the date of the gangland shootings, which might help him pin down the date of Rab's execution – because that's what it was now, not just a routine murder, if there ever was such a thing, but a made-to-order gangland assassination. But if he thought about it, if the police had carried out their duties in a professional manner as one would expect, then Cannon's report of Rab missing would have been filed in the records – which would give him a more accurate time of death. But from the way Cannon described it, the police had ignored him, and likely filed nothing. Still, it was worth a shot.

'Do you remember when you reported Rab missing to the police?' he said.

'Naw, my heid was a mess back then. Fucked with the drink and drugs, the usual.'

'Did anyone in the police station take notes, can you remember?'

'You're joking. They treated me like I was some fucking tramp. Couldnae get me out of the place fast enough. Nothing more than a heap of shite, was what I felt like.'

'Did you keep any records of sales?'

'No chance. It was all cash back then.'

Gilchrist grimaced. Cash businesses were as good as red flags to HMRC. Without any records for proof of sales or income, these businesses thought they could minimise income tax and VAT. But the taxman rarely gave the benefit of the doubt, and more often than not would come down hard, with fines and penalty payments, forcing many businesses to go to the wall. Which was really self-inflicted if you thought about it.

He stood upright, was about to leave, when he said, 'What was Rab like? As a person.'

Cannon squinted at him. 'A gentleman. And absolutely fucking harmless. No like that brother of his.'

'Was he gay?' Gilchrist asked, just to throw it out there.

'Bent as a nine-bob note,' Cannon announced, then frowned with a look of suspicion. 'Why did you think that?'

'The diamond ear studs.'

Cannon smirked. 'That was Rab's problem, I'd say. Not that he flaunted it like some of them, standing there like a fucking teapot. And he wasnae in your face. He just went about his business, but didnae hide it. And him being big Jock's brother and all. It didnae sit well with some of them.'

'Them?'

'Jock's sidekicks.'

Gilchrist nodded, letting that thought filter through. 'So what did Rab do?'

'What d'you mean?'

'He went about his business, you said. Which was what?'

'Worked in a bank. Did the accounts, or something. Smart as fuck he was with the numbers.'

'Like a bookkeeper, you mean?'

'Aye, maybe, he never really spoke about it.'

'Did he ever work for Jock?'

'He did, aye, but no full-time, only part-time, and never in the main office. Big Jock mostly kept him away from the business. Tried to keep him out of sight, more like. But Rab was proud of the way he was, and refused to be hidden away.' Cannon shook his head, and looked off to some point over Gilchrist's shoulder. 'That's what probably got him killed, in the end.'

Silent, Gilchrist watched Cannon's gaze return to the button in his hand, and stare at it as if it held the secret to Rab's murder. In the criminal underworld, where points were won for being tougher than the next guy, if you showed any sign of weakness, you suffered. Big Jock had tried to keep his gay brother out of the mainstream. So, if big Jock had tried to protect his brother, who'd had the brazen nerve to go against the family patriarch and kill Rab?

He retrieved the button from Cannon, thanked him for his help, then walked back along the slabbed path to his car.

CHAPTER 12

Jessie pushed through another door into yet another jewellery shop. When she'd entered the first shop about an hour earlier, she'd felt a shameful thrill in eyeing its wares – glass cabinets stashed full of diamonds and earrings and bracelets and brooches and necklaces of all sorts; gold, pearls, rubies, emeralds, all glistening and sparkling in enticing lighting that encouraged the casual shopper to part with their hard-earned money. Oh, if she could only afford to buy one, she thought, she would die a happy woman. But now, on her fifteenth jeweller's, or was it fourteenth? – she'd lost count – the stores had lost their initial appeal, now little more than packed shops that displayed glittering wares that could be baubles and trinkets, and manned by smartly dressed store assistants who aspired to be upper class and whose expectant smiles tripped when she produced her warrant card.

She held it out again to yet another young assistant with white teeth, glossed lips, and blonde hair with black roots. Her eyebrows could be paint or tattoos, and a name tag pinned above her left breast gave her name as Anne Marie. Jessie fished in her pocket and pulled out the wrapped tissue paper, which she placed on the glass top and unfolded with gentle care to expose the diamond and gold ear stud.

'Can you tell me if this was sold in your shop?' She'd already had it valued from everything between fifteen hundred pounds to two and a half thousand, which told her that either no jeweller truly knew what they were talking about, or they were all crooks.

'When did you say it was sold?' Anne Marie asked.

'I didn't. But about twenty years ago. When you were still in nappies.'

If she meant to offend, it didn't work. 'I'll need to ask Mr Levy to have a look at it,' Anne Marie said. 'I'll take it through to him.'

'No you won't. Get him out here.'

'Certainly.' Again, spoken without a sign of fluster or offence. She turned and stepped away from the counter through a curtain of sorts into the back room, to return fifteen seconds later behind a small man with a bald head on which was mounted a contraption – a headband magnifying headset, as it turned out – and a tired look on his face that told Jessie he was as sick at looking at diamonds as she was.

'You have something you want me to look at?' he said, in a voice so quiet you would have thought he was ashamed he could talk.

She nodded to the ear stud on the counter. 'That.'

Levy reached up and pulled the headset down over his eyes, clicked on the LED light, swung in the magnifying eye loupe, then leaned forward and handled the stud with tongs as small as twee-zers. Jessie watched with fascination as he examined the diamond, mumbling all the time to himself, 'Nice stone, yes . . . good . . . good clarity . . . very very slightly included one, I'd say . . . maybe two . . . no, one . . . definitely one . . . lovely, lovely . . .' When it seemed as if he'd examined it from every angle, he looked at her, and said, 'When did you say this was sold?'

'Best guess, about twenty years ago.'

'And how did you come by it?'

'I can't say at the moment.'

'I see.' He released the stud from the tongs, picked it up and pulled the stud from the metal leg. Then he made an adjustment to the magnifying loupe, and peered at the stud as he twirled it round in the light with his fingers. 'It's unusual,' he said. 'You don't see too many of these around any more.'

Jessie frowned. No one in any of the other jewellers had mentioned anything odd about it. 'Why's it unusual?' she asked.

'It's solid gold. Not gold-plated. And twenty-two carats, by the look of it. I have to ask you again, how did you come by this?'

'It's an exhibit in an ongoing investigation, so I'm afraid I can't say.'

Again, he said, 'I see,' then placed the diamond onto the tissue paper, and pushed the headset up and over and onto his crown. He pinched the bridge of his nose between his thumb and forefinger, and shook his head. 'I can't help you.'

'Can't or won't?' Jessie said.

'Can't.'

'Why not?'

'Do you know how many diamonds we sell each year?'

'I'm guessing a lot.'

'We process up to twelve hundred diamonds in any one year. That's close to twenty-five thousand in twenty years. And you're asking me to remember if I sold this one out of all these—'

'*No*. I'm asking you to remember this one out of twelve hundred, twenty years ago.'

'You're playing with words.' He shook his head. 'I'm sorry. I can't help you.'

Jessie took care to refold the tissue. 'You said it's unusual. Solid gold. Not your cheap stuff. So how much would you say a pair of these were worth?'

'For an accurate evaluation I'd need to separate the diamond from the clasp and weigh it to determine how many carats, then I would need to—'

'Rough estimate is all I'm asking for,' Jessie interrupted. 'Best guess.'

'At today's prices?'

'Yes.'

'Somewhere around three thousand pounds.'

'And twenty years ago?'

'Fifteen hundred, two thousand, thereabouts.'

'And you don't remember selling a pair, or coming across them, even though they're unusual?'

A silent shake of the head, and a lowering of his eyes warned Jessie that he was lying. She'd known he was lying. Call it gut feeling, natural instinct, or whatever, but she would bet the farm that Mr Levy with the swivelling headset and the magnifying eye loupe knew more than he was letting on. Without another word, she returned the wrapped-up diamond stud to her pocket, gave him a parting glare, then left the shop.

The covered walkway of the Argyle Arcade echoed with the shuffling of footsteps on the tiled walkway, the whispered chatter of shoppers and visitors – hordes of them, it seemed – and locals taking a shortcut between Buchanan Street and Argyle Street – normally to stay out of the rain, but with the heatwave, most likely to avoid the sun. Jessie eyed the length of the arcade

72

towards Buchanan Street, then to the Argyle Street end. She'd looked at enough diamonds for the day, but more than that, her instincts were telling her that she need go no farther than Levy's shop. As if on cue, her mobile vibrated, and she pulled it from her pocket.

'Hi, Andy. Any luck?'

'I think we've got a name for the victim,' he said, 'but it would be helpful to have that verified from another source. How about you?'

'Not sure. But if you give me the victim's name, I could throw it out there.'

'Rab Shepherd.'

'Shepherd? Any relation to that bastard big Jock?'

'Younger brother.'

'Holy *shit*, Andy. Are you sure?'

'Pretty much.' A pause, then, 'Where are you? I'm pulling in behind the St Enoch Centre. You need a hand?'

'No, I'm just about done. But the last shop I was in, I think the guy recognised the stud, but wouldn't tell me. I could see it in his eyes. I could tell from the way he looked at the stud, that he knew who'd bought it.' She forced herself to slow down, stop rattling on like a babbling brook. She took a deep breath, then said, 'I'd like to try something. If you're up for it, that is.'

'Not sure I like the sound of that.'

She gave him the name and address of Levy's jeweller's shop, then said, 'Could we have Jackie look into this Mr Levy for us? Don't know his first name, but I'm convinced he's hiding something.'

'Will do. But it sounded like you wanted me to do something other than have Jackie carry out routine research.'

73

Jessie held her phone to her ear, and tried to settle her breathing. Jackie would take some time to come up with the goods on Levy, but she felt she needed to know more about him there and then. Which was where it could become difficult. 'Well, if you're up for it, could you do that magic trick of yours again?'

The line fell silent for several long seconds, making her think she'd stepped over the line this time. Then his voice came back with, 'What are you looking for?'

'He might be completely innocent,' she said, all of a sudden regretting having asked the question. 'I could be wrong. It's just a feeling I had. I don't know. I just . . .'

He said nothing until she fell silent, then repeated, 'So . . . what are you looking for?'

'I want to go back in and give the jeweller a shock. I want to tell him that the ear stud belongs to Rab Shepherd. Then I want to know who he phones as soon as I leave the shop.'

'We can't give out that name yet,' Gilchrist said, 'until we know for sure. And even if we do formally identify the victim as big Jock's long-lost wee brother, we might not want that to be made public. Not just yet, anyway.'

She felt herself deflate. She'd screwed up this time, big. She'd asked her boss to do something illegal – *that magic trick of yours again* – and he'd slapped her down in that quiet but firm way of his.

'And besides,' he continued, 'if this Levy is as suspicious as you say, whatever call he was going to make, he's probably already made it.'

Jessie could kick herself. She'd shown herself in a bad light, come across as being someone prepared to skirt the law to get a result. 'I'm sorry,' she said. 'I shouldn't have. I just thought it might—'

'Forget it, Jessie. I've been onto Sam Kim again to expedite the DNA results. If the victim's who I suspect it is, we should get a familial DNA match through his brother Jock. And I've got Mhairi working with Jackie to find out everything they can on Rab Shepherd. We don't need Levy's input. We've already got a result. And we'll pick up a couple of coffees for the drive back.'

'Okay, good, that's good.' It was all she could think of saying.

CHAPTER 13

Gilchrist ended the call from Jessie, then dialled another number. He didn't know how long it would take her to walk to his car, but he knew he didn't have much time. The number rang out without going to voicemail, and he cursed, and tried again.

After ten rings, it was picked up. 'Andy, long time, long time. Sorry about that. Was in the loo. What can I do you for?'

Gilchrist said, 'Dick, I've got another one for you, if you can fit me in.'

'Of course, Andy. No problemo.'

Gilchrist rattled off the address Jessie had given him. 'The boss's surname is Levy. Sorry, that's all I can give you. But I'm interested in any calls he's made from, say, fifteen minutes ago through the end of the day.'

'Does he seem legit?'

'Let's assume that he is.'

'I'm asking, because if he's got a burner, then there's not much I can do.'

'Just give me what you can, Dick. It's a bit of a longshot anyway.'

'Anything else?'

'That's it.'

'And you'll need this for when . . .? Yesterday?'

Gilchrist threw out an appreciative chuckle. 'Tomorrow's fine. But maybe you could give me a heads-up if he's made any calls within the last fifteen.'

'Gotcha.'

The line died.

Gilchrist slipped his mobile into his pocket, and breathed a sigh of relief as Jessie rounded the corner of the shopping centre. He hadn't wanted her to know that he still called Dick, which was why he'd lied to her. She'd caught him out once before, in a rare moment of carelessness – on his part – which was how she knew about Dick. But what Dick did was illegal, and Gilchrist was definitely breaking the law, which was the main reason he'd kept Jessie out of it. Dick was his go-to guy whenever he needed a phone number or phone records quickly, or even recordings of phone calls, without having to go through the correct but often time-consuming protocol of applying for a legal warrant.

The passenger door opened, and Jessie slipped in. 'It's like an oven in here. How can you stand it?'

'I like the warmth. It's an odd feeling, isn't it, being hot in Scotland.'

'Can you please start the engine, and put the AC on for crying out loud? I'm sweating like a sumo wrestler's jock strap.'

'That's quite the image.'

She responded by flapping her blouse at her neck, then pressed a button to open the side window. As Gilchrist pulled into traffic, she leaned her face into the breeze. 'This must be some kind of record,' she said. 'You can almost see a heat haze.'

Gilchrist worked through town onto High Street, and ten minutes later powered up the slip road to join the M8. 'The AC works better with the window up,' he said.

'But I'm loving this breeze.'

Gilchrist switched off the AC and lowered his own window. Warm air swept through the cabin, ruffling his hair, carrying with it the rumbling noise and petrol smell of traffic in full flow. He exited onto the M80 and a couple of miles later indicated left and pulled off the motorway.

'Where are we going?' Jessie said, as he negotiated a roundabout.

'Coffee. I noticed a Costa Coffee on the way down.'

'Do they have ice?'

'Don't know. But I think they have iced coffee.'

'Don't like the sounds of that. Coffee's for drinking hot.'

'How about some ice cream from one of the other shops?'

That seemed to do the trick. Jessie shuffled back from the open window, and swept a hand through her hair as she pulled down the passenger visor and unfolded the mirror. She gave a whispered hiss of, 'Jeez,' as she tugged at her hair, pushed her fingers through it, then tried to fluff it up. 'Rat Woman the second.'

'How about Spaghetti Lady the first?'

'How about you just park over there, and I'll meet you on one of these bench seats outside Costa?'

Duly chastened, Gilchrist pulled into a parking spot and switched off the engine. Jessie was about to trot off for her ice cream, when he said, 'Would you still like a hot coffee?'

'Is the Pope a Catholic?'

'Cranberry, or blueberry?'

'Surprise me.' And with that, she moved away.

Costa was strangely quiet and Gilchrist was served in no time at all. He was seated outside when Jessie arrived, half-finished ice-cream cone in hand, eyes gleaming with the delighted satisfaction of a child in a sweetie shop.

'You look as if you're enjoying that,' he said.

'I thought of getting you one, but it would be dripping all over the place by the time I got here.' She sat opposite him, and licked her cone. 'I remember being a wee girl and trying to lick these things without ever dripping onto my clothes. You had to keep turning it round and round like this.' Which she did, then pressed it to her mouth for another white-lipped mouthful. 'But I could never manage it. I'd come home with ice-cream stains all down my front.' She chuckled. 'Used to drive the old dear crazy. Served her right, the *bitch*.'

Using his fingers, Gilchrist broke the muffin into four pieces. 'Cranberry,' he said. 'Your favourite.'

'You ever think of using a knife?'

'I keep forgetting to pick one up.'

'Typical.'

'Would you like me to get you another muffin?'

'What for?' She picked up one of the broken-off pieces, spilling crumbs onto the table, and squeezed it with care into her ice-cream cone.

'You're not going to eat it like that, are you?'

'Why not?' She smiled at him, then opened her mouth wide and took a bite.

Gilchrist nibbled a piece of muffin, washed it down with a mouthful of coffee, then said, 'Enjoy that?'

'Delish.' She dabbed her lips with a napkin. 'So tell me, how did you get on?'

The next fifteen minutes were spent exchanging details of their meetings – Gilchrist with Cannon, Jessie with Levy. From the way Jessie talked, he wasn't as convinced as she was that Levy was hiding something, but it would be interesting to see what Dick came up with. His mobile rang – ID Mhairi. A table close to them was occupied by a couple more interested in their mobile phones than each other. So rather than put the call on speaker for Jessie's benefit, he walked towards his car, and listened to Mhairi bring him up to speed.

'From what I can find from Jackie, Rab Shepherd didn't appear to have led a criminal life, sir,' she said. 'We can find no record of him on the PNC. No record of having ever been charged, not even for the slightest infringement. He's never had so much as a parking ticket. And we haven't found any mention of him anywhere at the time of the Glasgow shootings twenty-one years ago in October. We do have a copy of his birth certificate, and also that of his brother, James—'

'You mean Jock?'

'I think so, sir, yes, but on his birth certificate his name is James, not Jock.'

'Jock would be his nickname. Any other siblings?'

'A sister, Nadine, sir.'

Well well well. After all these years, he was only finding out now that big Jock had not only a brother, but a sister, too. 'Same mother and father?'

'Yes, sir. Their father is Alex Shepherd, and their mother is Mary Cannon.'

'Cannon?'

'Yes, sir.'

So Hugh Cannon and the Shepherd brothers were more than

80

likely related, and most likely cousins, he thought. Which made a difference to what? Not a lot, came the answer.

'Keep going,' he said.

'Nadine's the youngest by fifteen years, then Rab, and two years between him and Jock, sir.' Mhairi went on to give details of Rab's early years – born and raised in Bridgeton, one of the more notorious regions of Glasgow. Rab as a young boy would have been bullied senseless if he'd shown any signs of homosexuality back then. Jock, as his big brother, could have stood up for him, or ignored him – probably nothing in between. But Rab had survived his childhood and school, and left after attaining five O levels, no mean feat for someone with his family background, and with intelligence sufficient for him to have gone on to take his Higher exams. He wondered for a moment about Sam Kim's comments on Rab's battered bones, but decided not to enquire further.

But Rab had left school and gone to work, first in the fruit market – no details of what he did there, but Gilchrist suspected it would most likely have been low-level labouring work, loading and unloading crates of fruit all morning long, humphing them from one stall to the next – then as a sales assistant in the Men's Department of C&A in Argyle Street, and finally to his last place of employment, the Bank of Scotland, where he worked initially as a teller, and later in the back rooms of the bank, which is probably where he got into accounting – *Smart as fuck he was with the numbers* – until the day he'd allegedly packed up and headed off to the Far East. Just then, Gilchrist's mobile beeped with an incoming call. He thanked Mhairi, told her to continue her research with Jackie, then ended the call.

Dick said, 'You asked me to get back to you if Levy had already been on the phone before you called me.'

Gilchrist pressed his mobile hard to his ear. Jessie might have been correct after all.

'Thought you might be interested to know that he made two calls in the space of thirty seconds, about twelve minutes before you called me. Both were about ten seconds long, the first to a mobile number, the second to a landline. I've checked and both numbers belong to the same person.'

'Ten seconds?' Gilchrist said. 'He's left a message, you think?'

'Or passed one on,' Dick said.

Gilchrist gave that some thought. Had Jessie's presence stirred something up? Or had Levy recognised the ear studs and was already spreading the word that Rab Shepherd – long believed to be living the good life in anonymity in the Far East – had turned up dead on Scottish soil?

'So who did Levy call?' he asked.

'Tony Dilanos.'

Gilchrist stared off to the horizon, his breath stuck in his throat as his world seemed to tilt on its axis. He might be a DCI with Fife Constabulary, some seventy-odd miles north-east of Strathclyde Police Headquarters in Glasgow, but he'd come across the name Dilanos more than once in his career. Glasgow and Edinburgh, Scotland's two largest cities, were home to numerous gangs, some nothing more than a group of drug-seeking youths having a raucous time breaking the law, while others were serious businesses that dealt in drugs, prostitution, trafficking, protection, and anything else that made money or increased their power. And the kingpin of Scotland's gangs had been big Jock Shepherd, now deceased, but whose surviving criminal business was run by none other than Tony Dilanos.

'You still there, Andy?'

'Sure, Dick. Sorry. Thanks for that. Get back to me if anything else turns up.'

He hung up, then signalled for Jessie to finish up her phone call and follow him.

CHAPTER 14

Gilchrist accelerated onto the M80, and set his speed control at 78 mph – within 10 miles per hour over the limit, an almost universally accepted margin that didn't attract police attention or fines. Then he placed a call through the car's speaker system.

Dainty answered on the second ring with a booming voice that could have come from a big man. 'DCI Small.'

'It's Andy Gilchrist here. You got a minute?'

'If you make it quick, Andy. It's fucking looney tunes down here.'

Gilchrist couldn't resist smiling. Although he and DCI Peter 'Dainty' Small had started their police careers together, Gilchrist had stayed on in Fife, while Dainty had struck out for a larger, busier scene, and since then had always let him know it. Gilchrist was never sure if Dainty regretted the move, or enjoyed the bustle.

'Got you on speaker with Jessie,' he said.

'Hope he's keeping you busy, Jessie. Right, Andy, what're you after?'

'Tony Dilanos.'

A pause, then, 'What about him?'

'He took over from Jock Shepherd, didn't he?'

'You know he did.'

'Is he giving you any grief?'

'As in . . .?'

'No challengers for his position, no fights for a power takeover, that sort of thing.'

'None that I know of,' Dainty said, then added, 'Haven't heard from you in a while, Andy, so I'm thinking this has to be something to do with that skeleton you found on the Old Course.'

Part of Gilchrist hadn't wanted to mention the name until he was one hundred per cent certain, while another part of him needed to find out what he could, and to do so he would need to take Dainty into his confidence. 'This can go no further, all right?'

'Lips as tight as a virgin's pussy. Sorry, Jessie.'

'It's not confirmed yet, but we've strong reason to believe that the skeleton is all that remains of Rab Shepherd, Jock's younger brother.'

The line fell silent for several seconds, then Dainty came back with, 'Holy fucking shite, Andy. Are you sure?'

'Ninety-nine per cent. Hoping to have a DNA match later today.'

'My the *fuck* . . . if that's true . . . *Jesus* . . . I don't know . . .'

Gilchrist glanced at Jessie, who looked as puzzled as he felt. He'd expected some reaction from Dainty, but hadn't known what, certainly not the stunned confusion being expleted down the line.

'This could get fucking serious,' Dainty said, seemingly back in control, as if his mind had finally worked through all the options and settled on one.

85

'How come?' Gilchrist said, trying to mask his own confusion. 'What am I missing?'

Dainty said, 'Can you keep this under wraps? The name, I mean. Don't confirm ID until we have a better handle on the situation down here.'

'What situation? You're losing me, Dainty.'

A sigh of exasperation, then, 'You wanted to know about Tony Dilanos? Well, here's the scoop. He's the top man, or so they say, the guy they all run to when decisions have to be made. But he's no Jock Shepherd. Far from it. Big Jock ran the business with a fist of iron. Pull one over on him, and you're done and dusted, end of. Retaliation was swift and brutal. But big Jock was fair, in a pragmatic sort of way. He knew what was what, who was who, and how much he had to pay out, and to who, to keep the status quo. But this cunt, Tony, excuse the French, likes to act tough just for the hell of it, it seems—'

'So they say,' Gilchrist interrupted. 'That's what you said. He's the top man, or so they say. So he's *not* the top man, is that what you're telling me?'

'No one'll come right out and say it, Andy. They'd get their balls stuffed down their throats if they did. But Arletta can give as good as she gets.'

'Who's Arletta?'

'I thought you knew,' Dainty said. 'Arletta's Jock's daughter, and Tony's wife. Tony is big Jock's son-in-law. With only days to go before big Jock passed away, he had a meeting with his top guys, his solicitors, everyone, the fucking lot, and told them what's what. Tony was to take over all executive matters, and take full control of the business with immediate effect. Jock effectively signed over the whole business two days before he died.

Rumour has it, though we'll never know for sure, that big Jock then had his solicitors draw up a separate agreement, signed by Jock, Arletta and Tony, whereby Tony would lose the lot if he ever betrayed Arletta, and by betrayed I mean dealt her out of some business deal, kept money from her, or divorced her.'

Although Gilchrist had listened to every word Dainty had spoken, he was still at a loss. 'But how does the discovery of Rab Shepherd's skeleton affect any of this?'

'When Rab went AWOL, the story was put about that he'd emigrated somewhere to the other side of the world. But the story goes that big Jock saw it as the start of a new turf war, some campaign to take over his businesses, so he instructed his men to retaliate. The place went wild for a couple of days, shootings in restaurants, stabbings in clubs, bodies with their throats slit turning up in the Clyde. Ten people were killed in total, as best I remember, all of them from the Schiavone family, who'd moved up from London and were starting to flex some muscle in the city.

'Those closest to Jock said the killings were nothing to do with Rab's disappearance, but were Jock's way of putting an end to a potential threat to his business, by having the entire Schiavone family wiped out. Jock being Jock came out of it squeaky clean, and we couldn't lay a finger on him. It took a few months for the place to settle down again, and a few years later, Tony Dilanos married Arletta in the wedding of all weddings. Famous people were invited. Singers, movie stars, You'd have thought that Jock was some superstar instead of a cold-blooded gangster. At the wedding, much was made of Arletta's relationship with her uncle Rab, who'd been missing by then. Cried her eyes out, saying how much she'd wished he'd been there, how much she loved her favourite uncle of all time, even though he was the only uncle she had.'

Again, Gilchrist interrupted. 'Hang on, you still haven't told me how finding Rab's body's going to upset things.'

'I was coming to that. And you didn't hear this from me. Okay?'

'Of course.'

'No, Andy, I mean it. You, too, Jessie. Not a fucking squeak. All right?'

'Cross my heart and hope to die,' Jessie said.

The line fell silent for a few seconds, before Dainty said, 'Rumour has it, and I mean fucking rumour, but rumour has it that Rab was a police informant.'

'So nobody knows who was running him?' Gilchrist said, unable to hide his surprise.

'That's what I'm saying. And with him turning up now after decades of speculation, like he's been seen with a couple of toyboys in darkest Thailand or deepest Philippines, or in a gay bar in downtown Sydney, that puts an end to that. But here's where the shit's going to really hit the fan. Tony Dilanos was the person who allegedly managed to convince big Jock that Rab was safe and sound, because he'd personally driven him to Newcastle to catch the Amsterdam ferry, the start of his journey to the Far East.'

'Now I see it,' said Gilchrist.

'And the biggest betrayal of all,' continued Dainty, 'is Tony's lie to Arletta. He couldn't possibly have driven her favourite uncle of all time to the ferry, because he was already dead and buried in Scotland.'

'Ah, shit.'

'Shit indeed,' said Dainty. 'And all of it backing up against the fan, just waiting to be spread.' The phone rattled, as if it had been dropped, then Dainty returned. 'So I need you to keep Rab's ID quiet, until we figure out how to handle it.'

'It may be too late for that.'

'What?'

This was the dilemma when you were involved in criminal activity of your own, you could never come clean, and certainly not to a policeman. 'All I can tell you, is to keep an eye on Levy.' He gave him the shop address in the Argyle Arcade, then hung up.

CHAPTER 15

It took four miles of silence before Jessie said, 'Never heard Dainty so worried.'

Gilchrist grimaced, flexed his fingers on the steering wheel. 'He's worried that some turf war is about to kick off.'

'He certainly wasn't happy when you told him about Levy.'

'No.'

Another mile of silence, then Jessie said, 'You surprised me.'

'In what way?' he said, but knew what was coming. Jessie was no fool.

'Levy,' she said, and left the name dangling for several seconds. 'You knew he'd passed Rab's name on to Tony Dilanos, didn't you?'

Gilchrist thought of denying it, which was the easier thing to do. But ever since Jessie had moved to Fife from Strathclyde Police, he'd come to depend on her, rely on her opinion, value her instincts, and in his own convoluted way to seek her advice on matters professional and personal. Now was not the time to jeopardise their relationship.

'Well, I have to confess that after giving it some thought, I decided to wave my magic wand.'

'I knew it.' She shook her head, stared at the passing country-side for a moment, then said, 'When you mentioned Levy's name to Dainty, I was worried that I'd screwed up with my interview with him, that I hadn't handled it right, and that somehow—'

'You did well, Jessie,' he interrupted. 'As always.'

She grunted a disheartened chuckle, and said, 'Flattery doesn't suit you.'

He kept his eyes on the road ahead – best to say nothing.

'I don't know, Andy,' she said at length. 'I thought you trusted me.'

'I do trust you.'

'Well why not share it with me? Why not keep me in the loop? It's not like I'm going to cough it up, am I?'

He thought silence as good an answer as any, and from the corner of his eye watched Jessie settle into her seat, and turn away from him.

Not until they had crossed the River Forth, with the sun shining on the slopes of the Ochil Hills and clouds rolling across the blue horizon like tumbleweeds of fleece, did he say, 'It's your turn now.'

She looked at him. 'What is?'

'While I was on the phone waving my magic wand, you were on yours. You haven't told me who you were calling. Not that I'm prying, but was it anything to do with Robert?'

'No, it was just that whatsherface . . . Fran Patten.'

The name confused him for a millisecond, until an image of *hair as tight as a dyke's* flashed into his mind's eye. 'So you got hold of her?'

'Yes.'

He turned left at the first roundabout, heading back to St Andrews. 'And . . .?'

'And we've agreed to meet up.'

'When?'

'Tomorrow night.' She turned to him. 'That's if there's nothing urgent going on with this case.'

'Or with Robert,' he added. She nodded in silence, and he had a sense that the mention of her son's name saddened her. 'Have you heard from him?' he tried.

'He'll be busy at work. They're building an extension to some mansion in the back of beyond. I never really hear from him during the day, anyway.'

'Maybe it'd be a good idea to send him a text.'

'Maybe,' she said, then faced the passing countryside again, leaving him to drive on in silence, wondering if his intrusion into her private life had been a mistake.

Back in the North Street Office, the afternoon passed by with annoying slowness.

Nothing seemed to advance his investigation. Hugh Cannon had spent six months in jail, having been found guilty of consistently failing to pay late payment fines, and additional interest charges, as a result of his failure to file his income tax returns in a timely manner, if at all. Jackie and Mhairi also came up with nothing more on Levy and his jeweller's business. On the face of it, Levy was legit, despite his first port of call being Tony Dilanos. Research into Arletta Shepherd – she'd kept her Shepherd surname, despite being married – turned up nothing of interest, other than the fact that she appeared to be squeaky clean, too clean in Gilchrist's opinion, for the daughter of a past, and wife of a present, criminal patriarch.

But what could he do about that? Nothing, was the answer.

He was wading his way through copies of newspaper articles printed around the time of Rab Shepherd's disappearance, when he realised he'd forgotten to give Irene a call. She answered on the third ring with what he thought sounded a tired, 'Hello?'

'Are you all right?' he asked.

'I was having a nap.'

'Sorry to wake you up.'

'That's okay, Andy. It's not something I do often, napping in the afternoon, I mean. It makes me feel guilty in some way, that I should be busy doing something else.'

'I'm a great believer in it – you won't fall asleep if you don't need it. So, don't feel guilty about it. Just enjoy the benefits of a nap.'

'Yes, Doctor Gilchrist.'

He smiled at the sound of her chuckling, then said, 'I was calling to ask about your appointment.'

'I'll tell you about it this evening, if that's all right.'

'Of course,' he said, then reconfirmed the time for him to meet her that evening. 'I'm looking forward to it.'

'So am I,' she said, but after she hung up, he thought she'd sounded more tired than enthusiastic.

Back at his desk, when he tried to pick up from where he'd left off, he found he couldn't concentrate. He revisited a printout on Arletta Shepherd, flipped through it, his eyes scanning the words, but his mind taking in nothing. He put it aside, then decided to give Sam Kim a call, and make a push for Rab Shepherd's DNA results.

'Your ears must've been burning,' she said. 'Was about to call you.'

Gilchrist felt a flush of excitement. 'You found something?'

93

'I put a priority on the DNA analysis, and the results are just in. Here we are,' she said, and the line rustled with the shifting of paper. 'I've done a bit of research on it myself, it's a kind of hobby of mine, genealogy that is. But we've got a match. Not a direct match. He's related to a Mr James Shepherd, who was on the system for all sorts. I haven't been able to put a name to the victim just yet—'

'No need to,' Gilchrist said. 'We've already identified him as Robert Shepherd, James Shepherd's brother. But it's good to get DNA confirmation, thanks.'

'But he's not.'

'What?'

'Rab Shepherd is not James Shepherd's brother.'

Gilchrist pressed the mobile hard to his ear. 'But . . .?'

'He's his *half*-brother.'

'Bloody hell,' was all he could come up with.

'They have the same mother, but different fathers.'

Even though he knew the answer, he said, 'But we've got his birth certificate, which states the father's name is Alex Shepherd, and the mother is Mary Cannon, which matches Jock's birth certificate.'

'DNA results don't lie. Without knowing anything about anyone, I'm guessing that Mary Cannon had an extramarital affair, and when she fell pregnant kept it from her husband by putting his name on the birth certificate.'

Gilchrist had to agree. He'd never known Jock Shepherd's father, but rumours were abound of him being a hardman, someone you didn't mess with. And if he'd found out that his wife had been having an affair behind his back, it didn't take much to imagine how he would have reacted. Better to tell a lie, than come clean with the truth. And Jock Shepherd's mother had lived out the remainder of her life with that lie.

But it did have him thinking what kind of man would have an affair with the wife of someone renowned as a Glasgow hardman. One who was completely ignorant of that fact? A transient, perhaps, who didn't stay anywhere long and moved on? Or someone who knew the facts, and took the risk regardless?

Not that it mattered, he supposed, but it did put a different light on how Jock might have viewed his brother – if he'd known. He'd been protective of Rab, according to Hugh Cannon, even though he must have known Rab was as *bent as a nine-bob note*. Would Jock have been as protective if he'd known Rab was only his half-brother? Or was there a darker reason that explained why Tony Dilanos perpetuated the lie about driving Rab to the ferry?

It seemed he was digging up more questions than answers.

He thanked Sam Kim then hung up.

CHAPTER 16

By six o'clock Gilchrist had uncovered nothing new, and found himself rushing to shut down his computer and leave the Office. The Rab Shepherd investigation was effectively a cold case, and didn't carry the same urgency that a fresh murder demanded. So, instead of working all hours day and night, he'd instructed his team to have a good weekend, and to hit the ground running on Monday morning.

He would have preferred to have driven home for a quick shower and a change of clothes rather than going straight to Irene's. But he'd left it too late, and arrived at her door in South Street, a tad overwrought, and some ten minutes late.

'Sorry,' he said, when she answered the door. 'Late as usual.'

But she smiled at him, leaned forward to give him a peck on the lips, then stood back to let him inside. The temperature had not fallen below eighty all day, and in the cool interior he felt his clothes sticking to him. 'Didn't have time to change,' he said.

'Have a shower,' she said as she escorted him upstairs to the lounge. 'You know where it is. Then I'd like you to try something on for me.' He gave a puzzled frown at that, and she said, 'It's a surprise. On you go.'

He didn't need a second telling, and took the stairs two at a time up to the master bedroom on the uppermost floor. Not that he'd spent any time in the master bedroom, other than to have a shower, which seemed to be becoming the norm rather than the extraordinary.

Ten minutes later, he was showered and refreshed, and standing in the bedroom with a towel around his waist, about to dress. He was beginning to cheer up at the thought of a cold pint of beer and a bite to eat, when the door rattled, and Irene said, 'Are you decent?'

'In you come.'

She entered, and smiled as she ran a light gaze over his semi-nudity. 'I've brought you this to try on. If you don't like it, it's not a problem, I have the receipt. But I do think it would rather suit you.' She laid a crisply pressed white shirt on the bed, as if taking care to spread a delicate sheet. Then she stood back. 'Go on, then. Try it on.'

'What's this for?' he said, all of a sudden feeling embarrassed that he'd turned up in his work clothes, and annoyed with himself for not organising his day better to give him time to go home and get changed. Not that she was teaching him a lesson, he knew, rather this was what he'd found Irene to be like – kind, generous, and always eager to pay her way, split the bill, despite his most manly objections.

'It's a gift,' she said. 'Nothing special. I thought you might like it.'

He lifted it from the bed, held it up, and realised it wasn't his typical M&S shirt, but an expensive-looking designer shirt of the whitest cotton, with a stitched logo on the front that he didn't recognise, and double stitching in dark blue thread on the cuffs that gave it a tailored look. Again, he felt embarrassment shift through him as he slipped one arm into the sleeve, then the other, and pulled the front together.

'How do I look?'

'It's not too tight, is it?'

He closed two buttons around his middle, then another at his chest. 'No. It's perfect.'

She gleamed at him, her eyes creasing with pleasure. 'I thought it would be. And I have to say that it makes you look rather handsome.'

'You mean I wasn't handsome before?'

She smiled at his weak joke, then said, 'Come on, let's go. It's a beautiful night for a walk.' And with that, she turned and left the bedroom.

She took hold of his hand as they crossed South Street, and almost pulled him along Church Street as they strode side by side in determined effort, he thought. He shortened his stride to match hers, and when they crossed Market Street into College Street, the clatter of glasses and the chatter of merriment from the tables outside the Central Bar had him almost calling a halt at the thought of a cooling pint of beer. But he resisted, and when they crossed North Street and stepped into Butts Wynd, which led to The Scores, he said, 'Where are you taking me to?'

'I fancied a walk along the beach first, if you don't mind.'

'Sounds perfect.'

On The Scores they walked towards the Royal and Ancient Clubhouse, hand in hand. In the far distance, by the Eden Estuary, he could make out the gentle flutter of the SOCO's crime scene tape, which he'd insisted be kept in place for a day or two longer, until he was certain they'd recovered all they needed from the crime scene.

'It's wonderful, isn't it?' Irene said, as she slowed down on Bruce Embankment and turned to breathe in the sea air. 'Such serenity. Wild open tranquillity, stretching for miles and miles, as far as the eye can see. There's nothing more beautiful than nature at her best.'

He had to agree. The sea was as calm as he'd ever seen it. Waves slapped against the seawall, as if exhausted after their journey landward. Kites flew in the distance. Swimmers ran in and out of the sea. Joggers jogged, strollers strolled, and seagulls strutted the water's edge, sending a flock of sandpipers scuttling across the sands with legs moving so quickly they could be wheels.

'It's one of my favourite places,' she said.

'The West Sands?'

'St Andrews.' She looked back along The Scores, her gaze shifting over the black rocks and cliff faces, and seemed to settle on one particular spot, as if imagining how little it must have changed over the centuries. 'I always think it's a photographer's dream. But not in this light,' she said, returning her gaze to the sea, then letting it settle on the white strip of Tentsmuir Beach on the far side of the Eden Estuary. 'This light is too hazy, too warm, not sharp enough. This light is more for walking along the beach and feeling the sand between your toes.' She released her grip, and strode off. 'Come on,' she said, slipping out of her shoes. 'It's so refreshing.'

He followed her, puzzled by her attitude, and silently worried by the unsettling sense that she was about to tell him some bad news, that her appointment earlier that day had not gone well. But he said nothing as he slipped off his own shoes and socks, and stepped onto the cool surface of the West Sands.

Together, they walked towards the sea, the sand becoming colder and wetter with each step, until water seeped between their toes.

'Are you going in?' he said, bending down and rolling up the bottoms of his jeans.

Her face wrinkled in a look of surprise and pleasure. Then she nodded.

This time it was he who said, 'Come on,' and reached for her hand and led her into the shallows. Despite the air temperature, the water felt cold and sharp, and swirled around his ankles with icy tentacles.

'This shirt,' he said. 'I love it. But you shouldn't have.'

'It's one of life's simple pleasures,' she said, 'buying a present for someone you love.'

He stopped, held on to her hand, and she turned to face him.

'I know I haven't said it before,' she said. 'But I find that I have come to love you. But I've also realised that I should've been more open with you, Andy, that you deserve to hear the truth.' She took a deep breath, then let it out as she stared over his shoulder to some point in the distance, as if she couldn't bear to look him in the eye. 'You've been the perfect gentleman,' she said. 'You've never pressed me for anything. You've never made me feel uncomfortable. You've just . . .' She looked at him then, her eyes strong and steady, but with just the slightest glimmer of uncertainty in their tell-tale moistening. 'You've just been there for me,' she whispered, 'even when I never knew I needed you to be. You just were.'

100

'I still am,' he said, and took hold of her other hand, and pulled her to him. She didn't resist, just let herself fall against his chest. They stood like that for a while, ankle-deep in swirling water, before he said, 'What's wrong, Irene?'

She smiled, pushed back and shook her head. 'A detective to your dying breath.'

'Don't know if I like the word *dying*,' he said, and chuckled, pleased and relieved in equal measure to see her chuckling in return.

'I don't like the word dying either,' she said, then let out a long sigh. 'But I am.'

He caught his breath as he struggled to make sense of what she'd just said.

'My cancer's returned.' She lowered her head, turned away. 'I never told you because I thought it would have been too unfair.'

'Unfair? I don't understand.'

'I know you lost your wife to cancer. Which is why I've never let you . . . well . . . you know . . . we've never been . . . well, we have . . . but not . . .'

'Come here,' he said, and pulled her to him. He pressed his lips to her hair, kissed the top of her head, and felt her arms encircling him in a tight hug. He'd suspected something had been troubling her, but not this, not this . . . this . . .

'You never told me you'd had cancer,' he said.

She sniffed, nodded into his chest, and said, 'It's one of the reasons I've never asked you to spend the night with me.'

He hugged her tighter, pressed his lips deeper into her hair.

'All the excuses I used to make up for you. It's too soon. It's too late. And that most original of all,' she said, and coughed out a laugh, 'I'm not feeling well. God, I don't know how you put up with me. Any other man would've run a mile.'

101

'It's okay,' he said. 'It's okay.'

'I had major surgery,' she said into his chest, her voice sound-ing pained from the memory. 'Seven years ago. They took off one of my breasts, the right one.' Again another chuckle. 'My daugh-ter tried to make light of it by telling me it was better than taking off the wrong one.'

Gilchrist gave a supporting chuckle in return.

'You've got to laugh,' she said, 'even when there's nothing to laugh about.'

'Laughter's the best medicine,' he said, and cringed at his silly words of wisdom.

She pushed back from him then, and he thought he'd offended her. Then she sniffed, dabbed a hand under her nose, and gave a tight smile. 'On the positive side, I got myself a free tummy tuck.' She caught his frown of confusion, then tapped her right breast. 'It's called a TRAM flap. Reconstructive surgery. A brand new boob and a fake nipple from the muscles and blood cells of a portion of my lower belly. They cut out an oval-shaped section along your bikini line, then tuck it up and under, all intact, then reshape it into what's supposed to be a new boob.'

'I never knew,' he said. 'I mean, I would never have known.'

She looked down at her chest and shook her head. 'It might look the same, but it's not. The feeling's different. But it's not only that. You lose a bit of yourself in the process, and develop the sense that you're not . . .' She paused, her lips moving, as if search-ing for the right word. 'That you're no longer a whole woman. That somehow you're never going to be the same person you were. That the very essence of womanhood has been removed. Well, partially removed, I suppose. The left one's still original.' She sniffed again, tried to brighten with a smile. 'And I also had to go through a course of chemotherapy that almost killed me. It was worse than the surgery, and I swore I would never go through it again if my cancer ever returned.' She ran a hand through her hair. 'God I must look a mess.'

'You look fine, Irene. In fact, better than fine. You look lovely.'

She cried then, large tears that welled and spilled down her cheeks to drop off her chin, and fell into him again. Silent, he held her to him, her body shuffling from quiet sobs, and made a promise to himself to do whatever he could to help this woman. Her cancer had returned. That was all he knew. Not what type of cancer, or even worse, not how long her doctor had told her she had to live. They stood like that until he felt her sobbing subside, then as they separated, pushed his fingers through her hair, held her head in both hands, and kissed her lips.

'Come on,' he said, and took hold of her hand, and waded onto the beach.

CHAPTER 17

They walked along the West Sands side by side, each silent in their own thoughts. Gilchrist couldn't tell if Irene felt as if she'd told him too much and was now regretting it, or if she was contemplating how to spend the remainder of her life. She'd had chemo before, and swore never to go through that again. Did that mean her cancer was incurable? He found he didn't have it in him to ask her, and placed an arm around her shoulder, and walked on.

'Penny for your thoughts?' Irene said at length.

Her question surprised him. But what could he say? Tell her he was thinking of asking how long she had to live? Or what options she might consider if she refused chemo? Or what medical horror lay ahead as the cancer spread through her system? He grimaced, and shook his head. 'I suppose I wasn't really thinking of anything,' he lied.

She seemed to give his words some thought then said, 'I've been selfish, Andy. I'm sorry. Talking all about me.'

'That's what I'm here for. To listen.'

She tucked a strand of hair behind her ear, then stopped walking and stared off across St Andrews Bay to the North Sea beyond. 'It's beautiful, isn't it? So many of us don't appreciate the beauty that surrounds our everyday lives until it's too late. I heard a story not too long ago, about someone who was bipolar, who suffered severe depression all her life, but when she was diagnosed with terminal cancer, only then could she appreciate her life, and enjoy living, knowing that it was about to end, that she had to take in as much of its beauty as she could before she passed away. It's sad when you think about it. All this beauty and we don't appreciate it.'

'My parents certainly didn't appreciate it,' he said. 'They had too much work to do just to put food on the table. They had no time to look around and admire the world. Just surviving day to day, keeping a roof over our heads, and raising a family – me.'

'That's rather a sad legacy is it not?'

'I think it's a generational thing,' he said, pleased to be able to talk about something other than the morbidity of terminal illnesses. 'The generations who went through two world wars were deprived of so much their entire lives, simple things like eggs or milk, or having enough money to pay the rent, not being able to afford a house of their own. My mother ran our home on a shoestring budget. Money just wasn't around. But they never complained. They just got on with it. Nowadays, they're up in arms when the price of flights to Spain or Cyprus or someplace exotic are put up. Overseas holidays were something my parents could only dream about.' He stopped, found himself smiling at Irene smiling. 'What?' he said. 'What is it?'

'You.' She leaned up and pecked him on the lips. 'You've never opened up like that before. I never knew you had it in you, all this war generational stuff.'

'I've never had anyone to talk to about it, really.'

She took hold of his hand, and pulled him around so that they were facing the old grey town silhouetted over the cliffs. 'And I've dragged you away from your pint,' she said. 'On such a nice evening. You must be thirsty. Would you like to head back?'

'It's up to you. I'm happy to continue walking and talking and thinking about . . .' He caught himself, then said, '. . . thinking about nothing, really.'

'I think you think about a lot more than nothing. Come on,' she said, 'I haven't eaten since breakfast.'

He let himself be led by the hand, relieved to see that all thoughts of cancer and major operations and the worry of what lay ahead were put on hold, if only on a temporary basis.

Their meal at the Doll's House went well, with them sharing a starter of prawn salad with a bottle of red wine. What did it matter if white wine was supposed to be for fish, and red was for beef? 'Whatever takes our fancy,' Irene had said. 'We can drink whatever the hell we like.'

He couldn't recall having ever heard her swear before, but it was a relief just to see her enjoying herself, even if it was in effect a mask to cover the painful truth. Another bottle of red was opened, but by the end of the meal they'd finished only half of it.

'Would you like to take it home?' he asked.

Irene shook her head. 'A doggy-bottle you mean?'

He smiled at her silliness, and found that he, too, was masking his innermost feelings. Deep down he felt a pained sadness for Irene, and whenever he held her gaze and watched her eyes sparkle, he couldn't help but wonder how he would feel if he'd been given the same devastating news. Could he even pretend to enjoy a meal out with a friend? Could he mask his darkest fears about the future? He didn't think so.

His mobile beeped – ID Mo – and he excused himself to take it outside.

'Hi, Dad. Thought I would give you a call before I leave.'

'You're leaving now?'

'Sorry. A day earlier than planned, but I've got a lift to Glasgow sorted, and I didn't want to miss out.'

'But I can drive you there tomorrow. The offer still stands.'

'I know. Thanks. But I'm meeting someone later tonight.'

'In Glasgow?'

'Yes.'

He glanced at his watch. By the time she'd driven to Glasgow and unpacked, *later tonight* would be well past his regular bedtime. 'Do I have your new address?' he said, almost cringing at the desperation that had crept into his voice.

'I'll text you once I'm there.'

'Okay.'

'Got to go, Dad. Bye. Love you.'

'Love you too, princess.' He wanted to add, 'Drive safely,' but the click on the line told him she'd hung up. He knew he shouldn't feel saddened by her departure, but should see it as the next step in her life, a golden opportunity to spread her wings, make a new career for herself, a new home, too, maybe even meet someone and settle down and start a family – isn't that how children move on? Her move to Glasgow should be something to feel happy about, a new beginning, a new life, but even so he struggled to shift a sense of sadness that settled like a heavy weight around his heart.

Back inside the restaurant, Irene took one look at him and said, 'Is everything okay?'

'Sure,' he said, and tried a smile. 'It's nothing in the overall scheme of things. Mo's leaving for Glasgow. It was supposed to be tomorrow. And I was intending to drive down with her. But she's got a lift from someone else, and she's leaving tonight. Surprise surprise. Out of the blue. I was hoping to see her before she left.'

'Oh, I'm sorry, I've held you up.'

'No you haven't,' he said, all of a sudden regretting his complaint. 'I hadn't planned on seeing her tonight anyway.' He shrugged. 'But what can you do? It's all spur of the moment for youngsters nowadays.'

'Another generational thing?' she said, and coughed out a laugh.

He found himself laughing, too. He took hold of her hand, and squeezed, feeling mildly chastened at having felt poorly about Mo, when Irene had life-threatening issues of her own to deal with.

On the walk back to her home, she said, 'The wine's gone to my head, Andy, and I'm feeling tired. I think I'll go straight to bed, if you don't mind.' For a moment, he wasn't sure if he was being invited to join her, but then she said, 'I'm sorry. I've had an awful day, although this evening's been lovely, thank you. You've been a great support.'

'A good listener, you mean.'

'That, too.' She smiled at him. 'I'll be all right. It'll all work out fine.'

He saw her words for what they were, nothing more than reassurance that life goes on, and she'll have to handle whatever comes her way. A quick peck at her door, followed by a promise to speak tomorrow, found him walking back to the Office to collect his car from the car park in the rear. Although he was over the limit, he felt alert enough to drive, and the road to his home in Crail was mostly through countryside after all, and quiet. Even so, he thought of having a quick one in the Central Bar, but wisely decided against it.

He drove with the windows down, the rare warmth of a Scottish summer's night blustering throughout the cabin as if with heated fingers. He kept to the speed limit, and was entering the old fishing town of Crail, the lights of the Golf Hotel straight ahead, when his phone rang.

He took it through the speaker system.

'That's it fucking started,' Dainty said without introduction. 'Big Mac's just been pulled from the Clyde, minus his fucking head, of course, as if that's going to make it harder for us to ID him. His tattooed dick's a dead giveaway.'

'Big Mac?'

'Joe McKenzie. One of Tony's bodyguards. Not much good at guarding anyone if he couldn't look after himself.'

'So why him?' Gilchrist asked. 'What's Big Mac got to do with Rab Shepherd?'

'He's been with the firm all his life, since he was a teenager. Knew Rab from when he was a wee boy. One of his first jobs for Jock was to look after Rab, keep him safe, make sure nothing happened to him. If he hadn't been on fucking holiday when Rab went missing, he'd have lost his head back then. As it was, Tony spoke up for him, and got him assigned as one of his own.'

Gilchrist still felt confused. 'But why kill him now?'

'Sending a message. Letting Tony know that no one's safe, not even himself.'

'Who's sending a message?'

'That's the fucking problem, Andy, we don't know for sure.'

'But you can make an educated guess?'

Dainty let out a hard sigh, as if he'd had enough of the day's

109

events and just wanted to go home and forget about it. 'I wouldn't want you spreading this around,' he said, 'but I'd put money on it being Tony himself.'

'You're telling me that Tony's killing his own bodyguards to send a message to himself?' Gilchrist said, unable to restrain the tone of disbelief.

'No. He's sending a message to Arletta. Letting her know that if she and him don't stay close together, then somebody else could take over their business.'

'Like a double bluff, you mean.'

'That's one thing you can say about Tony. The man's as sharp as a cutthroat razor and twice as dangerous. I'm letting you know this, Andy, because I don't know how this is going to play out, who's going to be next to take a headless swim in the Clyde.' A pause, then his voice lowered. 'Or even the Tay.'

'Are you suggesting I could be in danger?'

'Well, you found that missing bugger. So why not?'

When Gilchrist ended the call, he parked his car and sat for several minutes before switching off the engine. His mind replayed the phone call, trying to pick through the not too subtle nuances of Dainty's words. When he exited the car, he locked it with his key fob, and felt the hairs on his neck rise as he turned to face his cottage.

The street ahead lay in semi-darkness, the late summer night casting shadows into darker corners. Despite the warm temperature, he slipped on his jacket and pulled the collar up tight to his neck. Then he strode downhill, the old town's night shadows shifting and dancing around him, the echo of Dainty's words still ringing in his ears.

You found that missing bugger. So why not?

Not the words he wanted to hear.

But if you thought about it, why not indeed?

CHAPTER 18

Saturday morning

Gilchrist woke to the raucous sounds of birds fighting in his garden.

As a country, Scotland is only equipped to handle cold weather, gale force winds, and battering storms, not heatwaves – meaning no air conditioning – and without a breath of air last night, he'd slept with his bedroom window wide open. Hence the early morning sounds of nature in the wild.

He slipped from bed and crept to the window to find one of his bird feeders – the one with the fat balls in it – covered in a mass of fluttering feathers. He counted a total of seven starlings pecking and harassing each other, flapping their wings, clinging onto the wire cage like acrobats, fluttering off then fluttering back, and stabbing yellow beaks at the fat balls at every opportunity. A family of sparrows hopped among the branches of an adjacent *Pieris* bush, watching and waiting, ready to fly into any short-lived gap to steal some crumbs. Even though he'd filled the feeder two days earlier, it looked as if it would be pecked clean before breakfast.

In the kitchen, he switched the TV on, set it to mute, then checked his mobile while he waited for the kettle to boil. Three texts only – one from Mhairi, and two from Jackie, letting him know that they'd left a number of printouts on his desk – which told him he was going to spend his Saturday morning in the Office reading reports. He accessed his emails, and noted a rare one from Dainty, which he opened.

Forgot to tell you Tony's wife is in hospital

Gilchrist frowned at that, pondering over the significance of Dainty's email. Why was Arletta in hospital? And did it matter? It must mean something, otherwise Dainty wouldn't have emailed it. Was he letting him know that Arletta's life was in danger, that she might die? Or was there some other more subtle message being sent. He couldn't say, and made a mental note to phone Dainty later and find out. He was scanning through his emails, none of which appeared of any real import, when he glanced at the TV to see a reporter standing on what he recognised as a modernised Clydeside, with the Squinty Bridge in the back-ground. He picked up his remote and rewound the scene until he came to the start of the reporter's interview.

Then he switched the mute off.

'The body of a sixty-year-old man was pulled from the River Clyde late last night. We understand he had not been in the water long. Estimates suggest less than a day, but it was reported that his head was missing. Strathclyde Police have been unable to identify him and are asking the public to come forward if they know of any missing persons.' A phone number appeared on the screen, then the scene changed to a view of the Clyde, further downstream where it widened, supposedly from where the body had been pulled.

But it could have been anywhere.

When the scene switched back to the television studio, Gilchrist muted the sound. Dainty had told him last night that the dead man was Joe McKenzie – *his tattooed dick's a dead giveaway*. Had he been joking? Had that been nothing but one of Dainty's throwaway comments? Or had some tattoo on the man's penis or elsewhere confirmed his identity? The TV reporter had said the police were seeking information on any missing persons, that they hadn't yet identified the body. So you didn't have to be a rocket scientist to understand the significance of that; Strathclyde Police did not want the man's identity to be made public. And with Dainty asking Gilchrist to keep Rab Shepherd's name from the media, it told him that Dainty *et al.* were taking the threat of a fresh turf war in gangland Glasgow seriously.

And if a turf war did break out as a result of Rab Shepherd's body being discovered after all these years, which in some way opened up old wounds and refreshed past arguments and feuds, just how realistic was it for the whole sorry mess to find its murderous way from Glasgow to Fife? Gilchrist felt a bead of sweat run down his spine at the question's simple answer – highly realistic.

That being the case, then who would they come after? Not the SOCOs, he was sure of that. They were too low in the chain of command, which pointed to himself and Jessie if you thought about it. The likelihood of anything happening to them was low, he felt, but even so, in the gangland underworld, family honour trumped rationale, and he hadn't yet worked out all the family connections to have a clear enough idea of where the danger

113

might come from – although Tony Dilanos had to be top of the list. He needed to speak to Jessie, alert her to his concerns, but it was still too early – not yet 7.30 on a sunny Saturday morning – so he made himself a cup of tea, found two slices of leftover pizza, and had breakfast outside.

Like him, Jessie was an early morning riser, and at 7.45 he phoned her and spent the next ten minutes bringing her up to speed on his conversation with Dainty, his own thoughts on their current investigation, but importantly alerting her to the possibility of some retaliation for being a member of the team who'd identified Rab Shepherd's body. He knew Jessie well enough to know she wouldn't be scared to death by hearing that – she'd been in more frightening scenarios before she moved up to Fife from Glasgow – but he thought it only fair that she be told the facts.

At the end of his call, before hanging up, he said, 'So how's Robert?'

'Better,' she said.

'Didn't get himself into any trouble then?'

'No. He was all apologetic when he came home, about leaving the way he did, and slamming the door. And after he'd showered, he tried to make it up by cooking a barbecue – surf and churf with mango sauce and red and yellow sweet peppers. Cooked to perfection, it was. I sometimes wonder where he came from, or if he really is mine.'

'Surf and turf, did you say?'

'No, surf and churf. Fish and chicken.'

Gilchrist could only mouth an Aahh as Jessie rabbited on about how tasty the mango sauce was, and how everything tasted flavourful . . .

114

'And of course a bottle of plonk didn't do any harm, although my head's a bit delicate this morning.' She let out a chuckle, and he found himself smiling along with her.

'Are you up for doing a bit of work today?' he said.

'I knew there was a catch. What d'you want?'

'Can you find out why Arletta Shepherd's in hospital? I don't think it's important, but it's a box that needs ticked.'

'You and your ticking boxes. You're worse than a bloody clock.'

'And while you're at it, can you and Mhairi get together and find out if Tony and Arletta have any kids?'

'Mine is not to question why, mine is but to do or die . . . or something like that.'

'Tennyson.'

'What?'

'Alfred, Lord Tennyson. It's a line from one of his poems, although I think you've bastardised it a touch.'

'And talking about bastards, do you want me to chase up Levy?'

'Not at the moment.'

'Why not? I mean, you're telling me there might be some backlash coming our way because we discovered Rab Shepherd. It's not our fault he was murdered. So I'm thinking we should stick it to them, meet them face to face and have it out with them right now.'

'Them?'

'Yeah. Them. Dilanos and his lot. How else are we going to move this investigation forward? We shouldn't have to cower. We should interrogate with power. And that's a line from a poem by Jessie Janes.'

Not too fast, Gilchrist thought. No need to prod a sleeping dog into action, or more correctly to give a gangland kingpin a couple of police faces to go after. Of course, he could be wrong. He could be focusing on the wrong spot. Tony Dilanos could be more intent on saving himself from the unavoidable wrath of his wife, Arletta – once she finds out that her beloved uncle Rab was not escorted to the ferry, but was already dead and buried – rather than making matters worse by killing anyone who moved . . .

'Earth to Andy? You still there?'

'I'm thinking.'

'Me too. I'm thinking Rab Shepherd must have been killed by someone high up in that organisation. Why else would the shit start hitting the fan so soon? Not twenty-four hours and bodies are already turning up in the Clyde without their heads. I mean . . . they're almost pointing fingers at themselves.'

Jessie had a point, he knew, but the business relationship between Arletta and her husband, Tony, didn't seem clear to him. According to Dainty, Tony was the puppet to Arletta's puppeteer. But you didn't take over big Jock's empire to be told what to do, or how to run it. You had to have a proven set of balls of your own. And if Tony really had told his wife-to-be at the time that he'd driven her favourite uncle Rab to the ferry and seen him on board safe and sound, never to be heard from again, how could he explain his reappearance in a hidden grave on a golf course seventy miles away? And why St Andrews anyway? Why not some other golf course,, or open field, or wooded area, or the bottom of some remote loch in the wildest Highlands? Many of them were deep enough. If you thought about it, Scotland had plenty of places in which to dispose of a body, never to be found again. So there had to be a connection to somebody, somehow, in St Andrews. But he couldn't see it through the haze in his mind, and at that moment it all seemed too much too soon.

'Let's not go in heavy-handed just yet,' he said at length. 'Let me go through what Jackie and Mhairi have dumped on my desk first. I need you to look into Arletta and get back to me. Hopefully then I'll have a clearer idea.'

'Will do, Andy, but from what I've heard so far, I have to tell you that Tony Dilanos is top of the list.'

'Or his wife, Arletta.'

'Her, too.'

'Which is why we need to tread with care, Jessie. Until things are clearer.'

A heavy sigh on the line warned him that his words weren't getting through to her. But even so, she was a top professional, and would do as instructed. 'Okay, let me look into it,' she said, 'and I'll get back to you as soon as.'

As he returned indoors, he had the uneasy sense that Jessie was about to step out of line. But in what way, he couldn't say.

CHAPTER 19

By 9.30, Gilchrist was no further forward in his investigation.

He'd read through Mhairi's and Jackie's printouts, but found nothing damning or incriminating in any of their paperwork – Daniel Levy the jeweller was clean; nothing more on Hugh Cannon or Rab Shepherd or big Jock's family tree – informative was about the best he could say of their effort. It just didn't provide him with the criminal connections he'd been hoping for. A glance at the window reminded him that the weather was far too good to be stuck in the Office on the weekend, especially as the forecast was for the heatwave to break that night.

He pushed back from his desk. Time to take a break.

Outside, the temperature was already close to seventy, not a cloud in the sky, although the occasional shift of wind carried with it the slightest hint of a chill off the sea, which from experience warned him that a haar could sweep inland before the end of the day and kill the heatwave in less than five minutes. It felt relaxing, almost holiday-like to walk along Market Street, already thriving with shoppers keen for a summer's day bargain, visitors wondering why everyone complains about the Scottish weather, and locals hovering outside the pubs hoping for the unlikely possibility of an early opening.

In South Street, he bought a bouquet of flowers from an open-air stall, and paid two-fifty extra for delivery to Irene – overpriced, he thought, for a short walk along the street, which was all it was. He strolled along Bell Street then down Market Street, bypassing Starbucks, heading for Costa Coffee instead. He'd just ordered his coffee – tall latte to go – when his mobile rang – ID Jessie. He mouthed to the barista that he would be back in a moment, then walked to the door as he took the call.

'You're never going to believe it,' Jessie said.

'I'm listening.'

'Arletta was allegedly assaulted on Thursday evening and spent the rest of the night in the New Victoria undergoing X-rays and scans and all sorts.'

'Assaulted? Who by, and where?'

'Hold your horses,' she said. 'I'm coming to that. She had two fractured ribs and a cut on the side of her head, at her temple, and another one above her right eye that she said was the result of a fall.'

'She *said*? So you don't believe her?'

'Of course not. She was beaten up. First around the body to hide the bruising, hence the fractured ribs. But when she fought back, that was when she was punched in the face.'

'Let me guess,' Gilchrist said. 'Her husband, Tony.'

'Got it in one.'

'And he beat her up at home?'

'You're showing off now.'

'So you've spoken to Arletta?'

'No chance. She checked herself out of the New Vicky yesterday morning, against her doctor's advice, and hasn't been heard from since.'

Gilchrist stepped off the busy pavement, onto the quiet of the road. 'That sounds serious.'

'I'd say so.'

'Is anyone looking into it?'

'Tony Dilanos has already been interviewed by Strathclyde Police, but he was out of town on Thursday, at some big meeting in Stirling, so he says. He's got a pile of witnesses to back him up.'

'And you think he's a liar.' More statement than question.

'Of course he's lying, for crying out loud.'

'So where's he at now?'

'Probably back home screwing one of his girlfriends now he's got an empty. Want me to have a chat with him?'

'Not yet.'

'Are you sure, Andy? He's just begging to be grilled.'

'Let me talk to Dainty first,' he said, and ended the call before Jessie could object.

Dainty picked up on the second ring. 'Tell me it's an emergency.'

Gilchrist frowned. 'Sorry?'

'The wife's been on at me to mow the lawn. Been putting it off for weeks. It's either that or a divorce, she says. Don't tempt me, I tell her.' A pause, then, 'If you know anyone looking to get rid of a few tons of concrete, I know just the fucking place. Cover the lot. It'd save us parking the car on the street.'

Gilchrist sent a chuckle down the line, and said, 'Why don't you strip to the waist and get a suntan? Pretend you're in the Costa del Sol.'

'Yeah, and out there on my tod. That'll be the day.' A sniff, then, 'So what's up?'

'Tony Dilanos.'

'Christ, Andy, it doesn't take you long.'

'Or more specifically, his wife, Arletta. She's missing.'

'She's always missing. It's par for the course. They have an argument. He thumps her about. She disappears. A week later, they make up. Life's hunky-dory for a while, then he thumps her again. And so it goes on.'

Gilchrist raked his fingers through his hair, let out a gush of breath at the futility of it all. Why do men feel the need to dominate their wives, abuse them physically? Nowadays, the police take marital abuse seriously. Not like in the past. When Gilchrist had been a child, physical abuse between husband and wife was put down as a domestic dispute, and often just simply ignored by the police.

He recalled the first time he saw his father slap his mother. He'd been only six. The speed with which his father's hand had flown across her face had shocked him, but it was the sharp crack of the flat of his hand against her skin that had terrified him, and made him burst into tears. Then his mother's response had confused him most of all – *Look what you've done now. You've gone and made the bairn cry.* And she'd lifted him up, cuddled him to her, and carried him from the room, her voice shushing and soothing in his ear—

'If she doesn't turn up in a week,' Dainty said, 'then we might consider it serious.'

'Has she ever filed a complaint to the police?'

'Are you serious? This is Arletta Shepherd. Big Jock's daughter. Tony's wife. The police don't enter into it.'

121

'But she must've filed a complaint this time, or you, meaning Strathclyde, wouldn't have interviewed Tony.'

'The doctor, some consultant, a Mr Grant Williamson, reported it to us as an incident of physical abuse. It's not the first time he'd attended Arletta, and he's hot to trot on the fight against domestic violence.'

'He's chancing his arm, is he not? Reporting her against her will.'

'Aye, well, be that as it may, but Tony's alibied up to the hilt, so there's fuck all we can charge him with.'

Gilchrist gave Dainty's words some thought, then pressed on with, 'You said she's always missing. Any idea where she goes to?'

'The short answer is: no. The long answer is: no complaint ever reached us, so we never put in the effort. Besides,' Dainty said, and Gilchrist had a sense that some secret was about to be shared, 'rumour has it that she's got a man on the side. So who are we to step in and spoil her fun?'

Gilchrist thanked Dainty for his time and information, then hung up, an idea tickling the back of his brain.

Back in his office, he retrieved Jackie's notes, and flipped through them. Something in Dainty's tone had triggered a fleeting image, words on the pages that might – or more than likely might not – give him a clue to Arletta's whereabouts. It took him only a few minutes to find it, a mention of big Jock's family tree – his father and mother, both deceased; his wife, deceased, too; his children, Arletta, and her younger brother, Jimmy, neither of whom had produced any children. But it was big Jock's siblings – his brother, Rab, and his sister, Nadine – that had caught Gilchrist's eye.

Until yesterday, he hadn't known Jock Shepherd had a sister. Not that there was any reason for him to *have* known about her. Her name had never popped up until Jackie had researched the family tree. Nadine had married then divorced a Freddie Thomson, but given birth to two children, one of whom, a boy, had died at birth. The other, Natalie, and Arletta's full cousin, was now married and had three children of her own. Gilchrist worked out the children's ages; nine, seven, and the youngest one having just turned three. But it was the name of the youngest child that sent ideas swirling through his mind – Arlene.

Had Natalie named her daughter Arlene in recognition of her aunt, Arletta? If so, why not just name her Arletta? But what if Natalie and Nadine wanted nothing to do with their criminal family? What if that was the reason he'd never known about them? What if they'd walked away from the family? Or what if Nadine had fought with Jock and been kicked out? Maybe naming her daughter Arletta would have been too much of a reminder of a family she was no longer willing to be associated with.

He pushed himself to his feet and walked to the window. Was he putting in too much time scratching the wrong spot? Was he trying to make a quantum leap in logic just to prove . . . to prove . . . to prove *what*? Did it matter to his investigation whether or not Tony beat up his wife, or that she went missing for days at a time? He found it simple enough to conclude that it didn't matter a toss, but no matter how many what ifs or maybes he could conjure up, the fact that Tony had claimed he'd driven Arletta's favourite uncle to the ferry, when he unarguably couldn't have, did it for Gilchrist.

He picked up his mobile and called Jessie.

'Would you like a trip to Glasgow?' he said.

'Thought you'd never ask.'

'I'll pick you up in fifteen.'

'I'm already waiting.'

CHAPTER 20

Gilchrist took the unusual step of inviting Dainty to join them, although he did wait a sufficient length of time before calling, to allow Dainty to finish cutting the grass.

Husband and wife, Tony Dilanos and Arletta Shepherd, lived in what had once been Jock Shepherd's home, one of the biggest houses in Pollokshields on the south side of Glasgow, with a lawn almost large enough to host the local football derby, it seemed.

'Who says crime doesn't pay?' Dainty moaned.

Gilchrist parked his car at the entrance to a gated brick-paved driveway that had to be at least a hundred yards long. At the far end reared an immaculate stone-built mansion. Three skylight windows lined the roof, as if to let neighbours know the mansion wasn't quite big enough. Two luxury cars – a white Bentley convertible, and a black Porsche with an aerofoil on the back – *big enough for a picnic table*, Jessie often said – sat parked outside the front door. Off to the side, four more glistening cars crammed the driveway, like the showroom of some upmarket dealership. Two security personnel stood alert at either corner of the building. Even from where he stood, Gilchrist could see their muscled build, the tight fit of made-to-measure suits that no doubt hid deadly weapons.

'Arletta would never sell this place,' Dainty said. 'It was left to her in Jock's will. She also owns the house next door. It's rumoured, although it's never been proven, that there's a tunnel connecting the two, so they can shift stuff in and out without anyone noticing.'

'I don't think they had this gate last time I was here,' Jessie said.

'Jock never needed it,' Dainty said. 'If one of his security team let anyone slip into the grounds uninvited, they were terminated on the spot. And I don't mean given their P45. But that was big Jock for you. Needless to say, it didn't happen too often.'

'And you couldn't prove a thing,' Gilchrist said, more conversation than question.

'Of course not.' Dainty stabbed a finger at the electronic buzzer, and a voice crackled in immediate response, to be cut off by, 'Tell Tony it's DCI Pete Small to see him.'

'What about?' the voice said.

'None of your fucking business. Now get this fucking gate opened before I kick it in.'

Jessie chuckled. 'I see you haven't lost any of your finesse.'

'A good booting in the fucking balls is what some of these bastards need, excuse the French.' Dainty pulled out his police ID and said, 'Warrant cards at the ready, please. I don't trust any of these bastards. Put your hands in your pockets, they're likely to shoot you.'

The gate gave a heavy click, then started to slide to the side, along the inside of the eight-foot-high boundary wall. At the same time two bodyguards stepped from the bushes to stand spread-legged on the middle of the driveway. Dainty squeezed past the gate before the gap was a foot wide. Gilchrist waited until it parted some six feet, before following Jessie.

Dainty's path was halted by one of the security guards, who held up an electronic wand, and said, 'We need to search you before—'

'That'll be fucking right,' Dainty snapped. 'Out of the way, sonny, before I cram that thing up your arse.'

The bodyguard gave a twisted grin in response, and flexed his neck to one side then the other, as if to say – I'd like to see you try.

Gilchrist held up his warrant card. 'We're here on police business, and we won't hesitate to arrest you for obstructing a murder investigation.'

A glance from one security guard to the other, resulted in a tiny nod, and a reluctant step back to allow Gilchrist and the others to continue unhindered. Even so, Dainty couldn't resist a parting quip. 'Radio ahead and tell that cunt, Tony, to put the kettle on.'

As they neared the end of the driveway, two more security guards converged on them from the corners of the mansion. One hesitated for a moment, and spoke into his sleeve. Then he nodded to the other, and together they both retreated to their positions at opposite corners.

'If only dogs were as well trained,' Jessie said.

'Or wives,' Dainty retorted, which earned him a cut-eyed grimace from Jessie.

At the front entrance, six stone steps, with low walls either side, led up to a vestibule beyond which a glass-panelled door gleamed with varnish. Gilchrist had taken only three of the steps when the door opened, and a man as tall as Dainty, wearing a black suit, white shirt and silver tie, and with a face that looked as

126

if it had spent ten seconds in a meat grinder, maybe longer, growled, 'Follow me.'

Dainty stepped in first, followed by Jessie, then Gilchrist.

They were led along a hallway that ran past the side of the main staircase, down a couple of steps, then into what Gilchrist would describe as a gentleman's study, although from what he knew about Tony Dilanos, he was certainly no gentleman. The entire room was wood-panelled; walls and ceiling in a mid-teak, with intricate framework; the floor in a dark oak polished so high it glistened. Black and white photographs of an older Glasgow adorned the four walls, each mounted on white backing and framed in a simple black frame. The effect was to create an almost panoramic view of the city.

'Mr Dilanos will be with you shortly.' The door closed with a soft thud.

'More trusting than I thought,' Jessie said. 'Leaving us in here on our owneo.'

Dainty nodded to CCTV cameras in the ceiling corners. 'Don't look now, but you're on *Candid Camera*.'

All three of them turned at the sound of the latch clicking, then a tall man in tight black chinos and a white open-necked shirt entered the room. Without a word, he strode past them as if they were statues, and took his seat behind a walnut-gnarled desk. Then he looked at Jessie, and said, 'We meet again.'

Jessie nodded. She'd been in this house before, but not this room, when she'd driven down from St Andrews to interrogate a terminally ill Jock Shepherd – well, to exchange one document for another. She remembered thinking that Jock looked as if he wouldn't see the end of the day, let alone the several months it had taken him to succumb to the inevitability of death. And in that room had been a younger man whom she'd thought was Jock's assistant, or aide, or some such thing. She'd not been introduced, but she recognised that man now as Tony Dilanos.

'You haven't changed much,' she said. 'Still as slimy.'

Dilanos gave her a dead-eyed grin in response, then turned his attention to Gilchrist. 'For whatever reason, Jock liked you. Said you were someone he could trust.' He grimaced at Dainty. 'Not like that wee piece of shite.'

'Well this wee piece of shite can have you arrested for assault,' Dainty snarled, rising to the bait.

'And my lawyers will get me released by the end of the day.' Another lizard-smile. 'And so it goes on. Life goes back to normal. So . . .' He examined his fingernails, as if lost for words, then said, '. . . what are you after this time?'

Gilchrist and Jessie had discussed their interview strategy and agreed that she should lead, with Dainty stepping in if anything backfired. 'Rab Shepherd,' she said.

Dilanos looked up from his fingernails, and frowned. 'Rab Shepherd? Jock's younger brother?' He stared at Jessie as if seeking confirmation, but she stared back at him in silence. 'Now that's a blast from the past,' he said at length. 'But Rab's been dead for years, so I don't know how I can help you.'

'He's been dead for years all right. Not in some godforsaken hole in the Far East, but in a makeshift grave on the Fife coast.'

'Oh dear. How sad.'

'Aye, I can see how upset you are.'

Dilanos's lips pressed into a toothless smile.

Jessie pushed on. 'I thought you drove him to the ferry.'

'Who told you that?'

'Didn't you?'

'What ferry?'

Dainty stepped in with, 'Cut the crap, Tony. The story's been on the street for years. And now Rab's body's been found, your darling wife Arletta'll be after your balls when she finds out that you didn't drive Rab to the ferry at all. Because he was already dead. And you knew all along he'd been murdered. If not by you in person, by someone instructed by you.'

Dilanos stared at Dainty. 'Well, arrest me then.'

'Don't fucking tempt me.'

Jessie said, 'So where's Arletta anyway?'

'With friends.'

'Recovering from being beaten up by you?'

'Don't be ridiculous.'

'We have her medical report,' Jessie said, and watched her lie work a furrow across Dilanos's forehead. 'Broken ribs. Stitched face. Is that how you treat all your women?' If she'd thought her innuendo on Dilanos's infidelity would upset him, she was sorely mistaken.

He laughed, then said, 'She fell down the stairs. Didn't you find that in her medical report? And now she's staying with some friends. Recovering, as you said, but not from being beaten up by me. Here . . .' He reached into his pocket and removed his mobile phone. 'Why don't we give her a call?' He dialled a number, and smiled at each of them in turn while he waited for the connection to be made.

Then he said, 'Arletta, honey, I've got some visitors I'd like you to talk to. From our friends, the police. I'll put you on speaker, and you can answer their questions. All right?' He pressed a button and laid the mobile phone face up on his desk. 'Can you hear me?'

'Yes,' she said, her voice strong and confident.

Gilchrist stepped closer. 'This is DCI Gilchrist speaking. We've never met. But I knew your father.'

'Good for you.'

'We've got a medical report from Doctor Watson who treated you at the Royal—'

'The New Victoria. Not the Royal. And it's *Mister*, not Doctor, and *Williamson*, not Watson. Who did you say you were? Put someone else on.'

Gilchrist nodded to Jessie, feeling somewhat chastened that his attempt to find out if the woman was someone other than Arletta had failed so badly.

'This is DS Janes, Arletta. I'd like to meet you to—'

'Not interested.'

'We're investigating the murder of your uncle Rab.'

'So I heard.'

'Who told you that?'

'Who do you think?'

'I'd like to talk to you about your uncle . . .'

'Not interested.'

'. . . About how he wasn't driven to the ferry, but in fact had been killed and—'

'I can't help you.'

'Can't or won't.'

'Both.'

'I could apply for a warrant.'

'Go ahead. It's not going to make any difference. I won't be talking to you lot.'

Jessie glared at the mobile, as if willing it to melt. But she wasn't finished. 'How did you sustain your injuries?'

'Fell down the stairs. How do you think?'

130

'I think you were beaten up by your husband—'

'He wouldn't dare.'

'So you're saying he's never beaten you up?'

'I think I'm done talking to you lot—'

'Where are you staying?' Jessie said.

But she was too late.

Dilanos smirked at her, then retrieved his mobile. 'Are we finished?'

'For the time being,' Dainty said, and stomped to the door, his heels clicking his anger on the wooden flooring.

Jessie followed, but Gilchrist held back. 'You said you were in Stirling when your wife fell down the stairs.'

Something on the nasty side of cunning slid behind Dilanos's cold eyes, but all he offered was, 'That's right.'

'And you didn't know that Rab was Jock's *half*-brother, did you?' He hoped his change in tack might derail Dilanos's cool demeanour. But it didn't work.

'I'd heard. But I don't believe it.'

'Why not?'

'Jock would've disowned him.'

'Why? They shared the same mother.'

'Jock's mother had a reputation as a bit of a tramp, so maybe I'm not surprised.'

'Nothing like Arletta, then?'

The air around Dilanos seemed to tighten, as if the entire room was waiting for an electric bolt to short circuit the place. His eyes narrowed, his lips whitened, and he stared at Gilchrist with a hatred impossible to mask.

Gilchrist returned the cold stare with one of his own, and thought of trying to wind him up further, by mentioning Jock's

131

sister, Nadine. But something told him to hold back, not let him know that he'd been researching the family tree. Instead, he said, 'Joe McKenzie, aka Big Mac. He's one of your men.'

'Was.'

'Do you know who killed him?'

'Not yet, but I'm working on it.' Something in the cold ring of his voice warned Gilchrist that Dilanos was a man who took no prisoners. Whoever killed Big Mac – if it wasn't Dilanos himself, of course – wouldn't last ten minutes if found out.

'Do you know why he was killed?'

'If I knew that, I'd know who killed him, wouldn't I?'

Gilchrist granted him a quick smile. 'So . . . why you?'

Dilanos frowned. 'Why me what?'

'Why are you running the organisation, and not Jimmy? He should've taken over after Jock passed.'

Dilanos smiled, as if a troubling weight had been lifted. 'Jimmy's a meth-head. And as thick as a butcher's block. Arletta runs rings around him. Jock knew that.' He pushed back from his desk, the move so sudden that Gilchrist found himself taking a step back. As Dilanos stretched to his full height, Gilchrist had a sense of the man's physical presence – tall and slim, but with shoulders that pulled the fabric of his shirt, and muscled biceps beneath the cotton material.

'Your wee piece of shite is waiting on you,' Dilanos said.

Gilchrist nodded, then followed Jessie from the room.

CHAPTER 21

Nothing was said as Gilchrist and the others strode down the driveway under the watchful eyes of the security staff, who seemed to have doubled in number as if warned to expect trouble. At the entrance gate, four guards stepped aside to let Dainty leave first, then one of them wolf-whistled as Jessie followed.

'Aye, in your dreams,' she said.

Only after they were all belted in and Gilchrist was driving away from the building did Dainty break their silence. 'What do you make of that lying fucker?' he asked. 'I don't think he's ever heard of the truth.'

'Well he did say you were a wee piece of shite,' Jessie said.

To Gilchrist's surprise, Dainty laughed and shook his head. 'I might be wee, but I'd like to think I'm not a piece of shite.'

'Have you met Arletta?' Gilchrist said, trying to set them back on track.

'Once. A few years back. When we'd pulled Jock into the Office for questioning. She came charging in with her solicitor, some big shot from Edinburgh of all places.'

'What did she sound like?'

'Loud. Demanding. Forceful. A bit like Jock, come to think of it.'

'No, I mean how does she speak? Any distinguishable accent?'

'Fancies herself as a cut above. A bit posh. In other words, she disnae speak wi' a Glesga accent,' Dainty said, leaning heavily on the slang. 'That answer it for you?'

Gilchrist thought back to the phone call. He'd detected no strong Glasgow accent from the woman on the line. Nothing that jumped out at him, anyway. He thought she'd sounded west coast, not east, but with none of the glottal sounds of colloquial Glaswegian. But was that a bit posh? Or more to the point, was that phone call enough to convince him? He needed to pry a bit more.

'So you couldn't say for sure that we were speaking to Arletta?'

'No,' Dainty said. 'But if you think about it, we caught Dilanos cold. He wasn't expecting us. So it's unlikely to have been anyone other than Arletta.'

Dainty had a point. A good one. Gilchrist tightened his grip on the steering wheel and eyed the road ahead while his mind worked through the rationale. For someone who'd been caught cold, Dilanos had come across as calm, in control, almost like he knew the answers to the questions before they were asked. So Gilchrist wasn't as convinced as Dainty that they'd been speaking to Arletta. But how could he prove that? He didn't want to phone Dick again. He needed to keep their contact on illegal business to an absolute minimum. And besides, for all he knew, Dilanos could have been using a burner phone, or a disposable SIM card, or someone else's mobile. So, that lead was a dead end before it even started.

But as he worked his way through traffic, back to Pitt Street to drop Dainty off, he thought he saw one way to check it out. A longshot, no doubt about it.

But it was as good a shot as any he had.

They drove on in silence, like sightseers lost in the old city's dark history.

On the M80, as the slip road to St Andrews neared, Jessie said, 'You wanted to know where Nadine's daughter, Natalie, had moved to, right?'

'Yes.'

'Well Jackie's just come up with an Edinburgh address.' She looked over at him. 'Do you want to give it a go?'

'Why not?' he said. 'You know how to work the GPS?'

'Of course not. But I've got it on Google Maps on my phone.'

'That'll work.' He pulled into the outside lane for the M9 to Edinburgh and beyond.

Minutes later, they drove past the Kelpies on their right, metal sculptures of the heads of two horses rearing out of an imaginary seascape in struggling desperation. Then the air seemed to thicken with the tongue-coating stench of petroleum and gas as they neared the exit for Grangemouth. To the left, the blue skies disappeared behind a haze as flat as low-lying clouds; discharged gases from Scotland's largest petrochemical complex.

Five miles later Gilchrist thought Jessie seemed quieter than normal, her attention taken up by messages beeping back and forth on her mobile. Again, he worried that her son, Robert, had got himself into trouble, so he said, 'Penny for your thoughts?'

'Just sorting out tonight's meeting with Fran. I hardly know the woman, but she says she can't wait to meet me.'

'Coming on strong, is she?'

'Aye, that'll be right. We're just meeting for a glass of wine and a wee chat.'

'I don't remember much about her,' he said. 'She seems a bit . . .' He searched for the politically correct word, but Jessie beat him to it.

'Gay?'

'Yeah. Gay. Don't you think?'

'Why would you say that?'

Gilchrist gritted his teeth, wishing he'd never opened up that can of worms. 'Just a feeling, that's all. Short hair. Boyish look. Not too feminine in the way she walks.'

'The way she walks? Wow, you must've been eyeing her up.'

'So where are you meeting?' he said, trying to change the subject.

'The Albany Hotel.'

'In North Street?'

'The one and only.' She glanced at him. 'You ever been to it?'

'Not for a while.'

'Aw, it's lovely. Got a cosy wee bar. A glowing gantry. Quite a romantic setting, if that's what you're after.'

He glanced at her, saw she was looking at him, a tight smirk on her lips.

Then she laughed. 'You should've seen your face. Jeez, Andy, I'm only going to meet her for a catch-up. That's all. From the look on your face you'd think I was going to get laid.'

'You know, Jessie,' he said, 'I think you could start an argument in an empty house.'

'And I think you've lost your sense of humour.'

'Well why don't you crack a joke, and tell me what you know about Nadine?' he said, keeping his gaze on the road ahead.

'Only what Jackie's texted me,' she said, scrolling through her messages. 'Nadine Shepherd's the youngest of the three siblings; Jock, Rab, Nadine. In her late fifties, which makes her what . . . fifteen, twenty years younger than Jock.'

'Jock was only sixty-seven when he died.'

'I didn't know that. He looked much older.'

'He'd had a hard life.'

'Aye, drinking, smoking, and shagging. And not necessarily in that order.'

'We know she's divorced,' Gilchrist said, 'with two kids—'

'One. The other died at birth. Natalie, her daughter, has three kids—'

'The youngest being Arlene,' he said, the memory of what he'd read from Jackie's notes coming back to him. 'What do you make of that name?'

Jessie frowned. 'What name? Arlene?'

'Yes.'

Jessie raised her eyebrows. 'Sounds French, I suppose, but other than that . . .'

'Don't you think she might have been named after her aunt Arletta?'

'Arletta? Arlene? I don't know. Why not just call her Arletta?'

'That's what's troubling me,' he said. 'But what if calling her Arletta was too close to the bone, meaning that it reminded her and her mother of the criminal business. Maybe they wanted nothing to do with it.'

'If that's the case, then why not call her Mary? That would sort it.'

Gilchrist felt himself deflate. Jessie was right, of course. He really was stretching the thinnest of leads – if it could even be called that – way beyond its limits, maybe even out of the universe. Still, there was only one way to find out.

He gritted his teeth and drove on.

CHAPTER 22

They found the home in Lauder Road, in the southern suburbs of Edinburgh, a red-sandstone mansion that stood in a well-groomed garden behind a tidy hedge trimmed above passers-by head height.

'I think Dainty was right,' Jessie said. 'Who said crime doesn't pay?'

'But they've broken away from all criminal ties, remember.'

'Aye, right.' Jessie stepped onto the pavement, and waited until Gilchrist came up to her. 'It looks quiet,' she said. 'No car in the driveway.' She looked around her. 'I'm thinking they're not at home.'

He had to agree. Something about the detached home suggested it hadn't been lived in for some time. Maybe they had gone on holiday. Or popped out for some shopping. It was Saturday, after all, and a beautiful day at that. Maybe too nice to go shopping? Maybe they'd gone to the beach. Portobello was the go-to beach promenade for Edinburgh locals. Or maybe he was just losing his touch, no longer capable of putting two and two together, and the house had been vacated. But yet again, a vase of flowers on the window sill looked healthy, and the lawn looked freshly mown, shaded lines in the grass still clear, which told him . . . what . . .? That the flowers had been recently bought, and the lawn cut yesterday?

Without holding out much hope, he said, 'Let's check it out.'

Sure enough, after several minutes of ringing the doorbell, walking round the back, checking door locks, and peering through windows, he had to conclude no one was home.

'We could try talking to some of the neighbours,' Jessie said.

Gilchrist felt reluctant to do that, as he'd hoped to speak to Natalie without intrusion into her private life. Police presence always seemed to find its way to the tongues of gossip merchants, and working behind the scenes gave him a sense of being in control – but in control of what, he couldn't say right then.

'Let's wait in the car,' he said. 'If no one turns up after a couple of hours, we'll conclude they're away for the weekend, or whatever.'

Jessie seemed put out by that suggestion, but went along with it without complaint, although she didn't wait in the car – too bloody hot, she said – preferring instead to sit on the wall opposite, fiddling with her mobile.

In the meantime, Gilchrist checked his own mobile, to find he'd missed a call from Irene. He rang her back.

'Oh, Andy,' she said, 'the flowers are beautiful. Thank you so much. You shouldn't have, really. And my favourites, too. Lilies. How did you know?'

'You told me once, I think. Or maybe I just got lucky.' He pressed the phone to his ear, loving the sultry whisper of her chuckle. 'How are you keeping?' he asked. 'Are you feeling better?'

'I don't feel ill at all. Well, not very often. That's the problem. One minute I'm fine, and the next it's like I've taken a dozen sleeping pills. But I'm not in any pain,' she went on. 'At least not yet. Which is a blessing. And I'm sorry about last night, Andy, I really am.'

Gilchrist frowned. 'You don't need to apologise for anything.'

'Well I feel as if I do. And I'm sorry. I told you why I've resisted you spending the night at mine, and in the next breath I'm inviting you back, only to turn you away at the door. You must have been so annoyed with me.'

'Not at all, Irene. I'm just happy to hear you sounding better.'

The line fell silent, making him think that he could have come up with some better response, then she said, 'I'm sorry to change the subject, but have you heard from Maureen?'

'Not yet. She's only just moved to Glasgow. If I know Mo, I'll be lucky to hear from her before the end of the weekend.'

Irene seemed to hesitate, then said, 'My daughter, Joanne, phoned me this morning. She said that Maureen's going to be sharing a flat with someone she's only just met.'

Gilchrist stared off to the distance. This was news to him, although he shouldn't be surprised. What either of his children got up to nowadays was entirely up to them, being fully grown adults. And in the normal scheme of things, being a father ensured he was the last to know. Even so, he couldn't prevent a shiver of worry from creeping into his tone.

'Is there something wrong?' he said.

The line filled with silence, as if Irene was giving thought to his question. Then she said, 'Joanne doesn't like him. And I have to say she's good at summing people up.'

'I hope she said some nice things about me,' he joked, struggling to shift a nip of anxiety that had him tightening his jaw.

'Well, she was biased, of course, being friends with Maureen. But she said right away that you were a lovely man. And she was right.' Another chuckle, which he tried to share.

But it was no use. 'Do you have a name?'

'I'm sorry, I don't. I didn't want to pry.'

'Of course,' he said, and changed the subject back to her side of the family, asking how her daughter was doing, when they'd last met, and how he would like to get to know her a bit more. It felt nice talking to Irene, the ease with which he could raise a chuckle from her, and how simply she relaxed him with her quiet way of talking. Jessie's presence at the side of his car caught his eye, and he cut the call short with a promise to catch up with Irene that evening.

The door opened, and Jessie slipped in. 'I think this is them,' she said, and shifted her position so she could look in the wing mirror.

Gilchrist had parked fifty yards from the driveway entrance. In the rear-view mirror he watched a white Mercedes convertible ease its way along Lauder Road. In such glorious weather, the roof was down, and the passengers seemed to be enjoying that rarest of Scottish phenomena – working on a suntan. The driver was female, dark sunglasses, blonde hair; the passenger female, too, sunglasses, auburn hair. Together, Gilchrist and Jessie watched in silence as the car cruised closer, then passed them, both women

142

oblivious to their presence, paying no attention to a young child strapped into a child's seat in the back.

Gilchrist took note of the number plate – it was them. Brake lights lit up, and the car slowed almost to a stop, swung into the drive without indicating, and disappeared from view.

'What is it about women drivers and indicators?' Jessie said.

Gilchrist fired the ignition, and eased forward past the entrance – the passenger with the auburn hair was lifting the child from the back seat; the driver was walking to the boot – then parked kerbside, out of sight.

Jessie had the door open before he switched off the engine.

'Let's take this slowly,' he said. 'We don't know if it's Arletta or not.'

'Bet you a tenner it is.'

'I don't gamble.'

'You're no fun.'

As they strode side by side up the driveway, something about the manner in which the passenger held the child to her warned Gilchrist to be careful. He had his warrant card held out in front of him as he introduced himself and Jessie from some twenty yards distant, in a firm tone which caused both women to stand still and face them.

Up close, the passenger was older than the driver – not motherly old, but close – and shifted her weight from one foot to the other as she patted the child's back. Then she leaned down, placed the child on the ground, and said, 'Go round the back and grab your toys. On you go now.'

The child, a girl with fine red hair, tottered off without a word.

'Can we help you?' the driver asked.

'Natalie Foster?' Jessie asked.

'I am, yes.'

Gilchrist faced the passenger. 'And you must be Arletta Shepherd.'

Arletta, if that was indeed her name, frowned. 'Why do you . . . who did you say?'

'Arletta,' Gilchrist said. 'Shepherd. Your father was Jock Shepherd.' He thought it odd the way her eyes shifted and her body tensed, as if in anticipation of being attacked. 'And your uncle was *Rab* Shepherd.'

Her lips tightened, but she acknowledged nothing.

Jessie said to the other woman, 'And *your* mother is *Nadine* Shepherd, Jock and Rab's sister.'

'I've no idea who you're talking about.'

For just that fleeting moment, Gilchrist felt doubt rise, then evaporate as the older woman sighed, and said, 'How did you find me?'

He noted the singular *me*, not us, and knew that his logic had been correct. Arletta was in hiding, and likely in hiding for her life.

'Tony doesn't know,' he assured her. 'No one does.'

She glanced over his shoulder. 'If you found me, he can, too. He's eyes everywhere.'

'We're working independently of Strathclyde Police,' he said.

She nodded, but didn't look convinced.

'Did Tony call you earlier?' he asked. 'On his mobile?'

She shook her head. 'No.'

Once again, his instincts had been proven correct. Tony had phoned some woman who could pass herself off on the phone as his wife, and stop their interview short by ending the call. 'When did you last talk to him?'

'Two days ago.' Then she hugged herself, as if cold. 'We should go inside. It doesn't look good standing out in the open.' She winced as she turned.

Without a word, Jessie and Gilchrist followed.

CHAPTER 23

The hallway ran through the centre of the mansion, and led to an open-plan kitchen in the rear, which in turn opened up to a conservatory with enough bamboo furniture to fool you into thinking you were in the Far East. A cloudless sky pushed the temperature into the high eighties, maybe nineties, and helped solidify that feeling. From another room off to the side, he thought he heard a child's voice, a woman talking, a nanny perhaps, with instructions never to answer the door.

Natalie opened two sets of double patio doors and a cooling breeze swelled into the room. Then she stepped onto a patio that covered most of the garden, and walked towards a set of chairs and table large enough for a party of ten. Arletta followed, arms wrapped across her chest as if cold. As she took her seat, Gilchrist realised she was in pain.

He pulled out a chair opposite. He thought her make-up was thicker over her right eye, as if to hide bruises, and her hair by her temple stiff, sprayed into place to hide stitches, perhaps. Jessie sat next to him. He caught Arletta's eye, and said, 'How many broken ribs?'

She shook her head. 'They're only bruised. I had Grant write up his report to make it seem worse than it really was.'

'Grant?'

'Grant Williamson. My consultant.'

Gilchrist nodded. 'Why would you ask him to do that?'

'To give him reason to notify the police, and hopefully scare Tony.'

'Tony doesn't look like someone who scares easily.'

'He isn't. But he won't do anything if he knows the police are watching. Not right away, anyway.'

'And the stitches?'

'They're real.' She shivered, as if from the memory, then her face saddened, and she said, 'Was it you who found him? Rab, I mean.'

Gilchrist nodded, his brain already working through the network connection – Levy to Tony, Tony to Arletta. But that made no sense. Rab's body being found proved Tony had lied to Arletta. No, he thought, she must have heard it from someone else, someone she knew she could trust.

'How was he . . .' Arletta closed her eyes for a moment, then said, 'How did he die?'

'Shot in the head.' He wanted to add *twice*, but thought it an unnecessary detail as he watched that image filter through her mind.

'I never believed Rab had emigrated,' she said. 'He wouldn't have left without saying goodbye. At least, I always thought he wouldn't. But Tony swore blind he'd driven him to the ferry, and that it all had to be done in a hurry. No one was to know. Jock's orders.' She shook her head, and her eyes shone with an anger that flared for a moment before being doused by tears. 'I trusted Tony back then,' she managed to say. 'God, I was so foolish.'

'We've all been tricked by men,' Jessie said. 'So you're not scoring any Brownie points.' She leaned forward. 'Did you not try to contact your uncle Rab?'

'Of course I did. I wrote to him. To an address I was given. A PO Box in Malaysia that was supposed to be a collection point for all his mail to be forwarded by special courier to Australia or wherever he was living at the time. But I never got any response.'

'Didn't you challenge your father, ask him to give you Rab's home address? Or even a phone number?' Jessie said, her tone rising with exasperation.

'Many times. But you could never win an argument with Jock. He would raise his voice, tell me he was fed up hearing about it, and order me to shut up, that if word ever got out where Rab was, it could put his life in danger.'

'Why would it do that?'

'He said Rab knew too much about the finances of the organisation. That's what I was told, anyway. And then, when he'd been gone for about four years, I was told he'd died.'

Gilchrist thought he saw Jock's logic. 'That story was created to stop you from asking about him, or insisting on flying out to see him.'

'Exactly. I was told to forget about him. Uncle Rab was dead. And that was that.'

'Do you think Tony was involved in his murder?'

She grimaced, and nodded. 'Tony might not have pulled the trigger, but he and Jock were in it together, I'm sure of that. When I heard that Uncle Rab's body had been found, I realised

148

he'd never left the country at all, and that they'd killed him and covered it up with the story of him going to Australia.'

'Who told you Rab's body had been found?' Gilchrist asked.

She shook her head. 'Doesn't matter.'

In a way, her answer was what Gilchrist had expected. She wouldn't give up her source so readily. He pressed on. 'So do you know who murdered Rab? Who pulled the trigger?'

'No. But I can guess.'

Guessing didn't help his investigation. He needed Arletta to name names, but that might come later. 'And where was your brother, Jimmy, when all this was going on?'

A look of disgust swept across her features. 'Either in rehab or stoned out his skull.'

Gilchrist saw now why Tony had taken over when Jock died. He'd been his right-hand man, taken care of troublesome family members, kept the secret of Rab's murder, then tightened the bond with the strings of marriage to Jock's only daughter. He leaned closer. 'Did you hear about Big Mac being pulled from the Clyde? Joe McKenzie,' he added, just to make sure there could be no misunderstanding.

She closed her eyes, and nodded. 'Yes.'

'Do you know who killed *him*?'

'No. But he was killed on Tony's orders, though you'll never be able to prove that.'

'Why was he killed?'

'Because he was my bodyguard, and because he knew who killed my uncle.'

'But he never told you who pulled the trigger?'

'No. But as soon as I heard about Mac's murder, I knew that Tony had stepped over the line, that he would have to shift gears, and that the next person on his hitlist was more than likely going to be me.'

Jessie said, 'Till death us do part. Jeez. Who needs enemies with a husband like that?'

'That's what you were told,' Gilchrist said to Arletta.

'Sorry?'

'Rab was killed because he knew too much about the organisation's finances. That's what you were told. Which tells me you don't believe it.' He held her gaze, letting her know that he wasn't going to let this go. He needed to get to the truth, no matter what that truth was. 'I'm thinking there's more to it than that,' he said. 'Did you know that Jock and Rab were half-brothers?'

She showed no surprise at the question, and instead gave a sad nod.

'Maybe it was something to do with who Rab's father was?' he tried.

She turned her head, looked off to some point in the far distance. Then she glanced at Natalie, as if seeking approval. But Natalie lowered her gaze, tightened her lips, and when Arletta spoke, her voice was no louder than a whisper.

'My paternal grandmother had an affair,' she said. 'I don't know who with. I could never find out. It was never talked about in the family, and I knew nothing about it until I was in my teens, and my aunt Nadine confided in me not long after Mum passed away.'

'Go on.'

'She told me that no one other than herself knew about that, although everyone knew Rab was gay.' She smiled at the memory. 'You couldn't not know Rab was gay. It was the jewellery and the clothes he wore, rather than what he said or how he acted. His clothes were always bold and colourful, even outrageous at times. He loved to dress to the nines, and he wouldn't harm a fly. He was the nicest man in that respect. It was one of the reasons I loved him. Not like some of the others who seemed to thrive on violence.'

Jessie said, 'Was Joe McKenzie violent?'

'Only when needed.'

'Could he have been involved in Rab's murder?'

Arletta frowned, as if that thought had never occurred to her. 'I don't know. He did as he was ordered. That's why he was trusted.'

'Clearly not trusted enough,' Jessie said.

Gilchrist stepped forward, a sign for Jessie to take a back seat. He needed to keep the interview on track, while Arletta was willing to talk freely. 'Did you believe Nadine when she told you she was the only person who knew about her mother's affair?'

'I did, yes.'

'And she never gave you a name? Just said she'd had an affair, nothing else?'

'Yes.'

'Not even how long the affair lasted?' He held her gaze, hoping for some indication that his questions were getting him closer. 'Could it even be called an affair?' he tried.

'What do you mean?'

'A wee knee-trembler up a close,' Jessie quipped. 'In and out in a flash, and nobody's any the wiser?' Which seemed to do the trick, but not the trick Gilchrist was hoping for.

Arletta's face darkened, her lips pressed tight in angered silence, before she said, 'I wouldn't have the foggiest. Not like you, by the looks of you. Nadine would've been able to answer that.'

151

'Okay,' Jessie said. 'We'll talk to her.'

'Good luck with that,' Arletta said.

'What do you mean?'

But Gilchrist already knew the answer.

'Nadine died five years ago.'

CHAPTER 24 ·

The flush of disappointment that coursed through Gilchrist's system could have been the aftermath of a dose of adrenaline. He'd felt confident that Arletta was the key to solving Rab Shepherd's murder, that once they'd interviewed her, it would become clear. He poked and prodded some more at her involvement in the family business, but other than saying she had no confidence in the direction the business was going, now being run by Tony, she gave nothing away. After a further ten minutes, he felt as if he was farther from the truth than ever before.

Up until then, Arletta had been helpful, but was now being difficult, refusing to give a statement, telling Jessie in an ever-threatening tone that doing so would put not only her life in danger, but Natalie's and her children's, too. Dainty was right. The discovery of Rab's body had initiated a family feud that could end in only one of the two – Tony or Arletta – surviving.

'You don't know Tony,' Arletta argued. 'If he gets wind that you've spoken to me, it's lights out.'

Gilchrist thought it would've been lights out for Arletta anyway – why else was she in hiding? – when Jessie said, 'Work with us, and we could apply for witness protection.'

'Not in a million bloody years. I'm not going into hiding for the rest of my life.'

Which in a strange way pleased Gilchrist, because Arletta hadn't been witness to anything related to Rab's murder. When it seemed as if Jessie and Arletta's shouting match was about to turn violent, Gilchrist stepped between them.

'There could be another way,' he said.

'Like what?' Arletta spat.

Jessie glared at her, lips tight as a scar.

Gilchrist looked at one then the other, waiting until he felt he had their full attention, that they wanted to know what the *other* way was. He wanted to know himself, because he hadn't thought it all the way through, and wasn't sure if what he was about to say would be acceptable, or that his rationale made sense. But he said to Arletta, 'I agree with you. I think Tony was behind Rab's murder. Directly or indirectly. It doesn't matter. He's guilty either way. He knew Rab was dead, evidenced by his story about driving him to the ferry. We just need to prove that.'

Arletta scoffed, 'Easier said than done.'

'But I need you to tell me who first told you that Rab had died in the Far East.'

Arletta narrowed her eyes. 'Maybe it was Jock. I can't remember.'

'Oh come on,' Jessie snapped. 'Your favourite uncle's been missing for years, you've never heard a word from him in all that time, and when someone finally tells you he's dead, you can't remember who? Pull the other one.'

'I was in Jock's office. Tony was there, too. I can't remember who

154

told me. Maybe it was Tony. I don't know. I just remember hearing that he was dead, and being devastated, and bursting into tears.'

Jessie's glance at Gilchrist told him she didn't believe a word of it. He wasn't sure he did either. But placing Tony and Jock together at the telling of Rab's death convinced him that both had to have been instrumental in his murder. But with Jock no longer alive, the only person he could go after was Tony. And Arletta was right. How could he prove it? All he had was circumstantial evidence – if it could even be called that – and the questionable word of a late crime patriarch's daughter slash current crime patriarch's wife. She might come across as being squeaky clean, with no criminal record on the PNC, not even a parking ticket. But per Dainty she was the one who wore the pants, and who everyone danced around. And here she was, hiding from Tony, in fear for her life. Nothing seemed to make sense.

He tried another tack. 'Let me ask you this. If Tony wasn't around, and by that I mean if he was held in custody for a long time, who would step in to run the organisation? You?'

She nodded. 'In the first instance.'

'Meaning?'

'I'm Tony's wife, and Jock's daughter. I'd be expected to take over. But Tony has friends, call them associates, who'd rather die than take orders from a woman. Eventually they'd try to get rid of me.'

'Kill you, in other words,' Gilchrist said, more statement than question.

She wrapped her arms around her middle. 'These guys don't mess around.'

'So if Tony and you were both . . . let's say . . . no longer part of the business. Who would take over then?'

'Eddie Cumbo.'

He thought the answer was given too quickly, as if she'd had the name sitting on the tip of her tongue in anticipation of his asking. He'd never heard of Eddie Cumbo, but a call to Dainty might enlighten him, and it could be worthwhile having Jackie dig deeper.

But first things first.

'And Eddie Cumbo is who, exactly?'

'Let's just say he's Tony's business advisor.'

'Meaning?'

'He's got Tony's ear.'

'And how long has Tony known Eddie?'

'They went to school together.'

'Could Eddie have been involved in Rab's murder?'

'He could've. But I don't think so.'

'Why not?'

'Back then, Eddie was a gofer, a small player in the business, not someone Jock would go to for . . .' She grimaced, as if unsure how to say it. '. . . for taking care of business.'

'So, Jock ordered Rab to be killed is what you're suggesting.'

'I'm not sure.'

'Why not?'

'It would've been too personal for Jock.'

Gilchrist gave that some thought. How personal was *too personal*? If Jock had found out that Rab had been fathered by someone other than his own father, and was only his half-brother, could he have seen that as a reason to order his murder? In nature, certain fledglings kill other fledglings in the same nest; the survival of the fittest. There was only so much of anything to go around. Maybe it wasn't a stretch of the imagination for Jock to murder his half-brother to keep the family blood pure, so to speak. But where did all this speculation take him? It seemed he was finding more questions than answers.

He forced his thoughts back to the task at hand.

'How safe are you here?' he asked Arletta.

She shook her head. 'You found me, so Tony can, too.'

'Do you have somewhere else you can go to?'

She gave a non-committal shrug.

'I can arrange for you to be put up in a safe house. Until things settle down.'

'And if you can't nail Tony, then what? I'm stuck there forever?'

'We'll nail Tony,' he said.

'And Eddie, too?'

Well, there was that additional problem to overcome. He chose to ignore her question about Eddie, and said, 'You're saying you can't stay here because Tony will find you, so you need to find someplace else to go. A safe house would be a good first step.'

'Not interested.'

'Your choice,' Jessie said.

'What do you intend to do?' Gilchrist asked.

She shrugged again, and glanced at Natalie, and in that shifting of her eyes he realised that she was two steps ahead of him, maybe more, that she was more devious than he'd ever imagined, a woman who could spill out lies, one after the other, and convince even the dead that they could rise again if she so desired. She had some other plan in place, of that he felt certain, but a plan she was never going to share with him.

He made sure Jessie had Arletta and Natalie's contact details. Then he handed over his card, told Arletta to give him a call if she changed her mind, and strode off, Jessie behind him.

157

CHAPTER 25

As Gilchrist drove off, Jessie said, 'Lying bitch. She's in it all the way up to her diamond-studded necklace. Did you see the size of these stones? And the matching bracelet? Here's me thinking those earrings of Rab's were expensive. But Jeez, these have to be worth tens of thousands.'

'Can't say I noticed,' he said, which pulled a curse from Jessie's lips.

He hadn't been looking out for jewellery, but it did have him wondering if Argyle Arcade Levy was the family's jeweller of choice, which might explain his calls to Tony. They drove on in silence, Jessie scrolling through her mobile – a glance at which told him she was checking out jewellery shops – while he struggled to work out how much of Arletta's interview was truth or lies, and where Eddie Cumbo fitted into events.

He waited until he was back on the City Bypass before calling Dainty.

'Eddie Cumbo,' he said. 'What can you tell me about him?'

'Jesus, Andy, he's as bad as they come. You don't want anything to do with that mad bastard. Why? Has he threatened you?'

Gilchrist caught the concern in Dainty's tone, and said, 'Why do you think that?'

'Because he's a fucking nutter who's threatened cops before. We've pulled him in umpteen times, but he's as slippery as an eel in a barrel of oil. We know he's responsible for a number of gangland shootings, but he's always alibied up to his oxters. And his solicitors are just as fucking slippery. Never get past Go with these bastards.'

'And his relationship to Tony?'

'Personal hitman.'

Well, there he had it. Rab's killer. He had to be. The logic seemed unarguable enough. Except, hadn't Jock ordered Rab's murder, and Eddie was a gofer back then? His thoughts were interrupted by Dainty saying, 'But . . .'

'I'm listening.'

'But rumour has it, and it's only fucking rumour, because no one knows for sure, or maybe best to say no one's prepared to mention it, but Eddie and Arletta are screwing behind Tony's back.'

Gilchrist let that thought simmer for a moment, then decided that Arletta's infidelity didn't really take him anywhere. He wanted to get back to the main point, and said, 'Let me run this past you.'

'Shoot.'

'Big Jock orders Rab's murder for whatever reason, it doesn't matter, but he's the guy who gives out the orders. Then he devises the story of Tony driving Rab to the Amsterdam ferry, while Tony and a few others drive Rab to St Andrews instead, and Eddie shoots him in the back of the head.'

'What proof do you have?'

'None yet, but I'll start the ball rolling by pulling Eddie in for questioning, and see where that takes us. From what you've told me, I can't see him coughing up and pointing the finger at Tony. But it's a good lead, starting off with Eddie's address. Do you have it?'

'Afraid it won't do you any good, Andy.'

Gilchrist glanced at Jessie who looked just as puzzled. 'Why?'

'Word on the street is that Eddie's gone missing.'

Gilchrist eyed the speaker. 'Missing? As in – no one knows where he is?'

'As in – we're expecting him to turn up in the Clyde. I tell you, Andy, the shit's hit the fan, big time. We're just waiting for the shockwaves to arrive.'

'Tony's behind it. He has to be.'

'No doubt.' Dainty gave out a heavy sigh. 'But proving that's another kettle of fish.'

Gilchrist frowned. He'd never heard Dainty so defeated. 'What am I missing?'

'Tony's untouchable, Andy. You can pull him in for question-ing, but he'll have an alibi forged in steel, and his lawyers'll have him out again in a matter of hours. As it stands, Eddie Cumbo's missing. No one knows where he is or if he's dead. Likely dead. But until his body turns up, you'd be wasting your time. Sorry, Andy, but there it is.'

Gilchrist didn't like what he'd heard. With Cumbo missing, his investigation had hit a stumbling block, maybe even a dead end. With reluctance, he said, 'Get back to me as soon as,' and ended the call.

'Now what?' Jessie said.

'We wait until Eddie turns up, with or without his head.'

'Or we could cut to the chase,' Jessie said, 'and pull Tony in for his murder, and see where that takes us.'

'Then we're showing all our cards, letting him know he's our prime suspect. And as Dainty said, he'll be alibied to the hilt. Better to lie low until we hear back from Dainty.'

'Yeah, I suppose,' Jessie said, and seemed to slump in her seat as if disappointed.

'On the bright side,' he said, 'it *is* Saturday. Go out and enjoy yourself.'

'You're forgetting I'm supposed to be meeting Fran whatsher-face tonight.'

'Sounds like you want to call it off.'

'I'm just not looking forward to it. I'd prefer to stay in with a pizza and a bottle of cheap plonk.'

'Phone her up and call it off then.'

'Might just do that,' she said, and stared off at the passing countryside.

Back in St Andrews, Gilchrist dropped Jessie off at her home, told her to enjoy the rest of the weekend, and that he'd see her on Monday. Then he drove to his cottage in Crail, intent on spending a rare few hours in the back garden before the heatwave broke, having a beer and working on his tan. Now when had he last done that?

In his shorts, stripped to the waist, he started off by rolling out the garden hose and watering his plants, then setting up a cheap sprinkler that seemed to leak more onto the path than water the grass. Surrounded by walls on all three sides, his back garden was a sun trap which exaggerated the ambient temperature by several degrees. Despite his best intentions to put his feet up and have a sun-warmed beer, he found he couldn't sit still, his thoughts

161

caught in a mental loop that replayed their meeting with Arletta over and over, like a video recording that kept repeating itself. He couldn't put his finger on it, or point to any one thing she'd said that caused him to doubt her, but something in her manner, her occasional glance at Natalie, the hugging of her arms across her chest, the way she told them more than he'd expected, all of it warned him it could be a smoke screen, that nothing was as it seemed, she was spinning them a yarn, she wasn't who they thought she was. But she was. Wasn't she?

She was the daughter of Jock Shepherd, now deceased; wife of Tony Dilanos, very much alive; and partner in a criminal organisation, but now in hiding for her life. But if she died, where would that put Tony? Head of the family business, with no Shepherds around to confuse leadership? But Tony was already head of the organisation, so what had he to gain by getting rid of his wife. Still, if you flipped the coin over, looked at it from the other side, Arletta Shepherd was the heir apparent to the family business if Tony just happened to have a fatal accident.

Was that what was now happening? A deadly power struggle between husband and wife for control of the family business, the firm, a criminal organisation built with blood and guts and sweat by big Jock Shepherd over a murderous lifetime to become a multi-million-pound enterprise that now seemed to be beyond the longest reach of the arm of the law? And all of this bonfire of bodies and criminal detritus triggered into gangland fury by the blue-touch-paper fuse of the discovery of Rab Shepherd's body?

He couldn't say. Not at that moment.

But he might if he found the answers to a few other questions.

He eyed the sun, wiped sweat from his face, then went indoors to text Jackie.

CHAPTER 26

Jessie approached the Albany Hotel, feeling nervous for reasons that defied her. She was only meeting Fran Patten after all, a friend of hers if she could be called that, someone she'd met a couple of times in Glasgow, years ago as best she could remember. So what was she worried about? Maybe it was because of what Fran had said when she called to arrange a meeting – *Looking forward to seeing you again, Jess. It's been a while.* Or maybe it wasn't *what* was said, but *how* it was said, with an enticing sense of innuendo that Jessie couldn't quite put her finger on. And no one called her Jess any more. So what was that about?

Oh well, she was here now.

She took a couple of deep breaths, and pushed through the door into the pleasant ambience of a boutique townhouse hotel. Fran had texted her and said she would meet her in the patio garden at the back, and Jessie walked along the entrance hallway, shuffling her hair, patting her blouse, last-second checking that nothing was out of place.

The patio had enough tables and chairs to accommodate every hotel guest and more. Jessie recognised Fran by the colour of her hair, seated by herself at the farthest end of the garden at a table for two. Before Jessie reached her, Fran stood and smiled with outstretched arms, and gave her a *haven't-seen-you-in-ages* hug with two air kisses, one on either cheek.

'You look great,' Fran said, taking her seat, and filling Jessie's empty glass with a dark red wine. 'I didn't think you'd mind,' she said. 'A bottle of your favourite.'

'Didn't know I had a favourite,' Jessie replied, flapping her blouse as she took her seat. Surrounded by walls and bushes, the garden area seemed stifled of air. Even at half past six, the temperature had to still be in the seventies. Or maybe she was having a hot flush. Jeez, what was this all about?

'You said you loved that wine last time,' Fran said.

'Did I?' Jessie eyed her glass with suspicion, while Fran raised hers, and held it out for Jessie to chink against with a 'Cheers.'

'So,' Fran said, sitting back, and eyeing Jessie over the rim of her glass. 'How have you been?'

'Busy.'

'I bet you have.'

Jessie returned Fran's gaze, struck by the hint of an impish grin that threatened to curl the corners of her mouth. She thought of asking what she meant by *I bet you have*, then chose to ignore it, and instead took another sip of wine. 'This is good. What is it?'

'A cheeky Ripasso.'

'I've heard of wines being cheeky, but I've never heard of Ripasso.'

'Oh, but you have. Last time we met, you were giving it laldy.'

'Aye, well, I must've been right gubbed.'

'We both were,' Fran said, and chuckled, her eyes never leaving Jessie's. 'It really is lovely to see you again. And I love your hair. It's shorter. It really suits you. And you've lost weight, too.' She paused, as if to wait for Jessie's response, then when it didn't come, added, 'I was watching you when you came in.' She leaned forward, lowered her voice. 'You have a certain air about you that you are completely unaware of. It's what makes you unique. And excitingly sensual, in a quiet way. You could steal the show, you know.'

Jessie replaced her glass to the table, harder than intended. 'Right, before you start asking me to take my knickers off, what's this about?'

Fran hid her face in a long sip of wine, a pink flush colouring the edges of her cheeks. When she then placed her glass on the table with slow deliberation, as if struggling to think of something to say, Jessie was already regretting her outburst. 'I'm sorry,' Fran said, her voice so quiet that Jessie had to strain to catch it. 'I didn't mean to upset you. That's the last thing I would do. I . . .' She looked at the tables around her, at other couples and groups lost in their own conversations, laughing and drinking and enjoying the warmth of a Scottish summer's evening. 'I . . . I'm sorry. I made a mistake.' She shook her head, gathered her handbag, and pushed her seat back.

'Wait,' Jessie said.

Fran stilled, her gaze fixed on Jessie's eyes.

'I'm sorry, too,' Jessie said. 'I didn't mean to be so . . . it's just . . .' She shrugged. 'When you texted me, I didn't know what to expect. I have this vague memory of the last time we met, and I think I made an absolute arse of myself. So, please . . .' She held out her wine, an invitation for Fran to finish her own glass. 'You don't expect me to finish the rest of that cheeky bottle of Ripasso all by myself, do you?'

Fran smiled, returned her handbag to the corner of her seat, and picked up her wine. Then she frowned, as if worried. 'I don't think you remember, do you?'

Jessie swallowed a lump in her throat. Now she was here with Fran, sitting opposite her, looking at her eye-to-eye, she *did* remember. At least she thought she did. It seemed as if her senses were firing in all directions, sending confusing messages to her brain. It had been a parting kiss on the cheek, which somehow found its way to her lips for a fleeting moment, an exhilarating instant that had her pushing away from the hard press of Fran's body. She'd been drunk, enjoying the moment, caught unawares, nothing more. That's all. She shook her head, and said nothing as Fran reached across the table. Her hand felt warm, her skin smooth and soft as if oiled every day, her fingers gentle.

Then Jessie pulled her hand free.

'I have a wee boy,' she said. 'Well, he's wee in the sense that he's young, but he's over six foot tall with shoulders out to here, and he's . . . and he's . . . he's my *son*, if you get my meaning.' Jeez, she was gibbering, and felt her face flush. 'Look,' she said, trying to pull her thoughts on track. 'I think you've misunderstood me somehow. To put it bluntly, I bat for the other side. I'm just not . . . you know . . . that way inclined.'

If she'd thought that was going to chase Fran away, she was wrong, for Fran offered her a comforting smile, and said, 'That's okay, Jess. I have a son, too. And a daughter. It took me a while to come to terms with my own sexuality. I denied it for long enough, years and years until I took action and filed for a divorce. Deep down inside, I always knew who I was meant to be. And who I am now.' She lowered her head, and eyed Jessie. 'And I sense you have the same feelings as I had.'

Jessie said nothing, just stared at Fran, wondering why she didn't get up and leave the bloody lesbian to enjoy her own company.

'And the same doubts, too,' Fran added.

Jessie shifted on her seat.

'I won't push you, Jess, I promise you. So why don't you stay with me? Have a chat. Finish our bottle of cheeky Ripasso.' She gave a husky chuckle at that. 'Maybe have another one. And if I haven't chased you away by then, we could go for a walk along the beach? It's such a lovely night.'

Jessie found herself resisting the urge to down her wine and just leave. What was it about Fran that she found so disconcerting, so . . . so . . . enticingly attractive? She couldn't explain it. All she knew was that the tone of Fran's voice soothed her, sent an exquisite warmth coursing through her body, like a current of electricity that relaxed and flexed and stimulated all her senses at the same time. She touched the stem of her glass, twiddled it with her fingers. What harm could a chat and a glass or two of red wine do? A cheeky Ripasso at that. But even so, she found her inner self offering resistance.

Fran raised her glass, held it out in anticipation of a friendly chink, a sign that all was well, that whatever had been said or done against the grain was forgiven, that the promise of not pushing was genuine, and that Jessie could leave anytime, or stay a bit longer and they could enjoy a walk along the beach.

Jessie lifted her glass, and chinked it against Fran's. 'No pushing?'

Fran gave her a white-toothed smile. 'Cross my heart.'

'And hope to die?'

'Of course.'

CHAPTER 27

At five minutes past seven, Gilchrist had showered and shaved and was splashing on aftershave when his mobile rang. He took the call on speaker, and said, 'Hello.'

'Told you the shit would hit the fucking fan,' Dainty proclaimed. 'Cumbo's body's just turned up. Washed ashore at Greenock. Minus his fucking head, of course. Right tit for tat going on. Fuck knows who's going to turn up next, but apparently Danny Levy's gone missing too . . .' For a moment, Gilchrist couldn't place the name. Then he had it. The jeweller in the Argyle Arcade. '. . . and another two of Tony's sidekicks have vanished.'

'Vanished? Jesus,' Gilchrist said. 'The Clyde's filling up with bodies.'

'No, not these two. Rumour has it that they've done a runner. They know they're on someone's hitlist, and didn't want to sit around and find out whose. There's fucking loyalty for you. When the ship goes down, the first fuckers off are the rats.' Dainty sniffed, then said, 'Anyway, I thought I'd give you a heads-up on Cumbo.'

'Any suspects yet?'

'Tony's men. No doubts about it. But trying to pin it on anyone's another matter. Tighter than a whore's purse, that lot. Could be any one of them, or all of them together. Who the fuck knows any more? On the bright side, if we, the boys in blue stay out of it, by the time they've finished hacking each other to bits, there might be no one left. A DI-fucking-Y city clearance. Now wouldn't that be nice.' A pause, then, 'But seriously, Andy, have you had signs of any trouble at your end?'

Despite Dainty's concern for Gilchrist and Jessie's welfare, neither of them had felt threatened in any way – so far. He thought of bringing Dainty up to speed, telling him that they'd found Arletta Shepherd, and confirmed she was in hiding in fear for her life. But until he had a better understanding of who was killing who, he decided not to. The fewer people who knew he'd met Arletta, the better. So he kept it simple. 'Not yet. But I'll let you know if anything happens.'

'Good, Andy. Be careful. These bastards are stir-crazy at the moment. They'd kill their own mother to save their own sorry arses.'

And with that, the line died.

Gilchrist held on to his mobile while his mind replayed Dainty's words. The mention of Danny Levy made him realise that he hadn't heard back from Dick yet, which told him that Dick had either found nothing, or was still working on it. A glance at the time confirmed he was running a few minutes early for his date with Irene, so he took the opportunity to phone Dick.

'Sorry, Andy. Meant to give you a call back, but got tied up. Haven't really got much for you. Levy placed a few more calls, a total of five in the space of thirty minutes. One to his wife;

169

another one to Tony Dilanos, in addition to those first calls; one to a mobile registered to an Edward Cumbo—'

'When was that call made?' Gilchrist snapped.

'Whoah, that got your attention. Let me see. At 14:42, and it lasted all of twenty seconds. Anything I need to know?'

'Any way you can give me a recording?'

'No chance, Andy. Didn't have time to set anything up.'

Damn it, he thought. It would've been good to know what was said, but he could go only so far with illegal tapping. 'Okay, that's fine, Dick. That got my attention because I've just heard that Cumbo's headless body was recovered from the Clyde today.'

'Holy shit, Andy. What's going on?'

'Maybe best you don't know.'

'Understand.'

'You said five. Levy made two more calls?'

'Yeah, one to another mobile registered to a D. Lynch, and the final one to a landline in the name of Julie Merton. Any of them ring a bell?'

The names meant nothing, and Gilchrist said so, although he asked Dick to text their details to him – phone numbers and names, and anything else he had on them. He'd have Jackie carry out some research. It might be worth knowing exactly who Lynch and Merton were, which could help explain why Levy had called them. But with Levy missing, and Cumbo turning up headless, did that mean Lynch and Merton's lives were in danger, too? Shit hitting the fan might be the understatement of the year. Another glance at the time, and he said, 'I've got to go, Dick. Get these details over to me as soon as you can.'

'Will do.'

Gilchrist slipped his mobile into his back pocket, reached for the car keys on a wall hook in the hall, and stepped outside into the unfamiliarity of a warm Scottish evening – not just warm, but hot enough to imagine you were stepping out for some tapas in Spain, or a walk along the beach in the Caribbean to catch the setting sun. Wouldn't it be wonderful if we could have another three weeks of it? Make that two. Even one would be enough, if you thought about it. Before he reached his car, his mobile rang – ID Mo – and he answered with, 'Hi, princess, how are you enjoying life in Glasgow?'

'It's early days, Dad. But yeah, so far it's fine.'

'You settling into your new place?'

'Just about.'

'Well, when you get a chance, it would be nice to have your new address.'

'I'll give it to you now,' she said, and rattled it off.

'I'm heading to the car, so I can't write it down.'

'No worries, I'll text it to you later. So you'll always have it on your phone.'

'You know me too well,' he said, then added, 'So what's your new place like?'

'It's nice. It's even better than nice. Plenty of room. On the fourth floor overlooking a cemetery at the back. So you don't feel as if you're being spied on from another flat across the road. And there's a common balcony at the front with a view up St Vincent Street.'

Gilchrist's knowledge of Glasgow was not good enough to pinpoint where the flat was exactly, but he was pleased to hear Maureen happy. The memory of Irene's comments to him earlier still niggled, and he decided to edge into it with, 'What are the flatmates like?'

'Flat*mate*,' she emphasised. 'Just the two of us.'

'Do you get on well with her?' he asked, and hoped his question hadn't sounded as conspicuous to Maureen as it had to himself.

'It's a *he*, Dad, and rather than try and finagle it out of me, his name is Mackenzie Baker, he's an architect, he's single, and he's extremely good-looking to the point of being handsome. And we're not sleeping together.' A pause, then, '*Yet*,' she added with what sounded like spiteful emphasis.

'I'm sorry, Mo, I didn't mean . . .' But the line was already dead.

Shit and fuck it. What was it about Mo that he was the lighted match to her blue touch-paper? Or maybe it wasn't Mo's fault, but his own unavoidable foot-in-mouth disease. Christ. He cursed himself as he beeped his key fob, took his seat behind the wheel, and fired up the ignition. He thought of calling back, but from experience knew it would take her some time to settle down, that she could nurse her anger for hours if need be, then let him have it back in spades. He let out a heavy sigh in resigned frustration, and eased his car from the kerb.

He was driving through Kingsbarns when his mobile beeped – a text from Jackie. He checked his rear-view mirror – nothing behind him – then with his knees against the steering wheel to hold his course, opened Jackie's message. A quick scan, at the same time as eyeing the road ahead, was sufficient to let him read that she'd found no death certificate for Nadine Thomson née Shepherd, and that she appeared to be alive and well and living in Cupar.

He gripped the steering wheel, slammed on the brakes, and pulled to a stop.

He read through Jackie's message . . .

Nadine now living with J Merton . . .

Bloody hell. He'd known it. That bitch Arletta had lied to Jessie and him through her back teeth. He read on, noted Nadine's address. She was alive, not dead, which meant . . .?

He phoned Dainty.

'Christ, Andy, can't a man enjoy a quiet pint on a Saturday night?'

'You've got contacts in Lothian and Borders, haven't you?'

'What d'you need?'

'Arletta Shepherd. She's in Edinburgh.'

'She's *what*? How d'you know that?'

He didn't want to say that he and Jessie had interviewed her earlier that day. It might make Dainty feel as if he didn't trust him, or was intentionally keeping him out of the loop, which he was in a way. So he ignored the question, gave Dainty the address, and said, 'I need you to have someone bring her in for questioning.'

'On what grounds?'

'Make something up. Anything. How about on suspicion of murder?'

'Who's she supposed to have murdered?'

'Danny Levy.'

'Jesus fuck, Andy, there's a lot of holes in what you're not telling me.'

'I'll explain later,' he said, and hung up before Dainty could grill him further.

Next, he checked his emails and found one from Dick with the details he'd asked for on Lynch and Merton. He forwarded them to Jackie, then phoned her.

173

Jackie answered on the first ring. 'Uh-huh.'

'Sorry to spoil your weekend, Jackie, but I've just sent over some info on a couple of names I'd like you to research for me.'

'Uh-huh,' she managed to say before he battered on.

'Who are they? Where do they live?' Even though he'd got Julie Merton's address, she might have some other properties in her name. 'Criminal records? Are they on the PNC? The usual stuff. And as soon as you can.' To someone listening in, it sounded as if he wasn't giving Jackie a chance to respond, but her stutter was so bad it could take her a minute just to say Hello, and with her mobility problems due to her cerebral palsy, she seldom spent time anywhere other than her home office. He pressed on. 'There's a connection between them all, I think, so it would be good to know how and what.' He paused for a moment, then said, 'Did you get all that?'

'Uh-huh.'

'Thanks, Jackie. You're a darling.' Not exactly PC, but if his heart would ever go out to anyone, it would have to be Jackie. He grinned when he heard her chuckle, and made a mental note to send some flowers to her with a big Thank You with smiley-faces and a few kisses all over. The line hung silent for a few seconds – she always waited for him to hang up – so he said, 'Thanks again, Jackie,' then ended the call.

He hated to do it, but he needed to call Irene.

'I'm sorry,' he said to her. 'But something's turned up that I can't ignore. I can meet you in an hour or so, or take a rain-check. Whatever works for you.'

'An hour's fine, Andy. I'm running a bit late myself.'

'Perfect,' he said. 'Chill that wine, and I'll see you soon?'

He threw his mobile onto the centre console, then entered Julie Merton's address into his satnav. He drove off, tyres scattering gravel as he accelerated hard, as good a reflection of his mood as any. He felt as if he'd been taken for a fool, that Arletta and Tony had played him, sending him round in circles as if to please their whim.

Nadine was dead, and now she wasn't.

He gritted his teeth as he settled down for the short drive.

Right, he thought to himself, enough is enough.

CHAPTER 28

Gilchrist found Julie Merton's address on the outskirts of Cupar, a modern bungalow which had once been a smallholding, on what appeared to be several acres of land. It still had the original facade – central door, windows either side. At first glance, the building looked in great shape, but as he walked between the gateposts – whatever gate used to hang there long since removed – he saw the natural deterioration of a place in need of better maintenance.

As he strode along the gravel driveway, weeds grew between flattened tyre tracks, wildness flourished around the edges of a lawn in dire need of a cut, sporting daisies and bald patches from lack of water. Potted plants of pansies, begonia, fuchsia, lined a strip of garden that could do with being weeded or turned over. A solitary car – a Toyota something – sat parked outside the front vestibule. A series of scratches that could have been done with a knife, or from clipping the roughcast gatepost, spoiled the near-side front panel.

He pressed the doorbell, and waited.

It didn't take long for the door to click open. An elderly woman with white hair tied back in a loose bun of sorts scowled down at him. It struck him that she didn't appear warm despite wearing a plaid shirt and heavy corduroy trousers more suited for winter rather than the heatwave Scotland was currently experiencing. And something in her features triggered a subconscious memory – the length of her face, the shape of her jaw, the piercing stare of blue eyes that had perhaps seen a harder side of life than most – a softer version of big Jock.

'Nadine?' he said.

Her forehead folded into creases. 'And you are?'

Even her voice sounded like a younger Jock. Gilchrist introduced himself as Detective Chief Inspector Andrew Gilchrist, and flashed his warrant card. 'Do you have a minute?'

'What's this about?'

'Your brother, Rab.'

'What about him?'

'He's been found.'

Shock flickered across her face, then softened into puzzled disbelief. Her lips moved as if she couldn't think of what to say, or how to say it. Then she came to and stared at him with undisguised suspicion. 'That's nonsense. Rab was never lost.'

Gilchrist thought it such an odd thing for her to say. 'What do you mean?' he said.

'Rab left Scotland and emigrated to the Far East, where he died several years later.'

'If I told you he never left Scotland at all, what would you say?'

'That you're off your bloody head.'

'Perhaps it's better if we had a chat inside?'

She narrowed her eyes at him, then shot a glance over his shoulder, as if to make sure he was alone, that his unexpected appearance was not some trap to overpower her, or worse, arrest her. Then she stepped aside. 'Just for a minute, then. And take off your shoes.'

Gilchrist slipped his shoes off as ordered, then followed her along a dark hallway.

The lounge could have been a morgue for all the light and sound allowed to enter it. Curtains as thick as rugs hung from beneath floral pelmets all the way to the floor where they lay curled like discarded clothes. A standard lamp stood beside a high-backed chair, as dull and still as a stone sentinel. As he stepped deeper into the room, his sock-covered feet silent in the thick-pile carpet, he felt as if he were invading a private moment between mourners at a wake. The room felt cool, the air redolent of mothballs, which cast up a memory of him as a young boy pulling open his grandmother's wardrobe and being frightened at the display of fur coats, some with fox stoles stitched to the collar, fierce eyes as fixed as beads. A shadow shifted out of the darkness to his left, to manifest into the form of another elderly woman.

'Forgive the poor light,' she said, her voice bruised with age or illness, maybe both. 'But old age doesn't come alone,' she added, as if that explained everything.

Nadine said, 'Over here,' and he felt himself being guided to an armchair.

He sat and waited while his sight grew accustomed to the dimness. Shadows lightened from blacks to greys to reveal themselves as armchairs, side tables, bookshelves, vases, framed pictures on dark walls.

'This is Detective Chief Inspector Gilchrist,' Nadine said. 'He's with the police.'

'Oh, really?' A heavy sigh, then, 'Well, this'll be interesting.'

Gilchrist said, 'Why do you say that?'

'It's been a while since your lot hounded us, so I'm interested to hear what we're supposed to have done now.'

Rather than ask why the police would *hound* her, or who the *us* referred to, he said, 'That's not why I'm here.'

Nadine said, 'He says they've found Rab.'

In the stilled darkness, Gilchrist could not fail to catch the sharp intake of breath, the whispered gasp of disbelief, and wondered why the mention of Rab would generate such a response from this other woman, whom he presumed to be Julie Merton.

The chair creaked, clothes rustled like dry paper as the woman leaned forward. 'I don't believe you. What proof do you have?'

'DNA.'

'Oh, aye. And what did that tell you?'

'That Jock's father wasn't Rab's father.'

'Mother of mercy,' the other woman said. 'It really is Rab.'

At that, Nadine leaned forward and wrapped her arms around her. 'It's all right, it's all right.' Then she straightened herself. 'We've always suspected that Rab hadn't gone away as they'd told us.'

'Why do you say that?' It seemed to be all he could think of asking.

'He wouldn't have left without saying goodbye to us. It just wasn't in him to do that.'

Gilchrist remembered Arletta's similar words, and felt as if he was beginning to see a picture of Rab, a gay man in the tough city of Glasgow, a member of a criminal family that could invite you to breakfast and have you shot and buried by teatime, the bastard brother of one of the underworld's most callous of kingpins. Rab's life would not have been easy, yet here he was – at least in spirit – a gentle soul who did no one any harm, and who was loved and missed by friends and family—

'Where did you find him? Rab, I mean. His body.'

Gilchrist spent a few minutes telling them of the renovation works on the golf course, how Rab's body was discovered in a shallow grave, all the while keeping his tone level, his voice clear, and missing out the gory parts, mentioning the unique buttons – which brought a sigh from Julie and a chuckle from Nadine at the memory – before he cleared his throat, and said, 'Without saying goodbye to us? And *us* are?'

Nadine said, 'Me and Julie. Who else?'

'That's why I'm asking. You meant just the two of you?' He waited several seconds, still puzzled by Julie's reaction. She had stopped crying, and sat sniffing in her chair, a tissue in her hand. 'So tell me,' he said, 'what was your relationship to Rab?'

She shifted in her chair, patted the hem of her skirt. 'I was his fiancée.'

Gilchrist suppressed a gasp as best he could, but wasn't sure he'd pulled it off. 'As in . . . you and Rab were going to get married?'

'Clever you,' Nadine said. 'The police never fail to amaze.'

He ignored the snipe. 'Had you set a wedding date?'

She sniffed, nodded. 'End of the year. The week before Christmas.'

A quick calculation had him wondering over the timing. 'So when you were told that Rab had emigrated to the Far East, you must've known something was wrong, surely.'

'We've always suspected,' Nadine said.

'Did you tell your suspicions to the police.'

'Here we go. What did I tell you?'

He couldn't fail to catch the hardening in Nadine's tone, but he said nothing, just waited for her to continue.

'You lot were a waste of time. You wouldn't listen to a word of it. Even when we showed you the letter, you weren't interested. We said it was wrong, but you lot said there's your proof. A Dear John letter. *Zero*,' she shouted. 'That was the number of manhours you lot spent on Rab's case. *Zero*.'

Gilchrist let a few seconds pass, to give Nadine time to settle down. Julie, on the other hand, had sat through the verbal onslaught with barely a murmur. 'The letter,' he said. 'Do you still have it?'

To his surprise, she had.

CHAPTER 29

Julie had kept the letter, held in a bunch of others, secured by tightly wound elastic bands, in a carboard shoebox at the bottom of her wardrobe.

Gilchrist slid it out of its dog-eared envelope, giving him the sense that Julie had read it a hundred times. Rab's Victorian-like handwriting sprawled across the page as if oblivious to lineal separation. Words on one line topped into words above, or tailed into words below, making it appear more of a coded puzzle to be untangled, rather than a Dear John letter. The paper itself was a faded pink onion-skin personalised with Rab's name – Robert Cannon Shepherd, no address – along the top in a bold burgundy scroll that twirled to a flamboyant fleur-de-lis ending.

As Gilchrist read Rab's final words to his fiancée, Julie, he came to see that what he'd first seen as untidiness, was in fact almost like a work of art, each word written with the self-assured flourish of fountain penmanship. Even so, on first reading, the letter made little sense.

He read it again.

Dear Julie,

Today, I have come to the decision that I have to leave. Only after I'm no longer around, will you see that my decision is the right one, even though it is so unwanted (I can't tell you how much it is so unwanted). Never before have I had such sad feelings of loss and waste and desperation, that I will never see you or my friends or my beloved country again. Yet, so it must be.

Yours forever lovingly,

Robert

PS: Although this may be the end, never lose sight of the beginnings. xx

Gilchrist read the letter two more times, puzzling over what looked like an underlined s in beginnings, as if to emphasise they'd had more than one beginning. Or had the underline simply been a slip of the pen, the nib catching the slightest of ridges in the onion-skin paper, an accidental stroke as he'd finished with the flourish of two parting kisses? He couldn't say. All he did know was that the letter as it read made little sense.

Rab had decided to leave, and clearly not by choice – *I can't tell you how much it is so unwanted . . . Yet, so it must be.* Had he known he was about to be murdered? Is that what he was trying to pass on, or leave behind?

Gilchrist folded the letter and slipped it back into its envelope – Julie's name printed in bold, no stamp, no address. 'How did you receive this?' he asked Julie. 'Was it hand delivered?'

But it was Nadine who answered. 'We found it on his bedside table. Just lying there.'

'We?'

'I did. I was given the task of getting his house ready to be put on the market.'

'Who gave you that task?'

'Jock. Who else?'

Who else indeed? he thought. He turned his attention to Julie, who seemed to have recovered her composure. 'When you read it, what were your first thoughts?'

It took a few seconds before she said, 'Disbelief, I suppose. I mean, I couldn't believe that Rab had just got up and left.' She shook her head, dabbed the tissue under her nose. 'Or that he could leave everyone without so much as a phone call, or a wee word of goodbye. It just wasn't him.'

'You said you took it to the police, but they did nothing with it. In fact, they said it was proof that Rab had ended your engagement. So what did you do then?'

Nadine said, 'We both knew something wasn't right. So I challenged Jock, of course, but I was wasting my breath. He just told me to get over it, that Rab had decided he couldn't face it any more, that he was struggling with the whole homosexuality thing, and that he and Rab had had words the week before.'

'An argument?'

'He said Rab had asked to speak to him about a personal matter, and it turned out he'd decided he couldn't marry Julie after all. He said he'd wanted to, that he thought he could, and that it would help him overcome the difficulties he had in his personal life. But the closer the wedding got, the more he felt like he was living a charade.'

Gilchrist turned to Julie. 'And did Rab say any of this to you, about his feelings?'

'Not a word. He'd always said he wanted to get married so he could start a family, and more than anything to have a daughter.

That was what was so hurtful.' She looked up at him then, and frowned, which appeared at odds with a weak smile that threatened to upturn the corners of her mouth.

He turned his attention back to the letter. 'Are you sure this is Rab's handwriting?' he said. 'It couldn't have been written by someone else, could it?'

'It's Rab's,' Julie said. 'It's perfect. He wrote often, and always with so much pride in his penmanship. When he was younger, he won a prize at school for the neatest handwriting in his class.'

'So you have other letters from Rab?'

'Yes. I kept them all.'

'I'm going to have to take this one for the time being, as part of our investigation, but it might be helpful if I could see the others, too. Would you mind?'

Julie cast a glance at Nadine. 'As long as I get them back.'

'Of course.' He slipped the envelope into his pocket, thinking that he might have it checked for DNA. But it had been handled by Julie umpteen times over the years, he was sure, and any secondary DNA would likely have been lost. Still, you never could tell.

He had one more avenue to chase down.

'Do either of you know who Rab's father was?' He sensed a tightening in the room, as if a lock had clicked and the outside world had been shut off. He thought he caught a shifty glance between Nadine and Julie, as if an unspoken question was being asked – whether or not to bring him into their confidence.

Then Nadine shook her head. 'No. We don't.'

Again, it was the shivering in her tone, a hint that the lie was not as convincing as intended. 'But you have your suspicions,' he said, more statement than question.

Another glance between them. Silence filled the room until Julie said, 'No one ever said for sure. But Nadine always had her suspicions.'

Gilchrist turned to Nadine, allowing her time to speak. But when she said nothing, he tried, 'Did you challenge your mother about it?'

'I did.'

'And did she tell you who she'd had an affair with?'

'Indirectly,' she said.

'Meaning?'

'That she didn't come right out and say it.'

Sometimes the way to get answers was not to ask, so he waited, his gaze locked on Nadine's. But again, she remained silent. 'So who did your mother indirectly suggest Rab's father might be?' he said, which was about as roundabout a way of asking as any.

'Someone famous,' she said. 'Not back then,' she added. 'Not when it all went on. But later. Famous later.'

'Is he still alive?'

'No. He died.'

Well, if he'd been looking for a dead end, there it was. 'And his name?'

'Does it matter?'

'It might throw some light on why Rab was murdered, or even who murdered him.'

'We *know* who murdered him,' Nadine said.

Now he knew she was lying. 'You thought Rab had died in the Far East.'

'Not fully,' Nadine said. 'We never fully believed that story. We always had our doubts. But now he's been . . . now his body's been found . . . we know Jock ordered him to be killed. But he

186

kept his hands clean. He gave out the orders, and his minions did as they were told, or suffered the consequences if they didn't.'

Gilchrist tightened his lips. He seemed to be going round in circles. 'What I don't understand is why Jock would order Rab's death. Even though he knew Rab was gay, rather than chase him from the family he gave him a job and defended him against all and sundry. What am I missing here?'

Again, he couldn't fail to miss the glance between them. They knew something, but didn't want to tell him. Thoughts swirled in his mind like slivers of light, not quite visible, but there, floating in the ether: Rab had been an informant. Was that it? Had Jock found out that Rab, who worked as an accountant slash bookkeeper, was not only cooking the books, but passing the recipes to others unknown? Or was it *other* unknown? Singular. One person. And Dick's earlier message that Levy had made a number of calls, one to Nadine, another to someone known only as D. Lynch. He thought he'd give it a punt, a ridiculous one, but he'd learned over the years that if you didn't ask, you didn't get.

'I think Jock ordered Rab's murder because he'd broken the family code,' he said, his gaze shifting from Nadine to Julie and back again. 'I think Jock knew that Rab was a police informant.' There. He'd said it.

Julie shifted in her chair. Nadine raised her head as if to look at him anew.

He focused on Nadine, and said, 'Does the name Lynch mean anything to you?'

Julie gasped, then hissed, 'He knows. For God's sake tell him.'

Nadine tightened her lips, then stepped closer.

CHAPTER 30

Nadine drew herself to her full height, nowhere near as tall as Jock, but above average for a woman. Then her body seemed to deflate before his eyes.

'That was one of the reasons Rab wanted to get married,' she said, stepping closer to Julie and placing a hand on her shoulder. 'To end his affair with David.'

'Lynch?'

She nodded. 'David was a detective sergeant in Strathclyde Police. He and Rab had a brief affair, a fling you could call it, back when Rab was in his teens. Years later, they met up after David had joined the police. No one knew David was gay. By that time, he was married with a wife and two young sons. But it turned out he had a problem with the drink, and his career was marked. He was going nowhere. Which was when he met up with Rab again and persuaded him to become a police informant. And what a feather in his cap. Big Jock's wee brother, giving them all the inside scoop on the business.' She let out a heavy sigh, while Julie patted her shoulder.

'But Rab didn't know that Jock owned a couple of cops higher up the food chain. He kept the status quo for a time, several months at least, letting Rab feed David harmless bits and pieces about the business, until one day it got back to him that Rab had passed on the name and address of one of Jock's firms through which money was being laundered. And that was that. Rab had to go. And that's how the story of Tony driving him to the ferry came about.'

Gilchrist said, 'And what happened to David Lynch?'

'Not long after Rab disappeared, he was suspended, pending an investigation. His police career was well and truly done, and he left to work with a security firm in Glasgow. But he knew what was what, that Jock had his card marked, so he handed in his notice and went into hiding.'

'Do you know where Lynch is now?' he asked.

Julie gave the tiniest shake of her head. 'He's left the country. That's all we know.'

'Or that's all you're going to tell me.'

Nadine stared at him dead-eyed.

It could have been worthwhile having a quiet chat with Lynch. But did it matter to his investigation if he didn't? He wasn't sure. Jock had sanctioned his brother's murder under the guise of Rab emigrating to the Far East. Tony Dilanos, the reigning Glasgow crime patriarch, had more than likely been the person to pull the trigger and shoot Rab in the back of the head. If he hadn't been hands-on in Rab's murder, he sure as hell witnessed it. So, with big Jock no longer alive, it seemed to Gilchrist that his prime suspect had to be Tony Dilanos.

Of course, having a prime suspect was one thing.

Nailing that suspect to the crime was another.

Back in his car, he opened the sunroof and fired up the ignition. What he'd learned from his meeting with Nadine and Julie was all good and well, but did it bring him any closer to the possibility of getting a conviction?

Not a hope in hell.

Before driving off, he texted Jackie, asking her to find out everything she could on the former Detective Sergeant David Lynch of Strathclyde Police. Next he phoned Irene, let her know he would be with her in under thirty minutes, then eased out of the driveway.

'Isn't it beautiful?' Fran said, facing the sea and holding her arms out wide as if to sweep up the panoramic vista before her. 'I love the sea. I always have. And this view is just to die for.'

Jessie followed her line of sight. 'It's not bad for Scotland, I'll give you that. But the Spanish Riviera it isn't.'

Fran took a deep breath, then exhaled. 'Fancy a paddle?' She pressed the heel of one shoe against the toe of the other, kicked it off, then slipped off the other. 'Come on,' she said, and held out her hand.

'I'll give it a miss, thanks.'

'Don't be a spoilsport, Jess. How often do you get evenings like this in Scotland?'

Jessie couldn't remember the last time she'd set foot in the sea. Years before Robert was born, she thought, when she'd skipped a day from secondary school and she and two of her friends – Anna and Val – got on the train to Gourock, in the days when train conductors were few and far between, and somehow managed to get a free ride. It had been November, with Christmas only four weeks away, but what she remembered most was how cold the sea had been – like ice, the water so cold it hurt like a burn if you stood in it for thirty seconds. Not exactly the memory to entice

190

you back again. But it was now summer, not November, so without a word she leaned down and removed her shoes, almost toppling onto the sand as she did so.

'Steady on,' Fran said, grabbing her by the arm. 'Anyone would think you'd had a few too many.' She pulled Jessie upright, then burst out laughing.

Jessie couldn't help herself, and joined in. The wine had gone to her head, the sun was still shining, and it was Saturday night after all, and she didn't have to go back to work until Monday. She had that rarest of rare events, a free weekend, and what the hell.

Fran waited while Jessie rolled her jeans up her calves, then said, 'This way,' and tugged her into the shallows.

With the sea sweeping over her ankles, the water felt ice cold. 'Bloody hell,' Jessie squealed. 'It's the middle of summer, for crying out loud. The water's freezing.'

'Only for a few seconds,' Fran said, and waded deeper. 'You'll get used to it. It's not too bad.' She was wearing knee-long denim shorts frayed around both thighs, which showed off a bit of well-toned skin – tanned, too, as if she'd spent some time in the sun.

Jessie on the other hand had legs as white as alabaster, and still too fat, she thought, nothing like Fran's slender limbs. And as she looked down at her jeans, already darkening from wave and wading splashes, she made a mental note to shave her legs in the morning.

Fran was standing still, letting the sea swirl around her calves. 'What do you think?'

'That it's not the bloody Riviera.'

'But it's not as cold as it first was. Right?'

Jessie nodded. 'I'll give you that. But not by much.'

'You know, I love this.' Fran tilted her head to the sun, and closed her eyes. 'The sun in your face. Enjoying the company of a lovely friend. Relaxing after a few glasses of wine. It takes the edge off the stress, it does. The wine. Don't you think?'

'One of my weaknesses,' Jessie agreed. 'Sometimes I think I'm not strict enough with myself, that I drink too much, especially after a hard day at the Office.'

'That's your problem, Jess.' Fran looked at her, a pained smile on her face. 'You've no time for anything other than work.'

Jessie looked away, locked her gaze on a girl in a wetsuit standing on a windsurf board that seemed to slice through the water with ease, despite the lack of wind. Off to her left, the West Sands spread out like a golden field. Kites ducked and dived and looped the loop off in the distance by the Eden Estuary. Couples strolled the sands hand in hand. Kids ran in and out of the sea, splashing in the weak waves, high-pitched squeals cutting the air. Dogs chased sticks or scurried after worn tennis balls across rippled sand—

'You mentioned the Riviera,' Fran said. 'When were you last there?'

'A year or so ago,' Jessie lied. Even if she'd had the time off from work to spend a week in the sun, she didn't have the money for any kind of holiday, not with all she'd put out on Robert's private tuition because of his hearing.

'Whereabouts?'

'Can't remember. Some place where it was hot.'

'I love Spain. I have a flat there. In the Costa del Sol. Close to Torremolinos. In the middle of summer it's scorching. The sand'll burn your feet if you're not careful. I know all the local places to go. Cheap food. Cheap wine. Late nights out. Dancing until midnight and beyond. Making love in the early hours.' She glanced at Jessie, as if to make sure she'd heard, then said, 'And the sea's warmer, too.'

'Now you're talking,' Jessie said.

'You should come.' A pause, then, 'No, I mean it, Jess. You'd love it. I always keep a week free for myself in September. It won't cost you a penny.'

'I thought it was euros.'

Fran chuckled. 'Or euros.'

'How many bedrooms does it have?'

'Two bedrooms. Both doubles.' Another chuckle. 'You'll be safe.'

'Do the doors have locks?'

'Of course. Besides . . .' She lifted her hand, brushed her fingers through Jessie's hair, tucking it behind her ear. 'I promised not to push. And I never break a promise.'

'I've heard that before.'

Fran let her hand drop to her side, as if disappointed by her response. 'You'll be safe, Jess. No pushing. Hand on heart.'

Jessie gave her a tight smile, and nodded, then turned to face the horizon. She took a deep breath, the smell of kelp and saltwater filling her senses. Beyond Bruce Embankment to her right, seagulls hovered and wheeled over cliffs as black as coal. Overhead, clouds were coming in from the west, high though, so still no threat of rain, even though it was forecast for tomorrow—

Her mobile rang.

She pulled it out, didn't recognise the number, and took the call with a sharp, 'Hello?'

'Jessie. Pete Small here. Is Andy with you?'

'No. Sorry.'

'D'you know where he is? I can't get hold of him on his mobile.'

Something akin to ice ran the length of Jessie's spine. How often had Andy warned her never to power down her mobile, always to be available 24/7, no matter what. But Dainty wouldn't be calling her number unless it was urgent. 'What's the matter?' she asked.

'It's Arletta Shepherd. Jock's daughter. Andy asked me to bring her in. But she's not where he said she was staying. She's flown the fucking coop. And no one can tell us where she is.'

Jessie splashed her way back towards the beach, conscious of Fran following her. 'So why's that a problem?'

'Because Tony's gone missing, too.'

'Which means?'

'That it's started. I warned Andy earlier that he could be in danger. That the both of you could. But I don't think he took me seriously. And now I can't contact him.'

'Leave it with me,' Jessie said.

'Get back to me asap.'

Jessie killed the call, and turned to Fran. 'Got to go,' she said, slipping her mobile back into her pocket.

Fran surprised her by coming up to her and holding her head in both hands.

Jessie pulled back. 'I thought you said no pushing.'

Fran smiled. 'But I didn't say no pulling.' And with that she pulled Jessie to her, let her lips brush her cheek, and gave her a whispered peck on her ear. 'Stay in touch, love.'

Jessie stepped back, half annoyed, but strangely thrilled at the encounter.

Then, without another word, she turned and strode towards town.

194

CHAPTER 31

Jessie tried phoning Andy several times, once by the R&A club-house, a second time as she approached the Golf Inn. No response. At the corner of North Street and Golf Place she stuck her head into the Dunvegan bar, one of his known haunts. The place was heaving, a rowdy mixture of loud Americans, red-faced caddies, and groups of sun-scorched golfers in shorts and golf shoes.

But no sign of Andy.

Out again, she phoned Maureen.

'Hey, Mo, Jessie here. Do you have Irene's phone number?'

'Sure, Jessie. Hang on a minute.' When Maureen came back with the number, she said, 'Is there a problem?'

'Just got to run something past her, that's all. Cheers, Mo,' she said, and hung up before she could challenge her further.

Jessie phoned Irene's number, but it rang out, dumped her into voicemail. She hung up and tried again. This time Irene answered, sounding a bit flustered, as if she'd struggled to find her mobile in her handbag.

'Irene, it's Jessie. Is Andy with you?'

'He is, yes. Is there a problem?'

'Jeez,' Jessie said, relief sweeping through her in a debilitating wave. She recovered her composure and snapped, 'Can you put him on?'

It took a few seconds of fumbling before Gilchrist said, 'Jessie. What's up?'

'And I'm the one who's supposed to be available 24/7? What have you done with your phone? Dainty's been trying to reach you.'

Gilchrist didn't respond, but from the fumbling noises in the background, she could tell he was searching for his mobile. Maybe he'd lost it. Or powered it down for his date with Irene. It was the weekend after all. Then he came back with, 'Sorry, Jessie. Battery's flat. It shouldn't be. But it is. I hadn't realised. So what's Dainty after?'

Jessie tried to keep her tone fierce, but she was so relieved that nothing had happened to Andy, that she found herself softening. 'That bitch Arletta's gone missing. Apparently Dainty was to bring her in, but she's gone. And get this,' she said. 'Tony's missing, too.'

'So,' Gilchrist said, 'it looks like we've stirred it up.'

'Don't know if that's good or bad,' she said, 'but Dainty sounded really worried. He wants you to call him back as soon as poss.' Dainty didn't, she knew that, but she said, 'So I'll leave that with you then. Okay?'

'Sure,' he said, then thanked her, and handed Irene's phone back to her. He and Irene had just finished their main course at the Doll's House, and she was now eyeing the dessert menu. He didn't want to spoil their evening any more than he already had by running late, but he found himself saying, 'Sorry, Irene, I've got to charge my mobile and make a quick call.'

'You can use mine if you'd like.'

'Can't remember the number I've to call. It's in my phone's memory.'

Irene smiled, and pushed her seat back. 'Well, why don't you charge it up at mine, and we can have after-dinner cheese and wine while you're at it?'

Gilchrist felt bad at having already delayed their evening out while he'd interviewed Nadine and Julie, and was considering not phoning Dainty right away, but later, when he got back home. But Jessie had sounded flustered, and he had told her he'd call Dainty right away. So he said, 'The restaurant must have a charger, so why don't I charge it up here, while you decide what dessert you're going to have?'

She smiled. 'Are you sure?'

'Of course. And we can still have that cheese and wine once we're all done. If that's still okay,' he added.

'Oh I can see why you're the boss,' she said, and chuckled as she reopened the menu.

Gilchrist checked with the waitress, who took his mobile from him and connected it to a charger by the till. No sooner had she plugged it in, than he heard it beeping with several incoming messages.

Irene caught his eye then, and said, 'Go on, check them. I won't be able to enjoy my dessert with you sitting there all antsy until you have.' She'd spoken to him with a smile on her face, but he had a sense that his workaholic attitude, and the demands of his 24/7 job, were putting a mounting strain on their relationship. And she'd asked him out that evening to tell him something. He still didn't know what, as they'd seemed to dance around the subject of her cancer having returned, without going to the heart of whatever it was she wanted to tell him. He hadn't pressed her, worried sick it was something along the lines of her cancer being incurable, that she had only months to live, maybe less, God forbid. So, he'd let her do most of the talking, while he nodded and listened with concern, all the while dreading the moment when she would tell him the worst. Which made what she'd just said all the more difficult for him, for the way he couldn't sit still, and always had to have his job at the forefront.

It could wait, couldn't it?

Damn it. He had to know.

'I'll just be a mo,' he said, and slipped from the table.

At the till, he picked up his mobile to find he had four missed calls from Dainty, two from Jessie, two text messages from Jackie, and one from Mhairi. He glanced at Irene, but her attention was still on the dessert menu, which seemed to be the most exciting course for any of the women he'd dated, or married for that matter. Gail had had one hell of a sweet tooth, and how she'd never put on any fat, or ended up with flaring diabetes, he couldn't fathom. As for his own dietary needs, he seldom ate dessert. A main course was sufficient. Not that he didn't have a sweet tooth, but he'd learned over the years that chocolate-based food late in the evening often gave him heartburn. Besides, it added weight where he didn't need weight added.

Another glance at Irene, then he opened the first text from Jackie.

Can't find any records for a D Lynch in Strathclyde. Only B
Lynch, N Lynch, and F Linch (spelling?).

Gilchrist grimaced, puzzled by that, then opened her second text.

D Lynch in Lothian and Borders? Maybe? Have attached brief cv.

He thought back to his meeting with Nadine, and wondered if he hadn't heard her correctly, or perhaps had assumed that as she was talking about Glasgow, that David Lynch worked for Strathclyde Police. But he couldn't say for sure. He opened the attachment, and knew immediately from the first name – Donald – that this Lynch wasn't who he was looking for. He wondered if he'd maybe picked it up wrongly from Dick, but a quick check of his earlier texts confirmed the name – D Lynch. No mistake.

He thought back to his meeting with Arletta, how she had lied to him, too, and now she was gone. And so was Tony. What was going on? It had to be something big for everyone to be fleeing, and headless bodies turning up in the Clyde. Irene seemed to be still undecided on the dessert, and he scanned the restaurant, Dainty's words echoing in his mind that his life – and Jessie's – could be in danger. He half expected to catch some unknown person's eye, and a victory smile to pass their lips before they rose to their feet and pulled the trigger.

Christ, his mind was running away with him. He forced his thoughts back to reality, and opened the text from Mhairi.

W Peterson assaulted in Dundee and admitted to Ninewells

Shit. Had Robert done what Jessie had feared he might do? But if so, it seemed so out of character for the lad. And someone like Peterson, who apparently ran about with a bad lot and skimmed the edges of the law with his ASBOs, must surely get his comeuppance from time to time. Maybe this was one of those times, and Robert had nothing to do with it. Still, just to be sure, he texted

Mhairi and asked her to look into the assault on the QT, and get back to him. He'd already decided he wasn't going to mention anything about it to Jessie.

Next, he phoned Dainty while his phone was still connected to the charger.

'Andy, thank fuck. You all right?'

'I'm fine. What's got you so uptight?'

Daisy paused for a couple of beats, then said, 'Word on the street is that there's going to be a clearing-out this weekend. And by clearing out, I mean a lot of fucking bodies turning up dead. Both Arletta and Tony can't be reached.'

'You think they've been killed?' He caught the look of shock on one of the waitresses faces, and he unplugged his mobile from the charger, and strode to the door. It didn't have much charge, but he wasn't intending to talk long on the phone.

'I'm not saying that. What I'm saying is, you need to be careful.'

He caught Irene's eye as he passed, raised a finger and mouthed, *One minute*. Outside, the street seemed more noisy than normal, as if night heat amplified every sound. He found a relatively quiet spot at the back of the Auld Kirk, and stepped into the shade. He felt as if his mind was spinning, that he'd been lied to throughout, and that it was time Dainty cut to the chase. 'You need to tell me what's going on,' he said. 'At the moment, it seems to be all smoke and mirrors.'

Dainty took a deep sigh, then said, 'Rab Shepherd's body was never supposed to be found. In fact, he was never supposed to have been murdered in the first fucking place. But that's by the by now. He *was* murdered, and more than likely by big Jock, so we'll have no chance of bringing that to justice. But the discovery of his body has stirred up more shit than the fan can handle.'

200

'But why?'

'Because of who he was.'

'Jock's brother?'

'*Half*-brother.'

'So you know.'

'Yes. But it's not just that he was related to Jock. It's who was in his past.'

'That's past tense,' Gilchrist said.

'There's too much going on for the powers that be to worry about the legacy of some punter who's dead and buried,' Dainty said, as if Gilchrist hadn't spoken. 'My money's on whoever was in Rab's past being alive and very much kicking. Hence all the fucking shite of the day going on.'

'Is it Rab's father?'

'That's just it, Andy. I don't fucking know. All I know is that we've got folks up from London, some big shots in the Met, talking to our top people. Word's going about that they're also from MI5 and 6. Jesus Christ, the mind boggles. James fucking Bond shooting all the punters in Clydeside. Maybe that's what this shithole needs.'

For MI5, the UK's domestic counter-intelligence and security agency, and MI6, the foreign intelligence service, to be working in cahoots with Strathclyde Police, something massive must be about to break. It had to be some terrorist threat, or major drug bust. But even so, Gilchrist was at a loss as to how the discovery of Rab Shepherd's body fitted into it. And all the lies he'd been told by those he'd spoken to. None of it made any sense. None at all. Unless . . .

He stared at the back of the Auld Kirk. It used to be a cemetery, many years ago, over which the current library had been constructed. Now all that remained of it was a grass strip at the rear of the church. Rab had been buried about a mile from where Gilchrist stood, with no marker, which pulled up something from the depths of his mind.

No marker. Everything hidden. Everything secret.

Everything created to throw him off the trail.

Even David Lynch could be a fake name—

'You still there, Andy?'

Dainty's voice jolted him back to the present, and he said, 'Let me get back to you,' then ended the call.

Jessie answered on the second ring.

'You busy?' he asked her.

'About to switch on the telly, and open a bottle of plonk, as if I need it.'

'I know it's Saturday night, but would you like to accompany me to make an arrest?'

'I wondered when you were going to let me loose.'

'I'll be with you in ten.'

CHAPTER 32

Gilchrist pulled to a halt outside the driveway, and Jessie was out and striding through the entrance gateway almost before his car had fully stopped. He caught up with her at the corner of the lawn, where she stood still, one arm out to her side, instructing him to stop.

'Something's not right,' she said.

The front door lay ajar, the entrance mat askew, as if someone had left in a hurry. He cast his gaze around and noticed disturbance in the gravel, scattered stones, and the hint of a skidmark from spinning tyres. If he looked closer, more than just a hint; clear definition in some places of a wide tyre track – a van, perhaps, or a large SUV? He stared across the open fields, half expecting to see the tail-end of some vehicle rushing from the scene. But it could be miles away by now. His attention drew back to the small-holding, its untidy garden, and the sense of a portentous silence about the place, as if all the wildlife had been frightened off.

'When did you say you were last here?' Jessie said.

Before his meal with Irene, he thought, and felt a stab of disappointment rush through him at the memory of the look on

203

Irene's face when he'd told her he had to go, something had come up, and he'd see her later – if she was still speaking to him, that is. But Irene in her inimitable way had simply smiled at him, and said she would love to see him later. Which made him feel all the worse, for some reason. He really couldn't continue to take advantage of her the way he felt he was doing.

But the scene before him now, if his worst fears were realised, was proof that he'd been right to leave, right to follow his instincts, right to phone Jessie. He crept closer, one foot on the first step, the memory of Nadine clear in his mind, of her opening the door and looking down at him with a direct stare that reminded him so much of big Jock.

He pushed the entrance door open with his foot, and let it swing wide into the dark hall. One step over the threshold, and he knew what they were going to find. It wasn't the smell that gave it away. Not directly, anyway. There wasn't enough time for decomposition to have taken place. Rather, it was the silence, the tiniest hint of a sour metallic taste as he breathed through his open mouth, that warned him to expect the worst.

'Anyone?' he shouted, more for his own mental strength than for any hope of a live response. Then Jessie was past him, shouting, 'Police. Police,' and halted at the door to the lounge.

The curtains lay open, not pulled apart with womanly care, but ripped off the rail by the desperate grip of a dying woman. Nadine lay on her side on the carpeted floor, one hand clutching the velvet material, as if she'd tried in her final minutes to wrap it around her. A bloodied spot in the centre of her chest stained the front of her sweater. A neat hole in the side of her head, an inch, maybe less, in front of her ear, trickled a thin trail of blood.

Julie was still seated in her chair, eyes open in the shocked look of disbelief as she'd taken a bullet to the chest. A blooming stain of blood suggested that the shot had not killed her instantly, but moments later. Perhaps she'd been the first victim, a disabled stationary target. Nadine, on the other hand, had tried in vain to escape.

'Jeez, Andy, we must've just missed them.'

He thought it odd that Jessie used the plural pronoun – them, not him, or her – but he didn't challenge her. Instead, he said, 'Get onto Glenrothes HQ and get them to check CCTV footage of all vehicles on the Cupar to Glenrothes road, focusing on the last thirty minutes. Let them know we could be looking for a van, or an SUV. And get a hold of Sam Kim to set her up with the SOCOs.'

Without a word, Jessie stepped from the room.

Gilchrist was taking a calculated gamble asking for CCTV footage on that back road to Glenrothes, as he didn't think the killer, or killers, would have driven into Cupar and its busy town centre, but would have escaped through the open country roads. It seemed the logical thing to do. If he thought about it, it's what he would have done.

He leaned down to Nadine, pressed a fingertip to her neck. Her skin felt warm, and he could tell without touching that the trickle of blood from the bullet hole in her temple had not yet congealed. Jessie had been spot on. They really had just missed them, and from what he could tell, by only a few minutes, maybe less. The thought of giving chase evaporated almost as soon as it appeared. At 60 miles per hour, each minute took the killer one mile farther from the scene. Three minutes after the killer had fled the scene, and he, she, or they, could be well on the way to Glenrothes by now.

Still, it was worth a shot. Glenrothes was over ten miles from Cupar, so whoever they were could still be on that road. He phoned Glenrothes HQ and instructed an unmarked car to drive immediately along the back road to Cupar. If they didn't waste any time starting out, it was possible – the slimmest of chances, he knew – that they could encounter the killer's vehicle on the way. Of course, what type of car he was driving, or what speed he was driving at, was up in the air. And when he studied the accuracy with which each kill had been made, he knew he was looking for a professional killer, someone experienced, who wouldn't panic, and could be sedately driving the back roads like a disinterested local.

He eased closer to Julie. Other than her bloodied chest, she looked as if she could simply rise to her feet and walk from the room. He resisted the urge to close her eyes. It always touched him as surreal that the eyes of the dead followed him as he studied the crime scene.

He pulled away from Julie, and looked around him. Nothing in the house seemed to have been moved, or handled, other than the curtain that now lay like a velvet curlicue on the floor. It seemed as if the killer had made his own way inside, and taken the pair of them by surprise. He couldn't imagine Nadine answering the door and letting the killer follow her inside. He felt certain that if she had done so – answered the door – the killer would have shot her on the doorstep, then walked down the hallway and killed Julie at his leisure.

Which told him what? That the killer was an experienced lock-picker? The door might not have been locked anyway. Had the killer let himself in unannounced? He wasn't really learning much by looking at it from that angle. But the opened door and the faint skidmarks on the gravel driveway were of more interest.

They told him that the killer had left in a hurry – an obvious conclusion, he knew – but if you asked yourself why both women had been killed not long after he had spoken to them, and why the killer had left in such a hurry only minutes before he arrived with Jessie, it raised the unsettling possibility that he was being followed – prior to his first meeting with Nadine and Julie, then later, on his return trip.

A phone call from the car tailing him to their murderous associate up ahead, and the double kill could have been completed and the escape then made in haste. Which told him something far more unsettling – that if his theory was anywhere near the truth, then maybe Dainty was right after all, that MI5 or MI6 were indeed involved, and that a whole team of intelligence experts had been assigned to Scotland to take care of his investigation, or to put it another way, to bring his investigation to a premature end by killing all and sundry, every living person associated with the discovery of Rab Shepherd's body.

His body gave an involuntary shiver at that thought, Dainty's words reverberating in his mind that his and Jessie's lives could be in danger. But if so, and if he'd been followed, why had they not killed both of them by now? He tried to shift the shivery sensation that he was being watched at that moment, then jolted when a shape appeared at the open doorway, and said, 'That's it. Done and dusted. Don't hold out much hope, but it's a shot at it at least.' She paused, her eyes fixed on him in a worrying look. 'You all right, Andy? You look as if you've seen a ghost.'

He swallowed a lump in his throat, worked up some spittle to clear the dryness in his mouth, and took a deep breath. He tried to give Jessie a reassuring smile, but didn't think he pulled it off. He really was becoming far too old for this sort of thing.

He nodded to the bodies, and said, 'Any thoughts?'

She stared at Julie first, then Nadine, studying the scene for fifteen seconds or so, before saying, 'Looks like a professional job.' She shrugged. 'Tony Dilanos's boys must be getting well trained.'

'You think it's a Glasgow hit?'

'Who else?'

He didn't want to mention MI5 or 6, not right there anyway, and instead said, 'To me, it looks as if it's too precise to be carried out by one of the Glasgow mob. Both shot in the centre of the chest. No wastage. Three bullets in total.'

'So who're you thinking?' she said with a smile. 'The SAS?'

Now it was Gilchrist's turn to shrug. 'Who knows.' He found his gaze searching the room again, and finding nothing different – the bodies of two elderly women almost spoiling the natural disarray of a lounge area packed with a lifetime of furniture, pictures and personal memorabilia. On impulse, he walked through the adjacent dining room and into the kitchen, and found what he was looking for – a telephone; not a mobile phone with which elderly people might be unfamiliar, but an old-fashioned yellow landline handset, sitting on the corner of the breakfast bar, surrounded by handwritten notes on scraps of paper, torn envelopes, Post-its.

He slipped on his latex gloves and fingered through the notes, finding nothing of interest – scored-through shopping lists, a gardening to-do list mostly unticked, two women's names that meant nothing to him, but which he would have his team check out – when his gaze settled on the handset. He picked it up and dialled 1471, and listened to the recorded voice saying, 'The last number to call your line was . . .'

He noted the date and time of the number – received less than an hour ago – and as he heard the string of numbers being read

208

out – a mobile number – he had the strangest sense of it being familiar to him. He'd always had a great memory for numbers, but even so, couldn't put a name to it. He followed the automatic instructions and dialled 3 for the call back.

It took half a dozen rings before a man's voice said, 'Two calls in one evening, Julie, darling. You certainly know how to make a man happy. What can I do for you this time?'

It wasn't the sound of the man's voice that made him remember where he'd seen that mobile number before, or the pregnant pause after the man's friendly introduction, it simply came to him in a flash of recall – one of the numbers Dick had given him.

'David Lynch?' he said.

The line fell silent for a couple of echoing seconds, then the man said, 'Who's this calling, please?'

Gilchrist told him.

CHAPTER 33

If what Nadine had told Gilchrist about David Lynch was true, then he appeared to have salvaged his career. Now a semi-retired solicitor, he lived by himself in a remodelled farmhouse with a glass conservatory extension to the back – far too large for a single resident – in the outskirts of the village of Torrance north of Glasgow. His wife, Nora, had died from cancer six years earlier, and both sons had moved overseas – one to Australia, the other to New Zealand – and barely kept in touch. He'd never remarried, or found interest in any other woman – at least that's what he told Gilchrist – all of which exposed tell-tale cracks in the truthfulness of Nadine's statement.

Despite Lynch's vociferous protestations during that initial phone call, Gilchrist had withheld telling him about this most recent double murder, believing it would be better if they talked face to face. He left Jessie in charge of the murder scene and set off to Glasgow on his own. He'd found the address easily enough, and been greeted wholeheartedly by a somewhat two-sheets-to-the-wind Lynch who barely blinked when Gilchrist broke the news of the double murder. In short order Gilchrist had been invited in, and offered a glass of Dom Pérignon – *as a way to drown one's sorrows, so to speak.*

It struck Gilchrist that Lynch had either the strongest control over his emotions, or the coldest of hearts, for he showed no signs of being upset at the news of *darling Julie* having been murdered. Of course, being on his second bottle of champagne – or maybe his third – might have had something to do with it. Even so, he still managed to maintain control of his speech, and his limbs.

'It's so damned tragic,' Lynch said, with a gap-toothed smile that defied the slightest signs of tragedy. 'Here's to Julie and Nadine. A lovely couple of old biddies. God bless the pair of them.' And with that, he emptied his glass.

Despite Gilchrist having declined the offer of a glass of champagne, he'd been handed one, and found himself tilting it in Lynch's direction, and taking a moderate sip.

'You're semi-retired,' Gilchrist said. 'What does that mean?'

'Keep my hand in giving legal advice as and when needed. Assist with the occasional house conveyancing, that sort of thing. You sure I can't persuade you with a top-up?' he said, tilting the bottle over his own empty glass.

Gilchrist shook his head, covered the glass with his hand.

'Oh, well, waste not want not.'

'And how did you know Julie?' Gilchrist pressed.

'Ever since we were teenagers, actually. Fancied her rotten back then. Gorgeous bit of stuff, so she was. And classy with it. Not like half the riff-raff that floated about the Barras back then. Definitely a cut above the rest.'

'And Nadine?' he tried.

'Friend of Julie's. Didn't meet up with Nady until, what, let me see, she'd have been in her early thirties, I suppose. Had to be on your best behaviour around Nady, of course, her being Jock Shepherd's sister. You heard of Jock?'

Gilchrist nodded.

'He was something else, I have to say. Stayed well clear of the man. And Nady did, too, for that matter. She never wanted anything to do with that family business. Which was why she and Julie hit it off. Two more honest people it'd be impossible to find.'

Gilchrist said nothing while Lynch seemed to slip back in time to relate stories of his dating Julie, youthful days boozing and partying, and disco clubbing the nights away. None of which brought him any closer to the answer to the burning question – why had Levy phoned Lynch after Jessie showed him the diamond ear stud from Rab's body? Time to cut to the heart of the matter. He reached forward, sat his champagne flute on the table with deliberate care, and said, 'So tell me, how does Jock's brother, Rab, fit into all of this?'

'Rab? Rab Shepherd?' Lynch snorted. 'Now there's a blast from the past.'

'Did you know him?' Gilchrist asked, just to test Nadine's story of their brief affair.

'Knew *of* him.'

'So you didn't have a . . . how should I say it . . . *close* relationship with Rab?'

'Good God, no. Didn't really spend any time in his company. As far as I know, Julie didn't have much to do with him either.'

Well, that's one lie out of the way. 'And have you ever worked in the police.'

'What, like a copper, you mean?'

'Or a detective.'

Lynch gave another gap-toothed smile and a shake of his head. 'No. Why would you think that?'

'No reason. Just a thought.'

Another lie done and dusted, which answered the question why Jackie hadn't been able to find David Lynch's name on any police records, and had him thinking that Julie and Rab's engagement was more than likely just one more untruth to be added to the pile.

'I always thought it slightly odd,' Lynch said, 'Rab being the half-brother.'

'Nadine's? Why?'

'And Julie's.'

The name was mentioned so casually, that for a moment Gilchrist thought he might have misheard. He sat upright. 'So you're saying that Rab was Julie's half-brother, too?'

'Which is why I thought it odd. Two half-sisters to the same half-brother. Which of course might be another reason why they ended up being so close.'

Well well well, out of nothing comes something. And so much for Julie and Rab's engagement; as expected, just one more lie. Gilchrist let the half-sibling connections filter through his mind, trying to work out what it all meant, or if it mattered. Of course it bloody well mattered. Rab's two half-sisters both murdered within a week of Rab's body being found in a secret burial spot? You couldn't make it up. Which told him it had to mean something. But what that something was, he couldn't yet say.

'Can I ask you?' Lynch said, and took some time to fill his flute again. 'Why did you mention Rab Shepherd?'

'Because his body's been found.'

'*What?*'

'Two days ago, in St Andrews.'

213

Lynch might have thought he had the strongest control of his emotions, but whatever strength he had failed him there and then. For a moment he eyed Gilchrist, as if time itself had stopped, then he slumped into his armchair, splashing most of his champagne over his white shirt, mouth agape in a stupefied look. He mumbled, 'I eh . . . I eh . . .' then roared, *'Jesus Christ Almighty,'* and gulped what was left of his drink.

Silent, Gilchrist waited and watched.

Lynch dabbed a hand at the mess on his shirt, and said, 'St Andrews?'

'Yes.'

'The east coast?'

'Yes.'

He frowned, shook his head, looked off to the side, then back. 'Two days ago? Are you sure?'

'Yes.'

Lynch scowled. 'But . . .' He looked around, eyes shifting left and right, as if his mind was searching through his years of experience for some irrefutable legal argument. 'That's . . .' He shook his head again, pressed a hand to his forehead. He hadn't reached for the bottle of champagne yet, but Gilchrist thought it was only a matter of time. 'That's . . .'

Then Lynch stilled.

His eyes narrowed to little more than slits, beneath which Gilchrist imagined he could see the speed of the man's brain as its neural connections fired like lighted crackerjacks. His lips moved as if in silent prayer, or recitation of some long-remembered rhyme. Then he lifted his right hand, squeezed the bridge of his nose between thumb and forefinger, and whispered, 'It has to be . . .'

Gilchrist leaned closer, not sure if he'd heard the spoken words, or if he'd imagined them. 'You've remembered something?'

Lynch stared at Gilchrist as if he couldn't understand. 'It's difficult to believe. But it has to be Stanton. It just *has* to be.'

Gilchrist leaned closer. 'I didn't catch that.'

'Stanton. Lawrence Stanton.'

'The Foreign Secretary? *Sir* Lawrence Stanton?'

'Yes. It's the only explanation. It has to be him.'

Now it was Gilchrist's turn to act confused. 'Only explanation for what?'

Lynch looked at Gilchrist as if puzzled by his presence. 'He's the reason Julie was murdered. Nadine, too.' He tilted his head as if to stare at the ceiling, and brushed a hand across his face, hard and fast, as if to clear it of all unclean thoughts. And when he looked at Gilchrist again, he could have aged ten years. 'So Rab Shepherd never died in the Far East after all?' he asked. 'Is that what you're saying?'

'It appears that way.'

'He never left Scotland at all?'

'We don't think so.'

'Now I understand,' Lynch said.

Gilchrist had to confess that he didn't understand a thing, only that the mention of Rab Shepherd's death seemed to have hit not just one of Lynch's nerves, but the core of his central nervous system. Which made no sense, because hadn't Levy phoned Lynch and told him, after Jessie had questioned him on the diamond stud – per Dick's illegal tapping?

'But I thought you knew Rab Shepherd's body had been found,' Gilchrist said.

'No. I didn't. I hadn't the foggiest.'

'Didn't Danny Levy tell you?'

Lynch seemed unsurprised that Gilchrist knew Levy, and simply said, 'He phoned me a day or so ago, out of the blue, and left a message saying he'd call me again.'

'And he never did?'

'No. And he's not answering his mobile, either.'

Gilchrist was still struggling with the rationale, and needed to pry deeper. 'You said that you now understand. Understand *what?*'

'Who killed Julie and Nadine.'

Gilchrist held his breath for fear that anything he said might close Lynch down.

'Tony Dilanos,' Lynch said at length, then reached for the champagne bottle, and drained the remains into his glass without offering to top up Gilchrist's.

When it seemed that Lynch was more interested in finishing his drink than offering anything else, Gilchrist said, 'Tony Dilanos? That's quite the quantum leap.'

'Not really, if you think about it.'

Gilchrist didn't have it in him to say he was thinking about it as hard as he could, and coming up with nothing. Instead, he raised his eyebrows and cocked his head, an unspoken invitation for Lynch to tell him more.

CHAPTER 34

'You know Tony Dilanos stepped into Jock's shoes when he passed away, right?' Lynch said. 'And you know he's a hardened criminal who manages to stay more than one step ahead of the law by having half the establishment in his back pocket. The same as Jock Shepherd had before him.'

Gilchrist thought that *half the establishment* was a bit of a stretch, but for the sake of argument, nodded his agreement.

'Well, what you might not know is that Tony Dilanos and Sir Lawrence Stanton, or *Larry* as he was known way back when, used to be the best of mates. Oh, yes,' Lynch said, cutting off Gilchrist's question before it was asked. 'Larry was born and raised in Balornock, as was Tony, and brought up the hard way. Rumour has it that they were closer than Siamese twins, and when the pair of them got into fights, they would stand back to back and take on all comers.'

Gilchrist puffed out his cheeks, and let out his breath. He could picture Tony Dilanos taking on all comers by himself. But an image of Sir Lawrence Stanton, the current Foreign Secretary, and former Deputy Leader of the Labour Party, a man renowned for his dapper suits and made-to-measure shirts, gold cufflinks and silk pocket handkerchiefs, being in any kind of street brawl as a young boy refused to manifest.

He said, 'So where does Rab Shepherd fit into this?'

'I'm coming to that.' Another sip of champagne. 'Tony Dilanos, as it turned out, had the dreams to match Larry's, but not the mental wherewithal.' Lynch shook his head. 'Where Larry was as sharp as a knife, Tony was as dull as wood, and as they grew older, they began to drift apart. Larry went to university and studied law, while Tony left school and worked in the fruit market. Which was where he met Rab Shepherd.'

Gilchrist raised a hand to interrupt. 'How do you know this?'

'Because I met Larry at uni. We became good friends. Not the best, but close enough to know what I know.' He drained the rest of his glass, stood up, and said, 'I'm going to open another bottle. Jesus Christ, for what I've just learned, it's the least I'm due.' Then he walked from the conservatory.

Again, Gilchrist thought the words odd, but he said nothing, just sat there in the latent warmth of the conservatory extension, and tried to make sense of what he'd just heard. Tony Dilanos was Julie and Nadine's killer. Of that Lynch had no doubt. But why? Or maybe more importantly, how could he prove it? All he had was Lynch's opinion – strong as it may be – that Dilanos was a double murderer. Which was nowhere near enough to make an arrest, let alone go through with a formal charge.

And somehow Sir Lawrence Stanton was involved?

He couldn't see the connection, other than that Stanton knew Dilanos – allegedly.

Which meant nothing as far as Gilchrist was concerned. Lynch was just mouthing off. For what reason, he couldn't say. And the man seemed to have a bottomless pit for alcohol. For all anyone knew, Lynch could be another compulsive liar. Christ, he'd been told enough lies in the last few days to last him a lifetime. Time to have it out with Lynch.

From the kitchen, Gilchrist heard a cork pop, then Lynch returned with yet another flute filled to the brim. He splashed some as he flopped into his chair, but seemed not to notice. 'Right,' he said. 'Where were we?'

'We got to Stanton at uni, and Dilanos in the fruit market,' Gilchrist said. 'So I don't see how that implicates Stanton in the recent murders in any way.'

'Of course you don't. That's where they were so clever.' Lynch seemed pleased with himself. 'Tony introduced Rab to Larry, and that was the start of it.'

'I'm sorry. The start of what?'

'Their affair, of course. His and Rab's. Not a lot of people know this, but Larry likes men just as much as he likes women. Never understood it myself, but who am I to judge?'

Gilchrist let out a sigh, sufficiently loud to express his frustration. 'You're going to have to do better to convince me.'

Larry smirked from behind his glass. 'When Larry met Rab, he was little more than a trainee solicitor with a Glasgow law firm, with hopes of entering politics. He ran for local by-elections, and as luck would have it, won the seat for . . . Christ I can't remember . . . Govan, or Pollok, I think. Not that it matters. What does, is that when Larry moved to Westminster and began to make a name for himself, he still saw Rab whenever he came back to Glasgow for constituency work. But Rab being Rab, was always on the lookout for ways to make an extra few bob, so he threatened to expose Larry if he didn't start paying.'

219

'Blackmail, you mean?'

'Yes, but with a slight twist.'

'A twist? I don't understand,' was all Gilchrist could say.

'Rab's idea of blackmail was not a monthly stipend paid into some obscure bank account. Oh, no, that would be too straight-forward for Rab. Instead, he insisted that at least once a month, Larry would take him out for a meal and a few drinks at the most upmarket restaurants in the city centre. Larry agreed. After all, it suited him to continue his affair, and at the same time not to be seen to hand over any 'cash, *per se.*'

'Payment in kind, in other words.'

'Exactly. So after Rab received a year's worth of monthly free-bies on the town, he wanted Larry to introduce him to some of his Westminster cronies. Not for sex, necessarily, although that would be a bonus, but for contacts.'

'Like networking?'

'Exactly, and you can imagine how that went down with Larry. Refused point blank.'

'Hang on a minute,' Gilchrist said. 'How do you know any of this?'

'Rab to Nadine, Nadine to Julie, Julie to me.' Lynch smiled that gap-toothed smile of his, took another sip of champagne as if it was lemonade – was the man's system immune to alcohol? – then, as if to explain the connection, added, 'For a while, Julie and me, we were pretty close. Not lovers, but friends, in the strange kind of way that men and women have a platonic rela-tionship. Completely unhealthy to my way of thinking. Not what nature intended. But not my choice. I'm not a rapist, so what can you do?'

'So Julie's gay, too,' Gilchrist said, finally adding two and two.

Lynch held his hand out palm down, and wobbled it. 'Let's just say Julie is, *was* . . . asexual.' He shook his head. 'Never known her to have had any kind of sexual relationship with anyone, male or female, myself included.'

Gilchrist had the sense of being side-tracked again, so he said, 'So, you were saying that Larry refused point blank to introduce Rab to any of his political friends. Then what?'

'Let's just say that Larry rekindled his friendship with Tony, who took care of the problem for him.'

'By murdering Rab, and devising a story that he'd emigrated to the Far East?'

'Yes.'

'And now Rab's body's been found, that story's proven to have been false, so . . . what are you saying? That Larry, now Sir Lawrence, has rekindled his relationship with Tony, who is now going about killing anyone who might know something about Rab's murder?'

'That's one way of putting it.'

'And another way?'

'Wiping the slate clean.'

'Including Nadine and Julie, too?'

'Yes.'

'Oh, come on.' Gilchrist hadn't meant to say it with such emphatic disbelief, but for Lynch to know all this really was stretching it to the limit and beyond. He let out a heavy sigh of frustration. He'd come across many a convoluted theory of conspiracy to murder before, but never one told with such certainty, despite raising so many ifs, ands or buts in his mind. He watched Lynch sip his champagne with a strange look of superiority, as if to say – you would never have worked it out on your

221

own, would you? But now I've explained it to you, what are you going to do about it?'

What indeed? Ignore it? Delve deeper?

But the thought of a sitting Foreign Secretary and former Labour Deputy Leader being complicit in a historical murder, and then for him to initiate a modern-day killing spree to ensure that the secret of that murder, with all of its intricate sexual details, is kept out of the public domain, was so explosive it needed the lid bolted on. But even if what Lynch was saying was in fact true, it had one unarguable major flaw – at least that's what Gilchrist thought as he watched Lynch sip glass after glass of champagne as if he hadn't a care in the world.

He leaned forward, and narrowed his eyes at Lynch. 'And you expect me to believe this?' he said. 'That Sir Lawrence is behind all those current murders?'

'You can believe it or not, but I'd bet my life on it.'

'You might already have,' Gilchrist said, 'because if there's any truth in it, then you, through your friendship with Nadine and Julie, must surely be on their hitlist, too.'

Lynch raised his glass as if about to announce a toast. 'You've hit the nail on the head, young man,' he said. 'Smack dab in the middle.'

Gilchrist gasped at the absurdity of the man's behaviour. 'And it doesn't worry you?'

'Not at all. Which is why I'm drinking like a fish.'

Again, Gilchrist found himself saying, 'I don't understand.'

'I'm dying, Mr Gilchrist. Bile duct cancer. Terminal diagnosis. I've been given two months to live at the most. Less, if I refuse any treatment.' He gulped another mouthful of champagne, then said, 'Which I already have.' Then his forehead furrowed with the deepest of frowns. 'I'm sorry, I don't mean to sound so ridiculously flippant about it all, but you've caught me at a rather unfortunate moment in my life. Or should I say, my imminent death.'

'I'm sorry,' Gilchrist said. 'I had no idea.'

'Of course you didn't. But one of these days, or should I say nights, in the very near future, I'm going to get myself seriously drunk, not too far from where I am at the moment, come to think of it.' He chuckled at his own joke. 'Then head off to bed with a good bottle of whisky, probably The Macallan 10, my favourite I have to say, and a bottle-load of sleeping pills, and pop the lot.'

As suicides went, Gilchrist had to say it sounded as simple and as surefire a way as any. But to know, or at least suspect, that someone is coming after you with the sole intention of killing you, that thought didn't sit right with him. If you could imagine yourself standing on the edge of a cliff, looking down, about to jump off, you would by natural instinct resist someone pushing you over, even though your intention was—

His thoughts were interrupted by Lynch saying, 'However, if I were you, I'd be more than worried.'

Gilchrist frowned, but said nothing.

'Because *you*, having found Rab Shepherd's body, and being so intensely focused on solving his murder, are as much on that hitlist as I am. Of that, I have no doubts, absolutely none whatsoever.' He tilted his glass, and said, 'Cheers,' leaving Gilchrist to weigh the truth of his words.

CHAPTER 35

The drive back to St Andrews took longer than normal.

Gilchrist found himself thinking of his meeting with Lynch, and wondering if his life – and Jessie's, for that matter – really was in danger. If so, then it could be argued that Sam Kim's life was in danger, too. She also knew the identity of the body. And let's not forget Rab's tailor and cousin, Hugh Cannon. If there was any truth in what Lynch had told him, then the discovery of Rab's remains had unwittingly unearthed a list of executions-in-waiting.

But why? That was the million-pound question.

If Sir Lawrence Stanton was indeed behind Rab's murder all those years ago, then surely initiating a fresh string of murders would be far more risky than simply denying all and sundry. If he were ever questioned on it, why not play dumb and insist he barely knew Rab Shepherd, they'd been friends as kids, nothing more, and there was no past relationship of any kind, homosexual or otherwise, and if anyone suggests something to the contrary they would find themselves in court *tout de suite*, answering a case for slander, or libel if the papers ever got their hands on it? That would put an end to it. No, there had to be something more. And the longer he let his thoughts simmer, the more it seemed to him that Dilanos was the driving force behind this recent spate. After all, he was the person who'd allegedly pulled the trigger on Rab as instructed by his friend and co-conspirator, Larry, the then up and coming MP-in-the-making.

And where did big Jock fit into this? Had he even been party to it? But he must have collaborated with them, for hadn't he emphasised the lie that Tony had driven Rab to the ferry? Or had Tony been smart enough to have pulled the wool over Jock's eyes?

Somehow, Gilchrist didn't think so. But the more time he gave it, the more it seemed to him that this line would put him on the right track. The discovery of Rab's body exposed Tony's earlier lie to Arletta that he'd driven her favourite uncle to the ferry and seen him off on his forced departure to the Far East. And now Tony was missing, and so was Arletta. What did that mean?

Had they been killed, or were they just in hiding?

But the two of them together? It just didn't seem to fit.

Then an idea came to him.

What if Tony had not gone into hiding for the purpose of carrying out a series of murders – as Lynch had suggested – but had done so to avoid Arletta's revenge? And what if Arletta had gone into hiding because she was afraid of what Tony might do to her, knowing that she now knew that he had lied to her, and was most likely the person who'd killed her uncle Rab? Revenge has no fury like a woman scorned – or perhaps like a woman whose favourite uncle had been murdered.

But if that was correct, then who was responsible for those latest killings?

Again, he seemed to be finding more questions than answers. To settle his mind, he phoned Jessie to make sure she was okay.

She answered immediately, and he said, 'What's the latest on the double murder?'

'We've recovered two bullets. The one that killed Nadine was found buried in the wall. The other that killed Julie in the back of her chair. Another one looks like it didn't exit Nadine's skull, so Sam Kim should recover that in the post mortem.'

Well, despite the gruesome discovery of two elderly women murdered at home, if he had to look on the bright side, it would be to say that at last they had some tangible evidence, instead of headless bodies being pulled sodden from the Clyde. 'All we need now is to find the gun,' he said, then added, 'Anything from Glenrothes yet?'

'Yes and no.'

Gilchrist found himself slowing down, his fingers tightening their grip on the wheel. Despite Jessie's equivocation, he thought he'd picked up a hint of success in her tone. 'I'm listening,' he said.

'A Range Rover was clocked on Cupar Road, just outside Kettlebridge.'

'Speeding?'

'They didn't mention that.'

'So why did they clock it at all?'

'A number of things. One: it was the first and only SUV they came across once they got out of Glenrothes. Two: it had tinted windows and oversized tyres. And three: when the crew turned around to follow it, lights flashing, the works, they couldn't find it.'

'Couldn't find it? How's that possible?'

'If you turn off that main road, you drive into a network of country roads that go left and right and straight on. Two turns

226

later, you could be going the wrong way. It's as good as any rabbit warren.'

Shit, and damn it. 'Did they get a registration number?'

'Yes and no.'

'Oh, for crying out loud, Jessie, we're not playing games here.' He hadn't meant to shout, but she really was pushing his buttons.

'Sorry, Andy. Only a partial. They didn't think anything of it until they'd passed it going the opposite way—'

'What the hell's not to understand about be on the lookout for an SUV? Jesus *Christ*.' He slapped his hand on the steering wheel, hard enough for his fingers to sting.

'They've checked their dashcam, but as luck would have it, at the moment of passing, the van in front of them slowed down and sort of obstructed their view. Hence the partial. We've got our techies going through the dashcam images, trying to enhance them. We could check the ANPR, but with only a partial we'd be spinning our wheels. Sorry, Andy. Best I can do.'

He was about to hang up, when he said, 'What colour was it?'

'Black.'

'Black. Tinted windows. Wide wheels.' He thought for a moment, then said, 'Where did you last see one like that?'

'Now you're asking. I'm not into cars.'

He nodded to himself. No, she wasn't. And neither was he. But the vaguest memory of a white Bentley convertible, and a black Porsche with a *picnic table* on the back, drifted into view. And off to the side of the mansion, the tinted windows of a Range Rover, its polished paintwork glistening as black as obsidian.

'Get hold of Dainty,' he said, 'and get him to give you a list of all cars and SUVs registered in the name of Tony Dilanos, or any of his associates.'

Jessie felt too chastised to question him, and said, 'I'm on it.'

'And better still,' he said, as the scale of that task seemed to swell before him, 'have him concentrate on black Range Rovers.'

'What are you thinking, Andy?'

'I'm thinking that Tony Dilanos might just have blown his cover.' At that moment, his mobile beeped – ID Smiler – and he said, 'Get back to me soonest.' He answered the call with, 'Yes, ma'am.'

'Where are you, DCI Gilchrist?' Chief Superintendent Diane Smiley asked without introduction. Never a good sign, compounded by the snap in her voice, and the formality of her question.

For a moment, he thought of telling her he was with Irene, enjoying some well-earned time off, but thought better of it. 'On the road, driving back to Crail, ma'am.'

'Well, this can't wait for a face to face,' she said. 'So, with immediate effect, you are to cease your investigation into the murder of Rab Shepherd.'

Gilchrist tapped his foot on the brake and slowed down, letting the car pull to a halt at the gated entrance to some farmer's field.

'Did you hear what I said, DCI Gilchrist?'

'I did, ma'am, yes. Can I ask why?'

'You can, but I'm under no obligation to explain it to you. Let's just say it's orders from above. *High* above.'

'As high as the Foreign Office, ma'am?' He thought he caught her intake of breath, almost hear the workings of her brain in the silent seconds that followed.

Then she said, 'The case is closed with immediate effect, DCI Gilchrist. Wrap it up and have a report on my desk first thing Monday.'

He listened to the hollow sound of a dead connection. Well, if he'd been expecting a detailed explanation, he was sorely disappointed. But he didn't need one. He had his answer. Sir Lawrence Stanton, Secretary of State for Foreign, Commonwealth and Development Affairs, the fourth highest cabinet position in Her Majesty's government, and Prime Minister-in-waiting – as the press would have you believe – was up to his ears in it. The case was closed, and Gilchrist and his team were off the investigation.

Or were they?

He thought back to Smiler's words – *cease your investigation into the murder of Rab Shepherd* – and realised she'd inadvertently provided him with a way to continue. Of course, it was all seman-tics. Which was something he could argue face to face when the time came. He knew Smiler had instructed him to shut down every single aspect of his investigation, but if he had to have his report on her desk first thing Monday, well, when you thought about it, that gave him one last day to solve the murders of Nadine Shepherd and Julie Merton.

And to do so, he needed help.

He tapped in a text message and sent it to Jackie.

CHAPTER 36

'You're kidding me,' Jessie said. 'She can't just stop the investigation like that, for crying out loud. Can she?'

'She can, and she did,' Gilchrist said. 'Orders from high above.'

'Jeez,' Jessie hissed.

'Ours is not to question why. Remember?'

'Anyone tell you you've got a memory like an elephant?'

'Someone once did, but I've forgotten their name.'

Jessie let out a chuckle, then said, 'I'll need to pass that one on to Robert.'

He hadn't heard back from Mhairi with anything more on Peterson's assault, and was still inclined not to mention anything of it to Jessie, regardless. So he said, 'How's he doing now, anyway?'

'Better. Seems to have come to terms with it. I had a nice wee chat with him earlier, and explained to him that getting dumped by your girlfriend isn't the end of the world, it's just part of life. It toughens you up, and how you handle it defines your character.'

'Wise words.'

'Yeah, coming from a numpty who can't keep any relationship going.'

'So how did you get on with Fran Patten?'

'None of your business.'

'Talking of which . . .'

A pause, then, 'What?'

'Business.'

'That sounds ominous.'

'I hope you don't have anything planned for tomorrow.'

'Thought I'd put on a bikini and head to the beach. How about you?'

'The weather's supposed to break overnight,' he said. 'Have you had a look outside?'

'Clouding over. Looks like winter. So I'll wear my wellies. What have you got?'

'One day to find Nadine and Julie's killer.'

A pause, then, 'You sneaky old bugger.'

'I don't think there's any need to call me old,' he said, and smiled at her chuckle. 'But I'll pick you up first thing in the morning.'

'Define first thing.'

'Eight?'

'That'll work.'

'Oh, and one final thing.'

'What's that?'

'Leave your bikini at home.'

'You're no fun.'

There wasn't really anything Gilchrist could do until the following morning, when Jackie would hopefully have provided him with what he'd asked for, and he and Jessie could then move his investigation forward. So he'd called Irene, really to find out if she was still speaking to him, and found to his surprise – one of the loveliest things about Irene, her ability to surprise in a pleasing way – that she was looking forward to opening a bottle of red wine and sharing some midnight cheese with him, if he was up for it. Although he knew he had a long Sunday ahead of him, he found he couldn't turn down her offer, not after all the times he'd let her down.

By the time he parked outside her home in South Street, it was almost half eleven. She answered the door with a welcoming smile, and held it open while he stepped inside. 'Did you manage to get the case all solved then?' she said, as she led him to the upstairs lounge.

'Not quite. Still working on it.'

'But you'll have Sunday off, won't you?'

'Got some loose ends to tie up,' he said, and hoped she hadn't planned to surprise him with Sunday lunch, or some such thing. 'But after tomorrow,' he said, thrusting some enthusiasm into his tone, 'then it looks like I'll have plenty of time off.'

'You haven't been fired, have you?' she said with a husky chuckle.

'Not yet.'

'But you're working on it.'

'As always.'

She smiled at him, then said, 'You go and have a seat at the breakfast bar while I pour us a couple of glasses of wine. The usual measure? A very cheeky *large*?'

'You talked me into it.'

She chuckled at his silly joke, and he pulled up a black leather-clad stool and said nothing as she poured equal measures from a bottle of Barolo that had been breathing with the cork off, into two glasses. Two minutes later, she sat beside him, tray of cheeses and biscuits and grapes and sliced apple in front of them.

They chinked glasses with a mutual 'Cheers,' and he took a sip. The wine tasted rich and heavy and smooth, and he nodded his approval.

'Lovely, isn't it?' she said.

'One of your favourites, no doubt?'

'I've got far too many favourite wines.'

Something about the way her eyes held his gave him the sense that she had other intentions on her mind, nothing to do with wine or cheese. But he returned her gaze, and smiled in response, and helped himself to a soft blue cheese on what looked like a Jacob's cream cracker. He would never have considered himself to be a blue cheese kind of guy, but something about the softness as he bit into it had him licking his lips, and searching for another one.

'This is nice,' he said. 'What is it?'

'Cambozola.'

'Never heard of it.'

'It's like a blue Brie. Here,' she said, and pushed a side plate of mixed fruit – apples, red and white grapes – closer to him. 'Try it with a slice of apple.'

Which he did, and found he liked it.

They spent the next twenty minutes sipping wine, nibbling cheese, sampling a red Cheddar with red grapes, mixing apple slices with a soft blue, then a hard Stilton, all the while chatting away and catching up on each other's day. He was surprised by the ease with which they communicated, how they seemed to fit into each other's thoughts, almost ask the same question of each other in concord. But all the while, Gilchrist made a point of keeping the details of the double murder, and his conversation with David Lynch, to himself.

Irene had spent most of the day at home, fiddling a little in her photographic studio, a spare bedroom she'd converted into an amateur's gallery. She'd felt so much better than she had for a while, and wanted to do something before the feeling of wellbeing wore off. Time spent in her studio felt relaxing and therapeutic. Not that her cancer was causing her any pain, she pointed out to him, well, not at that moment, but in its present form it caused her to feel especially tired now and again, which sometimes turned into overwhelming exhaustion.

'And I printed out some photographs I'd taken last month, shots around town when the light was right, which I'd almost forgotten about, what with all this medical stuff going on, consultations here, scans there. God, it felt never-ending at times.'

Gilchrist wondered where he had been when all these exploratory examinations were going on, and realised there was a side to Irene that she hadn't wanted to share with anyone, not even him.

'I'd like to show some of these photographs to you, and ask your opinion. You've got such a good eye. But not just now. I'd rather have some more wine,' she said, then crinkled her eyes in an impish smile. 'To work up some Dutch courage.'

Gilchrist frowned at her, not understanding why she would seek Dutch courage, but before he could ask, she finished her glass, and said, 'Would you like another?'

'Here, let me get the bottle for you,' he said, slipping off his stool and reaching for a Barolo on the kitchen counter top. He uncorked it, and filled up both glasses without letting it breathe. Then he returned the bottle to the corner of the breakfast bar, held out his glass to hers, and said, 'Dutch courage?'

She eyed him over the rim as she took a sip. Then she placed her glass down with careful deliberation, and looked him directly in the eye. 'I hope you don't mind my asking,' she said, 'and forgive me if I come across as being too forthright, but I'd like you to spend the night with me.' She paused, as if to gather her breath, or seek some more of that Dutch courage, then added, 'Tonight, I mean. To stay over. In bed. Together. You and me. If you don't mind, that is.' Then she pressed a hand to her lips, and closed her eyes. 'I'm sorry,' she whispered. 'I'm so sorry. I'd been working out how best to ask you, and then it just came out all wrong.'

He took hold of her free hand, and waited until she opened her eyes. When she did, he grasped her other hand, held them both, and pressed them to his lips. 'I thought you were never going to ask.'

She burst out laughing, more from relief than finding his words funny, he knew. She dabbed a hand to her eye, sniffed, and reached for her wine. She took a sip, well, more of a gulp that took it down past the halfway mark. 'I feel such a fool,' she said. 'You don't have to stay over if you don't want to. I know you're so busy, and you said you've got to go into the Office tomorrow, and I . . . and I . . .' She stilled when she noticed he was holding up a finger to his lips in a don't-say-anything-more gesture.

Then he slid off his stool, pulled her up by her hands, and said, 'Shall we?'

CHAPTER 37

Gilchrist had never been in Irene's bedroom before. Any time he'd stayed over he'd slept in one of the spare bedrooms, other than on two occasions when he'd fallen asleep through exhaustion or having had too much to drink – passed out, might be more appropriate – and he'd woken the following morning on the sofa downstairs. So the bedroom décor surprised him. Of course, what else would he have expected from Irene but another surprise?

He hadn't expected her bed to be a sleigh bed. At least, that's how he would describe it, with its high curved headboard of polished dark wood, and matching footboard which gave the impression that the whole thing could be harnessed to a horse and dragged outside onto the snow. And to finish it off, a king-size mattress covered in more fluffed-up pillows and cushions and tartan throws than he'd ever seen before. Oh well, yet one more surprise.

'Do you mind if I keep the lights off?' Irene whispered.

'Of course not.'

'I'll open the curtains. No one overlooks this room, so we're quite private.'

As she slid the curtains open, moonlight spread a soft glow through the room.

'I'll go first, if you don't mind,' she said, then stepped into the ensuite bathroom and closed the door behind her.

In the dim light he noticed a pair of reading glasses on top of a book on the bedside table, which at least told him which side of the bed he should take. From the bathroom came the sounds of running water, scuffling feet on tiled flooring, cupboard doors clicking, which had him thinking it would be more courteous of him to nip downstairs and recover the wine rather than listen to the sounds of Irene undressing for him. He might even carry up another bottle. Who was seeking Dutch courage now?

In the kitchen, he took a generous sip of wine, then topped up both glasses with the remains of the Barolo. He found a large bamboo tray, and removed another bottle from the wine rack, while overhead he followed Irene's exit from the bathroom by the gentle cracking of ancient floorboards. He waited until the creaking ceased before he carried the loaded tray upstairs.

When he entered the bedroom, Irene was under the covers. 'Thought we might need some more wine,' he said.

'That's very thoughtful of you.'

He placed the tray on the dresser by the window, picked up both glasses, sat on the edge of the bed, then handed Irene her glass. He raised his to hers, then took a sip, conscious of her struggling not to spill any.

'Maybe this isn't such a good idea,' he said.

'Oh . . . do you think not?'

He caught the concern and hurt in her voice, and said, 'I mean, it's not a good idea to sit in bed drinking *red* wine. It'll stain the sheets if we spill it. We should be drinking *white* wine.' He offered a soft chuckle and hoped he'd help smooth over the awkwardness of the moment. Then he stood, returned his glass to the tray, and said, 'My turn?'

In the bathroom, he looked in the mirror, saw the tiredness of working too many long hours, or perhaps it was simply the inevitability of ageing. He washed his face and hands then rubbed some toothpaste over his teeth with his fingers, and gargled his mouth. Stripped to his undershorts, he returned to the bedroom, loosely folded clothes over his arm, aware of Irene watching him every step of the way. He draped his clothes over the back of the dresser chair, then slid under the sheets. He wasn't sure whether to roll over to Irene, or lie on his back for a while. But Irene helped him out by searching for his hand under the sheet, and holding it.

'Are you okay?' she said, and squeezed.

'Yes, but a bit tentative, I have to say.'

'We don't have to do this, you know, if you don't want to, I mean . . . it all feels rather . . . rather . . . what's the word I'm trying to say . . .?'

Gilchrist rolled onto his side, and said, 'Lovely.' He kissed her cheek. 'It all feels rather lovely. And perfectly natural.' He tried another peck on the cheek, but she turned into him, and their lips met. He could feel the shiver through her body as she pressed against him, and knew it wasn't from desire or some desperate need, but from nervousness and anxiety in exposing her scarred body to him – and very likely anyone – for the first time.

He held her gently as they parted, and said, 'Yesterday, when we were walking on the West Sands, you said something that took me by surprise.'

'I did? What was that?'

'That you'd come to love me.'

'Yes. I have.'

'Well, I'm finding I have the same feelings for you.'

'You do?'

'Of course. I mean, what's not to love about you? You're loving, you're kind, you're generous, you're funny, you make me feel at ease, oh, and before I forget, you're attractive. *Extremely.*'

'It's nothing to do with the fact that I'm lying semi-naked next to you in bed, is it?'

'Oh that, too,' he said, and found himself laughing along with her.

They held each other close, cuddling more than kissing, and he found he liked being physically close to a woman again, and Irene's gentle touch, her hands rubbing his chest, her fingers caressing his face. He was careful where he placed his own hands, not wanting to brush against her scars or touch her surgically created breast in case he upset her. Then, without warning, she pushed away from him. For a moment he thought she was going to reach for her wine, but she sat upright, and peeled her night-dress over her head.

When she dropped it to the floor, she said, 'There. That's me as nature intended.'

'My turn?' he said, and slipped off his undershorts with surprising ease.

Then Irene said, 'I have to do this. I hope you don't mind.' And before he could say anything, she took hold of his hand and placed it on her right breast.

He did as he was expected, and ran his hand over and around her breast, taking care not to press hard, in case she was sensitive to his touch. 'It feels absolutely normal,' he offered. 'I don't feel any ...' He wanted to say *scars*, then said, '... anything different.'

'The surgeons did a wonderful job. They were very pleased with it.'

'And are you pleased with it?'

'I am, yes, but it hasn't aged like the other. Here,' she said, and offered him her other breast. It felt softer, slacker, more saggy, the nipple flatter, but something in the touch aroused him, and he found himself stretching over to kiss her.

Then she faced him, arms out wide. 'See the difference?'

In the soft moonlight, her body glowed white, her breasts before him, enticing him to touch, one higher and firmer than the other.

She ran the palm of her hand over her right breast. 'They made me a new nipple by stitching the skin in a kind of puckering way. They had to do it twice before they were happy with it. But it sort of sticks out all the time, so I'm on permanent nipple alert.' She gave a childish giggle, and he joined in.

He didn't think he should choose that moment to inspect the nipple in question, and instead said, 'You don't have anything to worry about, Irene.'

'And my tummy tuck,' she said, as if gaining confidence from his words, 'although it felt wonderful losing a bit of flab around the middle, it left a scar, too. See?' She took hold of his hand. 'Feel?'

He did, and ran his hand along the welt, from one hip to the other.

'So, my body's a bit of a mess,' she said. 'And even though it's been years since the operation, I suppose I'm still coming to terms with it.'

He knew she was putting a face on it all, talking as if she'd recovered from her cancer and all she had left to remind her of it were scars. But her cancer had come back, and she'd made the decision not to have any more chemo, and he knew that the worry of how it would spread and eventually take her life was something that could drag you to the bottom and not let you go. And for that strength of character alone, he could love her. He reached out, ran a hand from her face, down under her neck, over her breast, to the scarred line on her stomach.

'In this moonlight,' he said, 'you look beautiful.'

'And in the daylight?'

'You look even more beautiful.'

She chuckled, and said, 'Andrew James Gilchrist, my oh my, where have you been all this time?'

He pulled her down to him, and whispered in her ear, 'Waiting for you.'

241

CHAPTER 38

The following morning, to Gilchrist's surprise – should he have expected anything else? – he woke to an empty bed. A quick glance at his mobile phone confirmed the time as just after 6.30. From downstairs came the sound of cutlery clattering, and he caught the mouth-watering aroma of bacon frying. He slipped his feet from under the covers, and from the spare bedroom – the one he usually slept in – pulled on a guest dressing gown.

He found Irene in the kitchen, bright and alert, hair tied up in a loose bun, still in her dressing gown and slippers – well, it was the early side of seven. She glanced at him as he approached and gave him a wide smile.

'Thought I'd make you a roll and bacon before you head off.'

He walked up behind her, put his arms around her, and said, 'How's your head?'

'A bit on the tender side if I'm being honest.' She smiled. 'We didn't finish that other bottle of wine, did we?'

'Only half of it.' He didn't feel particularly well himself, not a full-blown hangover, but wine often did that to him, left him feeling sluggish in the morning.

'Would you like an egg with it?' she said.

He let her slip free from his grip. 'Are you trying to fatten me up?'

'Just trying to make sure you don't go through the day without eating, which I know you're prone to do. Now,' she said, 'how do you like your eggs? Scrambled, poached, fried, or boiled? And . . . runny or hard?'

He couldn't recall the last time he'd had an egg for breakfast, probably on holiday in the States when he'd gone to a greasy spoon one Sunday morning and ordered an egg sunny-side up with hash browns. He wasn't sure how that translated into Scottish, but said, 'Fried, please, but not too runny, and not too hard.'

She chuckled. 'I'll do my best. I've made some tea. Have a seat at the breakfast bar and I'll have this with you in a few minutes.'

The toast popped and he removed four slices from the toaster.

'I'm fussy with my toast,' she said. 'I don't like it buttered when it's hot. It makes it too soggy.'

He found a toast stand and slipped the slices into it. He'd never given any thought to how he ate toast, with or without butter sometimes, or margarine, whichever was available, and hot or cold, it didn't matter – just something to tide him over, a bit like cold pizza, he supposed. But what he did like about toast was that lovely home-baking smell that filled the kitchen just after it popped. He remembered his grandmother in her smallholding, making toast on the open range – a slice of bread stuck onto a long-handled two-pronged fork, then held over the flames. How the world has come on from these days. He organised two seats at the breakfast bar, making sure Irene's had everything she needed – fork, knife, napkin, salt, pepper, tomato ketchup. He preferred HP Sauce, but couldn't find any nearby.

'So what do you have on for today?' Irene asked as she placed a side plate with a roll and bacon and fried egg dripping butter in front of him.

He didn't want to talk about his murder investigation, especially not about the details of Nadine and Julie's deaths, and instead said, 'I'm picking up Jessie at eight, and then we're going to check on a few things, see if we can ID that skeleton we found on the Old Course a couple of days ago.'

'No luck with that, then?'

'Not yet,' he lied. 'But first, I need to head home for a change of clothes. What about you?' he said, changing the subject.

Irene sat beside him, poured two cups of tea. 'Nothing planned. I'll go for a walk along the beach, I think, take my camera and see if anything pops up that I think might be worth capturing.'

Gilchrist glanced out the window. 'You may want to take an umbrella. The weather's turned. Looks like it's going to rain.'

'Thunder and lightning's forecast later this morning. With heavy rain.'

'A thunderplump as my mother used to say.'

She chuckled, then said, 'Don't worry. I'll dress appropriately. Watch yourself, your yolk's dripping.'

Gilchrist dabbed the edge of his roll into the egg, and soaked it up. Another bite had him nodding and saying how much he liked her cooking. For some reason, he found himself reluctant to talk about the previous night, hoping instead that Irene would raise the subject, if only in passing. It seemed that the two of them could talk about anything other than their intimate evening together. He finished his roll, glanced at his watch, took a swig of tea, and said, 'I need to get going.'

'Nae man can tether time nor tide,' Irene said. 'The hour approaches—'

'Tam maun ride,' he cut in, then shrugged. 'Robert Burns, "Tam O'Shanter".'

She raised her eyebrows. 'You're full of surprises, Andy, I have to say.'

He saw an opportunity to broach last night. 'Pleasant ones, I hope.'

'Extremely pleasant ones.'

He leaned forward, gave her a hug, kissed the top of her head. 'I'll give you a call when I know what's happening later.'

'That would be lovely.'

He parked his car in Castle Street, just a short walk from Rose Wynd where his home – Fisherman's Cottage – stood, one in a row of terraced homes in the quiet street. He slid his key into the lock, and the door swung open as if of its own accord. Only then did he notice scratches and scrapes around the keyhole that told him he'd been broken into.

At 7.30 on a Sunday morning, it was unlikely that whoever had broken in was still there. Even so, his senses were on full alert as he eased along the entrance hallway and stepped into the lounge.

Nothing appeared to have been touched. Some notes he'd been working on were still scattered over the coffee table. A magazine on DIY kitchen renovations lay on the floor, its pages opened to the same chapter he'd last read. He walked through to the kitchen, which also looked untouched – plate and mug in the drying tray, dishwasher door ajar, just as he'd left it. He tried the back door and confirmed it was still locked and secured, so entry and exit had been through his front door only.

His bedroom was a different matter, though.

The door frame was splintered and cracked where the door had been kicked in, booted so hard that the brass handle had burst through the plasterboard on the inside wall. His gaze searched the room, as his mind worked out what had happened. The killer – because he now knew that's who had entered his home – had arrived some time during the night, more than likely this side of midnight, when the skies had been at their darkest from clouds that had moved in overnight, and seen his home in darkness; how many times had Maureen told him to draw the curtains when he knew he'd be home after sunset, and leave a light on indoors? But on hot August days, it seemed incongruous to do so.

Back to the killer.

Suspecting Gilchrist to be in bed and asleep, he would have crept through the cottage to be confronted by a closed bedroom door. Maybe the killer had stood in the night darkness and listened for signs of movement – bed creaking, light snoring, sleep-laden cough – then, hearing nothing, had decided to go for broke.

Silencer fitted, gun at the ready, a heavy kick to the interior door, and follow through into the darkness to shoot, not once, but three times as best Gilchrist could tell from the mess of his pillow and splintered bullet hole in his headboard. Would he have heard him as the killer made his way through his house? It was difficult to say. The door exploding open would have shocked him awake, but only for the length of time it took for the bullets to kill him. What he did know was that, if he hadn't spent the night at Irene's he wouldn't be standing where he was now, alive and well.

All of a sudden, ice ran the length of his spine.

Surely never. Dear God, please no.

Dainty's words came back to him – *You found that missing bugger* – their urgency over the possibility that he and Jessie could be next to lose their lives. If an attempt had been made on his life last night, it was no stretch of the imagination to conclude that a similar attempt might already have been made on Jessie's.

He rushed from his bedroom, mobile in his hand.

CHAPTER 39

Gilchrist gasped a sigh of relief when Jessie said, 'I thought you said eight o'clock.'

'Are you all right?'

'Bit hungover, now you're asking. Why?'

'Is Robert okay?'

'Still sleeping.' A pause, then, 'What's going on, Andy?'

He didn't mention his fears over Dainty's words, or his worries that Robert could somehow be involved in Peterson's assault, and told her only about his cottage being broken into.

'I'll call Colin and get the SOCOs over to yours asap,' she said, as if she'd sensed something in his tone that warned her she needed to take charge. 'Stay put,' she added, 'and don't touch a thing.'

As if he needed to be told that. Meanwhile, he had work to do.

Even though it was still early on a Sunday, he phoned Jackie – relieved to find she was wide awake – and fired questions at her. She answered with an Uh-huh for yes, or a Nuh-huh for no, sufficient to bring him up to date, but which took him no further forward.

She'd found nothing of interest on Eddie Cumbo, other than that he was a renowned Glasgow hardman who'd spent a total of six years and nine months in Barlinnie Prison for a series of assaults, more than likely instructed by Tony Dilanos.

A call to Mhairi, too, uncovered nothing new on Nadine or Julie. Forensics were still going through the property, although Gilchrist was surprised when Mhairi said, 'And you wouldn't believe the artwork they found, original paintings on the walls, several others stored in the attic. The killer could've made off with a few of them, and no one would've been any the wiser.'

'So we're looking for someone who's not interested in art,' he'd said, more to put his thoughts into words, than define a criminal profile. 'Or just doing as he was ordered.'

'And I've had no luck in identifying the SUV on the back road to Glenrothes. Not yet, anyway.'

He thought he caught a glimmer of excitement in her voice, and said, 'Not *yet*? So you're still hopeful?'

'I tried following it through town, one CCTV camera after the other, and I managed to get a good image at a set of traffic lights. I've run the number plate through DMV and PNC databases, but it's clean and registered to a Mr Alec Hoddle in Wolverhampton. I've phoned him, and he confirmed the number was his.'

Gilchrist let out a heavy sigh. 'So they've used fake plates.'

'Yes, sir, but I thought that whoever was driving wouldn't drive the SUV all the way to their home, because he'd know we might be able to follow it on the ANPR, which would lead us to a home address. So I think the plates might have been changed in the Kingdom Shopping Centre in Glenrothes, and probably back to the originals, sir.'

'You think?'

'Yes, sir, the time between two CCTV sightings, one before it went into the shopping centre, and one after, seemed longer than normal.'

He almost groaned with despair, but managed to keep his tone level, the frustration from his voice. 'He could've stopped off for a coffee, or done a bit of shopping, or gone to the loo.'

'I know that, sir, but I don't think you would if you were fleeing from the scene of a double murder. You wouldn't continue to drive a car with fake number plates. At least, I wouldn't. I don't think so, anyway. And I don't think he would either. That's what I . . . what I thought. Sir.'

He'd sensed her rising doubts, her worry that maybe her logic was flawed, that her rationale could be challenged and shot down. But he knew she must have spent hours on it, and he didn't have it in him to give her a hard time. Automatic Number Plate Recognition was now such an indispensable tool used by law enforcement agencies throughout the UK, it seemed pointless to take Mhairi off that task. She should continue with her research, at least for one more day. She didn't need to know he'd been pulled off the case. Not until tomorrow at the earliest, he thought.

So he said, 'How close are you to ID-ing it?'

'I've got three more SUVs driving out of the Kingdom Centre, same colour, same model, that I'm trying to rule out. So, within the hour, maybe? Earlier, perhaps, sir.'

'Stay with it, Mhairi, and let me know as soon as you come up with something.'

'Yes, sir, and before I forget, sir, you asked me to look into Peterson's assault?'

'I did, yes. Anything?'

'Managed to find something on CCTV. But it's poor quality. He was assaulted by two males in one of Dundee's back streets. Punched to the ground, kicked around the face, then the assailants ran off.'

'Can you identify the assailants?'

'No, sir, the quality's too poor.'

'Any witnesses?'

'No one's come forward, sir.'

The fact that two people had assaulted Peterson convinced Gilchrist that Robert hadn't been involved. He couldn't say for sure, but he had a sense that Robert was man enough to confront Peterson alone, without the help of anyone else. And with no witnesses and poor CCTV images, it was likely that no one would ever be charged with the assault. He thanked Mhairi, told her to close the report on Peterson, then phoned Dainty.

'Fuck's sake, Andy, I was about to nip out for a McDonald's. What's it this time?'

'Someone tried to kill me last night.' The line hung in silence long enough for him to say, 'Are you still there?'

'Anybody hurt?'

'No one.'

'Thank fuck. What happened?' Dainty listened without interrupting, until Gilchrist mentioned his bedroom door. 'That bastard, Dilanos, is decompensating,' Dainty said. 'He's losing it.'

'You think so?'

'Breaking into someone's house to shoot them?' He tutted. 'That's too up close and personal for my liking. Slitting throats and dumping bodies in the Clyde is more his style. And those other two, Nadine Shepherd and Julie Merton, both shot indoors?

251

Tony's feeling the heat, I tell you. He's speeding up the killings. He's changing his MO.'

Gilchrist didn't want to say there were too many quantum leaps in Dainty's thought process, as if he were trying to fit Dilanos to the crime, instead of the other way round. 'So you're thinking what?' he tried.

'That he's beginning to make mistakes.'

'And you don't think it could be anyone other than Tony? Like one of his men simply carrying out his orders?'

'Word on the street is that not only has Tony gone missing, he's gone mental since Arletta ran out on him. He's not thinking straight. Too many people missing, or hiding. Too many bodies turning up in the Clyde. He's turned reckless. It's only a matter of time until he's caught.'

'And when he is, his hotshot solicitors'll get him off.'

The connection seemed to die for several seconds, then Dainty came back with, 'You didn't hear this from me, Andy, all right?'

'All right.'

'No, Andy. I mean it. I'm sticking my neck out.' A heavy sigh, followed by a hissed curse, then, 'When you're no longer safe in your own fucking home, that's it. An unwritten line's been crossed, and it's time we wiped these fuckers off the face of the planet.'

Gilchrist mouthed a silent *Oh*. He'd listened to Dainty vent steam from time to time, but never before with such bitter venom.

'You've heard the joke – what's the difference between a prostitute and a solicitor, right?'

'I'm listening,' Gilchrist said, just to play along.

'A prostitute'll stop screwing you when you're dead.' Dainty laughed, then added, 'Well, let's just say that Tony's solicitors are living up to their name.'

'What's happened?'

'They've had a right good talking-to by none other than representatives of the Scottish government.'

'Hang on, hang on,' Gilchrist said, struggling to make sense of what he was hearing. 'I don't follow.'

'No one can. But it's happening, apparently. Tony's solicitors have been caught with their pants down, well . . . knickers in this case. And again, you didn't hear this from me.'

'Got it.'

'Right. Here it is,' Dainty said, and seemed to take a deep breath before saying, 'Big Jock Shepherd was a canny old bastard, and paid top whack for legal services on the mutual understanding that as long as he kept himself clean – in inverted fucking commas – in other words, alibied to the fucking hilt, then Strickland Pettifer and Associates would continue to represent him. Innocent until proven guilty. That sort of shite. It helped of course, that old man Strickland and big Jock went way back. Not that Strickland did anything criminal per se, but let's just say they had a mutual *respect* for each other.

'Knowing big Jock worked well for old man Strickland, particularly when his daughter, Penny, joined the firm, with Jock putting a word in here, slipping a few bob there, as Penny worked her way up the legal ladder to become an advocate. Now she's effectively out of private practice, and been seen rubbing shoulders with the high and mighty. Rumour has it she has her eyes on becoming Lord Advocate, the top legal position in Scotland.'

Other than the connection between big Jock and old man Strickland, Gilchrist failed to see what any of this had to do with Tony Dilanos. But he didn't want to ask questions and interrupt Dainty in full flow, so said, 'And will she?'

'Almost certainly. And here's why. Old man Strickland struck a deal with a friend of his in Parliament, not Westminster, Holyrood. I don't know his name, not that it matters, but the deal is that they, the Scottish government, want Tony out of the family business. Gives Scotland a bad name. Too much of a loose cannon. Unreliable. Not right in the head. Can't be trusted to keep the status quo. Even though old man Strickland's retired from the firm, he still keeps his hand in, and as far as he's concerned they're going to wipe the firm's hands clean of Tony, and dob him in.'

'How can they do that?' Gilchrist protested. 'What about client confidentiality, all that stuff that criminals hide behind?'

'Because the government are pulling the strings. End of. They want to be seen to be doing a clean-up act in all the major cities, starting with Glasgow. Tony runs Glasgow, and he's out of control, and only going to get worse. And to do so, they need the assistance of old man Strickland, who wants to see his darling daughter, Penny Strickland QC, become Lord Advocate before he dies, which won't be too much longer. So he doesn't give a shite. He's going to spoon-feed the Scottish law enforcement agencies with copies of whatever they need to put Tony down. Illegal as fuck. But it's *quid pro quo*. Old man Strickland helps the government, and the government makes sure his daughter becomes Lord Advocate.'

Well, Gilchrist had often heard the saying – I'll scratch your back if you scratch mine – but what Dainty had just told him took mutual back-scratching to a whole other level. It all sounded down and dirty, too down and dirty for the police to be involved. But not too down and dirty for politicians and solicitors. However, getting rid of Dilanos might look like a cure, but it was really only a bandage, a loosely fitting one at that.

'So who's going to take over the business when Tony's out of the picture?' he said.

'Arletta.'

Gilchrist thought Dainty's reply was too quick, as if he was being told the answer to some equation that had already been worked out. 'And if Tony gets to Arletta first?' he said, just to test his theory.

'He won't.'

It took a few seconds for the rationale to filter through his brain. 'So you know where Arletta's flown to, where she is?'

'Let's just say we know where that fucker Tony is.'

Gilchrist frowned, troubled by that comment. If what Dainty had said was correct, then it couldn't have been Dilanos who'd tried to kill him last night, surely. If they had eyes on Dilanos, then he'd already have been arrested for last night's attempted murder. 'So when are you going to arrest Tony?'

Dainty remained silent for five long seconds before saying, 'That's above my pay grade, Andy.' Another pause, then, 'You understand what I'm saying?'

'Jesus *Christ*,' Gilchrist hissed.

'It's going to take more than heavenly assistance to save that bastard now.'

And with that, he hung up.

CHAPTER 40

Fifteen minutes later, when the doorbell rang, Gilchrist was surprised to see Jessie at the end of the hallway, not Colin and his team.

'The SOCOs'll be here in five,' she said, as she entered, feet covered in latex booties, hands latex-gloved. In the lounge, she said, 'Where's the damage?'

He nodded in the direction of his bedroom door.

She frowned as she took in the mess. 'Bloody hell. They weren't fooling about, were they?'

'They?'

'Turn of phrase.'

Like the good detective she was, she didn't enter the bedroom, but steered clear of the door and viewed the damage from a dispassionate distance. Forensics would recover all they needed. 'I take it you weren't home, then,' she said.

'I stayed at Irene's.'

'That figures.'

'What do you mean by that?'

'Nothing,' she said, as if regretting her comment. 'Just that, well . . . if you hadn't been there . . . you know . . . you were really lucky.'

He nodded his agreement, and stared into his bedroom. Lucky didn't come close to it. Miraculous might be closer. His mobile beeped, and he opened it to find a text from Mhairi –

Permission needed to access archived ANPR files.

He thought for a moment. Granting Mhairi permission would almost certainly leave a trail, paper or digital, it didn't matter. What did matter was that he'd been pulled off the case by CS Diane Smiley, as instructed from high above. But Mhairi had proven herself to be as aggressive as a Rottweiler on a fresh bone whenever she was on to something. He texted her back with one word – Granted – then led Jessie into his kitchen, where he sat her down and told her about Dainty's call.

'Jeez,' she said. 'Have I just heard you correctly? Was Dainty saying that Dilanos is on the government's hitlist?'

Gilchrist found himself grimacing. The problem with Dainty was that the man had a hand in almost everything going on in Strathclyde Police. If he shared Dainty's conversation with Jessie it might inadvertently create unintended consequences; backfire on one or both of them, in other words. But another glance at the damage to his bedroom, and the timely arrival of the SOCOs, had him saying, 'Let's go outside.'

He helped Jessie into a patio chair in his back garden, the legs of his own screeching on the garden slabs as he pulled his close to hers. 'Have you ever heard the name, Strickland Pettifer?' he asked her.

'Family-run law firm in Glasgow? That Strickland Pettifer?'

He nodded. Jessie had spent her early years as a detective in Strathclyde Police, so she knew more about Glasgow and its goings-on than he did, although less than Dainty. Most people knew less than Dainty. 'And how about old man Strickland?' he tried.

'Grumpy old bastard, is how I remember him. Why?'

Why? indeed. He wasn't sure how much he should tell her, then came to understand that she needed to know his own convoluted thoughts on the matter, even though they were still in nascent form, swirling through his mind as vague as rolling mist.

'How about his daughter, Penny Strickland?' he tried.

'Don't know a lot about her. I hadn't much dealings with them, to be honest. But I did come across old man Pettifer when he was defending some perv we'd pulled in for attempted rape after he'd been caught flashing his cock at a drunken hen party. He got off with it due to insufficient evidence, and an alibi that couldn't be broken. One of the hen party had taken a photo of his cock, for crying out loud, but she'd zoomed in on it and hadn't caught his face. In the end, our case got shafted. But what I also got, was a real flavour of old man Pettifer. As slimy and as sleekit as they come.'

Gilchrist savoured Jessie's words. An alibi that couldn't be broken? That sounded about right. Dainty's words came back to him; as long as big Jock kept himself *alibied to the fucking hilt*, old man Strickland was prepared to represent him. And now he was no longer an active solicitor, he was willing to breach client confidentiality so his daughter's aspirations of becoming Lord Advocate would be realised. But at the expense of someone's life? Christ, it didn't bear thinking about. Which was causing his imagination to catch fire.

He again considered running his thoughts past Jessie to find out if they made sense to her. Would they? He couldn't say. He wasn't even sure if they made sense to himself.

But at least she could hear him out.

'I told you what David Lynch said to me,' he began. 'How he was convinced that Sir Lawrence Stanton, aka Larry, is instrumental in initiating these recent murders.'

She nodded. 'Yes.'

'And how Larry and Tony had been school friends. And how Tony introduced Larry to Rab Shepherd. And their homosexual affair that ended up with Rab trying to blackmail Larry, after which Larry conspired with Tony to kill Rab and hide his body.'

Silent, Jessie nodded again, her eyes encouraging him to press on.

'Fast forward, and Larry is now Sir Lawrence Stanton, a prominent and highly respected minister in Her Majesty's government. Nothing can touch him. No one has anything on him. His homosexual past has been well managed or forgotten, almost certainly swept under the carpet. Everything is going great for him until *wham* . . . out of the blue, Rab Shepherd's body turns up on the Old Course, when everybody thought he'd headed off to the Far East years ago, and died there.'

Gilchrist pushed to his feet and took his time walking around the table, one moment behind Jessie, the next in front of her. Her gaze followed him, but still she said nothing, as if puzzled as to where this was leading. If she'd asked him then, he would've told her that he was just as puzzled. Even so, he let his thoughts air themselves.

'So,' he said, 'what to do now with that little hot potato? Therein lies Sir Lawrence Stanton's problem. And it's a very big problem, a *huge* problem, for someone whose political dreams are finally about to be realised. He knows with his political savvy that Rab's body will be ID'd because his familial DNA is already on the PNC. He also knows Tony Dilanos is in trouble because it was Tony who repeatedly confirmed the rumour about Rab going to the Far East.' Gilchrist stopped, took hold of the back of his chair, and eyeballed Jessie. 'So what does the holier-than-thou Stanton do?'

Jessie shook her head. 'Surprise me.'

Gilchrist paused for a moment, then said, 'He decides to take control. That's what he does. He contacts Tony, and calls in an old debt. After all, they are the two people who know the truth about Rab's murder. Or are they? Are they the only two? That's Stanton's second and now his most worrying problem. He can't know for certain that Tony's kept silent, that he's kept the secret of the murder to himself, and no one else. He should have, of course, because he'd only be pointing the finger at himself if he did. But Stanton isn't willing to take that risk, not when his political peak is almost within his grasp. So he comes up with a plan.'

'Which is?' Jessie said.

'Which is that everyone and anyone who might have had a shared history, whether that history was in fact shared or not, is to be killed. And who's going to do the killings? No one other than Tony Dilanos, who once again has been pulled into murder, to save not only his own skin, but that of Sir Lawrence bloody Stanton.'

'Hold on,' Jessie said. 'I thought Dainty said that Dilanos was on the government's hitlist.'

'Yes,' Gilchrist said. 'But which government?'

'Westminster?'

'How about Holyrood?'

It took Jessie all of ten seconds of puzzled expression to say, 'Are you implying that Stanton's somehow pulling the strings? That he's manipulating the Scottish government from Westminster? That he's somehow coercing them into assassinating civilians?' She shook her head. 'That doesn't work for me, Andy.'

'It might if you remember old man Strickland's dying ambition, to see his daughter become Lord Advocate of Scotland.'

'I don't follow.'

'She's the driving force behind the move to clean up Scotland's cities and rid them of the gangs and gangsters who make millions out of trafficking women and selling drugs, not to mention controlling the casinos and God knows how many protection rackets they run. And what better way to do that than to have Tony Dilanos taken out of circulation? Permanently.'

'And what does that do? Someone else'll take over. And we're back to square one.'

'Not if that person's Arletta Shepherd.'

'You think she'll take it on?'

'More than likely, yes.'

'Jeez,' Jessie said. 'Lying bitch, is what she is.'

Well, there was some truth in what Jessie had said, he had to acknowledge. But he thought he'd seen a side to Arletta that reminded him of her father. Tough, but fair, and cruel only to those who truly deserved it. No way to run a business, of course, but in the criminal world big Jock had proven himself to be an honourable crook, if there ever was such a thing.

Jessie interrupted his thoughts. 'So what has this to do with old man Strickland?'

What? indeed. He let out a deep sigh, then said, 'I can't say with one hundred per cent certainty. But here's what I think's going on.'

'I'm all ears.'

'The Right Honourable Sir Lawrence Stanton has his old friend and co-conspirator to murder, Tony Dilanos, pick up where they left off years ago, and Tony sets about killing anyone who could possibly associate either of them with Rab's murder—'

'So why try to kill you?' Jessie argued. 'That won't stop the investigation.'

Gilchrist shrugged. 'Dotting the last i. Crossing the final t. Maybe just a fuck-you-very-much for finding the body. I don't know. But when Tony's done what he believes has to be done, there'll be no one alive who can provide any evidence against him.'

'Except Sir Lawrence Stanton.'

Gilchrist nodded. 'And Stanton knows it. Which is why, once Tony's cleaned their slate, so to speak, he's going to be taken out for good.'

'Jeez,' Jessie said. 'Which then leaves Sir Lawrence free and clear to continue his career in Parliament.'

'And old man Strickland purring like a cat as his daughter is made Lord Advocate.'

Jessie's eyes danced left and right as her mind worked through the logic. 'Jeez,' she hissed. 'It's government-sanctioned assassination is what it is.' She grimaced, and stared at him. 'Is that possible? I mean, in this day and age?'

'I'd say *particularly* in this day and age.'

Jessie shook her head in disbelief. 'Then that makes Strickland just as much of a cold-blooded murderer as Stanton.'

'And all as a *quid pro quo*. They both want rid of Dilanos. Stanton to cover his past involvement in Rab's murder. And Strickland to pave the way for his daughter's promotion to Lord Advocate.'

'Partners in crime, you mean?'

'You could say.'

She pushed her chair back and stood. 'So what are we waiting for?'

'Smiler's pulled us off the case, remember?'

'Not this case. Smiler doesn't know about this one. This is a new investigation into government-sanctioned assassination. Besides,' she said, 'I'd love to get one back on that grumpy old bastard, Strickland. Your car or mine?'

'I'll drive.'

'Perfect. Let's go.'

CHAPTER 41

Gilchrist and Jessie didn't leave as quickly as intended. Gilchrist had to discuss the break-in with the SOCOs and log a formal statement with the Office; a necessary formality if he was going to make a claim against his insurance policy. It took Jessie some time, too, to trace Strickland's home address, landline and mobile numbers, and a further fifteen minutes for Gilchrist to send and respond to text messages to set his plan into action.

They didn't set off from Crail until the back of nine. By that time the sun was hidden behind thickening clouds. Even though it felt warm enough for shorts, gone was the sticky humidity of earlier days, replaced by a cooling breeze that promised to return temperatures to seasonal normal. The forecast was set for thundery downpours, the usual break in the weather after a hot spell.

Being Sunday, the roads had light traffic and were clear of heavy vehicles, and they arrived at Strickland's home in Milngavie on the outskirts of Glasgow a few minutes before eleven.

'Looks like we're definitely in the wrong business,' Jessie said, as she eyed the architect-designed facade. 'Is that a statue in the fountain, for crying out loud?' She tutted, then said, 'You know,

I'm kind of disappointed. This place doesn't relate to my image of him being a grumpy old bastard at all.'

'How about a very rich grumpy old bastard?'

'Probably can afford to get himself a new-model wife, too.'

'Why would you think that?'

'Experience. Do you want to bet?'

'I don't bet.'

'What is it with older men and young wives, anyway?'

'You're asking the wrong person.' Gilchrist pressed his fob to lock the car.

The front door was solid wood coated in a rich varnish. Reinforced glass panels down either side enabled the visitor to see through the core of the house, from front to rear, where the far wall seemed to consist of a floor-to-ceiling sheet of glass that overlooked a walled garden in the back.

Jessie poked a finger at the doorbell, then again. 'Is it working?'

'I can hear it chiming.'

'Anyone tell you you've got bat ears?'

'They did, but I wasn't listening.'

She chuckled, and said, 'I think old age is beginning to suit you.'

'Right.' He rang the doorbell again, and through one of the windows followed the path of an elderly woman as she hobbled to the door.

'Not sure if she's the wife,' Jessie said. 'Could be the house-keeper. Or maybe the mother. Looks like you could've won the bet.'

A few seconds of fumbling with the lock and the door opened to reveal a silver-haired woman, face powdered and eyes mascaraed, wearing a silk dressing gown that trailed to old-fashioned parquet – or was it Amtico flooring to look like parquet? A downturned mouth with wrinkled lips had to put her in her eighties, if a day.

Gilchrist introduced himself and Jessie, then said, 'Mrs Strickland?'

'Yes?'

'Is Mr Strickland available?'

'Why?'

'We'd like to speak to him.'

'Why?'

Well, so much for Sunday manners. Before Gilchrist could respond, Jessie chipped in with, 'We're investigating a murder.'

'A murder?'

'A double murder.'

'Who's been murdered?'

'That's why we need to speak to Mr Strickland.'

'What's a double murder got to do with Julian?'

'So, is he in?'

'Julian wouldn't harm a soul.'

'Jeez,' Jessie hissed.

Gilchrist decided to take over before Jessie ran out of patience. 'Would you prefer if we came back with a warrant?' he said. 'Or we could have a quick chat with Julian and be in and out in a few minutes? Either way we *will* speak to him. Your choice.' He smiled, to show her how harmless he was, but her lips pressed into a scar.

Then, without a word, she stepped back, and pulled the door wide.

Gilchrist entered, Jessie behind him, and waited until the door closed.

They followed the elderly woman as she shuffled along the hallway, slippered feet scuffling along the floor, down a couple of carpeted steps that led to an open-plan living room too large for furniture that looked dated and didn't quite match the modern interior, and too high-ceilinged for the array of paintings and photographs that hung at eye-level in dark frames around the walls.

'Lovely home you have,' Jessie said.

'Our old home was much nicer,' she said. Her voice was nowhere near as frail as her appearance suggested, and failed to mask her bitterness. 'It had more character. Not like this heartless hovel.'

He caught Jessie rolling her eyes, and hoped she wouldn't come back with a quip of her own. But Jessie said, 'Most people would give their right arm to live in a home like this.'

'They'd be welcome to it. *Julian?*' she shouted. '*Julian?*' Her high-pitched screech echoed off the bare walls. 'Where is that damned man? Julian? There are two police people to see you. For God's sake, man, where in the blazes are you?'

Gilchrist turned at the sound of metallic rattling, and was faced with a silver-haired man easing towards them in a wheelchair.

'Can't a man have his morning constitutional without interruption, woman? What is it anyway?' He scowled at Gilchrist, then at Jessie. 'Who are you?'

Gilchrist held out his warrant card as he introduced himself and Jessie. 'Are you Mr Julian Strickland?'

'With an OBE last time I looked. What do you want?'

'We're investigating a murder,' Jessie said.

'Good for you. Why don't you go away and get on with it, then?'

'We intend to,' Gilchrist said. 'But first, we'd like to ask you a few questions.'

'Don't you need a warrant for that?'

'You know perfectly well we don't.'

Strickland grunted, then spun his wheelchair around and pushed his way to the far end of the lounge where, to Gilchrist's surprise, he pulled himself upright, took two steps, turned around, and more or less collapsed into a leather chair large enough to seat two. 'Better make it quick, then,' he said. 'I'm busy.'

'Yes, I can see that,' Jessie said, which earned her a scowl from Strickland.

'Haven't we met before?' he grumbled at her.

'I don't think so,' Jessie said. 'I'm sure I would've remembered.'

Strickland's scowl deepened, causing Gilchrist to step forward. 'What can you tell us about Jock Shepherd?'

'Jock Shepherd? The man's dead for God's sake. Don't you know that?'

'You used to represent him. You were his solicitor. Am I right?'

'You know you're right. Otherwise you wouldn't be here. Stop playing me for a fool, otherwise you're perfectly welcome to leave.'

Gilchrist decided to hold back, before cutting to the core. 'And Tony Dilanos?'

'What about him?'

'Didn't your daughter, Penny, represent him at one time?'

'What're you trying to imply? Keep Penny out of it.'

'Keep Penny out of what?'

Strickland's eyes narrowed, as if seeing in Gilchrist something he hadn't come across in a while – a sharp mind, faster and smarter than his own. Then he fixed a dead-eyed stare on Gilchrist, and said, 'I think you should leave now.'

Jessie said, 'If that's what you want, sure, we can do that. But we'll just come back with a warrant.'

Before Strickland could snap back at her, Gilchrist said, 'How about we agree to keep Penny out of it? If you agree to answer a few questions.'

'Are you threatening me in my own home?'

'What we're trying to do, Mr Strickland, is investigate a double murder. I said to your wife when she answered the door, that we could be in and out in a few minutes. We'd very much like to keep to that. And not waste anybody's time.'

'I don't think I particularly like your tone, young man. Or your veiled threat. Now as I said before, I think you should leave.'

This wasn't going anywhere near as well as Gilchrist had hoped. But the chances of obtaining a warrant to question a retired solicitor, the father of the Lord Advocate-in-waiting, no less, and OBE to boot, which in any way could link him to a double murder, was in the zero to fifty-below category. Maybe even colder.

'All right, Mr Strickland.' Gilchrist nodded to Jessie that the interview was over. The trouble with Jessie was, that you could never tell when she was going to speak out of turn, or what she would say when she did. But on the drive to Glasgow, they'd had a chat about their interview strategy, how they would handle it if old man Strickland refused to cooperate.

She didn't let him down.

'Now I remember where you've seen me before,' she said.

Strickland frowned.

'You got that guilty perv off, you know, the one that flashed his cock at a hen party. You convinced the jury that the cock didn't

269

match the face. I was a member of the arresting team. I remember you now. You could spin a right yarn. As sleekit as they come. If you'd put your mind to it, you could've convinced them that the cock in the photo was your own.'

Strickland looked fit to explode, but when he spoke, his voice was sharp and precise, and cut the air like an executioner's axe. 'I will personally see to it, young lady—'

'Detective Sergeant Janes,' she snarled.

'—that you will be walking the streets next week handing out parking tickets.'

'I don't think that would go down too well with Penny. Don't you agree?'

'What in the name of hell are you implying?'

'Are you going to ask Westminster to step in? Maybe ask your old chum, whatshisface, for advice, or a helping hand?'

They had discussed when and how to bring up Stanton's name, and decided that they didn't want to show their hand, or prompt Strickland in any way, that it was better to dance around the name, rather than say it out loud. But Gilchrist found it interesting how the planted seed shuffled through Strickland's mind – from silence, to disbelief, through to an anger that seemed to swell from deep inside his body and strove to have him on his legs, frog-marching them to the door, and throwing them out in person if he could, but which finally erupted in an explosive, '*Get out!*'

Without another word, Gilchrist turned and walked to the door, Jessie by his side. From behind them, Strickland was letting them know just how far down the rungs they were both going to fall, how many pensions would be lost, and how many heads would roll. Well, if he'd had any doubts that old man Strickland was a grumpy old bastard, they were quashed right there.

Back in his car, he eased around the fountain and exited onto the main road.

'Jeez,' Jessie said. 'I was expecting a reaction, but not as bad as that. Maybe he had a hangover.'

'Maybe not the best person to make an enemy of.'

'I know, but I really enjoyed that.' She chuckled, then said, 'You think we've given him a heart attack?'

'That's a possibility.'

'Who do you think he's going to contact first?'

This was where it could all come tumbling down. Gilchrist was under no illusions that Strickland had powerful contacts – politicians at local and government level, Holyrood *and* Westminster, and possibly in other countries for all he knew. And from the way the old man had raged at them, Gilchrist was certain his verbal threats would be followed through. By the end of the day, all things being equal, he supposed he would hear from Smiler, maybe even big Archie McVicar himself, and be ordered to report to the Office first thing Monday for a fresh reaming, likely demotion, maybe even a sacking.

Not what he wanted, though. He just hoped his intuition was correct.

Otherwise, heads for the chopping would almost certainly be his and Jessie's.

'I don't know,' he said, and drove on, his heart heavy with the misery of his doubts.

CHAPTER 42

Gilchrist waited until they'd crossed the Firth of Forth before finding a suitable spot and pulling to the side of the road. He'd thought about keeping Jessie out of it, but they were both so deep in the quagmire that it seemed pointless. Instead, he put the call to Dick through the car's speaker system, and held his breath as it was picked up on the second ring.

'He's made only one call in the last thirty minutes,' Dick said. 'Ten minutes ago.'

Gilchrist felt his stomach turn over. He'd had it wrong. He thought Strickland would run wild as soon as he and Jessie left, called all and sundry, anyone and everyone to ensure that the careers of Detective Chief Inspector Andrew James Gilchrist and Detective Sergeant Jessica Harriet Janes would be dead and buried by sunrise. He had hoped – slim hope, he knew – that by doing so, Strickland might provide them with possible leads, and maybe even to Tony Dilanos himself.

'And . . .?' Gilchrist asked, more in hope than expectation.

'The call was made to a landline number,' Dick said. 'Ex-directory. Haven't been able to put a name to the recipient yet, or an address, but I'm still working on it.'

'Did you record it?'

'Of course. Hang on.'

Gilchrist and Jessie stared at the speaker as the line buzzed for several seconds then changed to the distinctive double burring of the British telephone service. He counted six rings before the line clattered and a man's voice said, 'Hello?'

'We have an issue that needs to be resolved.' Even from those few words, Gilchrist had a sense of lawyerly control, that Strickland was a solicitor who knew what he was about, an eloquent speaker who could command an audience, and stand in front of judge and jury and argue his case without so much as an um or an ah.

The line seemed to hiss with silence for several seconds before the recipient said, 'But it's an issue that *can* be resolved, is it not?'

Gilchrist glanced at Jessie, and saw that she'd caught it too, the residual Glaswegian accent worn thin with spending too many years in London and hobnobbing with the Oxbridge set, and with a hint of a lisp and once-heavy smoker's rasp, which they'd both heard often in the news, the unmistakeable voice of the Right Honourable Sir Lawrence Stanton MP.

Jessie hissed a Yes, and offered a high-five, which Gilchrist ignored.

'Of course.' A clearing of the throat, then, 'With some help.'

Another lengthy pause, then, 'I'll be in contact.'

The line died.

Gilchrist frowned, and glared at the display. 'Is that it?'

'Afraid so. And not a squeak since. No calls in or out. So rather than sit with a digit up my butt, I did a bit of digging, back-tracked through his phone records, and found that he's called that number on three separate occasions in the last two days, but nothing for over two years, which was as far back as I got by the time you called.'

'Doesn't mean to say they haven't spoken to each other in all that time,' Gilchrist said. 'They could've used a mobile, or FaceTimed each other, or even met in private.' Just saying that made him realise how insurmountable a task he'd set himself.

'That's true,' Dick conceded.

'Did you recognise the voice?' Gilchrist asked.

'Can't say that I did. No.'

Dick spent most of his time in the netherworld of the dark net, so it wasn't beyond imagination that he never watched the daily news.

'Want me to keep digging?'

For a moment, he thought of asking Dick to search Stanton's phone records, but being a member of the cabinet, God only knew what government service might be vetting his calls. Private phone calls were never meant for eavesdropping, but in this digital day and age, and with security scrutiny in the guise of national defence, you could never be sure.

With reluctance, he said, 'No, that's it, Dick.'

'Want me to find out whose number it is?'

'No, we have our own suspicions, but thanks.'

'Sure thing. Give me a shout anytime.'

When the call disconnected, Jessie said, 'I thought we were on to something there. But all it proves is that Strickland knows Stanton. And what's this? – I'll be in contact?'

'They must have a way of reaching each other.' Gilchrist shook his head. 'It could be any number of routes, but most likely hand delivery, face to face, nothing over the internet, and certainly nothing in writing. You heard how bland their conversation was.

No names mentioned. And all spoken so that even if anyone overheard them, they couldn't prove a thing.' He smirked at the absurdity of it.

'What now?' Jessie said.

What indeed. Again, he was of a mind to keep his thoughts from Jessie, but she was as implicated as he was. They'd more than ruffled Strickland's feathers, for which they were both about to have their heads placed on the block, ready for Smiler to execute the fatal blow. And to what avail? They'd achieved nothing, other than their own downfall.

But even as the hopelessness of their situation sank in, Gilchrist could not help but ponder – why had Strickland phoned Stanton? What did he mean by *we have an issue that needs to be resolved*? Which of course could be resolved. How silly was Stanton in asking? And Strickland's closing words that it could be resolved *with some help*. What help? Or more correctly, *whose* help? What could Stanton do to help resolve the issue? Was the key figure in all of this none other than Tony Dilanos, who knew Rab Shepherd and Stanton all these years ago? Was the help that Strickland was asking for, nothing more than Stanton's instruction to Dilanos to get rid of a pair of troublesome detectives, to set in motion a freelance killer?

Christ, it didn't bear thinking about. His home had been broken into, for the purpose of killing him. So it was no stretch of the imagination to see your name at the top of some Glasgow hardman's hitlist, bearing in mind that Dilanos was nowhere to be found, probably hiding from his wife. Which raised a pile of other questions. Why would Dilanos be afraid of his wife? Because he knew how ruthless her father had been, and how the genetic code had been transferred from father to daughter—

'Earth to Andy? Hello?'

'Sorry. Just thinking.'

'Me too. And d'you know what I think? I think we've screwed up big time.'

Well, what could he tell her? He grimaced, and nodded. 'On the bright side, if there is one, at least Strickland hasn't phoned anyone other than Stanton.'

'Oh that'll come,' Jessie said. 'Don't you worry about that. He's probably putting it in writing, even as we speak, a formal complaint filed in the correct and proper manner, every i dotted and t crossed.' She gave a heavy sigh, and said, 'Smiler's going to have a field day tomorrow.'

No matter how Gilchrist tried to shuffle Jessie's words through his mind, he couldn't come up with a suitable defence. He'd ignored Smiler's instruction to cease his investigation; well, bent the rules slightly, choosing to halt the investigation into Rab's cold case, and focus on the double murder of Nadine and Julie. Semantics, if you like.

All he could do was go home, and prepare for tomorrow's onslaught.

'I'll talk to Smiler in the morning,' he said. 'Tell her that you were only following my instructions, against your better judgement.'

'I don't think so. I'm as guilty as you are. But guilty of what, I don't know. We're trying to solve a couple of murders, for crying out loud. How can we get our jotters for that?'

'Because of the way we did it. And because of who we did it to.'

'You have a point. But if I'm going to get my wrists slapped—'

'It could be worse than that.'

'Okay, kicked up the arse. Then I'm going to give as good as I get.'

Gilchrist gave a wry smile. He'd seen first-hand how disciplinary interviews could go. But he didn't want to dampen Jessie's pyrrhic victory speech. 'I'll put in a good word for you,' he said. 'Best I can do.'

She gave a high-five, and this time he reciprocated.

He fired up the ignition, and headed back to St Andrews.

CHAPTER 43

Monday morning

By mid-morning, Gilchrist had seen neither hide nor hair of Smiler. She hadn't turned up at the Office for her usual Monday morning briefing, in which she'd set the targets for the day and the week ahead, usually at Gilchrist's expense. She hadn't called in to explain her absence, or to arrange a meeting later that day with Gilchrist. So, rather than sit around in misery, waiting for the axe to fall, he'd instructed his team to carry on with the double murder investigation, but to drop everything associated with Rab Shepherd's cold case.

At least he could explain away the semantics.

Come midday, he was no further forward.

Mhairi's attempt to track the Range Rover on the back road to Glenrothes came to a dead end. Whoever had driven it seemed to have knowledge of the far-reaching powers of the ANPR, so much so that in the end Gilchrist concluded the number plates must have been changed twice – once in the Kingdom Centre, and again on the country roads of Fife, out of range of any CCTV cameras.

Sam Kim had come up with nothing out of the ordinary on the ballistics of the bullets found at the double murder scene. She'd recovered the bullet from Nadine's skull, which confirmed that the same gun had fired every bullet, but wasn't the gun used to kill Rab.

Gilchrist was on the verge of phoning Irene to see if she'd be interested in having a snack lunch, when his mobile rang. He looked at the screen – Private Number – and was about to decline the call – he'd had enough of salesmen phoning him out of the blue – when he remembered that one of the techies had adjusted his phone's settings so that calls from commercial sales centres – those with the 800 numbers – couldn't get through.

He swiped the screen to accept the call, placed the mobile to his ear, and said, 'Yes?'

'DCI Gilchrist?'

'Who's this?'

'Natalie,' she said. 'Natalie Foster.'

It took all of three seconds for the name to register; Arletta Shepherd's cousin, the woman who'd been with Arletta when he and Jessie had talked to them in Edinburgh. He pressed his mobile hard to his ear, and said, 'Where are you?'

'That's not why I'm phoning.'

'Is Arletta with you?'

Silence, which was as good as any Yes.

'Her life could be in danger,' he tried, which brought a guttural sigh in response. 'She should hand herself in to the nearest police station.'

'And what good would that do?'

'She'd be safe.'

'She's safe where she's at now.'

'With you?' he tried, but again she didn't respond. 'Talk to me, Natalie. I can help you. Put Arletta on, if she's nearby.'

For a moment, he thought she was going to comply, then she said, 'I need to meet you. Alone.'

'What about Arletta?'

'It'll just be me.'

'Does she know where Tony is?' Again, the line hung in silence, and he worried that he'd pressed too hard, that she was about to hang up, and that he'd blown his chance of a meeting. 'Okay,' he said. 'Okay. I'll meet with you. And I'll come alone.' When she didn't answer, he said, 'So where do you want to meet? And when?'

'At the end of the harbour pier. Fifteen minutes.'

'St Andrews's pier?'

But she'd already hung up.

He slipped his mobile into his pocket, and walked to the window. Outside, the car park glistened with puddles. The skies lay heavy with grey clouds. Low pressure had moved in. The heatwave was over. By the end of the day, it would be back to temperatures below the seasonal normal. He let his mind replay the phone conversation. Arletta was with Natalie, of that he had little doubt. And if he was to meet Natalie in fifteen minutes at the end of the pier, then Arletta had to be close by. He'd heard no chatter in the background, so she hadn't called from a public place, which ruled out most of the local bars. If he was a betting man, he'd put money on her having called from a hotel room. But which one?

The Old Course Hotel was one of the upmarket hotels in the area. With the money Arletta had – allegedly – she could proba-bly afford to stay there for months on end. On the other side of the coin, a little-known hotel on the outskirts of the town might grant them more cover, make it less likely for them to be located by Tony, or whoever else was after them.

For a fleeting moment he thought of alerting his team, having them set themselves up within sight of the pier – by the cathedral ruins, or the East Sands, or even by Kinkell Braes with a set of heavy binoculars. Then just as quickly, the thought evaporated. The harbour pier was several hundred feet long, a narrow stone promontory that reached into the sea like an outstretched arm. On one side lay the calm waters of the harbour, and on the other, the wilder waters of the open sea. But he understood, too, that Natalie would have full view of him as he walked the length of the pier. Any unusual movement from others in the Force could be readily seen, and might cause her to abandon the meeting.

No, he decided to go alone.

He arrived at the harbour early, only ten minutes after Natalie had called. He stood on the shorehead, facing the sea, his gaze scanning the pier. Although the weather had broken, the temperature was still warm enough for couples to enjoy a walk along the pier. Built from stones pilfered from the cathedral ruins – as many of the older houses had been, too – the pier had survived countless storms without harm, and had become a place where visitors could safely view the open waters without fear.

Gilchrist recalled taking his children to the pier in the teeth of a storm when they were still in primary school – Jack seven, Mo nine, if his memory served. On the harbour side of the pier, protected by the seawall, they were all perfectly safe. He'd intended it to be a lesson, to show them how fierce the sea could be, how dangerous it was to play in wild surf. Waves hit the pier with a thunderous force they could feel through their feet, then rose up and over the wall in spindrift that drenched them. Jack loved it, but Mo was less enthusiastic, and hugged her father's legs for support and safety. They ventured only some forty feet along the pier, which was sufficient for Gilchrist's lesson.

Now, the harbour lay calm, the waves on the open side clapping and surging as they broke against the wall. Off to his right, anchored boats rocked in the harbour, their work done for the day. Empty lobster creels littered the walkway like abandoned baskets. Somewhere in the distance, an engine fired up, then just as quickly shut down. Two pairs of swans paddled the calm waters effortlessly, while above the sandwich bar, gulls circled and swooped over visitors snacking lunch, in the hopes of a spilled chip or two.

From where he stood, Gilchrist could see only couples on the pier. Up ahead, where stone steps led to a raised platform that formed the end of the pier, only one couple, a pair of women, stood side by side facing the open sea. He was too far away to identify them, but he wondered if Arletta had changed her mind, and decided to come along with Natalie.

Only one way to find out.

He strode onto the pier and walked seawards, all the while keeping his gaze on the solitary couple at the end. He passed other couples and several individuals, all of whom paid him no attention, despite the direct examination he gave them as he walked by. It took him only a couple of minutes to reach the end of the pier, by which time he realised the couple were not Arletta and Natalie, but a pair of visitors to the town enjoying the fresh air.

He checked his watch. If Natalie was being fussy, he figured he was two minutes early. He stood with his back to the sea and eyed the shorehead, searching for anyone who might be Natalie. But it seemed the longer he scanned the harbour, the more unsure he was of what she looked like. He hadn't paid much attention to her while they'd spoken to Arletta, and worried that he might not recognise her. Would she recognise him?

His mobile rang – the same private number.

He accepted the call, and said, 'Hello?' He shifted his gaze, ran it along the harbour to the sandwich bar, then over the East Sands, hoping to catch sight of someone with a mobile to their ear, watching him. But he saw no one, and the line lay quiet. 'Well,' he said, 'as you can see, I'm standing at the end of the pier all alone.'

'There's a sandwich bar by the bridge at the other end of the harbour,' she said.

He fixed his gaze on it.

'Do you see it?'

'I do.'

'Go inside, and ask for an envelope in your name. I told them you were with the police, and that you would show them your warrant card.'

'Hang on. Before you go.' He sensed the connection was about to die. 'Can you tell me what's in the envelope? Just in case I'm asked,' he said.

'Photographs.'

'Of what?'

'Of what you need.'

The line died.

Gilchrist cursed and set off at a fast jog along the pier, glancing towards the sandwich bar in the hope that he might catch a glimpse of Natalie. But when he reached the harbour walkway, he knew she'd outsmarted him. He slowed to a fast walk, and by the time he reached his destination, he was breathing heavily.

He bullied his way to the front of the queue with, 'Excuse me. Police. Excuse me,' and when he reached the counter already had his warrant card in his hand. 'DCI Gilchrist,' he said to the young girl serving. 'You have an envelope for me.'

'Here it is,' she said, and handed it to him with barely a glance at his ID.

He thanked her, then pushed his way out of the small shop.

He found a quiet spot on the East Sands, sheltered from a stiffening wind, far enough away from prying eyes to feel comfortable opening the envelope. No sooner had he sat on the sand, than his mobile rang. He removed it from his pocket, thinking that it might be Natalie following up, making sure he had the envelope, but his heart sank when he read the screen – ID Smiler.

This was it. She'd been in meetings all morning, no doubt being grilled about the formal complaint filed by Strickland. He thought of powering his mobile down, telling her later that the battery had died, then realised he was simply putting off the inevitable.

He swiped across the screen, and said, 'Yes, ma'am.'

'I've been looking for you, DCI Gilchrist. No one in the Office seems to know where you are.'

He thought she sounded more irritated than angry, but Smiler had a way of keeping her moods hidden. He let his gaze drift down the beach to the water's edge, where waves splashed onto the sand with invigorating claps. Here, at the East Sands, the waters were calm, protected on one side by the extended arm of the pier, and on the other, by the black cliffs of Kinkell Braes. He used to bring his children to this beach, with their plastic buckets and spades, and his wife, Gail, too, a long time ago, it seemed.

'DCI Gilchrist?'

'Sorry, ma'am. I was distracted. I'm having a short break for lunch.'

'Where do we stand with the investigation into Shepherd's murder?'

Her question had him on full alert. 'You instructed me to put it on hold, ma'am.'

'I did, yes, but I see your team are working away like beavers.'

He thought he detected a hint of pride in her voice, as if she were a teacher pleased by the effort her pupils were putting in. On the other hand, it could be the quiet before the storm. Even so, there was only so much he could keep hidden. Nothing for it, but to come clean.

'We're continuing with the investigation into the murders of Nadine Shepherd and Julie Merton, ma'am.'

'And how's that going?'

'We have a lead on the suspect's vehicle, ma'am, but haven't been able to locate it so far. Likely switched number plates. Or maybe switched vehicles,' he said, and wondered where that idea had popped up from.

'And do you have a suspect?'

'Early days, ma'am, but we're thinking maybe Tony Dilanos.'

The line held in silence for a few seconds, then she said, 'Very well, DCI Gilchrist. Give me an update by close of play.'

'Ma'am?'

'Yes?'

He hesitated, as his mind tried to sort through the logic of what was happening.

'DCI Gilchrist?'

'Sorry, ma'am. Yes. Of course. By close of play.' He ended the call, and pressed his mobile to his mouth, trying to make sense of it all. Smiler didn't know that he and Jessie had spoken to Strickland yesterday. That much was clear. Had Strickland not filed his formal complaint yet? Or had it not filtered down to the St Andrews Office? But neither made sense. It was Monday afternoon, plenty of time for the complaint to have been filed and for Smiler to have been informed.

Strickland's words, as he and Jessie had left his home yesterday, came back to him with their fierce vitriol, an impassioned solicitor giving a pair of mere underlings a blast from hell. Then the memory of Strickland's call to Sir Lawrence Stanton, the calm manner in which he spoke – *we have an issue that needs to be resolved* – and his final words, confirming that the issue could be resolved – *with some help*.

As Gilchrist replayed those words, a cold chill stroked the nape of his neck. He let his gaze drift to his right, along the beach. Couples walked hand in hand, or sat on the sand having a drink or a bite to eat or just enjoying the view. Children paddled in the sea, or searched the rock pools. Others splashed around in deeper water, as waves rose and fell around them. He gave an involuntary shiver at the thought. Even in August, the waters of the North Sea could be ice cold. He rolled to the side, pushed himself upright, and in doing so was able to take a three-sixty sweeping view around him.

With some help.

What did that mean? But Gilchrist feared he knew what it meant.

This was why Strickland hadn't filed a formal complaint. He had no need to. He was the man who chose the victims. Stanton was the man who gave the orders. And Dilanos, the reigning crime patriarch, was the man who pulled the trigger, or instructed someone to pull the trigger for him.

Gilchrist let his gaze shift across the East Sands, back to the sandwich shop, along the harbour front, over the pier, then return and sweep the length of the beach to the dark rocks beyond. If Dilanos was still out there, evading arrest, was it possible that Stanton could get in touch with him and pass on one final instruction?

Gilchrist didn't know.

But he wouldn't want to bet against it.

CHAPTER 44

It seemed surreal, but the more Gilchrist thought about it, the more he realised that he might have uncovered a criminal group that had worked together under everyone's radar, unquestioned and unchallenged, for years. And if his thinking was correct, had Strickland's call to Sir Lawrence Stanton set in motion the order for a pair of troublesome detectives to be . . . what was the word he was looking for? . . . *eliminated*?

Surely assassinating police officers went beyond every unwritten law of the criminal underworld. But if this is what happened to you if you confronted Strickland face to face, it was no stretch of the imagination to understand that nothing and nobody ever stood in that man's way. Which had Gilchrist's thoughts veering off on another track, a slim possibility, he knew, and an unlikely one at that, but it was worth checking out, if only to put his mind at ease. He spent the next five minutes sending texts to Jackie, asking her to do some deeper research for him, and to get back to him by the end of the day, if possible.

He slipped his mobile into his pocket, and returned to the envelope.

He ripped it open and removed six ten-by-eight coloured photographs, held together with a paper clip. Even just a glance at the top one told him they'd been taken by a mobile phone, both subjects unaware they were being photographed, out-of-focus leaves of some houseplant in the foreground.

He pulled the image closer. Two people seated at a table in some restaurant he didn't recognise. The corniced ceilings and intricate wall panelling suggested they were dining in a club of sorts. A men's club? A private club? In London? He couldn't say. What he could say was that Julian Strickland was cutting into his meat with relish, while Sir Lawrence Stanton was studying the label on a bottle of red wine.

The second photo showed the two men at the same table, talking to each other. They could be discussing the dessert, or how to overthrow the government, for all he could tell, but it did provide a clearer image of both men's faces. He felt his breath catch at the next image. A third person now at the table, facing the camera and, like the other two, unaware of being photographed. Tony Dilanos looked young compared to Stanton, who in turn looked young next to Strickland. Out of interest, Gilchrist flipped the photograph over, but found nothing written on the other side.

The fourth photo had been taken in a different setting, which looked vaguely familiar for some reason. It had been taken with a telephoto lens, and provided a zoomed-in close-up through a window of three men talking – again, Strickland, Stanton, Dilanos – seated around a table in the same arrangement as before, as if each man knew his place. The fifth photo was of the same scene, but taken from farther back, showing the facade of an adjacent stone mansion, and the corner of the neighbouring home. The sixth and final photo was taken from farther back still, providing confirmation that the three men were meeting in the house in Pollokshields next to that in which Tony Dilanos and his wife, Arletta, lived. It seemed that the rumours of there being a tunnel between the two houses might be fact after all.

Gilchrist flipped through the photographs again, checking the back of each for any writing. But that's all they were. Photos of Strickland, Stanton and Dilanos, together. He looked around him, half expecting to see Natalie standing close by.

But she was nowhere to be seen.

Back to the photos.

By themselves, the photographs were more or less worthless. All they showed were three men dining and chatting, and the location of one next door to the home of Scotland's crime patriarch. Gilchrist didn't know what he was supposed to do with them. Shred them, sounded as good an action as any. But as he shuffled through them, he came to understand that they represented only a sample of what Natalie might be able to provide him with.

There had to be more.

And was that why Natalie had sent them to him, a taster of worse to come, or a warning to watch his back? Again, he felt a chill on the nape of his neck, and he could not resist the urge to take a long, slow look around him. On the beach, nothing seemed to have changed. Kids and couples, parents and families, played or relaxed. No one of any interest jumped out at him. The same, too, at the sandwich bar, and the walkway along the head of the sands. The harbour, too, showed nothing. But still that sixth sense of his was niggling. His mobile vibrated. He slipped it from his pocket, and recognised Natalie's number.

He swiped the screen, and said, 'Natalie?'

The line remained silent for several seconds, as if he'd surprised the caller.

Then she said, 'It's not Natalie.'

He thought he knew who she was, but said nothing for a moment, just let his eyes scan around him, searching for a woman with a phone to her ear. He was convinced she could see him, but even so, he couldn't find her. 'Arletta?' he said.

'What did you think of the photographs?'

He ignored her question, and said, 'Where are you?'

'What are you going to do about them?'

'We need to meet. Talk face to face.'

'Isn't going to happen until you tell me what you're going to do about the photos.'

'There's little I can do about the photographs. They're interesting, I'll give you that. But they don't provide me with much.'

'They provide proof of contact,' she said, and he couldn't fail to catch the biting nip of frustration in her tone. 'They're in it together. The three of them.'

He decided to play it long, in the hope that he might force some more information from her. 'They're in *what* together?'

'For fuck's sake. Are you serious?'

'I've been instructed to drop the investigation,' he said. Not strictly true, but he thought he'd throw it out there to get a reaction. 'So my hands are tied, unless . . .'

Seconds passed in silence, then, 'My father once told me he trusted you. He said you were the only one.' She sighed, then said, 'Can I trust you now?'

'You can trust me to follow the letter of the law.' He almost cringed as he said that, the memory of his dealings with Dick still fresh in his mind.

'Are you being followed?' she said.

The question was so unexpected, that he found himself looking about him. 'Why do you say that?'

'Because Tony's on the loose. And Tony's in the photographs. Jesus Christ, I thought you were supposed to be a brilliant detective.'

'So you know where Tony is,' he said, more hope than question.

'If I knew that, I wouldn't have to show you the photographs.'

'So you sent them. Not Natalie.'

Another sigh, followed with, 'I'm beginning to think you're thicker than two short planks. Of course I bloody well sent them. And why d'you think I did? So's you could get an arrest warrant and pick the lot of them up. For fuck's sake, do you get it now?'

It would have been easy to lose his patience with Arletta, tell her to stop fooling around with him, and if she didn't agree to meet him, he would get an arrest warrant for her instead. But he bit his tongue, and said, 'What I don't get is – how no one in Strathclyde has ever put two and two together, or I should say, three and three together.'

'The answer to that is, they're dumb as fuck, and twice as thick. Next question.'

'When can we meet?'

'Why?'

'Photos can be doctored. Face-to-face meetings can't.' Although something in the way Arletta was dictating their conversation warned him that he could be wrong on that count. He pressed on. 'I met with your father in Dundee. The King's Arms. Do you know it?'

'Of course.'

'Meet me there in an hour,' he said.

'And if I don't?'

'Then I'll take it you've not been truthful. And whatever you expected me to do with the photographs will have died on the vine, so to speak.'

He ended the call before she could object, and slipped his mobile into his pocket. If Arletta really thought he could find and arrest her husband, Tony, along with the other two, she was living in a dream world. Without more definite proof, he couldn't even think about applying for a warrant to arrest Sir Lawrence Stanton. He'd have his head in his hands before he could finish the first sentence. But maybe Arletta would meet him. He stuffed the envelope back into his pocket, and walked off the beach.

CHAPTER 45

Jackie never failed to amaze Gilchrist.

He was two minutes shy of the Tay Road Bridge, less than an hour since he'd texted her, and here she was – researcher extraordinaire – messaging him back with answers to his earlier questions. He pulled off the road to read her email, and after a quick skim through the attachments would have given her a high-five if she'd been within reach.

According to Jackie, Penny Strickland's road to becoming Lord Advocate-in-waiting had been smoothed over by the deaths of three practising advocates who, as more senior or experienced members of the legal profession, could arguably have been better suited candidates for the position of top solicitor in Scotland.

The most recent demise had been Nathan Butler QC, who had died in a boating accident at the beginning of the year. Despite being a strong swimmer, and an excellent sailor, his Hobie Cat had capsized in relatively calm but freezing cold seas and his body washed ashore on the sands of Leith. Toxicology analysis confirmed high levels of alcohol, despite his having sworn off the booze two years earlier. No investigation was undertaken due to a statement issued by his ex-wife that he'd recently gone back to heavy drinking, which his son and daughter vehemently denied. His ex-wife committed suicide three weeks later to the utter bafflement of her family. No note was found, and no explanation was given for her having taken her own life.

Gilchrist's thoughts fired alive. Two suspicious deaths within weeks of each other?

He read on.

The previous year, Ravi Manou QC, a highly respected judge in Edinburgh's High Court, was found dead in his car in his garage outside his stone villa in Aberlady, its engine still running, and a rubber pipe connected to the exhaust stuffed through the rear window. No explanation was given for his apparent suicide. He had a history of bouts of depression, but despite his family insisting that he'd been looking forward to an imminent and long-deserved holiday in Tunisia, and therefore had no reason to commit suicide, the procurator fiscal concluded death by his own hand, and no further investigation was initiated.

Around the same time, Mark Cummins QC, an energetic solicitor with political aspirations in the Scottish government, and whose peers in the legal profession had predicted him for the top job, was killed in a road accident while vacationing in England. An articulated lorry inexplicably ran into the back of his car while sitting at a red light. Both Mark and his wife of fifteen years died instantly. The lorry driver, a Polish immigrant who lived outside Perth in Scotland, claimed his brakes had failed, and was charged with manslaughter. A forensic examination of the lorry revealed there was nothing wrong with the brakes. Three weeks later, the driver committed suicide by overdosing on sleeping pills while awaiting trial.

Well, there he had it, although Gilchrist couldn't say at that moment exactly what *it* was. A conspiracy to murder the top legal brains in Scotland? A murderous plan to clear the way for the next most suitable candidate, Penny Strickland, to take up the position? Had it become an interview process of the last man standing? Or perhaps more correctly, the last woman standing? Or did he have it wrong? Was it nothing more than a series of unfortunate accidents and deaths that coincidentally provided an opening for one remaining candidate for the top legal post in Scotland? He couldn't say.

But if you didn't believe in coincidence, where did that put you?

Smack dab in the middle of a devious gang of three who would stop at nothing for their own personal gain. A murderous *quid pro quo* scheme, in which each had plenty to gain. Old man Strickland, for personal or conceited motives, ensures his daughter, Penny, becomes Lord Advocate for Scotland. Sir Lawrence Stanton reaffirms his hold over Dilanos to ensure his homosexual relationship with Rab Shepherd and involvement in his decades-old murder remains a deeply buried secret, never to be uncovered, allowing him to continue with his quest to become Prime Minister if Labour wins the next general election. And Tony Dilanos strengthens his position as Scotland's crime patriarch with powerful contacts and far-reaching arms in Scottish politics, the legal system, and probably beyond.

All they needed was a blessing by the Pope, and they would be untouchable.

Gilchrist sent a quick text to Jackie, thanking her for her great work, and told her to meet up with Jessie. Then he called Jessie, and instructed her to touch base with Jackie and locate copies of the police reports on each of the deaths, including those of the wives of Nathan Butler and Mark Cummins, and of the Polish lorry driver, too. Anything else she could find on any of them might prove helpful. He wasn't sure what he was looking for, or if it would be helpful if she found something. But at least he felt he was moving something forward.

Then he told her where he was going, who he was meeting, and what he wanted her to do. With his plan set in motion – if it could be called any plan at all – he powered down his mobile, and resumed his journey to Dundee.

The King's Arms hadn't changed much over the years. The bar, tables, chairs, and the seating around the walls, hadn't been renovated. If anything, the décor was a tad brighter than he remembered. It had been in this pub that Gilchrist had first met big Jock Shepherd all those years ago. Back then, Jock – all six foot six of him, with shoulders out to here, and a scowl that could scare rats – had been accompanied by four bodyguards armed to the teeth, and who could have been mistaken for a bunch of hardmen looking for a fight. Thankfully, they had behaved themselves, but as Gilchrist ordered himself a pint of Deuchars IPA then sat at a table by the back wall, he couldn't shift the overwhelming feeling of déjà vu, that instead of meeting Arletta, big Jock was about to surprise him by striding through the door, bodyguards in tow.

He checked the time – six minutes early – and took a sip. Around him, the midday crowd had already arrived; working men in boots and jeans or paint-stained overalls, and scruffed-up students – at least that's what they looked like – in shorts and T-shirts and sockless deck shoes, paying more attention to their mobile phones than their drinks on the bar. An old man in one corner lowered his copy of the *Daily Mail*, its pages opened to a half-completed crossword and filled-in sudoku puzzles, and was eyeing him up as if to say – *I remember you from the last time you were here, sonny.* Then the moment passed, the man's gaze shifted to his pint, and his attention returned to the crossword. Another man in denim shorts and a loose-fitting linen jacket carried his pint to his table, and sat down, oblivious to everyone and anything except his mobile phone. Gilchrist sipped his pint, and as the meeting time came and went he resisted the urge to power up his mobile and phone Arletta back.

Maybe she would come, maybe not.

When she did eventually turn up, fifteen minutes late, he'd been about to call it a day and finish his pint, and tell Jessie not to bother driving over.

She stood in the doorway for a moment, silhouetted by a burst of sunlight, before catching his eye and stepping inside. She was by herself, Natalie presumably close by but out of sight, no doubt within easy reach in case Arletta decided on a quick getaway. Without a word, she sat opposite, and clasped her hands together, as if to show she was harmless. He wasn't sure he could trust her that far, but at least it was a start.

'I was about to order another pint,' he said. 'Can I get you anything?'

'Pellegrino and ice. Slice of lemon, not lime.'

'Natalie not with you?'

'Does it look like it?'

He didn't answer her, and ordered the drinks at the bar.

Two minutes later, he was back at the table. 'There you go.' He placed her iced water in front of her, then raised his pint, and said, 'Cheers,' which she ignored.

A delicate sip was followed by, 'Okay, now we're face to face, what do you want?'

'The truth.' He slipped his hand into his pocket, and hesitated for a second when he sensed her alarm. He smiled, and said, 'There's no need to worry. I don't carry a gun,' and laid the photographs on the table. He turned one of them around so she could see it right way up. 'Looks like rumours of a tunnel between yours and the neighbouring house have been proven to be correct.'

She said nothing.

'And this one.' He turned another image around. 'Where was this taken?'

'A private club.'

'Which one.'

'I can't say.'

'Can't, or don't know?'

She shrugged.

He leaned closer. 'Why me?'

She frowned, looked around her, as if expecting someone to step towards her with a set of handcuffs. Then she stared at him, and said, 'What do you mean?'

'Why me?' he repeated. 'Why not Strathclyde Police, the local bobbies? Why Fife?'

'I already told you. My father trusted you.'

'But I have a sense that *you* don't trust me.'

She fiddled with her glass. 'I've learned the hard way, not to be loose with my trust.'

He nodded. 'And you don't trust Tony?'

She scoffed, but said nothing.

'And you don't know where he is?'

'If I did, I wouldn't be here.'

299

Gilchrist felt troubled by Arletta's answers. She wasn't opening up to him the way he'd hoped, and he didn't know if he could trust her. So far, she'd kept her cards hidden, not given him an open sight. Maybe it was best to run a few checks of his own.

He spread the photographs wide. 'How does Tony know Julian Strickland?'

'He was Jock's solicitor.'

'And Sir Lawrence Stanton?'

'Through my uncle Rab.'

Two out of two so far. 'What can you tell me about Penny Strickland?'

The frown that crossed her face told him she had no idea who Penny Strickland was, so by logical default knew nothing of the scheme the three of them had hatched – if his theory was correct, that is. But it had to be. It was staring him in the face, or rather, the photos were there in full colour, lying on the table between them for all to see.

'I don't know her.'

So far, so good, but he needed to dig a bit deeper. 'How about Nathan Butler?'

She frowned, shook her head.

'Mark Cummins?'

Another shake of the head.

'Ravi Manou?'

She sat back, let out a sigh filled with frustration. 'What is this? I don't know any of these names.' She shook her head. 'Is this why you wanted to meet me? To throw names at me? Try and catch me out?'

He took a sip of beer, returned his glass to the table with slow deliberation, and said, 'I needed to know that I could trust you.'

'You've lost me.'

Truth be told, he might have lost himself. But he'd learned from experience that it was sometimes just as safe to wade deeper than to return to the shore. 'Tony never mentioned them to you? These names? Who they were?'

'Why would he?'

He returned her gaze, tried to see the truth through her eyes. 'Do you trust Natalie?'

'With my life.'

'Where is she?'

'Safe.' She looked around her once again, as if expecting to find Natalie seated behind her. But when her gaze returned and settled on him, she said, 'Why are we here?'

'It's where I used to meet your father.'

'No. Why are we meeting? Here? Today?'

'I want to ask you if you've heard from Tony today?'

'Are you for real?'

He couldn't fail to catch the hardening in her tone, and said nothing as he watched her sip her iced water and almost finish it. He could tell she'd almost had enough of him, thought he was wasting her time, and was about to leave. 'Listen,' he said. 'I'm sorry. Don't go. Why don't you answer this?'

'If it's any more names, forget it.'

He shook his head. 'Tell me this,' he said. 'What happens to your family business *once* Tony's no longer involved?'

That seemed to work. She'd caught his emphasis – *once*, not *if* – and stilled, her grip frozen around her glass, her eyes fixed on his in an unblinking stare. 'What do you know?' she said.

'I know that you and Eddie Cumbo were close.'

Time stopped. The world, too. Arletta's eyes never wavered, her body froze as if its muscles had locked. Then slowly, as if the universe was trying to recover a missed beat, she raised her iced water to her lips, her eyes shifting left and right until they settled on his again.

Some decision had been reached, but he wasn't sure if it was a decision between fight or flight. So he helped her with, 'When did Tony find out that you and Eddie Cumbo were lovers?'

CHAPTER 46

'Who told you?' Arletta said.

Gilchrist gave a shrug of his own. He didn't want to give too much away in case it got back to Dainty. In the criminal world, and in the police world, too, you always had to keep something back. Much safer that way. 'Let's call it an educated guess.'

She tightened her lips.

'Did you never think that Tony would find out?'

She fixed him with a cold stare that could cut steel. And in that moment, he saw how ruthless she could be.

'You haven't worked it out, have you? I *wanted* Tony to find out.'

He thought he'd kept his surprise hidden. Not the answer he'd expected. But now he had it, his mind fired alive with so many questions that he struggled to put one in front of her.

'But what about Eddie?' he managed to say.

'He's dead,' she said, and flickered a smile.

It took a few seconds for the meaning of her words to filter through. Whatever he'd mistaken for kindness in her was wiped out there and then. Over the years, he'd interviewed murderers, psychos, rapists, paedos, the worst of the worst, the utter dregs of society, people for whom compassion and empathy were no more than words in a dictionary. And here he was, sitting in front of a woman whose method of ending a relationship was to let slip word of her infidelity to her husband, so he could take his revenge and kill her lover.

'Okay . . .' he said, dragging the word out, giving his thoughts time to recover. 'Once Eddie was out of the picture, what did you expect Tony to do?'

'The obvious.' She shrugged. 'Try to talk me into keeping the affair quiet. Get me back on side. Things back to normal. Manage the status quo. Put it behind him. Us. You know. What every husband tries to do with the wife he loves. Or in my case, the wife he *needs*.'

Gilchrist thought he saw what she was telling him, a possible reason for the killings and beheadings that had followed. 'But Tony knew he couldn't do that, could he? Because we'd uncovered the remains of your uncle Rab. You now knew he'd lied to you about driving Rab to the ferry all those years ago. So, the game had changed. Gloves were off, so to speak.' He paused to give her time to affirm his words.

She didn't disappoint him.

'Time to move on,' she agreed.

'With or without Tony.'

It hadn't really been a question, but she said, 'Without.'

'And without Eddie, too.' Another statement.

'Eddie had limits.'

'And you decided that he'd already reached his limits.' Again, not a question. 'He wouldn't make a good husband?' he asked. 'Or a good second-in-command?'

'Either or,' she said.

'So while the shit hits the fan and the police run about like chickens with their heads cut off trying to work out who's killing who and where the next body's going to turn up, you go into hiding.' He raised his eyebrows. 'Why?'

She frowned. 'You already know the answer to that.' She leaned forward, and slid the photographs across the table to him, as if to direct him to the right conclusion.

But he'd already worked it out. With Tony Dilanos and Arletta Shepherd in hiding – other than the fact that Gilchrist had managed to meet her . . . *semi*-undercover – and both of them knowing that their marriage, business relationship, criminal part-nership, whatever you want to call it, was over once and for all, then the only outcome was death for one of them, maybe both. So why not throw another part of the puzzle into the mix, and let the boys in blue track Tony down via Strickland and Stanton? Of course, on the assumption that the boys in blue couldn't put two and two together, a nudge towards the target could help acceler-ate the process. And once Tony was out of the picture, Arletta could return to her rightful place at the top of the family table, and take over from where her father had left off.

Maybe he didn't have it all correct, but he felt certain that he was moving in the right direction. The problem he now had was, what to do about it? He could arrest Arletta, bring her in for ques-tioning. But what would that achieve? She hadn't killed anyone as far as he was aware, although now he had spoken to her face to face, he had a strong sense that she was more than capable of doing so. Giving her the benefit of the doubt, he said, 'I can have you and Natalie put up in a safe house. Until we bring Tony in.'

She shook her head. 'We're safer where we are.'

He glanced over her shoulder at the clock on the wall, but it seemed slow to him. It had to be later than that, surely. He reached for the photos to ingather them, and in doing so managed to sneak a peek at his watch.

But he hadn't been discreet enough, and Arletta hissed, 'You bastard. You've set me up,' and pushed her chair back as if to stand and leave.

Gilchrist reached for her. 'No. Don't,' he said, then froze.

Arletta must have caught the shock in his eyes, for her lips parted as if to shout, and she spun around as someone at the bar shouted, 'Gun. Gun. Watch out.'

Another voice roared, '*Police. Drop it.*'

Then she stumbled to the side and gasped, 'Don't—'

A bullet hit the bench by Gilchrist's shoulder with a hard crack that sent splinters into the air, at the same time as Arletta fell to the floor, and a man staggered towards them. It took Gilchrist a fraction of a second to recognise Tony Dilanos who looked strangely puzzled, as if he couldn't understand how he'd missed with his shot, and wanted to ask Gilchrist. Then his arm fell to his side and his gun clattered free and he toppled over and crashed face-first onto the pub floor with a thud that could break bone.

Before Gilchrist could pull himself to his feet, the man in denim shorts and linen jacket was already kneeling by Dilanos, fingers on his neck, Glock in his free hand. A quick glance at Gilchrist, and an almost unnoticeable shake of the head, confirmed that he was dead. Then, without a word, he slipped the Glock into the back of his shorts, turned to Arletta, and helped her to her feet.

'You all right?' he asked her.

She nodded, but said nothing.

Around them, the bar was stirring into action again. Chairs clattered. Glasses chinked. Someone cursed. A door slammed. While Arletta brushed herself down, the man removed his mobile phone, eyed Gilchrist, and said, 'DS Harrison. Strathclyde. I'm calling it in.'

Gilchrist didn't have it in him to ask Harrison for ID, but just sat back and watched Arletta walk to the corner of the bar and remove her mobile. He didn't know who she was calling. Probably Natalie. Or maybe her solicitor to set in motion the paperwork that would place her at the top of the family business, no doubt where she always believed she should have been.

DS Harrison ended his call, then turned to face the bar, warrant card held out for all to see. 'Everybody *out*,' he shouted. 'That's it. Come on. Bar's closed. This is a crime scene. Finish your drinks and leave the bar *now*.' Then, satisfied that his instructions were being followed, he turned to face Gilchrist. 'DCI Small sends his regards, sir.'

Well well well, Dainty at large. Gilchrist nodded. 'I might've known.'

Harrison frowned, then leaned forward. 'You're bleeding, sir.'

Gilchrist dabbed a hand to the side of his face, then looked at it. A minor cut from the splintered wood. 'It's nothing.'

Harrison grimaced. 'You were lucky, sir.' He nodded over Gilchrist's shoulder. 'A few inches to the left, and you would've had a right sore one.'

'Can I ask you?' Gilchrist said, struggling to sort his thoughts in order. Whatever had just happened must have been in the planning for some time. And all without his knowledge. If he needed anyone to run a covert operation, who better to have than Dainty? 'How did you . . .?' He shook his head, annoyed with himself for not being able to work it out. 'You were tailing Tony Dilanos?'

'Arletta, sir. She doesn't know it, but we've been on to her for the last few days. Got her phones tapped. So we knew she was meeting you here, and well, we just got it set up before you arrived.'

'And Tony?'

'We got the occasional sighting of him, but he's slippery. We knew if we followed Arletta, he would eventually turn up. We can place him at the scene of several killings, but couldn't keep track of him. More SIM cards than Tesco, and changes cars like underwear.' He shook his head. 'We knew from his double murder in broad daylight that he was getting desperate, that it was only a matter of time. But . . .' He looked down at Dilanos's body. 'To try to take out his wife in a pub, in the middle of the day, well . . . that's just crazy.' His mobile rang, and he said, 'Excuse me, sir,' and strode to the other end of the bar.

Gilchrist tried standing, and gave himself a couple of seconds to make sure he could move without pain. His left ear still hummed from the near miss, and he pushed a finger into it and gave it a hard shake. By the pub doorway, three uniformed PCs had arrived, and were taking names and addresses of those who were leaving. No doubt statements would be called for later.

Arletta had finished her call to whomever, and he walked over to her in the corner, and said, 'Did you know anything about this?'

She shook her head. 'Natalie told me to lie low. But I didn't . . .' Her voice faded, and tears filled her eyes as she looked at the prostrate body of her dead husband. Gilchrist wasn't sure if she was shedding crocodile tears, or not. Maybe she'd had some feelings for Tony at one time. Or maybe what he was witnessing was simply the aftermath of shock.

He took in Tony's body, and realised that Harrison had been well trained in firearms. A single shot to the centre of Tony's back was marked by a bloodstain on his jacket the size of a side plate. Armed police use low-velocity bullets to limit collateral injuries from bullets passing through, and Sam Kim would no doubt recover Harrison's bullet from the body during her post-mortem examination.

Back to Arletta, who had dried her eyes, and looked as if she was ready to go home. 'I need you to come back to St Andrews with me,' he said. 'I want a formal statement from you, and to question you further on your late husband's association with Julian Strickland and Sir Lawrence Stanton.'

'Can't it wait?' she said.

He ignored her question. 'And get in contact with Natalie right away, and tell her to deliver herself to the North Street Office.'

Arletta nodded, with some resignation he thought.

He removed his mobile. One more call to make. Probably one that would spread more shit from the fan. He dialled her number, and when Smiler answered, he said, 'I need to meet with you right away, ma'am.'

CHAPTER 47

Tuesday

Gilchrist had taken separate statements from Arletta and Natalie, debriefed Smiler, and obtained approval to initiate cross-office investigations into the suspicious deaths of advocates Nathan Butler, Mark Cummins and high-flying solicitor Ravi Manou, as well as reopening the suicides of Butler's ex-wife and the Polish lorry driver.

But what to do about Julian Strickland OBE and Sir Lawrence Stanton?

Smiler's initial reaction had been one of resistance, against what Gilchrist could only guess. It seemed to him that she was reluctant to involve Fife Constabulary, or the police in general, in the unravelling of political favours in not only Holyrood, but Westminster, too. Gilchrist managed to allay some of her concerns by convincing her that Penny Strickland, as the Lord Advocate-in-waiting, knew nothing of her father's alleged criminal input into her meteoric rise to the fore. Even so, it was inevitable that shit would stick, and Penny would be hard-pressed to accept the position in light of her father being accused in a conspiracy of murders that paved her way to the top job – allegedly – whether or not he was found guilty. Gilchrist was convinced that guilty would be the default result, and Smiler had agreed to take the matters of Julian Strickland and Sir Lawrence Stanton higher, again with some reluctance he noted.

With evidence of Dilanos's involvement in three Glasgow murders being presented by Strathclyde Police, and two in Fife, there was only so much resistance Smiler could put up. The photographs that showed Strickland and Stanton in the company of Dilanos were inarguable proof of their connection to the head of Glasgow's crime family. With such a hot political potato, Smiler could do little to stall the inevitable, and called in Chief Constable Archie McVicar to make sure the police hierarchy was on board, and that the correct protocol would be followed to the letter. Gilchrist had never seen Smiler so slick in action, and came away with the feeling that he'd witnessed the perfect lesson in how to cover one's arse.

And with Dilanos now dead, Gilchrist would never be able to question him on his relationship with Rab Shepherd, or answer his suspicions that Jock had ordered the hit on his half-brother, or that Dilanos had been responsible for the kill, and was in fact the individual who'd pulled the trigger and performed the coup de grâce. However, Gilchrist did take some solace from Mhairi's interpretation of Rab's Dear John letter to Julie Merton, when she noted that reference to the *beginnings*, with the *s* underlined, could be the key to a coded message that pointed to his killer.

'I'm not sure, sir,' she said, holding out the letter to him. 'But if you take the first letter of each sentence . . .?'

He took it from her, and scanned through it. Then checked it again to make sure he wasn't mistaken. No mistake – T.O.N.Y.

Christ, it had been there all along, Rab's attempt to tell them who his killer was. It struck him then, that Rab must have known on that fateful drive to St Andrews that there was no coming back, that his life was about to end. It must be a terrible thing to know that you're going to be killed, and there's nothing you can do about it. But to have the mental wherewithal to come up with the idea of a coded letter, then to sit down and write it, well, that took a special kind of courage indeed.

He handed the letter back to Mhairi. 'I think you're right,' he said. 'But I suppose we'll never really know for sure, will we?'

'I suppose not, sir. Thank you, sir.'

A warrant to arrest Julian Strickland and search his home had been applied for. His daughter, Penny, was scheduled to be interviewed by Lothian and Borders Police later that day. Gilchrist thought it unlikely she would become a suspect in any of the goings-on behind the scenes, but he knew from experience that you never could tell.

But charging sitting politicians was always tricky, and meetings had been scheduled with the London Metropolitan Police to strategise how to deal with Sir Lawrence Stanton. A few heated telephone calls had been exchanged, with Scotland's First Minister phoning the Prime Minister, calling for Stanton's immediate arrest, and insisting that the proverbial book be thrown at him.

Despite their best attempts to ensure the press had minimal knowledge of what was about to happen, the shooting in the King's Arms had hit the social media channels, with mobile-phone videos of people fleeing the pub spreading like wildfire. In consequence, the media had flocked to Dundee like vultures to a slaughterhouse, and had already made their way to the North Street Office.

Despite Gilchrist's resistance against holding a press conference – his least favourite task, and one he always tried to avoid – Smiler had instructed him to organise one in the car park at the rear of the Office. He did so, reluctantly, and set it up for eleven that morning. By the time he stepped outside, the pack had swelled to forty-plus journalists and media crews, and in front of a row of TV cameras, he simply stated that a suspect in the shootings of both Nadine Shepherd and Julie Merton had been killed in the King's Arms while resisting arrest, and was yet to be identified. He aggravated the ensuing clamour by announcing that a further statement would be issued by Chief Constable McVicar later regarding far-reaching political connections to the killings.

He then stepped back inside the Office to the resounding roars of a frenzied media frantic for more information. He had overstepped the mark by bringing McVicar into it, he knew, and was no doubt in for it. But Smiler could fire him for all he cared. He felt as if yesterday's near-death experience had changed him in some subconscious way. The bullet fired by Dilanos had missed his head by no more than a few centimetres – as measured by DC Harrison – and the shockwave of its passing had left him with a high-pitched ringing in his ear, and a sense of dizziness, which might explain why he'd been so slow to gather his thoughts in the immediate aftermath of the shooting.

But by mid-afternoon, Smiler still hadn't reacted. It was just before 3.30 that a gentle rap on his door had him looking up to find her standing there, blouse and trouser suit as smart as a dummy's mannequin, mascaraed eyes and hair short and brush-perfect. Rather than show fury at his press briefing, she surprised him by expressing some sympathy.

'Are you okay, Andy? You look pale.'

313

The use of his first name was always a sign that their conversation was informal, and that whatever was about to be discussed was off the record. He shook his head. 'I'm fine. Just feeling a bit . . . dizzy.' He clapped a hand to his ear, but it seemed to exacerbate the ringing. He shook his head, but it seemed only to increase his sense of imbalance.

'You should see a doctor, Andy.'

'I've already had someone look at it,' he lied. But if it didn't clear up by the end of the day, he would have to make an appointment.

'Archie would like to have a word with you,' she said.

Gilchrist returned her gaze, but said nothing. Not like Smiler to use first names when it came to talking about the Chief Constable. He had the strangest sense of some plan being hatched behind his back, but for the life of him couldn't think what. A sacking, perhaps? A reprimand for passing the media buck to McVicar? But if so, Smiler's demeanour would have been much more formal.

'I hope it's nothing serious,' he joked, and was again puzzled by a friendly smile that stretched her lips, and gave him a glimpse of white teeth so perfect they could be mistaken for falsers. If there was one thing he could say about Smiler, she was always immaculate.

'Shall we?' she said, and held out her arm.

'Ma'am?'

'He's already here.'

Gilchrist could only mouth an Aahh as he pushed himself to his feet.

Following Smiler along the corridor was like trailing a perfume advert, an almost intoxicating fragrance of flowers and something else . . . something musky that somehow didn't quite suit her.

She opened her office door and stood back to let Gilchrist enter – another first.

He almost stopped at the sight of McVicar in his full Chief Constable outfit, standing straight-backed and regal as a monarch, white hair cut short and tidy, eyes bright and focused – like an eagle settling on its prey, Gilchrist always thought. By his side stood a woman much shorter than McVicar, a tad on the stocky side, which exaggerated her height, or lack of it, in a navy-blue business suit – skirt, not trousers. A white blouse with a mandarin collar, and a fine necklace of intricate gold and silver, if he were to guess, hinted at things oriental.

Gilchrist didn't recognise her from Adam – or should it be Eve? – although at a guess he would put her somewhere high up in the current Scottish government, or maybe even Westminster – although he suspected he might have seen her face on some media channel before now if she had been. Despite his congenital dislike of politicians, he took hold of her proffered hand while McVicar introduced him.

'Ms Simington, Detective Chief Inspector Andrew Gilchrist,' he said, his voice booming.

Her name didn't strike any bells, although something about it – the three syllables, perhaps – niggled his subconscious. Her grip was a quick dab, as if she feared picking up some infection. But at least she didn't follow it up by wiping her hand on her suit.

'A pleasure to meet you at last, DCI Gilchrist.'

Her polite English accent surprised him. Maybe she was with some governmental department in darkest Westminster. 'Andy.

Please.' Well, now he was here, he might as well be as friendly as he could.

But she seemed not to have heard, and started off in what sounded like a prepared speech. 'Chief Constable McVicar and Chief Superintendent Smiley have advised me of the effort put in by Fife Constabulary, and most notably yourself, in bringing an end to the reign of one of Scotland's most despicable criminals, namely Mr Anthony Dilanos. Apparently, Mr Dilanos had been on Strathclyde Police's radar for some time now, and over the years was personally responsible for . . . and I don't think I exaggerate here when I say it . . . *tonnes* of illegal drugs entering this country, for subsequent onwards distribution.'

Gilchrist resisted correcting her – up until Jock Shepherd's death last year, Tony had not been involved *personally*, *per se*, big Jock had. But it was a small point, probably not worth mentioning, and he nodded in silent agreement.

'It's a major problem for Scotland, and probably the most significant failure in your current government's mandate. I'm sure you're aware that Scotland has the worst statistic in Europe with respect to drugs, the highest number of deaths by drug users, a deplorable record of which no government should be proud.'

She paused, as if for feedback, but he didn't feel up to pointing out the government's other failings regarding social services, healthcare or education. So he shook his head at the deplorable record in drug-user deaths, then nodded in agreement that it was not something to be proud of – about as non-committal a response as he could possibly give her. Then it struck him that she'd said *your* current government, which told him that she wasn't with Holyrood, maybe not even a politician at all.

She continued. 'What you most certainly don't know is Operation Mindset, which is not directly related to the drug war we're currently fighting, but is a cross-border task force created to investigate money laundering associated with the disposal of these drugs, and how funds have been historically moved between our four nations.' She frowned at him, and said, 'You look as if you want to say something?'

'I do, yes. I didn't catch who you worked for.'

McVicar lowered his head. Smiler's lips tightened. Simington almost smiled.

Gilchrist pressed on. 'You're with the UK's security services. That's where I've heard your name before.' He thought her chest puffed out at his words.

'I didn't know I was known north of the border,' she said, and flashed a quick smile that told him that was as much as she was going to tell him.

'You're first desk at MI5's Homeland Security,' he said, which earned him a deep harrumph from McVicar, and a widening of Smiler's eyes. 'Which begs the question – why is MI5 interested in a Scottish drug lord, or even Scotland's drugs problem, when investigation of these matters is fully devolved?'

Simington's lips tightened. 'You're right. And I have to say I'm surprised you've heard of me. Not something we ever want to bandy about. Do we? So yes, I am First Desk. And I do work with MI5. But not Homeland Security. Westminster Oversight.'

Now he had it. 'You're here because of Sir Lawrence Stanton.'

She nodded her agreement. 'Among other things.'

'What other things?'

McVicar said, 'DCI Gilchrist, Ms Simington appreciates your interest, but it's not your place to interrogate her.'

'Yes, sir. I'm sorry, sir.' So much for first names. He returned Simington's forced smile, and waited for her to continue.

'I'll keep this short and to the point,' she said. 'Thanks to you, DCI Gilchrist, Sir Lawrence Stanton will be formally arrested by close of play today. We are looking at two other Members of Parliament with close ties to Sir Lawrence, whose names we may never disclose if our investigation turns out to be fruitless.'

He couldn't fail to catch the change in her tone, a clipped sharpness that warned all within earshot that she would harbour no defectors, and would not be questioned.

'Over the coming weeks and months, you may be required to provide assistance to certain members of my office. Chief Constable McVicar and Chief Superintendent Smiley have assured me that in that event you will provide uninhibited access to your files and to members of your staff.'

It took him a few seconds of silence before he realised she was waiting for his response. 'Of course,' he said.

'You may also be required to attend meetings in London at short notice, expenses for which will be fully compensated on evidence of receipts.'

He hadn't been to London for a few years. Not his favourite place to visit, but he nodded, and said, 'Of course.'

'Good. Thank you. I'll be in touch.'

Well, that was that. He took hold of her hand again – another quick dab – nodded to McVicar. 'Sir.' And to Smiler. 'Ma'am.'

Then he turned and walked from her office.

CHAPTER 48

Two weeks later

Jessie rapped on Gilchrist's door. 'Just in,' she said, entering his office, and holding up what looked like a printout of an e-newspaper article. 'Thought you'd love to hear it.'

'I'm listening.'

She read, 'The body of Sir Lawrence Stanton was discovered earlier this morning in the dining room of his mews apartment in Knightsbridge, London. Sir Lawrence, who many in Westminster believed would become Prime Minister one day, was a leading advocate for the fight against homophobia and racial abuse. Born in Glasgow, he first entered politics by winning the Labour seat in Govan with a landslide win . . . blah blah blah . . . hang on, hang on . . . Sir Lawrence was a well-respected and influential figure in Westminster, becoming a cabinet member . . . blah blah blah . . . here we are . . . He'd complained of feeling unwell recently, and is believed to have died from natural causes.'

She looked at him, eyebrows raised. 'You believe that?'

'That he's dead?'

'That he died from natural causes.'

'As opposed to . . .?'

'Being taken out by that snooty MI5 bitch, whatsherface. Here.'

Gilchrist took the article from her, and scanned through it. Not that he believed MI5 had a hit squad on the sidelines, ready to take out whomever First Desk Simington decided was becoming too much of a nuisance. But the timing was troublesome if you thought about it, and especially if you didn't believe in coincidence.

The article showed two photographs; one of a younger Stanton staring shyly at the camera, the other of a flamboyant Stanton, bow-tied, carnation in his breast pocket, giving a speech on the front benches in Parliament. Gilchrist thought he recognised the background behind the younger Stanton, a row of houses that looked similar to those in which he'd interviewed Hugh Cannon, and which had him thinking that Cannon and Stanton might once have been neighbours in their youth. Not that it mattered, he supposed, but the connection was intriguing—

'So what d'you think?' Jessie said.

He handed the article back to her. 'That it brings the matter to a close, whether we like it or not.'

'Yeah, and good riddance.' She scanned the article, then folded it. 'Doesn't mention anything about him being gay.'

'Does that matter?'

'Just saying.' She livened, and said, 'And before I forget, that arsehole Strickland's been on the news again today. Did you see it?'

He shook his head. 'No. When?'

'Ten o'clock, the Beeb. Denying anything and everything. What an absolute plonker he is. They should throw away the key. And his daughter, Penny, there, standing by his side for support.' She raised an eyebrow. 'Didn't realise she was so pretty, though. Can't imagine her in one of those wigs. She's not for stepping down either. Fully supporting her daddy.' She scoffed. 'What is it with the upper class? All hoity-toity and above the law.' She shook her head. 'I hope the bitch goes down with him.' She paused, then said, 'What's wrong? You don't look happy.'

He tried a smile. 'I'm fine,' he said, even though he wasn't. He had to drive Irene to the hospital that afternoon, which had been weighing on his mind all morning. Not something either of them were looking forward to. But he said, 'I agree with you. I'd be disappointed if Strickland got off with it.'

'Disappointed? I'd be *raging*. But he won't, will he? That would just be so . . .' She shivered her shoulders. 'So . . . *shite*.'

'It would indeed be shite. But there's justice, then there's the law. And never the twain shall meet.'

'Burns?'

'Gilchrist.'

She laughed, and looked as if she was about to say something, when his mobile rang. He looked at it – ID Dainty. She gave him a toodle-do wave as he answered the call.

'Just calling to give you a heads-up on the shite that's splatter-ing bonny Glasgow,' Dainty said. 'You want to hear about it?'

Not that he had any choice with Dainty. 'Shoot,' he said.

'We had Arletta Shepherd in yesterday morning. Came in on her own free will.'

'That's got to be a first,' he joked.

'No, the first is coming,' Dainty said. 'Wait till you hear this.'

'I'm all ears.'

'Came in with her solicitor, some hotshot from a firm in Edinburgh I'd never heard of before. Young guy. Dressed to the nines, and sharp as fuck. Read out a prepared statement which basically said that she wasn't aware of, or was party to, any illegal activities carried out by her late husband, Tony-the-slimeball-Dilanos. My words, not his.'

Gilchrist chuckled to let Dainty know he got his joke.

'Anyway, in exchange for immunity from prosecution, Arletta will supply evidence of Tony's involvement in a number of drug-related crimes.'

'What?' Gilchrist stood and walked to the window. 'She could have her property seized. She could lose her home if it's ruled that they were purchased from the proceeds of drug crimes, regardless of any immunity.'

'That's where her hotshot solicitor comes in. He says Arletta's prepared to give up the names of up to ten of Tony's associates involved in the drug business, including evidence in the form of emails and . . . get this . . . video recordings taken on mobile phones of drugs and money changing hands.'

Gilchrist let out a whistle. 'Wow. That's quite a coup. But presumably she'll only agree to this in exchange for full immunity, and total absolution from any association with her late husband.'

'Precisely.'

'And it was accepted?'

'Almost.'

'What do you mean?'

'Well, our boys down here – bunch of fucking wallies that they are – didn't seem to understand what they were being gifted, and tried to play hardball with her. Why don't we just arrest you and get a warrant to search your home and business premises? they say. And as calm as you like, hotshot says that if we go down that road, then certain other phone and video recordings will find their way to national media outlets, which show certain members of Strathclyde Police and other Scottish police forces in . . . for want of a better phrase, he says . . . poor light.'

'And he didn't say what these phone or video recordings show?'

'Of course not. Then it all kicks off. Chief Superintendent Martin's red in the face, like he's going to blow up, threatening them with this, that, and everything from a parking ticket to murder. But Arletta says nothing, while hotshot doesn't bat a fucking eyelid, just takes hold of her by the arm after a few minutes, and says, Excuse us, gentlemen. I can see we've wasted your time.'

'They get up and leave?'

'Managed to get hold of them before they left the Office.' Dainty paused, as if to catch breath. 'And this is where it gets fucking unbelievable.'

It took Gilchrist a few seconds of silence to realise Dainty was waiting for him, so he said, 'I'm listening.'

'A meeting was arranged for this morning, again attended by Arletta and her hotshot solicitor. But by this time, CS Martin's handed in his notice and in his place comes Assistant Chief Constable Drew Ellencourt, who accepts everything hotshot's got to offer, signs an agreement, then sets in motion a series of arrest warrants that more or less closes down Scotland's drug business. It's like it was all prearranged and prepared the night before.'

'And have arrests been made?'

Dainty laughs, a chuckle that could have come from a big man. 'You remember that phone call we listened to in Tony's office, where the woman pretended to be Arletta?'

'I do, yes.'

'She was one of them. Turns out she'd been shagging Tony behind Arletta's back, or so she thought. Arletta'd had her card marked for ages. Should've heard her. I know I swear like a linty, but Christ, you could patent some of the stuff she was spouting out. And as for Ellencourt, I think he signed off on it before his name popped up on Arletta's list.' Dainty laughed again, which brought a smile to Gilchrist's lips.

'And where's Arletta now?' he said.

'She's given assurances that now she's in charge, her father's business will become legit. Not sure I believe her, but it's a start.'

A thought struck Gilchrist. 'Penny Strickland's been pushing for cleaning up the big cities, so I suppose in a roundabout way Arletta's assurances help Penny Strickland's chances of being appointed Lord Advocate.'

'If she distanced herself from her father, I'd agree with you,' Dainty said. 'But she's standing by his side, which I think is a big mistake, in fact it's a *huge* mistake. Word is that those high up in Holyrood are having second thoughts about her candidacy. It's only a matter of time until she goes down with the ship.'

Gilchrist noticed the time on his computer, and said, 'I've got to go, but thanks for the update, and keep us posted.'

'Will do.'

Gilchrist grabbed his jacket, and hurried from his office.

CHAPTER 49

The drive from St Andrews to Dundee was done in almost total silence.

Irene felt as if she couldn't find the right words to say without breaking down. Every now and then she sensed Andy chancing a glance at her, but she continued to sit tight-lipped in the passenger seat, gazing out the side window, lost in the depths of her own thoughts and fears. Not until they crossed the Tay Road Bridge and were working through the city traffic did she finally search for his hand, and squeeze – tight.

He squeezed back. 'You're doing the right thing,' he said. 'You know you are.'

'You're very convincing when you put your mind to it.'

He took his eyes off the road for a moment, gave her a smile, another squeeze of her hand, as if trying to reassure himself that his powers of persuasion really were for the good.

But she had to believe that. They both did.

He slowed down to enter the car park, and in the turning managed a quick glance at her again, and she caught his eye. And as he drove around, searching for a parking spot, she returned to her thoughts, worried sick about the horror of what she was about to go through.

Chemotherapy.

She'd sworn she would never have it again, convinced that it would now kill her. She'd witnessed a childhood friend of hers go through a course of chemo, ten or so years earlier. As the end neared, her face had become so pale that Irene could see her veins pulsing beneath the skin, eyes sunken dark as bruises, head glistening as bald as the day she'd been born, hands and fingers like bones covered with skin, arms so thin and frail that Irene feared she could break them just by touching her.

And all for nothing.

Weeks of vomiting. Tiredness that sucked the strength from her friend. Sleep that overtook her for hours and hours, and which turned into days and weeks, until she eventually sank into a coma from which she never recovered.

No, she'd told Andy. *Chemotherapy's not for me.*

But somehow he'd managed to convince her.

Not for me, he'd said. *But for your daughter, Joanne. And for yourself, too.*

But if she were being honest, what finally persuaded her was when he'd reminded her of her son, Jamie, who'd committed suicide four years earlier. *If Joanne lost her mother to cancer*, he'd said, *who would she have left? You have to try. You have to give it a go.*

So she'd agreed to give it a go. And now here she was – Ninewells Hospital, Dundee – to begin her course of chemo. And she was terrified. No amount of hand-squeezing, powers of persuasion, motherly responsibilities, or comforting words of reassurance could ever lift that fear from her, or shift the sickening worry that hung in her gut like poisoned lead.

The car jolted as Andy parked and switched off the engine.

'You ready?' he said.

She tightened her lips, lowered her head, and nodded.

When he walked to the passenger side and opened her door, she found she didn't have the strength of belief to look at him, but sat staring out the windscreen, seatbelt still on. She ignored his helping hand, and shook her head.

'I'm sorry, Andy, I'm having second thoughts.'

'I know you are.'

She looked at him then, and knew her words had pained him.

'Take my hand,' he said.

Oh, no, she thought, please don't force me to do this.

'Please?' he said.

So she did as he asked, but to her surprise he didn't try to pull her from the car, but instead covered her hand with both of his, and crouched down beside her.

'I know this is hard for you,' he said. 'I know how you feel about it. And you know how I feel about it, too. But . . .' He pressed her hand to his lips, and held it there. He closed his eyes, and tears squeezed from under his lids.

When he looked at her again, she could see his resolve.

'But . . .?' she said.

'But . . .' He tried a smile. 'You don't have to do this, if you don't want to.'

She pressed her lips tight, afraid that if she tried to speak, she would break down.

'Would you like me to drive you back home?' he asked.

She closed her eyes, lowered her head, and nodded.

He kissed her hand, gave a parting squeeze. 'We'll find another way. Okay?'

'Okay.'

When he took his seat behind the wheel again and switched on the ignition, it felt as if a weight had been lifted from her being. She risked a glance at the hospital building as he left the car park and eased onto the road. Just the sound of his car accelerating, the power of its engine as he slipped into traffic and raced through the lights, seemed to lift her. She reached for his hand, and held it, pleased to feel his response.

'I'm sorry,' she said. 'I've wasted your time. Driving me here, then driving home.'

'You haven't wasted any time at all,' he said. 'Only by making the journey did you find out how you truly felt about it. It was worth every second.'

She dabbed a hand at her eyes, then looked at the passing townscape.

As the car swept back onto the Tay Road Bridge, she marvelled at the slow movement of the River Tay, as if she were seeing its expanse for the first time and only now coming to understand how rivers flowed, how the world worked, how these waters would continue to run to the sea for centuries to come, while she and other human beings lived their lives, and died in the end.

And that's what she knew was going to happen to her.

She was going to die. And so would Andy.

We are all going to die.

Maybe she would die soon. Or maybe she would die later. But at least she'd made the choice as to how she would die – not hooked up to some chemical-dripping contraption that had to kill you before you could recover; but to be at home with someone she loved, and who loved her.

She reached for his hand, and gave another squeeze.

He glanced at her and gave her a smile and a squeeze, too.

'How do you feel?' he said.

'I don't know,' she said. 'Sad in one way. Strangely elated in another. But mostly . . . I don't know . . . relieved, I suppose.'

'That's good to hear.'

'Just having you with me, Andy, when I needed you . . . it helps. It helps a lot.'

'I'm here for you.'

'I know you are.' She didn't want to try to guess how long he would have to be there for her. It was just so comforting having him with her for now.

Later would come. Or sooner.

It wasn't up to her to choose.

She put her head back, and closed her eyes. Air from the open sunroof ruffled her hair. She breathed it in, and settled down for the drive home.

ACKNOWLEDGEMENTS

Writing is without question a lonely affair, but this book would not have been published without considerable help and advice from the following: Ian, Sheila, Tom, Jane and Anna, for advance reader comments; Howard Watson for professional copyediting to the nth degree; Rebecca Sheppard, Editorial Manager, Sean Garrehy, Art Director, Brionee Fenlon, Marketing Manager, and John Fairweather, Senior Production Controller, for working hard behind the scenes at Little, Brown to give this novel the best possible start; Krystyna Green, Publishing Director, Constable, for placing her trust in me once again, and especially for relenting after considerable resistance to leaving the sex scene in. And finally Anna, for putting up with me, believing in me, and loving me all the way.

Enjoyed *Dead Find?*
Read on for T. F. Muir's
heart-warming short story
featuring DCI Gilchrist:
'A Christmas Tail' . . .

A Christmas Tail: A Short Story

T. F. Muir

23 December
North Street, St Andrews, Scotland

DCI Andy Gilchrist never noticed the woman as he left the office.

He pulled his jacket collar tight to his neck to fend off a bitter chill that came in off the Eden Estuary. Snow that had been forecast for that evening was now falling – flakes as light as feathers that seemed to place themselves with care on the pavements. Within a few hours, the town of St Andrews would be blanketed white.

Even when Gilchrist turned into College Street, thoughts of a meal in the Central Bar – the first food since breakfast – were foremost in his mind, and he didn't hear the running patter of footsteps chasing him. Twenty yards farther in, he glanced over his shoulder, but even then he paid the woman no attention.

Not until he was about to enter the bar by the side door did he notice her.

'Andy?' she said. 'Andy Gilchrist?'

Gilchrist stopped, his mind struggling to place a name to a face he hadn't seen since he'd been a teenager. 'Isabelle?' he said.

'You remembered.' Her breath puffed in the cold air. 'I wasn't sure you would.'

He leaned towards her, pressed his face to her cheek, surprised to hear how hard she was breathing. Her whole body seemed to pulse with a nervous energy that shivered through her heavy winter coat. When he pulled back, her smile was still as attractive as ever, but tainted with a hint of sorrow that seemed to stitch the corners of her lips.

'Can we . . . can we talk?' she said. 'I mean, I'm not interrupting anything, am I?'

'No, I'm almost done for the day. I was just taking a break, popping in for a bite to eat. Would you like to join me?'

She glanced at the door, then shook her head. 'I . . . I can't. I've got to get back.'

'You wanted to talk?'

'To ask for a favour . . . for your help, really. I . . . I hope you don't mind.' She gave a nervous laugh, and a quick flash of teeth. 'It sounds silly. But . . . but . . .' She smiled at him again, but tears welled in her eyes, and he reached out to her, took hold of her hand.

'What's the matter?' he asked.

She sniffed, nodded, then shook her head. 'I'm sorry,' she said. 'I shouldn't have come . . . it was just a thought, that's all.'

He turned from the bar's entrance. 'We can talk somewhere else, if you want.'

She hesitated, as if undecided, then said, 'I'm . . . we're staying nearby.'

'I can walk you there, if you'd like,' he offered.

'Yes . . . yes . . . that would be kind of you . . . thank you.'

She took hold of his arm and clung to him as he retraced his steps along College Street, both of them silent in their own thoughts until they reached North Street.

'Which way?' he said.

She tugged him to turn right, and said, 'We're staying in a flat along the road. I've rented it for the week. Over Christmas.'

He held her firmer as they walked along North Street, taking care not to slip in the settling snow. In the dark distance, the cathedral ruins stood silhouetted in a moonlit sky. Cars eased past, the sound of their tyres on the road oddly muted by the bitter cold.

'You haven't changed,' she said to him. 'I'd recognise you anywhere.'

'Older fatter stiffer,' he said, and lifted a hand to his head. 'Greyer, too.'

'It suits you.' She clung closer, tightened her grip.

'I haven't seen you in, I don't know how many years,' he said, 'since you . . .'

'Ran away?'

He felt a nip of regret at bringing up the moment of their break-up all those years ago, but said, 'I was going to say: since you left this wonderful old grey town of ours.' He gave a chuckle. 'How long's it been?'

'Over thirty years,' she said. 'The year before you married Gail. I take it you're still married. I would like to think so. That at least it wasn't all for nothing.'

He waited a couple of beats. 'Gail passed away a few years ago.'

'Oh, Andy, I'm sorry to hear that.'

335

He was about to mention his children, Jack and Maureen, but Isabelle had sought him out to ask for a favour, not to listen to his moaning about the past. So he changed the subject with, 'And how about you?'

'I'm afraid I've been unlucky in love,' she said. 'Twice married, twice divorced. But I never really fell for anyone . . . anyone else . . .'

Her body shivered with a nervous pulse again, and he stopped when he realised she was crying. He said nothing, just pulled her to him, and waited for the moment to pass.

She pulled free, dabbed a gloved hand to her cheeks, then ran it under her nose. 'I'm sorry,' she said, and sniffed again. 'I must look a mess.'

He brushed snowflakes from her hair, tugged a strand behind her ear, surprised by the strangest sense of familiarity in doing so. 'Well, in that case, you look a lovely mess,' he said.

She stared away from him then, as if searching for some memory from the past, and he found himself thinking back to the last time they had kissed, remembering how empty he had felt when she had turned and walked from his life, all those years ago—

'I have a son,' she said. 'From my second marriage. To Dan.' She shook her head, as if to rid herself of the memory. 'He'd been having an affair. I didn't know anything about it until he just left one morning without a word of goodbye.' She faced him, her eyes bright, reflecting the fire and steely resolve that he knew she possessed. 'We never heard from him again.'

'I'm sorry.' It was all he could think to say.

'He did leave me with a child, Thomas, a beautiful boy, who will soon . . .' She pressed her hand to her mouth, shook her head. 'Who will soon be ten.' Tears spilled down her cheeks, dripped from her chin. 'I'm sorry . . .'

Silent, Gilchrist waited.

Then she looked up at him, a hint of a tremor on her chin. 'Which is why I'm here,' she managed to say. 'To ask for your help.'

'To help you and Thomas?'

She nodded.

Gilchrist was not sure what he could do for her, but said, 'If I can.'

'I'd like you to meet him.'

'I would like that, too,' he said, but caught a flicker of concern in her eyes.

'He wants to ask you himself.'

'Ask me what?'

'He's not well,' she said, as if that explained everything, then added, 'This way.' She pushed a tall metal gate open, and entered a narrow pend that led to the back of the terraced buildings. Staircases to the right and left rose to upper floors, but Isabelle walked into what looked like an alcove, and fumbled with her key. She pushed the door open, and in a hushed voice said, 'He was sleeping when I left. Which is why I couldn't stay.'

She entered what Gilchrist assumed had once been the main lounge, but which had since been converted into a small living and dining area, with a fitted kitchen and breakfast bar off to the side. A small Christmas tree with flickering lights sat on a table in the corner, its base hidden by presents neatly wrapped in Christmas paper. Rows of cards strung along the walls, not all Christmas cards, he noticed, but Get Well cards, too.

Isabelle scuffed her feet on a hard-bristled doormat, and kicked off her shoes.

Gilchrist slipped his shoes off, too, intrigued as to why he was here. The tiled floor felt cold, but he said nothing as he watched Isabelle tiptoe to another door and push it open. From where he stood, he saw that it was a modernised bedroom with a king-size bed that seemed to swamp the space. A blue and pink patterned duvet as thick as pillows covered the bed. Matching curtains were drawn across the windows, the only light in the room coming from two bedside lamps. It took Gilchrist a few seconds to realise the bed was occupied.

Isabelle leaned forward, pressed her lips to her son's face, then fiddled with the duvet cover. 'I've brought someone to see you, Thomas,' she said, then signalled for Gilchrist to come closer. 'He's my old friend I told you about. The policeman. He's going to help.'

The boy said something which Gilchrist failed to catch, then Isabelle slid her hand under his head, and helped lift him to a more upright position.

Gilchrist caught his breath.

Thomas's tenth birthday might be soon, but the boy who stared back at him must have weighed no more than someone half his age. Blue eyes dominated a too-thin face, and an arm no thicker than Gilchrist's wrist tried to lift from the cover. Gilchrist was taken by how like his mother Thomas was, and how handsome a young man he would one day become.

He reached the side of the bed and took hold of Thomas's hand. It felt cold, and he clasped his other hand over it to warm him. Thomas tried a smile, revealing white teeth too big for his face it seemed, and when he spoke his voice was no more than a dry rasp of a whisper.

'Mum said you'll help . . .'

Gilchrist nodded. 'Of course I'll help.'

'Help find Hamish . . .'

Gilchrist glanced at Isabelle, but she had her hand pressed hard to her mouth, her gaze locked on her desperately ill son. Gilchrist found himself racking his brain, trying to recall anyone by the name of Hamish. But his memory came up blank. 'Hamish?' he said.

'McHamish . . .' Thomas said.

'Hamish McHamish,' Isabelle said to Gilchrist. 'He's missing.'

Now Gilchrist had it. He smiled at Thomas. 'You want me to find Hamish?' he said. 'And bring him to you?'

Thomas's eyes widened with hope. 'When?' he whispered.

Gilchrist gave Thomas's hand a squeeze of reassurance. 'I'll find Hamish as soon as I can,' he said.

'Will you find him tonight?'

Isabelle said, 'Mr Gilchrist will do his best, Thomas. I know he will.' She placed a hand on Gilchrist's shoulder, and squeezed, and Gilchrist gave Thomas a nod of assurance. He would find the missing cat, and bring him to Thomas. But if the truth be told, he had no idea where to start. Hamish, the beloved local stray, could be anywhere in the town. He gave Thomas's hand a gentle shake. 'I'll find Hamish,' he said, and Thomas replied by smiling and closing his eyes.

Isabelle leaned forward and stroked her son's hair, kissed his cheek.

Back in the main living area, Isabelle made Gilchrist a cup of tea, and opened a box of chocolate digestives. 'They're the only biscuits I've got,' she apologised, holding the plate out to him. 'It's all Thomas will eat, and even then it's only to have no more than a broken-off piece or two.'

Gilchrist took a biscuit to please her, and found his gaze shifting to the bedroom door – open just a touch, so Isabelle could hear Thomas's slightest call. The silence in the bedroom told him that Thomas was asleep. He took a sip of tea, and said, 'Are you able to tell me what's wrong with Thomas?'

Isabelle gave a nervous glance at the door, then said, 'He was diagnosed four months ago with non-Hodgkin lymphoma.' Her voice was so quiet that Gilchrist had trouble hearing her. 'He was not expected to live this long,' she said, her eyes welling.

Gilchrist hid behind a sip of tea.

'He was fine one morning, then later that day I thought he looked tired. He said he wasn't, but I could tell. Two weeks later I took him to the doctor. It all happened so quickly,' she said. 'It's . . . it's . . . I can't believe it.'

'Why Hamish?' Gilchrist asked.

She gave him a nervous smile, as if embarrassed. 'We often come to St Andrews,' she said. 'We were here last year and stayed for a week.' She smiled at the memory. 'The first time I ever brought Thomas to St Andrews, he found Hamish when we went to the East Sands. Well, it was more like Hamish found Thomas. He wouldn't leave him, and followed us around for an entire afternoon, as if Hamish had found his best friend. Every day after that, no matter where we went in town, Hamish would always find Thomas. And the strange thing is, every time we visited St Andrews, Hamish would be there the very next day, almost as if he was waiting for Thomas.'

Gilchrist smiled at the image, made all the more amusing because Hamish was no one's cat. Originally a house cat, over the years he had embarked on longer walks away from home, until one day he never came back, and that was that. At least once a year, his owner made a point of tracking him down and taking him to the vet for his annual check-up, but other than that, Hamish had become the town cat. He was often seen around the streets of St Andrews, sitting at the butcher's entrance on Market Street, or popping in and out of shops on South Street as if considering a purchase, or taking shelter from the rain in some doorway. From time to time he would move in with a group of students, then just as simply move out again.

For a young boy on holiday, befriending Hamish must have been irresistible.

'But we haven't seen Hamish since we arrived two days ago,' Isabelle said. 'I asked around, thinking he might have died, but it seems he is still about, but no one knows where.'

Gilchrist crunched his biscuit, sipped his tea, then said, 'So you want Thomas to see Hamish for . . . for . . .' He almost said *for one last time*, but Isabelle saved him.

'The first time they ever met, Thomas had the flu. The next day he was as right as rain. Another time, Thomas had an ear infection, which cleared up within a day of seeing Hamish.'

Gilchrist said, 'They have antibiotics for infections.'

Isabelle nodded. 'Thomas was nearing the end of his course of antibiotics,' she said, 'but he believed that meeting Hamish cured him. And last year he had toothache, which he said disappeared the instant he saw Hamish.'

Gilchrist smiled. It was almost a proven fact that the power of positive thought and self-belief was as good as any medicine. And what could be more powerful than a young boy's imagination?

Isabelle's gaze shifted to the bedroom door for a moment, then she said, 'The doctors told me last month that Thomas wouldn't see Christmas, that he should be transferred to the

Marie Curie Centre.' She shook her head. 'I couldn't do that to him. Hospitals and clinics frighten him.' She pressed her hand to her mouth again, stifled a sob. 'So I went against the doctors' advice and brought him home to . . . to . . .'

Gilchrist said, 'Is he in . . . any . . .?'

'He's on morphine. He's not in pain. He's comfortable. Well, as comfortable as I can make him.' Then she took a deep breath. 'I'm sorry, Andy. I know it sounds ridiculous, and I wouldn't blame you if you said you were too busy, but I thought if Thomas could see Hamish for just . . . for just one last time . . . that it might . . .' She squeezed her eyes. Tears spilled onto her cheeks, and she whispered, 'That it might make his last moments happy.'

Gilchrist placed his teacup on the table, and removed a couple of business cards from his jacket. He placed one beside the teacup, and gave Isabelle time to recover. He then asked for her mobile number, wrote it down on the other card, and slipped it into his pocket.

He pulled himself upright and walked to her, helped her to her feet. She looked up at him, and in her eyes he saw the reflection of the girl he once knew, who had told him that she wanted to see more of the world than old stone buildings and a cold Fife coast, who had then struck out for the deep waters of an uncertain future, only to find herself back in her home town, wounded and desperate and all alone, with the only person in the world she loved on the verge of dying.

'Leave it with me,' he said to her.

Back in the North Street Office, Gilchrist instructed Jennifer to tell all units to be on the lookout for Hamish McHamish. Only recently transferred to St Andrews, Jennifer said, 'Can you give me a description, sir?'

342

'Orange long-haired cat with a bushy tail, white chest and paws. And it's cold outside, so he'll be hanging about somewhere warm. Try the library, the Students' Union, the Halls of Residence for starters. Ask around. Someone must have seen him. I mean, how many places are there in St Andrews for an orange cat to hide?' An image of Thomas hit him – blue eyes in hollowed sockets – as if to remind him how close to death the young boy was, how little time they might have. 'And find a photograph of Hamish, and email it to everybody.'

A grumbling stomach reminded him it was time to eat.

In the Central Bar he ordered fish and chips and a pint of Deuchars, and asked the barman, 'Has anyone seen Hamish recently?'

'The cat?'

'The one and only.'

'Can't say that I have.'

'Ask around,' Gilchrist said, and on the spur of the moment added, 'I'm offering a hundred pounds to anyone who finds Hamish and brings him to me.' He passed over a card as his mobile rang. In the bustling din of the busy bar he had difficulty catching DC Mhairi McBride's words.

'Did you say you've found him?' he asked her.

'No, sir. We have one definite sighting in Waterstones this afternoon. He slept there for an hour before walking off. And a couple of sightings in South Street.'

'Where was the last place he was seen?' Gilchrist asked.

'The most recent report we have, sir, is walking past the Byre Theatre about three-thirty, just before it got dark.'

'Going uphill or downhill?'

'Heading uphill, sir. Back towards South Street.'

'Keep looking,' he said to her, and ended the call.

He spent the next ten minutes trying to think where to search, and pulled up memories of the last time he had seen Hamish – two weeks ago, in Market Street outside the fish shop, sitting on the pavement as if waiting to be fed. Then last week walking along Murray Park, as if checking out the prices of the local B&Bs. But none of that was really helpful in figuring out where Hamish was now.

He had just ordered another pint when his fish and chips came up, and he took a seat by the back wall. He spread a healthy dollop of HP Sauce over his chips, and squeezed sliced lemon over the fish. Peppered and salted, the first mouthful had his taste buds fizzing. He dabbed a chip into the sauce, and glanced outside. The snowfall was thickening, the forecast proving correct for once. So Hamish would not be outside, he felt certain of that, but likely snuggled up for the night someplace warm and cosy. And with that thought it struck him that if Hamish hadn't found refuge before the snow began, then it was possible he had left tracks. Enthused by that, Gilchrist decided to take a quick walk around town before driving home to his cottage in Crail.

On leaving, he checked with the barman, only to be told of reported sightings that stretched from Madras College to the Golf Museum to the harbour. In a small town the size of St Andrews, these landmarks were almost diametrical opposites. It seemed that he might have underestimated the number of places for a cat to hide around town.

Outside, he called the office for feedback, but Jennifer had nothing to report. 'Spread the word that there's a hundred-pound tax-free Christmas bonus to anyone who brings him in,' he said to her, then ended the call. He crossed the cobbles of Market Street, walking away from the main thoroughfare towards where the street narrowed to a single lane, and in the general direction of where Hamish had last been seen.

In the lane, Gilchrist kept his eyes to the ground. Footprints, both fresh and covered, spoiled the thickening bed of snow. But by the time he reached South Castle Street, he hadn't come across animal tracks. He turned in the direction of the Byre Theatre, and exited South Castle Street.

To his right, the lights of South Street beckoned him, but he chose to walk in the opposite direction, towards the darkness of The Pends. His gut instinct told him to cross the road and he waited for a gap in the traffic before jogging to the other side, onto the pavement that ran along the front of the cathedral ruins. Landscape lighting lit up the old stone walls and cast shadows into the darker reaches of the cemetery. Overhead, twin stone spires reared into a black sky.

He reached the entrance gate to the cathedral grounds when he heard a woman call out from his right. A brown animal – a fox he first thought – streaked from the cemetery and shot across the road. The woman screamed as another figure, a young girl this time, darted through the gate opening and chased the dog across the—

Gilchrist caught her, swept her off her feet—

A van powered past, its horn blaring, brake lights red as it pulled to a slippery halt.

The woman rushed up to Gilchrist, arms outstretched as she took the girl from him. 'I asked her to hold his lead for a moment,' she gasped, 'and off he runs. He's far too strong for her.' The girl clung tight to her mother, sobbing quietly, frightened by the close rush of the van and the hard grasp of a stranger. The woman

345

glanced at the van driver striding towards them, and said to Gilchrist, 'If you hadn't been there, she would've been—'

'Somebody wants to put a lead on her,' said the van driver, 'and not the dog, yeah?'

Gilchrist faced the driver. 'She's okay,' he said, and flashed his warrant card. 'Have a merry Christmas, pal.'

The driver stopped, then did an about-turn, and Gilchrist waited until the van drove into South Street before saying, 'What's the dog's name?'

'Codger,' she said.

Gilchrist crossed the street and strode towards the dog, who stood facing the scene as if expecting to receive a good telling-off for running away. As Gilchrist approached, Codger hung his head, tail down, as if undecided whether to run or not, until Gilchrist said, 'Sit, Codger, *sit*,' and to his surprise, he did.

He retrieved the lead from the ground, and chucked Codger behind the ears. 'Good dog,' he said, and together they returned across the road. At the sight of Codger on his lead, the girl stopped crying. 'Where are you walking to?' he asked the girl's mother.

'Car's parked round the corner.'

'Come on,' he said. 'I'll escort you, and make sure Codger doesn't run off.'

At the sound of his name, Codger glanced up at Gilchrist, then trotted beside him, step for step. They reached the car, a Range Rover with a dog cage in the back, which Codger leapt into as soon as the hatchback was opened. The woman thanked Gilchrist again, and he wished her a merry Christmas, and resumed his search.

He retraced his steps to the entrance to the cathedral cemetery and strode on. To his surprise, he picked up some paw marks on the steps of the War Memorial. He had no way of knowing if these were a dog's or a cat's, and the likelihood of them being Hamish's defied the odds. But, curiosity got the better of him, and he found himself following them.

Into Gregory Place, along the side of the Cathedral Wall . . .

Across the stone foundations of Culdee Church . . .

Down Kirkhill to the harbour front where . . .

Gilchrist stopped. The paw prints just seemed to end. What had he missed?

He retraced his steps, but sure enough, the prints just faded from view. But as if to replace them, another set of prints, not animal prints, but deep footprints from someone heavy led to the stone pier. The prints were fresh, but no footprints back.

Who would walk along the pier on a night like this?

Intrigued, he followed the footprints.

The wind had strengthened. Icy spray blasted the pier. He could hear the sea thudding into the stone wall with a force he could feel, then ebbing with a powerful surge and sucking sound of water rushing over rocks. No one could survive for long in these ice-cold waters. As he stared into the darkness ahead, he thought he could just make out the shape of someone standing on the high wall at the end of the pier.

A minute later, he stood at the foot of the metal ladder that led to the high wall.

The figure had morphed into that of a man, who stood with his back to him, unaware of his presence, arms hanging by his side. Gilchrist thought the man must be frozen to the spot, until he leaned down and tugged at something by his feet – a lump of concrete, or a large rock – connected to his ankle by a rope.

'Can I help?' Gilchrist shouted up to him.

The man jerked upright with surprise, and faced him. 'Stay away. Leave me alone.'

'Can I join you—'

'No. I mean it.' The man tottered on the brink.

Gilchrist took two steps back, arms raised in defeat. 'It's too cold for a swim.'

'I'm not going for a swim.'

'You certainly aren't. Not with that thing tied to your leg.'

The man looked down at his feet, as if contemplating just getting on with the job.

'Can I ask why?' Gilchrist said.

'It's none of your business.'

'I know it's not. But it'll soon be Christmas, and I'd like to swap with you. Well, actually, Thomas would like to swap with you,' Gilchrist corrected.

Silent, the man stood silhouetted against a grey sky.

'Thomas would give everything to have what you have.' Gilchrist went on. 'His mother would do the same.' He turned his head, stared off across the darkness of the East Sands and the black cliffs beyond. 'You see, Thomas will soon be ten years old, except that he probably won't live that long. He has cancer, and is expected to die any day now. It would be a miracle if he even made it to Christmas. But you have what Thomas doesn't have.' He turned to look up at the man on the wall again. 'You have your life to live. You have a life ahead of—'

'How do you know I'm not dying, too?' the man responded.

'Oh that's easy,' Gilchrist said. 'If you were dying, you would want to live.'

Neither of them spoke for what seemed like minutes, until Gilchrist said, 'I don't have a knife, but I'm good at untying knots,'

348

and without waiting for a response, gripped the metal rungs and pulled himself onto the top wall. The man stood still as Gilchrist wrestled with the knot at his feet and managed to untie it. Then he pushed the lump of concrete over the edge where it hit the water with a deep splash.

Gilchrist helped the man down, and escorted him the length of the pier. By the time they reached the shorehead, a police car was waiting for him – no flashing lights, as Gilchrist had instructed – where he was helped into the back seat for the drive to the hospital for treatment.

Gilchrist waited until the car drove from view, before heading back to the Office for his car. At the brow of Kirkhill, he decided to walk along the East Scores, with the cliffs on his right. The wind was at its strongest and coldest there, but at least the snow had stopped.

He came across no fresh paw prints by the time he reached his car. He pressed the key fob, took his seat behind the wheel, thinking it strange how his search for Hamish had helped him to save one life, and possibly two if the girl had run onto the road. Maybe there was more to Hamish McHamish than anyone knew. He flicked on his headlights, slipped into gear, and was about to exit the car park when he put his foot on the brakes.

He peered through his windscreen.

Was he mistaken? Had the brightness of his headlights tricked his eyes?

He flicked off the full-beam, and held his breath as he opened the door.

The car's dipped headlights enabled Gilchrist to see the top of the wall that bounded the edge of the police car park. And there, looking down at him as if he hadn't a care in the world, sat

Hamish, thick fur as dry as fluff, bushy tail wrapped around his front paws to keep them warm.

Gilchrist approached, fearful that Hamish might turn around and leap into the garden on the other side of the wall. Then how would he find him? Slowly, he reached up with both hands and, to his surprise, Hamish let himself be lifted down as if Gilchrist were his one and only master.

He cradled Hamish with his left arm, and stroked his chin with his right, whispering, 'Puss, puss,' worried that Hamish might leap from his grip if he thought he was not being given the correct amount of attention. Rather than risk scaring Hamish by placing him in his car, Gilchrist tightened his grip, and switched off the engine and headlights. Then he pressed the fob to lock his car, and walked through the pend onto North Street.

Five minutes later, he stood at Isabelle's door.

The curtains were drawn, but the lights were on. He pressed the bell. Hamish stirred in his arm, as if fearful of the chiming sound within, and for one troubling moment Gilchrist thought Hamish was struggling to free himself from his grip—

The door opened. Hamish stilled.

Isabelle's eyes widened with surprise. 'You've found him,' she said.

Without a word, Gilchrist stepped inside, and waited until Isabelle closed the door behind him before he placed Hamish on the floor.

'He's just as lovely as I remember him,' Isabelle said.

As she leaned down to stroke him, Hamish snubbed her. He turned and walked away, tail held high. He crossed the patterned rug, rubbed himself around the corner of the sofa, and brushed the door frame with his tail as he entered the bedroom.

Isabelle placed her hand to her mouth, and whispered, 'It's as if . . . as if he knows.'

Gilchrist said nothing as he followed Isabelle to the bedroom doorway.

Hamish was already on the bed, sniffing out a suitable spot near the pillow next to Thomas, who was asleep. His too-thin face looked a pasty shade of white, across which veins ran like thin ink. For one heart-stopping moment, Gilchrist thought he had arrived too late, until he caught the tiniest of movements in Thomas's fingers.

'How is he?' Gilchrist asked.

'He's comfortable,' Isabelle said.

Gilchrist watched Hamish curl up on the duvet cover next to Thomas. 'Looks like Hamish has claimed your side of the bed,' he said.

'That's all right. I can't really sleep anyway.'

'Would you like me to stay with you for a while?'

She took hold of his hand, and squeezed. 'Go home,' she said. 'Get some sleep. I'll potter about in the kitchen for a while, and put out some water and food for Hamish. If I need to sleep, I'll curl up on the sofa.'

Gilchrist retreated to the door.

'Thanks for all your help,' she said, and leaned up to peck his cheek.

Gilchrist gave her a gentle hug in response. 'I've got a busy morning ahead of me, so I won't be able to pop in until later in the afternoon.' She looked tired, he thought, her eyes dark and lined, but he detected the tiniest sparkle of something behind them – hope, perhaps. 'If you need me for anything,' he added, 'anything at all. Just call.'

Then he turned and walked through the pend.

Although the wind had died, it felt as if the temperature had dropped ten degrees in as many minutes, and his breath puffed in white clouds before him. All around, snow glistened with sparks of ice. He looked to the sky, surprised to see that the clouds had cleared. Stars glittered like a million diamonds on a black backdrop, and he caught his breath as a shooting star streaked across the sky with impossible speed, leaving him to think he had only imagined it.

But he closed his eyes and made a wish, nonetheless.

Christmas Eve

By the time Gilchrist freed himself from the mundane duties of the Office, the day was already dying. He made his way into town and bought a Christmas card, and signed and sealed it before leaving the store. Market Street thrummed with the bustle and buzz of last-minute shoppers, or revellers intent on earlier festivities, or passers-by just looking at fairy lights that brightened shop windows. More snow had fallen that morning, and with the temperature hovering around zero, the promise of a white Christmas was more or less sealed.

As he made his way to Isabelle's, he worried that she hadn't called him, or left any messages on his mobile, not sure if that was good news or bad – if anything had happened to Thomas, she would surely have called. Yet again, she could be too distraught to think of phoning anyone.

He stood outside her flat, his heart heavy with dread at what he might find. For one long moment he thought of just slipping the card through the letterbox, then decided that the least he could do was to be there for her. He pressed the doorbell, caught the melodic chime within.

He counted to thirty before he rang the bell again, and breathed a sigh of relief when he heard footsteps approach, then the lock click open.

Isabelle stood before him, her eyes welling. She blinked, and tears spilled down her cheeks. Behind her, he noticed the bedroom door was closed.

'Come in, Andy,' she said. 'Please.'

Silent, Gilchrist entered. He stood in the centre of the room while he listened to the click of the door being shut. The smell of home-cooking invaded his senses, and he noticed a covered pot on the stove. At that moment he felt utterly helpless, the pointlessness of his gift of a Christmas card all too apparent to him.

Isabelle came up behind him, and said, 'Can I take your jacket?'

How could he stay at a time like this? But if Isabelle felt she needed someone to talk to, then how could he not? He nodded, slipped his jacket off, and she took it from him and hung it over the back of a kitchen chair.

Then she surprised him by taking hold of his hand. 'Come,' she said.

Gilchrist let himself be led to the bedroom door.

Isabelle pushed it open.

The first thing that struck Gilchrist was that Thomas was propped up on a high pillow, eyes sparkling with the light of life. The second was that Hamish was snuggled on the duvet cover on Thomas's lap, eyes closed in that look of pleasure that only cats seem to possess, and purring away like a thrumming motor as Thomas stroked his neck. And the third was an empty soup plate and spoon abandoned on a tray on the bedside table.

'Thank you for finding Hamish,' Thomas said in a rasping whisper.

'I . . . it's . . . I'm glad I found him for you.'

'Would you like to stroke him?'

'Will he let me?'

Thomas whispered something to Hamish, which Gilchrist failed to hear, but one of Hamish's ears twisted back as if to listen. Then Thomas looked at Gilchrist, and said, 'He'll let you.'

Gilchrist stepped into the room, and up to the bed. As he stroked Hamish he felt the hairs on the back of his neck rise, and the strangest sensation of something warm shivering through every part of his being. Then Hamish opened his eyes and looked at him, and the feeling evaporated.

Gilchrist smiled at Thomas. 'I think Hamish wants only you to stroke him.'

'Okay,' Thomas said, and worked his fingers into Hamish's fur.

Hamish closed his eyes, and purred as if with renewed energy.

'Would you like some more soup, Thomas?' Isabelle asked.

'Yes please, Mum. And could I have some toast soldiers, too, please?'

'Of course you can.' Isabelle beamed. As she walked from the bedroom, she said to Gilchrist, 'Would you like me to make something for you?'

Gilchrist felt confused at what was happening, his mind firing a thousand questions that seemed impossible to answer. But he also felt he was invading a moment of extreme privacy between mother and son, and said, 'I've already got a casserole cooking at home.'

Isabelle didn't pick up on his lie as she closed the bedroom door behind them. 'I worry that Hamish will escape if I leave it open,' she explained.

'I think Hamish has found a soulmate,' Gilchrist said. 'I don't think he's going anywhere. But it's good not to take any chances.'

Silent, he watched Isabelle slip two slices of bread into the toaster, then lift the lid off the pot, and ladle a portion of soup into a bowl. 'I can't believe it,' she said to him. 'He's not had anything to eat for over a month, and now he's had a small bowl of soup, and asking for toast soldiers.' She stopped what she was doing then, placed the ladle on the draining board, and covered her face with her hands. 'I know I shouldn't raise my hopes, but . . .' She shook her head, dabbed her nose with a tissue that she pulled from the sleeve of her cardigan.

Then she sniffed, and faced him.

'The doctor came to see Thomas this morning,' she said. 'He said he couldn't feel any lumps under his arms, or anywhere else. He checked his eyes, took his temperature, and said everything seems normal. He asked Thomas if he felt any pain, but Thomas said all the pain had gone. The doctor said he couldn't understand it, said he'd seen nothing like it.' She raised a hand as if to silence Gilchrist before he interrupted her. 'I know it's early days,' she said, 'but the doctor said that the only thing that seemed wrong with Thomas was that he needed to put some weight on.'

She shook her head again, and said, 'Do you believe in miracles, Andy?'

What could he tell her? That he had wished on a shooting star? That by searching for a magic cat, he had followed tracks in the snow and saved two lives? Instead, he shrugged a non-response and retrieved his jacket from the chair, slipped his hand inside the pocket, and handed her the envelope.

Isabelle took it from him, grinning with surprise. 'I didn't get you a card, Andy. I'm sorry.' She removed the Christmas card and smiled at the cover – a snow scene with a star streaking across a night sky. She opened it, and gasped. 'What's this? It's a voucher. For one hundred pounds. Oh, Andy.' She frowned a silent question at him.

'The reward for finding Hamish.'

'But . . . you . . . I don't . . .'

'It's for you to take Thomas out for a treat,' he said. 'When he's fit and well.'

She came up to him then, and hugged him. 'Thank you,' she said. 'For everything.'

When they parted, she led him to the door, and unlocked it. As he was about to step into the evening chill, she gave a worried glance at the bedroom door as if to ask something. But he silenced her with a finger to his lips, and said, 'Tomorrow's Christmas. The time of year when miracles sometimes happen. Hold on to that thought. And believe in it.' He leaned forward and pressed his lips to her cheek. 'For Thomas,' he whispered. 'Merry Christmas.'

On North Street, he stopped for a moment and eyed an overcast sky, not sure what he was looking for, or expecting to see. Maybe he was hoping for another shooting star on which to wish. Or maybe he was just giving silent thanks for one Christmas wish that had indeed come true.

He tugged up his collar and walked into the night.